PRAISE FOR *DOWN TO THE RIVER*

"*Down to the River* is a deeply absorbing family saga that unfolds in the vicinity of Harvard Square during the turbulence of the late Sixties and early Seventies. Anne Whitney Pierce captures those vanished days—the collapse of the old order, the sexual experimentation, the hovering threat of the war in Vietnam, the uneasy sense that anything might be possible—with uncanny precision and an empathy that does justice to both sides of the generation gap."

—Tom Perrotta, author of *Election* and *Little Children*

"Anne Whitney Pierce has written a novel so richly imagined and finely observed that it casts a sort of spell. The extended Potts family—flawed and loveable, dissolute and striving, solitary and connected, real—will live long in the mind and heart."

—Elizabeth Graver, author of *The End of the Point*

"Some books you read, others you inhabit. *Down to the River* is in the latter category. Anne Whitney Pierce writes about Cambridge, Mass in the late 1960's with the kind of rich, textured detail that's missing from a lot of contemporary fiction. Without sentimentality or nostalgia, she brings the period alive with all of its political unrest, social anxiety, and sexual experimentation. More importantly, the Potts family becomes real and familiar, especially Chickie and Hen, the teenage cousins at the center of the novel. Their complicated relationship is a moving portrait of a particular stage of life in a specific time and place."

—Stephen McCauley, author of *My Ex-Life* and *The Object of My Affection*

DOWN TO THE RIVER

Anne Whitney Pierce

Regal House Publishing

Published by
Regal House Publishing, LLC
Raleigh, NC 27587
All rights reserved

ISBN -13 (paperback): 9781646031887
ISBN -13 (epub): 9781646031894
Library of Congress Control Number: 2021943783

Interior layout by Lafayette & Greene
Cover design © by C.B. Royal
cover image from Shutterstock/Can Pu
Author photo credit: Steven Monahan

Regal House Publishing, LLC
https://regalhousepublishing.com

Printed in the United States of America

For the Avon Hill Gang
And in memory of my parents, Olive and George

PROLOGUE

The barnyard names were just coincidence; the rest was by design. Chickie was Minerva, a nickname shortened over time from Chickadee. Hen was short for Henry. They were first cousins, born third and last children at the tail end of 1951 at the Women's Lying-In Hospital in Boston. Fathered by identical twin brothers, they grew up, side by side, in high Victorian houses, one plum-colored, one olive-colored, across the river in Cambridge. They were not the first. By the time Chickie and Hen arrived, older siblings roller-skated, bickered, played April Fool's jokes, Slap Jack, Cat's Cradle. By the time Chickie and Hen came along, their parents were long enough done with diapers and tantrums and sleepless nights to have forgotten their toll—dim the days of sitting zombie-like on a juice-stained armchair in a garment that had once borne the shape and sheen of a decent blouse, bearing bits of three meals running, staring at the ravaged carpet, littered with toys and crumpled paper, thinking that if you could only bend down to pick up that one petrified Cheerio in the corner, the rest would follow. The toys would march back onto their shelves, the puzzle pieces snap back into their frames, the garbage fling itself into the can. Teeth would get brushed and sheets would turn themselves down on the bed. Long gone, those days of drone and diaper rash and snotty noses, those fleeting moments of crushing joy, those nights when you ached and the children climbed all over you like monkeys, tugging, whining, always needing to talk and poke and tug at your face:

Elsie Marley is so fine
She can't get up
To feed the swine.
I'm hungry! I'm cold! I'm bored! I'm sad!
FEED-THE-SWINE!!!

Chickie's father was Naylor Potts, better known as Nash. Nash's twin brother, Remington, was Hen's father, Remi for short. They'd grown up riding the frayed coattails of an old and dwindling fortune made by their great-grandfather in frozen food. Their black-sheep father, "Jocko" Potts, had squandered his money and died young, leaving the twins fatherless, in the care of their mother and paternal grandfather,

Mercy Potts—sons of a moth-ravaged legacy. Cambridge born and bred, the twins went to prep school and then on to Harvard, as all Potts men had, as all Potts men did. They muddled through on athletic prowess and capable if not brilliant minds, riding the tide of sturdy genes, a shaky sense of entitlement, and the old family name. Reveling in the sport of identical twins, Nash and Remi plotted the final dupe in the summer of 1943, blindfolding their girlfriends and proposing to each other's intended on a roller coaster ride one summer night at Revere Beach. Voices muffled in the wind, stomachs lurched, faces blurred. In mid-swoop, deceptive kisses led to wind-swept vows. Back on the ground, the twins confessed to the ruse and reproposed. On shaky legs, with cotton candy breath and open eyes, the girls accepted their rightful suitors, not sure what had scared them more—not having caught on right away or how sweet the stolen kisses had been.

A double wedding ceremony was held in the fall at the boat club, upriver, near the private boys' school, champagne by the bucket and a swing band that played long into the night. Tuxedoed stragglers were found on the riverbank the next morning, kicking through the maple leaves, singing a much altered "Get me to the Church on Time." For days afterward, straggling balloons floated upriver. Mercy's last gifts to his grandsons before he died, not long after the wedding, were the down payments on two neighboring houses: old, rambling Victorians, shaded by hulking oaks and elms, bordered by sprawling porches, tilted carriage houses in the rear, on Hemlock Street, one of many wide, tree-lined avenues that connected Brattle Street to Memorial Drive.

The first children came quickly, as they did in those days. Nash and Violet had two daughters, Persephone "Seph" and Janie, sleepless little girls who spoke early and had the twins' fine hair. Remi and his wife, Faye, had a son, Cameron "Buzz," and then a daughter, Victoria, "Tory"—handsome, serious children with large hands and feet. With what was left of Mercy's inheritance, the twins started a sporting goods store in Harvard Square. The store did well in its early years, a comfortable fit in the prospering, postwar Ivy League square. The twins could be seen jogging together along the river paths, their store logo on the backs of their polo shirts, "Potts Pro Shop." Former lettermen in track, they cut fine figures, fit and swarthy, long in the leg and jowl. They strode the riverbanks with their babies in carriages, kites and pinwheels, a series of lanky rust-colored dogs. At the store they sold squash rackets, scuba masks, and tennis whites and regaled customers with sports trivia and old Cambridge lore. The twins moved entwined together through the years, as they say twins will do, going to the Head Of The Charles Regatta and Harvard football games, tailgate martini parties on the riverbank, foreign beer at the Wursthaus, skiing at Mount Sunapee, skating at the tennis club in winter, and weekends and summers spent at the family cottage on Nantucket.

The twins' wives, Faye and Violet, were more alike than they knew. Both had come from hard work and character, and hard work and character would see both of them through. They'd made their way East for college from the Midwest and stayed on to find husbands or careers, whichever claimed them first. After marriage they set out to be good wives and mothers, hosting dinners and bridge parties, appearing at the proper social functions, properly tailored and curled, with just enough lipstick and cleavage, just enough opinions. They went to football games and tennis matches, the symphony and the annual fireman's ball. They could be seen at the beauty parlor once a week, and at a lecture every third Tuesday—on butterflies, say, or Alfred Lord Tennyson. If some-one handed them a martini, they drank it; if someone suggested an outing, they went along. If someone ventured an opinion, they tended to agree, if only because to raise an eyebrow or an objection had simply become too much trouble, and perhaps too much of a risk—of the comfort and privilege they'd accepted in marriage to their husbands. Raised to be God-fearing, if not religious, both Violet and Faye came to think of all this—their lives as silent, fettered wives and mothers—as the tradeoff for marrying well.

Knowing it to be part of the bargain, the wives took on the task of mending the twins' fraying family quilt. They made plans together—picnics and bridge dates, bike rides and cocktail parties, fresh lettuce and pearly corn from Wilson Farms. On Sundays and holidays, the two families gathered for overcooked roast beef dinners, crusted potatoes, and shriveled-up peas. The children ran over the rude bridge in Con-cord, went to the Science Museum, rode the Swan Boats religiously each spring. They strolled the coiling path around Walden Pond and the white sands of Crane Beach off-season, the wives in stretch pants and velveteen sweaters, loosely curled hair and dark shades of lipstick. The children played vicious card games of Spit in the Plum Island dunes, keeping the cards down with driftwood and horseshoe-crab skeletons.

By the late forties, the plum and olive houses on Hemlock Street had regained some order, some calm. The baby toys had been given to Goodwill and no one had a taste for Cheerios anymore. Soiled rugs had been replaced. Silk curtains hung on the plate-glass windows of the plum-colored house and a Wyeth painting found its way above the mantelpiece in the olive. A basketball hoop went up on one of the carriage houses; the children gave up their training wheels for shiny two wheelers. In Nash's house landed an aquarium with brightly colored fish that died routinely and were replaced. In Remi's, the greenhouse overlooking the yard slowly filled with cacti and exotic plants. By 1949, Nash's house boasted one of the first TV sets. As the new decade approached, things were looking up. All was well.

The fifties rolled in. The new rug, not such a good one after all, started to fray. One of the children was asked to leave the Shady Lane School for a reason that was never spoken about but involved a teacher, a cactus, and a jar of Vaseline. Another child, Remi's, still wet his bed at eight. One of Nash's girls, it became clear, never *was* going to outgrow her baby fat. The other, though smart as a whip, was as plain as her given name. The twins no longer held their liquor all that well, gone to flushed faces and worn khaki and a bit of flab. They no longer ran along the river but walked a huffy walk. Grandfather Mercy's money was long gone. Business at the sporting goods store bumped along on the sale of sweat suits and squash rackets and bathing suits. Ski poles went out of vogue and hung limp from their leather straps on the pro shop walls. Despite the wave of post-war prosperity that was sweeping the country, the two families felt strapped. Somehow, in their feckless fashion, they'd fallen off mid-ride. Gone suddenly the yearly new car, the European vacations, the family Christmas portraits. Gone the Wyeth painting before the wallpaper around it had time to fade. The modern furniture got scratched and dull. The stained-glass window was smashed by a hardball and never replaced. Broken the piano bench, tarnished the candelabra, shattered the ancient glass mirror in the hall. Mercy's ghost frowned down upon Hemlock Street as the houses fell into disrepair, as the children sprouted weeds and the grown-ups lived on beyond their means. And as affluence dwindled, so did the gaiety, the bravado, the shiny veneer of their comfortable lives. But because no one knew what else to do, they kept pretending.

The twins spent more and more time away from home during these years, no longer sure what was required of them there. One wintry night, they got to drinking hard at Cronin's Bar, down by the trolley car barns in the Square, as they had in college days, men of thirty now, and not eighteen. The whiskey bottle sat on the wooden table of the booth; the empty beer mugs slowly gathered. Slipping dimes into the jukebox, they chased beer with shots of whiskey, and whiskey with swigs of beer. They waited for something to happen—a pretty girl to pass by, a drunk to tell a rambling tale, a fight to break out, a million-dollar scheme to rise from the beer foam, all the while listening to the sultry strains of Doris Day.

"So, how goes it, brother?" Nash said to Remi. Younger by a few minutes, heavier in the chest and cheek, Nash usually spoke first.

"Goes it?" Remi ran a wobbly finger around the squeaking rim of his glass. "Round and round it goes…"

"And where it stops…" Nash raised his glass and tilted it toward the jukebox. Someone had played a Supremes song. "Hey. Listen. Hear that? 'Where Did Our Love Go.'" Nash sang along drunkenly.

Remi looked up, hoisted his lips in a twisted smile. "Don't look in my house," he said. "Izn't in my house anymore."

"Studs." Nash brought his glass back down. "Maybe that's all we ever were, Rem. Studs."

"Remember, Nash, that first time I met Faye? I knew she was the one."

"Vi was a goddess," Nash said. "A goddamned goddess."

"Those days—"

"They were good days," Nash said. "The kids—"

"I *love* my kids." Remi pounded down his fist. "They don't even know."

"We made 'em, Rem. We goddamn made 'em. Doesn't that amaze you sometimes?"

"Hey, we still got it." Remi looked up, hiccupped.

"Goddamn right we do."

Remi caught the look in Nash's eye and laughed. "Whoa, brother."

"We're not so old…"

"I could…"

"Any time…"

"Hundred bucks says…"

"I could knock her up in a month."

"Make it five hundred."

"Make it a goddamned week."

"Twins, maybe!" It wasn't important which of them had the last drunken word.

As boys, the twins had sliced flesh and tasted one another's blood in pacts of secrecy and loyalty. Now approaching thirty, they clinked their glasses together in a drunken toast, grasped hands as if they were set to arm-wrestle, and watched the beer foam drip down the sides of their mugs. An idle notion come alive in a smoky Cambridge bar, a reprieve from impending mediocrity, from descending middle age. It seemed so simple that night, so clear. They'd go home and make love to their wives, over and over again. The wives would hold out their arms and smile, fold the way they used to, soft and powdery, murmur, stroke, and rise. The sheets would twist; the sweat would pour. And maybe up from the steam of passion, hope would once again rise. Nash poured the last of the whiskey, the last of the last beer. The foam shot up above the rim of the glass—fizzled, spit, and held. The twins toasted again, to manhood, to family, to the future. They'd go home and make babies, create new life. This is what men *did*. Had done, since the beginning of time. This is what made men *men*. Nash pounded his fist on the counter. Remi shuddered with a thrill. In the smoky, dim light of the bar, the yellow haze of drink and the relentless, age-old affection they felt for each other, the twins imagined that the love of one last child might sweep them off the path of the way it was bound to be and back to the way it might have been.

At closing time, Nash and Remi crossed the arc of Brattle Street and roamed Harvard Square, arms slung around each other's shoulders, weaving and singing a drunken song. A woman dozing in the Cardells storefront with a purple beret and a bird on her shoulder woke up when they passed noisily by.

"Hey, lady." Nash bent down to the woman and scared the bird away. "You wanna *know* something? You wanna *hear* something, lady?"

"Sshh!" she scolded. Out of her mouth flew an obscenity. Then another. The bird flew up to the ledge of a building in Harvard Yard with a reproachful screech. The woman saw the other man then, leaning over the first one's shoulder, the same man it seemed, but thinner, darker, breathing hard. There were two of them. Both drunk as piss-potted skunks.

"Tell her, Nash." Remi nudged him from behind. "Go on. Tell her what we're gonna do."

"We're gonna go home..." Nash wobbled from the weight of his leaning brother. "And we're going to make *babies*." His hands crumpled on the last whimpered word. "Little, tiny, beautiful babies."

The woman snorted. "Babies cry," she said. "They break. They puke. They stink. Goddamn babies die."

"No. No." Nash shook his head back and forth. "They're angels," he said. "They melt in your arms. They smell like the earth."

"They cry," the woman said. "They cry and stink and fight and walk right out the door."

"But they love you," the drunken shadow said from behind—swaying, leaning into his brother's shoulders, slurring his words. "No matter what…in the whole goddamned world, lady…" he leaned closer to make her understand. "They still love you."

"Pray then," the woman said.

"Pray for what?" Nash looked up at her.

"Pray for the babies." The woman made the sign of the cross, then let out a barking sound. "Pray for the stinking babies."

"Pray for the babies!" The twins rose wobbly to their feet, making a drunken song of the bird woman's words as they wove a crooked path toward home. *"Pray—for—the—babies! Oh yeah, I say PRAY—for the baaaa-bies."* The words fell, slurred and careless back into the night. Watching them go, the bird woman made clucking noises with her tongue. The offended bird flew back down from the Harvard rooftop and landed on her shoulder.

The next year, Faye and Violet looked into the faces of their newborns with something between hysteria and joy. They were almost thirty years old, and they had babies again. Their breasts were swollen and leaky, bellies rubbery and sore. They got weepy over piles of dirty laundry, paralyzed by puddles of spilled milk. Dusty cribs and rusty strollers were pulled out of the cellars, toys and highchairs from the attics. The older kids knew exactly where babies came from and now—abracadabra—here they were. Neither Faye nor Violet could imagine reliving those baby years in the same trapped and frenzied way. Calling upon old instincts and drives, they took charge. They lost their postpartum weight, restyled their hair, drank strong cups of Turkish coffee. They put the babies on bottles and in far-away rooms at night in order to get their sleep. They scoured the classifieds for jobs and filled out applications for night courses—art, business, finance, Freud. Faye and Violet kissed the babies and let them cry, went out into the world to find work, to find salvation, to find themselves.

The twins peered at their new babies with something between

religious fervor and fear. They, too, had to wonder what strange, warped wind had swept them home that night from the bar. Knowing the feel of uncertain arms around them, the babies fretted and squirmed. The fathers rocked them uneasily, jiggled and patted, pecked a soft cheek here, raised a rumpled smile there. The woman with the bird on her shoulder had been right. Babies did puke and they did cry. They did stink sometimes, but they also smelled like powder and the cool dark loam of the earth. They were soft and fragile, but miraculously they didn't break. They were angels—innocent, feral—full of memory, forgiveness, wisdom. They were eminently good and trusting. And they *did* love you, no matter what—at least for a while. But oh, you'd forgotten, how they humbled and terrified you all over again. Made you small, shook you, wooed you, filled you, took your breath away, scared you half to death. Who can say how it might have been, if Chickie and Hen—the last children—had remained no more than drunken nostalgia, idle whimsy come alive in a smoky bar?

Mistakes, such children are often called.

Live-in babysitters came to roost in the attic rooms of the olive and plum houses on Hemlock Street, eaved rooms piled high with clothes and books, candles shoved into bottles covered with dripping wax. They'd stay for the better part of a year, sometimes more. They wore oversized men's shirts, holey tennis shoes, and stretch pants. They talked of reincarnation and D.H. Lawrence and the Jean-Pauls—Belmondo and Sartre—of infinity and hell and boys, booze and bitten nails, boys some more. Every day they walked up Brattle Street and brought Chickie and Hen to the park on the Cambridge Common. They'd sit all morning on the benches while the two babies played, swiping pebbles or cigarette butts from their mouths, wiping a tear or a runny nose on a shirttail from time to time, building elaborate forts and castles in the sand. They doted on the two cousins in distracted rushes, loving to play mothers for a lazy, surreal while, reveling in the bounce of a baby on a hip and the clutch of a sticky hand, adoring to be adored so unconditionally, and still be free.

People watched Chickie and Hen playing in the park with something between suspicion and wonder, thinking them in cahoots, otherworldly, twins maybe—the family resemblance strong and the intimacy so real. They played for hours together, sang songs and spoke in a language all their own, bounding in and out of the sandbox and onto the swings.

They had the swagger of gypsy children, barefooted, bare-chested, dirt-smudged. Their clothes didn't match; their hair wasn't combed; their fingernails were rarely clean. Not used to being coddled or entertained, they played with sticks and mud and leaves and socks and frazzled bits of trash. They didn't clamor for treats or special toys, didn't whine about being hungry or cold, didn't beg to go home. People who watched them wondered. Hen was a pretty blond boy, and Chickie, though not so much to look at so soon—too much feature for the face and nearly bald until her third birthday—was an agile, triumphant child, dancing and spinning her way through the sand, bounding over the rungs of the jungle gym and up the slope of the slide with no hands. She wore a tutu over her denim pants and hand-me-down saddle shoes—part monkey, part dragonfly, part long-necked swan. She put on shows in the sandbox, charging twig and stone admission. Hen would hold her towel cape and scuffed-up shoes. When it was over, Chickie would bow and put on her dandelion crown and cover Hen's face with kisses.

Hen's mother, Faye, always thought there was something slightly off about her last child, so quietly did he slide into the world, so dark his feathery blue eyes, so vacant his toothless smile. Buzz and Tory had been born restless and sharp. Hen was different. It was a relief to have a baby that didn't fret and cry, didn't cringe when a stranger came near or fuss when a bottle was too cold. Hen would fall happily into anyone's arms, drink anything put to his lips, and sit on the floor contentedly as the outblow of the vacuum blew up his hair. He'd march off the backdoor step and fall silently into the dirt, pick himself up with an eerie smile. Hen worried Faye because he seemed to have no fear, no caution, no sense that life was a matter of survival, as well as course, even for the very young. Still, Hen was an easy, pretty child, one who'd sit by the hour with a piece of pink cardboard, backdrop packaging for some toy which didn't interest him—chewing it, waving it, vrooming it. For a time during those years, when other children his age began their babbling and Hen was silent, Faye worried.

"What's wrong with him?" Remi would ask. "Why doesn't he say anything?"

"Nothing's wrong with him," Faye said. "A watched pot and all. Give him time, Remi. He'll talk when he's ready."

"Leave it to me to produce the only retard in the family."

"He's not a retard, for goodness' sake. That's such a terrible word."

"Well, if worse comes to worst…" Remi would soften, reach out to tousle his son's curls. "He can always be the next Cary Grant."

Remi seemed to love Hen, far more attentive to this child than he'd been to the other two, even changing an occasional diaper and filling a small silver spoon with green peas and guiding it to Hen's mouth airplane-style, kissing him goodnight. *Patty-cake, patty-cake, baker's man. Bake me a cake as fast as you can.* A man gone to midlife mush over a sweet, dumb child. These moments warmed Faye, and she clung to them, to the feelings Hen could raise like magic from them both. It often felt like the only real love left between them, those times when she watched Remi swoop Hen up from the floor and give him a clumsy squeeze or hum him an old college tune. Sometimes at the end of a long day, while the older children pounded and bickered and banged, Remi and Faye would stop and watch Hen in mid-yawn, bathed and pajamaed on the living room rug, and they'd beam, thinking for a moment that to have made such a beautiful child was almost enough of a thing to have done with a life, no matter how random or empty the moment of the making had been, no matter how slow the workings of his brain turned out to be, no matter how big the space between them in bed later that night would feel.

The Studebaker's muffler was dragging when Hen and Chickie went off to kindergarten at the neighborhood school in the fall of 1956, the first Pottses ever to join the public-school pack. The teacher patted Faye's arm on PTA night and told her not to worry, and so, of course, Faye did.

"We're just the slightest bit concerned about Henry," Mrs. Mooney said. "He doesn't defend himself; he doesn't fight back."

"Isn't that what we try to teach our children?" Faye asked. "To turn the other cheek? To be gentle, to be fair? Isn't that just the point?"

Well, yes, of course that *was* the point, said Mrs. Mooney. No one liked a bully and civility *was* important. But after all, Hen was a boy, and a special one at that. Hen pulled endless 'buts' from his teachers' lips, an exception to all their rules. With his curls, dark eyes, and translucent skin, Hen cast a certain spell. He didn't like what he saw in the mirror; it didn't feel as if it belonged to him. In the third grade, he took scissors to his hair and chopped it all off, including his eyelashes and what he could manage of his eyebrows.

"What'd you do to your hair?" Chickie asked him, running her hand over the rough clumps.

"I killed it," he said.

"Cool," she said, understanding completely. "It looks really, really dead."

God bless that child, they said. God love him. God save that precious Henry Potts. Chickie listened; she heard. She knew what they said about Hen, that he was sensitive, dreamy, slow. But she didn't believe it, that he was stupid or helpless. She knew him better than anyone. But if it were true, and he *did* need saving, she would be the one to do it. Not the teachers. Not God. And damned if those curls never really did grow back.

"Minerva has great p-p-potential," Chickie's third-grade teacher told Violet. "But she lets her emotions get in the w-w-way of her work." And it was such a shame, said Mr. Carbunkle, because Chickie was so smart. Maybe even too sss-mmmart, sometimes, for her own g-g-good. Violet smiled at the handsome young teacher, imagining for a moment his hand sliding under her silk blouse. Where she came from, there was no such thing as being too smart for your own good and a stern young man with a stutter was fair game for mid-life fantasy. Even at PTA night.

Chickie and Hen's names rose up often in the smoky haze of the teachers' lounge at the Curley Elementary School. You'd either had one of the Potts cousins in your class or you were bound to get one. These children weren't quite normal somehow, not easily understood. They'd never developed the proper social skills—not outcasts exactly, but without real friends. They spoke their own language, seemed to read each other's minds. They weren't attentive, but still, somehow, they managed to learn. The boy was either a dullard or a saint, the girl brilliant or maybe mad. And stubborn as a mule. When Hen was kept back in the third grade, Chickie refused to be promoted without him. And so ferocious was her will, so strong her resolve, that no grown-up had the stamina to prevail.

Hen was a dreamer, it was true. By 1960, when they were in the fourth grade, people were starting to talk about rocketing into outer space. Right from the start, Hen wanted to go. Chickie couldn't understand. Lots of kids said they wanted to be astronauts, to twirl in space drinking Tang and plunk back down into the ocean and have medals hung around their necks by President Kennedy. But they didn't really mean it. Hen did.

"What would you *do* up there?" she asked him.

"Think," Hen said.

"You'd just hang in space all day, thinking, until you died?"

"Maybe you don't die up there," he said. "Or maybe dying is different. Maybe it's like dreaming. Anyway, what's so great about being on the earth?"

"Gravity, Bozo." Chickie stomped her feet. "Our feet touch the ground. We can walk and run and eat Bit-O-Honeys. God, I wish I had one right now. I'm starving. We're *human*, Hen."

"So?"

"So we can *feel* ourselves." Chickie pinched herself. "Ow. See? We're real." She pinched herself again. "See? Ow!"

"How do you know you're really real and that your whole life isn't just a dream?"

"Shut. Up." Chickie covered her ears with her hands. "Don't say that, Hen."

He pried her hands loose. "Maybe *they're* real and we're not."

"Who?" Chickie asked through a grimace.

"The aliens," Hen said. "The Martians. The Mercatoids. The Jupitarians."

"There's no such thing as Jupitarians," Chickie said. "Or Mercatoids, stupid."

"You don't know it all, Chickie." Hen let go of her hands. "Anyway, what's so good about being real?"

"Everything!" Chickie pinched him and laughed. She loved being real. She didn't want to be anywhere else than here on the earth, walking, skipping, twirling. She believed that when you died, you were really dead and your flesh rotted away from your bones, even if your hair and fingernails kept on growing. She didn't want to die ever. She'd miss everything—red licorice, Christmas, their new TV set, crickets chirping, Hen, her sisters, even her mother. She didn't want to be weightless, forgotten, a pile of bones and teeth and curling fingernails rattling in a coffin buried deep under the ground, a memory drifting in space. She didn't want to be all over with, finished and done. She wished she could live forever; it made her crazy that it couldn't be true. This is why Chickie couldn't believe in God. Only people.

In the days when Chickie and Hen were small, the bird woman with the purple beret came to the Common and watched the children play. She sat on a bench just outside the playground, arranging her bags and birdseed around her. The little blond boy and the bald dancing girl came nearly every day, even when the weather was bad and others stayed away. She watched those two children playing together in the park on the Common, lost in a world of their own making, where the sun rose and fell at their feet, where their laughter echoed in the dark, long after the children had gone home, and the bums wandered in through the gates with their blankets and bottles. Every day they came, the blond boy and bald ballerina girl. First they were babies. Then they rose up on their feet. Toddled, swung, climbed, and fell. Said their first words. Sang a crooked song. *I know an old lady who swallowed a bird…to catch the spider… to catch the fly…I don't know why…*

In time, Chickie and Hen grew too old for babysitters and sand-boxes, and they came to the park no more. But the bird woman kept coming, kept watching, kept feeding the birds on the bench near the playground gate, all through one year and part of another, before she understood that they wouldn't be coming back. And to this day, when the bird woman is very old, not always clear on time and space, her once-reddish hair hanging in a wispy silver V down her back, she can still be seen wandering near the park, now filled with a glittering metal castle and tunneled slides, children who've known no heroes, breathed no clean air, fought no wars. She can still be heard to say to someone, or to no one at all, in a throaty hiss, impatient now, with people, pity, and time, "Where did those happy children go?"

1

SUMMER 1966

As Chickie lifts the lid of the cookie jar, the smell of damp sugar rises. She flattens her hand against the crumb-covered bottom of the jar and licks her sticky palm clean. Out in the hallway, her father, Nash, is talking on the phone. Chickie can always tell when he's talking to his twin brother, her uncle Remi. His voice is different, softer, sputtered out in jumbled bits that wouldn't add up to anyone else—code words, half mind reading—twin talk.

"Take the babies. Right. Ball four," Nash says. "Who knows? Jesus, no, Rem. Cock a doodle. Make a night of it. Hey, Chick!" her father calls out.

Following the line of the coiled black phone cord, Chickie pushes through the swinging door. Brass hooks in the shapes of elephant trunks line the hallway wall. A full-length mirror hangs next to the closet, shattered in spiderweb lines in one corner. Nash leans against the stair post in khaki pants and a Prep Shop sweater that's unraveling around the V at the neck. He puts his hand over the receiver. "Remi's got tickets to the ball game tonight," he says. "You want to go?"

"Is Hen coming?" Chickie shoves her sleeves up over her elbows.

"Is the Pope Catholic?" Nash says.

"How should I know?"

"Hen's coming." Nash speaks back into the receiver. "My daughter, the religious idiot."

Chickie sticks out her tongue. Nash gives her the vampire look, fangs bared.

Back in the kitchen, Chickie opens the refrigerator door. She's fourteen years old. Her hair's almost long enough to sit on. It hasn't been cut in five years, since her mother, Violet, made her get a pixie cut at the beauty parlor in the third grade and she had to wear a baseball cap all year to save face. She likes her hair, feels naked without it, has early memories of playing in the park with a cold head. She's wearing a boat-necked cotton shirt, maroon and black striped, a pair of white Levi's jeans and loafers. Violet calls it her preppie-convict outfit. Chickie loves the shirt, even though it's old and starting to fray. She can't help it. Like her father, she gets attached to things.

Chickie finds chicken leftovers wrapped in tinfoil and goes at a drumstick in a way that makes Violet say "there's a bit of the Neanderthal in you, Minerva," which is Chickie's real name. She straddles a chair and tears off a piece of skin with her teeth. Nash comes in through the swinging door to hang up the phone and goes at a chicken wing in a way that makes Chickie see how much like her father she can be. She looks around. The kitchen's just barely clean. The pipes clank and bang with a shudder. The countertops are scratched and dull. The telephone, mounted on a wall filled with the pencil marks of old family measurements, is crusted with years of crud. As Nash closes the refrigerator door, Chickie wrinkles her nose. It's not quite cold enough inside; the food smells on the edge. Over the sink, venetian blinds do a crooked dance down a window spattered with the salt of old blizzards, splats of dried Ivory liquid, petrified bits of food.

"God." Chickie puts her foot on the pedal of the trash can and throws the half-gnawed drumstick away. "I can't believe I live here sometimes."

"Home sweet home," Nash says cheerfully. "I'll just grab a drink, honey, and then we'll hit the road." He chews the crackling tip of a chicken wing, pulls Chickie into his arms. "Should be a great game. Lonborg on the mound. Balmy night. Me and my gal..." He waltzes her around the kitchen, chicken wing riding his teeth like Casanova's rose. "Yankees, oh yes! Sweet revenge."

"Calm down, Dad." Chickie ducks out from under his arms. "It's only a game."

"*The* game, Chick." Nash stops dead in his waltzing tracks. "Lonborg's fastball's about to hit ninety miles per hour. And that, my dear, is faster than a speeding bullet."

"Yeah, he's fast." Chickie takes a swig of nearly sour milk from the carton and wipes her mouth on her sleeve. "But he stinks against the Yankees at home, one win out of the last six starts."

"One out of six?" Nash pauses as he takes an ice tray out of the freezer. "Is that true?"

Chickie points to the newspaper, folded open on the kitchen table to the sports page. "Read it and weep, Dad," she says. "Read it and weep."

Chickie doesn't mind being the boy her father never had. He wasn't sorry when she came out another girl. He liked what he was used to, and he liked girls. Once, though, when she asked her mother if she wished she'd been a boy, Violet sighed and said, "Well, of course, sweetheart, you want it all, don't you?" Chickie shoves her shirtsleeves up over her elbows and takes another swig. Maybe it's being the boy her mother never had that's hard. Gets more and more of a gyp being a girl, Chickie's two older sisters, Seph and Janie, keep telling her. Once you get your period. Bam. You're a prisoner in your own home, your own skin. The rules start to change. No second servings of dessert. No wrinkled T-shirts. No loud voices, running races, taking risks, talking back. They're older, these sisters, supposedly wiser, done with college, out on their own now. But who can really trust them? They ditched her a long time ago. Chickie's seen the green in her mother's eyes turn to gray lately, the line of her thin lips tighten. Violet tries to groom her like a poodle—plaid skirts and ironed blouses, lip gloss and barrettes, stockings and deodorant tucked into her drawers. Chickie feels the leash tightening. She has to cross her legs in company now, curb her tongue, chew her food ten times before she swallows. She's supposed to walk, not traipse; nibble, not gobble; laugh and not guffaw.

"Grow up, Chickie," Violet says with a sigh, always a sigh now after her name. It feels more to Chickie like growing back down—withering, stiffening, closing back up into an old, shed cocoon. No jumping on the bed anymore or sliding down the banister. No ruffling your eyebrows to look like Dracula. No food jokes at the table. Now, when Chickie burps "Baa, Baa, Black Sheep," Violet says, "Stop it, Chickie. That's disgusting."

"Why wasn't it disgusting last month?" she asks.

"It was," Violet says. "It just hadn't made it to the top of the list yet."

How long can the list be? Chickie wonders. She's only fourteen.

Chickie takes the wishbone and wraps what's left of the chicken in the crumpled tinfoil. Her mother's voice comes through the door from the hallway as she shoves it back onto a rusty refrigerator shelf.

"Hello! Anybody home?"

"In here, Vi!" Nash calls out.

"I'm going upstairs to change!" Violet says. "I'll be right down. Chickie? You there?"

"No! I'm just a Fig Newton of your imagination!"

"My daughter the comedienne," Nash says.

"My father, the father," Chickie says, taking another swig of milk.

"No drinking out of the milk carton!" Violet's voice barrels down the stairs.

"Je-sus." Chickie's fingernail loosens the crusted edge of a scab on her elbow. Don't drink out of the milk carton. Don't wear your underwear inside out. Don't draw mustaches on magazine covers. Stop picking at your skin, Chickie. No man will ever want a wife covered with scars. Don't stand on your head, pick your nose, go up the stairs two or three at a time, kiss things that aren't alive—or even worse, things that are—don't eat chicken like a cave dweller. And for god's sake, Chickie. You're such a smart girl. Don't ask such stupid questions.

"Does he have to be Catholic, Dad?"

"Who?" Nash reaches for the whiskey bottle in the liquor cabinet.

"The pope. Only the Catholics have a pope, right?"

"Right."

"What do we have?" Chickie asks.

"Nothing." Nash rinses out a dirty glass from the sink. "I mean, we have nothing in the sense that we aren't religious."

"Why aren't we, by the way?"

Nash shrugs. "We just never have been in my family. And your mother is what you'd call lapsed. I guess in the end..." He twists the bottle to end the pour. "You either are or you aren't."

The swinging door gives no warning. Violet catches Nash in mid-pour, her arms loaded with dirty laundry. Looking up at the wall clock, she frowns. "Bit early, isn't it, Nash?" she says.

"Just a shot, Vi," Nash says quietly, wincing with a sip of whiskey.

"I'm going out with Dad." Chickie picks the scab from her elbow and licks the blood clean.

"What about homework?" Violet raises one eyebrow. She's wearing stretch pants and velveteen slippers, mascara but no blush.

"I did it at school."

"I often wonder why they call it *home*work," Violet says. "Give me that shirt for the wash, Chickie. You've been wearing it since the Alamo. It must stink to high heaven."

"Just one more day. I promise."

"The socks then. Give me the socks. I can smell them from here. They're beyond the pale."

Chickie kicks off her sneakers and peels off her socks. "No one's going to smell my feet at the ballpark, Mom."

"Ballpark?" Violet turns to face Nash, losing hold of an undershirt.

"Yankees," Nash confesses, lowering his eyes to meet the rim of his glass.

Violet drapes Chickie's dirty socks on top of her pile. It gives her a pang that Nash no longer asks her to come to the ball games, though she long ago willed him to stop. She never really enjoyed them—the hard, sticky seats and long, idle stretches, the endless talk of hits and numbers and balls. She never liked the maleness of it all, so often feeling she'd just been brought along for the ride, to fill a seat and hold the popcorn, good for a wifely kiss or a squeeze, someone to fill in the score sheet neatly, to share the memory of a great play.

In the early years of their marriage, baseball was one of the social graces. They'd get babysitters; Faye and Remi'd come along. The twins would empty the change out of their pockets and make bets—who'd strike out first, who'd get the first home run, who'd be up last. With each swig of whiskey from an old army flask, the bets would get more remote, more absurd—what word the plane would end up writing in the sky, the age of the bleached blonde in the third row, the size of the catcher's shoes—bets with no consequence, no reason, no rhyme. Violet would sit in the stands and think of all the work that needed doing at home, and when, in her mind's eye, she'd smothered herself in a pile of dirty laundry and strung the bathtub ring around her neck, she'd slowly give in to the ballpark's magic. Something deep and nearly dark would stir inside her. Slowly she'd rise up out of her weary self as someone with second chances—lighthearted, sexy, brave. Looking out over the field, she'd watch the batter get the feel of his bat on deck, switching his hips and tugging on his cap, and she'd see him not as a player anymore, but as a man. She'd begin a list of things that needed changing in her life—a new hairdo, another degree, a new paint color on the wall, a better sex life. She'd vow not to turn bitter, bent, resigned. Choosing a nameless man in the crowd, she'd hedge her own bets, imagining that *he* was the one she'd married, wagering what their children might have looked like, what exotic vacations they'd have taken, what positions in sex, what stands, while beside her, wiping his lips after a belt from the flask, Nash bet Remi which pitcher in the bullpen would scratch his crotch first.

"Clean socks, Chickie." Violet stoops to retrieve the fallen undershirt. "And run a comb through your mane while you're at it."

"I'm not a horse," Chickie says. "Sorry, guys. You wanted a horse. But all you got was another kid."

"Next time we'll try for the horse," Nash says, with a neigh.

"Next time?" Violet gives him a sideways glance as she pushes back through the door. The last words boomerang back on the in-swing. "Clean socks, Minerva!" she says.

"Why didn't you ask Mom to come?" Chickie says, when they're alone again.

Nash pours himself a refill. "Your mother gave up on baseball a long time ago," he says.

"Maybe she's changed her mind."

Nash stirs his drink with a knife. "Maybe," he says.

"You always do what Mom says."

Nash raises his hands in mock defense. "Hey, do I look like a guy who's looking for trouble?"

"Let's just go, Dad." Chickie pulls on a sneaker over one bare foot. "I don't need to change my socks. It's pointless."

"'We must learn to live together or perish as fools,'" Nash says.

"Says who?"

"Martin Luther King."

"Martin Luther King doesn't care if I wear clean socks to the ball game."

"Do it for peace, Chick." Nash raises two fingers in a V. "In the end, it's a small price to pay."

"Why does everything have to cost something?" Chickie says. Then, "Never mind, Dad. You don't have to—"

But Nash has already launched into the answer with a sigh and another sip of whiskey. "It's the capitalist way, sweetheart. The argument is, if there were no prices, then nothing would be of value, and there'd be no incentive to work. If every kid had the same doll you had, then yours wouldn't be special, and if I didn't have to work to buy it for you, then I'd get no pleasure from giving it to you or you from having it. Do you see?"

"I don't even like dolls, Dad. I never did. But I get the point."

"I can see how it all started." Nash digs his chin into his palm, swirls the ice in his glass, no longer really talking to her. "A good day's labor for a good day's pay. Pride in your work. Hungry mouths to feed. Every man for himself. Problem is, somewhere along the line it all got so lopsided, so loaded. Just like this goddamned war."

"What goddamned war?"

"Vietnam. And don't swear." Nash takes a gulp of his drink.

"You did."

"Do as I say, not as I do. It's mayhem, Chick. We went in there to help. Our moral obligation. That's the official party line. But Johnson's dropping bombs like a madman. He just sent over 170,000 more troops, but he claims we're not there to win. Bullshit. Excuse my French. Moral obligation to who? Or is it whom?" He shakes his head and puts his glass down on the table. "You just hope this thing doesn't get too out of hand. That someone takes a stand."

"Like that Quaker guy who burned himself up?"

Nash's face falls. "The ultimate protest," he says.

"Did anyone even care except his family?"

"You've got to hope so, Chick." Nash tips his empty glass back and forth. "You've just got to hope so."

"Baseball, Dad," Chickie says. "Yankees. Revenge. Remember?"

Nash's eyes turn back to her. "Clean socks, Chickadee," he says softly.

Upstairs, choosing one orange and one white sock from her drawer, Chickie grabs her Red Sox cap and hangs the wishbone on a crooked nail sticking out of her dresser. She kisses the cross of her fingers and spits through the diamond she makes with her thumbs, a Greek prayer a girl at school taught her, praying first for all good things and then for a clean house. She likes this prayer, the play of fingers and spit. But why would any god listen to her? Any real god, if there is one, knows who the fakers are. Wishing is her kind of religion. Wishing is free. No prayers. No strings attached. No guilt. No broken promises. She picks up the wishbone and runs her fingers over its rough-edged arc, bits of damp meat still clinging. When the wishbone dries, she'll wish for peace—in her head, at home, in Vietnam, peace for the family of the Quaker guy who burned himself to a crisp. She'll do the wishbone with her father. He always pulls with his pinkie.

Hen steps up into Fenway Park in the June dusk, up from the dark tunnels of cement into a cool, green world, maybe feeling the way that first guy is going to when he opens the space capsule onto the moon. He loves the ballpark—the sudden muffling of sound, the smells of popcorn and newly mown grass, pitchers milling in the bullpen, masked catcher rocking in his crouch, organ music drifting across the field. The Coke is sweeter, the white of the players' uniforms whiter, the grass greener than Hen has ever seen. He could live at Fenway Park forever, in a pup tent pitched out in left field, living on ice cream bars and fast-balls, stolen bases, stats and swings. Baseball saves Hen. It's one of the few things that as a boy, as a Potts, he's supposed to love—one of the few things that makes him his father's son.

The vendors make their way through the stands, trays slung around their necks, unfolding thick wads of cash, ice cream bars sailing through the air, money passing hands down the line. Hen's stomach rumbles. Out in the park, the grounds crew grooms the infield. Pitchers warm up in the bullpen. The players hit fungoes out into the field. Nash and Remi start up the stadium seats to the bleachers, crimson-and-white-striped scarves wrapped around their necks. After one of them had a bad sore throat the winter before, the scarves became a fad. The twins are often given matching gifts; they borrow and wear each other's things. Chickie and Hen trail behind. They're all used to being watched. Eyes always turn to the twins, not so much in awe anymore, but still with curiosity. The four of them climb high into the bleacher seats and settle against the Green Monster, a thirty-seven-foot, left-field wall. Nash bangs the Jim Beam billboard with his fist. "Evenin', James," he says, feeling for the flask of whiskey in the inside pocket of his corduroy jacket. Remi takes the seat beside his brother, binoculars dangling around his neck in a battered leather case. Chickie and Hen sit a few rows down below.

The Red Sox take the field. Lonborg strikes out two Yankees in a row and the crowd starts to stir. Chickie does sit-ups on the bleach-ers, the tips of her hair brushing the soda-splattered ground with each downward roll of her spine. Looking down upon the seizing belly of his niece, Remi feels a jolt at his center, swallows an old and sour taste of shame. He slides back in time, to a stadium in prep school days. Prentiss Academy. He used to sit on the bleachers, smaller than these, sharp-edged and tippy, and wait for his race to be called, watching the runners circling the track. But his eyes were really on the legs of the cheerleaders that came on a bus from the Miss Porter's School to cheer their meets. The girls' legs would shoot up and down on the ratty grass, from out of the flouncy felt skirts, peach and pale green. He'd imagine the girls splitting in half, half a ponytail, one breast, one leg, one flared nostril, half a frozen smile. He'd watch those legs at the widest part of the thigh when the skirt flopped up and try to imagine what went on underneath those thick tan tights, behind the bared teeth of the mascot bulldog.

Remi was given the chance. May Day, senior year. After a track meet, during a victory party, Marcia Lacey offered to do him and Nash the favor in the back seat of her father's Dodge. It would be a gas, she said, to do it with twins. Marcia Lacey was pretty, sea-green eyes and curly black hair, pretty enough it didn't matter what else she'd ever done in her father's car or with whom. Nash went first—he always did—came out flushed and beaming, with a whistle and a grin.

"Your turn, big brother," he said.

Inside the car, Marcia Lacey was ready, stretched out, cool and steady, hair brushed, fresh red lipstick applied.

"Wow," she said, as Remi climbed in. "It's crazy. *Deja vu.*"

But when Marcia leaned forward, Remi's tongue froze halfway through a French kiss, his body stone-cold and still. By the time Marcia Lacey had pulled down his zipper, it was all over.

"It's okay," she said, as he pulled away. "It's kind of strange, though, twins and all. Your brother's such a...stud." The bulldog on Marcia Lacey's skirt sneered. When Remi replays that night, he wishes she'd been nastier, more disgusted, that she'd shamed him, scared him into it. He wishes she'd talked dirty, begged him, bit him, hurt him in some vicious way. He wishes he could have wiped that look of pity from her face when she told him, "Don't worry, slugger. I won't say anything. It happens. Really. It doesn't mean anything..." She put her hand on his arm. "You know. About being a man."

Back out on the grass, Nash flung an arm around Remi's shoulder. "Now is that a girl or is that a girl?" he said.

Remi ran his fingers through his hair, stuck his shirttail back into his pants, reached for words that wouldn't betray him, and settled for silence. At that moment he invented the look that would protect him from that day forward, eyes narrowed, grin half-cocked, the look of a conquering liar. Since then, he's been living the lie—of the rakish twin, the man of few but forceful words, the sexy, passionate brooder. In truth, his moments of real passion have been starkly few. He still remembers the stolen kiss with Violet on the roller coaster all those years ago, when he and Nash duped the girls for a last lark, blindfolding them at the last minute before the ride. He can't admit how much time he spends dwelling on those few silly minutes of his life; he finds obsessions like these pathetic. For that one moment, whirling through the air, trying to keep his tongue rolling in Vi's wet, greedy mouth, he'd forgotten that he was Remi Potts, the moody, bad-tempered twin, the one who hadn't been able to get it up with Marcia Lacey in her father's Dodge Dart. Violet pushed him up against the metal railing of the rolling car, thinking him to be Nash, or maybe knowing all the while, rubbing, pressing, until he thought he might explode in midair. For a minute, Remi knew what it was to be someone else, to have absolute sexual power. If that ride had gone on and on, he would have found a way to give it to Violet, right then and there, and she would've loved it. It would have changed him forever. That's how good it was, that moment of airborne deception, that twisted kiss, that mobius swoop in the sky—when he forgot why it was Faye that he'd asked to be his wife.

Remi had to have someone like Faye—thin, smooth, plaster-of-paris Faye. She was the kind of girl some men wanted without knowing why—pretty in a modest way, quiet and contained—classy was the word they'd used. A girl like Faye would never bleed or second-guess, embarrass or browbeat or one-up a man. Pity, kept in the deep reaches of Faye's heart, Remi knew he could stand. He'd been lucky to get her. She came with that fine, honeyed hair, that troubled heart, that stiff upper lip, all that dignity and caution.

Remi looks over at Nash on the bleacher seat to make sure he hasn't been caught in regretful thought, in lascivious gaze. *Do not covet thy brother's wife or, god forbid, his daughter.* Nash is busy filling in the score-card, oblivious, while Hen piles up coins for betting—quarters, nickels, dimes. But Chickie, done with her hundred sit-ups, has caught the look in her uncle's eyes and parries it with a flip of her hair down over her eyes and then back over her head. Remi buys an ice cream bar, bites off a chunk, and presses it with his tongue against his cracked gold filling until he feels the pain.

The Sox start hitting in the fifth. With runners on first and second and no outs, a hot dog, Coke, and ice cream bar downed, Hen burps long and loud and lowers his head onto Chickie's lap.

"Good one," Chickie says.

"Learned from the master," he says.

"I'm losing my touch," she says. "Burping's against the law in my house these days."

Hen tosses pieces of popcorn into the air and catches them one by one in his mouth, bouncing his head up and down on Chickie's thigh. The muscles in her leg slink underneath his neck. She smells damp like moss, sweet like gum—Beeman's, Cinnamint, Teaberry's, Blackjack. Hen watches her fingers folding the paper wrappers into tiny wing-tipped strips, tucking them one by one into the open links of the chain she's making.

"Number six," booms the loudspeaker. *"Shortstop. Rico Petrocelli."*

"Do something, Rico," Remi says.

"He's going to choke," Nash says. "Quarter says he pops out to left."

"Quarter says he gets on base."

"How do you like it, Hen?" Chickie dangles the gum wrapper chain in his face. "It's almost six feet long."

"It stinks," he says, wrinkling his nose. "What are you going to do with it when it's done?"

"I'm going to wrap it around your neck and strangle you." She slides the chain around his neck, her long hair falling to make a tent around his face, voice slipping into a raspy whisper. "And then I'm going to suck your blood!"

"Aaagh!" Hen sticks out his tongue, shivers in fake *rigor mortis*, as Chickie's minty breath spreads over his face.

"Hen!" Remi says sharply.

"What?" He sits up, startled.

"Come on down and get a hot dog with me." Remi's already up on his feet, hiking up his khakis, fiddling with the buckle on his belt.

Hen unwinds the chain from his neck. "I just had a hot dog," he says.

"Have another." Remi tosses the end of his scarf around his neck and leads the way. They climb down the wide cement steps into the underground pit of the ballpark, dark and cool, smelling of boiled hot dogs, ketchup, and beer.

"Want to talk to you, old man." Remi buys a hot dog in a cardboard sleeve, squirts it with neon yellow mustard.

"About what?"

A drunk leans against the condiment stand, staring at Remi's steaming hot dog. Remi motions Hen with a jerk of his head and they walk a few feet away.

"Thing is," he says. "You and Chickie are getting too old to be horsing around like that."

"Like what?"

"The vampire bit. Your head in her lap. You can't do that stuff anymore."

"Why not?" Hen asks.

"Let's just say," Remi takes a bite of his hot dog, "that a woman's lap can be a very dangerous place."

Hen watches the drunk man sway as he takes a few unsteady steps, reaching out to prop himself against the wall.

"Listen." Remi puts his hand on Hen's shoulder. "I know you two have always been like a couple of puppies together," he says. "But you're getting too old for all that now. What can I tell you? Things change. Everything starts to get a lot more…complicated. Boys. Girls. You with me here, Hen?"

The drunk's hand doesn't quite reach the wall and he falls. Hen starts over to help him.

"What are you doing?" Remi says, grabbing his arm.

"I'm going to help that guy get up."

"What's the point?" Remi says, taking another bite of his hot dog. "Poor bastard'll just fall back down again. Am I right, Hen?"

Giving up the fight of gravity, the drunk curls his arm around his head where he lies and tucks his legs up into his stomach. A trickle of blood oozes from a cut on his cheek. Hen looks around to see who else is watching. The hawkers wave banners and programs and stuffed animals dangling from flimsy sticks. The cop at the gate twirls a toothpick in his mouth, gazing out onto Lansdowne Street. A wet patch forms in front of the drunk's hunched-up legs. Above them, in the ballpark, the crowd noise rises. Hen feels suddenly sick to his stomach.

"So as I was saying." Remi makes a ball of his mustardy napkin and tosses it into the trash. "About Chickie, Hen. About women—"

"Women?" Hen says.

Above them, the din swells high into a roar. Remi's bloodshot eyes rise to the cement ceiling. He had a drink before he came, one or two blasts earlier at Potts Pro, a shot in the bathroom, four or five swigs so far in the bleachers. There are bottles all over the house on Hemlock Street, stashed like forgotten eggs in an old Easter hunt, under the radiator, lurking at the backs of high bookshelves. The policeman finally saunters over and nudges the drunk man with his shoe. "Hey, Billy Budd," he says. "Can't stay here all night. Get yourself up now." He bends to shake the man's arm. "Let's go, old man."

Hen looks over at his father, down at the drunk, and back up at his father.

"'Nough said?" Remi says.

Hen turns away. The drunk man's moan turns into a swampy laugh.

"Do we understand one another, Hen? *Hen!* Good god. Have you heard anything I've said?"

The drunk rolls over on his back with an enormous belch. Hen feels his stomach heave. His father's asking him for something. He'd try to give it to him if he only knew what it was—a nod, a word, a stupid joke. But he can't do anything but stare at the drunk, at his swollen feet, his shoes, crushed and bloody at the heel. If he were his own man, he'd go over and help the cop get the drunk guy back on his feet. But he's not. He's just a chickenshit kid who's afraid to tell his old man where to go. More than anything, Hen wants to get away from his father, out of this dungeon, away from the bum and the cop and the sickening smells of mustard and peanuts and piss. He wants to go back up to the stands and the soft night air, to see what made the crowd go wild, to see what it is about Chickie that scares his father so much. And so, not knowing which of them is the bigger coward, he says, "Yeah, Dad. I catch your drift. Come on, let's get back to the game." Remi smiles and slaps him on the back. And because Hen hasn't braced himself, he stumbles.

Upstairs, a mist shimmers around the park lights as darkness falls. The fielders move deep back into left as Yaz comes up to the plate with the bases loaded. The crowd rises to its feet and starts to chant. A man sitting on top of the Marlboro sign waits to catch a hard-hit ball with an outstretched glove. Johnny Kiley's organ plays its swirling, staircase riffs. Yaz hits a foul ball and breaks the bat. The ball flies into the stands and a batch of young boys scramble. In the distance, the CITGO sign's red neon pyramid rises and falls. The bat boy retrieves the splintered lobe of Yaz's bat and runs back to the dugout for another.

Nash puts his hand on Chickie's knee. "Just like old times, honey."

"It still *is* old times, Dad." Chickie pulls her leg away.

Yaz gives the new bat a few test swings.

"Look at that stance." Nash hikes up his pants and props his hands on his knees. "That arm control, that grip. He's so calm, so focused. There's enough power in those arms to send a rocket ship to the moon. You notice how there are no fights in this game, Chick? You take hockey, football, it's all part of the show. There's glory in a good brawl. They actually hire goons to get the job done. But baseball's civilized; it's a thinking man's game. These guys can be big shots without throwing any punches. These are *real* athletes, Chick. This is a real sport. That's why this is—"

"*The* game," Chickie says softly.

"Right." Nash unscrews the top of his flask. "You remember what you said the first time I brought you to a ball game, Chick? You must have been all of four. You looked out over the field—"

Chickie rolls her eyes. "And I said, 'where're the womens?'"

"That's right." Nash chuckles. "You said, 'where're the womens?' And I said, 'They're coming, Chickie. They're a comin'. Just you wait and see.'"

"Yeah, big surprise." Chickie crosses her legs underneath her, looks out over the field. "Still not here yet," she says.

Yaz finally connects with a mighty crack of his bat. As the ball spins through the dusty light, the heads of the fielders rise. The man on the Marlboro sign takes off his cowboy hat and waves the ball out over the Pike. Yaz rounds the bases slowly, an easy lope, as the crowd goes wild.

"Grand slam! All the way home." Nash is up on his feet, yelling, cheering. "Unbelievable! You can always count on Yaz in the clutch."

"Hen's going to be pissed." Chickie smooths out a lime-green Doublemint wrapper and makes the first fold. "He didn't even want another hot dog," she says.

"Damn," Remi says softly, as he climbs back up to his seat. His eyes rise to the scoreboard as the 4 slides up beside the Yankees' 0.

"Moon-bound, Rem." Nash gives him the recap. "That ball went straight to heaven and no looking back. Baylor didn't even bother to reach for it."

"I thought we didn't believe in heaven," Chickie says.

"Oh, there's baseball heaven, for sure," Nash says. "Where all the fly balls go and baseball lovers follow. To watch the eternal seventh game."

"Sports pages open on every table," Remi says. "Fountains spouting whiskey."

Hen slides into an empty bleacher. Chickie slides along with him, pressing him up against the wall. "What'd he say to you down there?" she whispers.

"Nothing."

"Come on. He gave you the third degree about something. What was it?"

"Nothing." Hen whips a pile of baseball cards out of his back pocket. Dr. Strangeglove. Mesner. Yaz. It will be worth a lot someday. He'll make the Hall of Fame. Easy. Don't meet her eyes. Chickie won't quit; she'll drill into you until you're so full of holes you go limp like Swiss cheese. Carl Lester. His stats are wicked. Stop looking at her bare leg. Some scout found him whipping fastballs at a cactus in a parking lot in Arizona and brought him up for a tryout. Now he's leading the league in strikeouts. God, how can Chickie's skin be so smooth?

Chickie comes closer. Hen feels her breath on his cheek. "Was it the old birds and bees speech?" she asks. "Oh my god, your face is bright red. It was, wasn't it? Little late, don't you—"

"Shut up, Chickie," he says.

During the seventh-inning stretch, the crowd noise rises from a hum. Chickie and Hen stand up on the bleachers to see. Out on the field, three men in brown jumpsuits give chase to a creature which finally bangs up against the scoreboard, flaps its wings helplessly, and flops to the ground. Hen sees a flash of color as a tail rises, spreads part way, and falls.

"I'll be damned," Remi says. "It's a bird."

"A peacock or something," Nash says. "See the colored tail?"

"A goddamned bird," Remi says. "It's a goddamned peacock or something."

"Let me see." As Hen takes the binoculars from around his father's neck, the thick, sour smell of whiskey floats up his nose. Narrowing his eyes into the lenses, he watches the bird struggle in short spurts, then fall still. A man hops into a baseball-shaped cart and corners it near the dugout. Two others come running over with a net. The bird bounces up and down, gaining a few feet and then losing them, trying desperately to fly. The crowd noises roll in waves across the bleacher seats. Nash takes a swig from his flask. The Yankee zero on the scoreboard slides to one side. Swinging the binoculars left, Hen sees a man's head peering out of the square black hole. Someone nearby turns on a transistor radio.

"Well, what do you know," says the announcer, Curt Gowdy, in his gravelly voice. "I've heard of a bird in the hand being worth two in the bush, but a bird in the outfield, what do you figure that's worth, Don?"

"Gee, at this point, Curt," the color commentator says with a chuckle, "I don't think even a peacock can turn this game around for the Yankees."

As the game starts up again, Chickie's suddenly up and gone, skipping down the steps to the Red Sox bullpen, orange sock flashing. With a four-run lead in the seventh and the bird causing delay of game, the Sox pitchers are easy, chewing tobacco, tossing the ball back and forth. Hen closes in on Chickie with the binoculars. Her shirt shimmies up as she leans over the railing, high-top sneakers loose on her ankles, hair streaming down her back. She blows her bangs away from her eyes with her lower lip stuck out on one side, hands a pen to one of the pitchers. Hen pulls her outstretched arm into the lens and sees the braided rope bracelet on her wrist, the one she got at the whaling museum the summer before. Dick Radatz writes his name on the back of Chickie's hand. Hen swings the binoculars back over to the bird, still struggling in the corner under the net, and catches the head of the scorekeeper disappearing back behind the Yankees' zero.

"We've just gotten word from the field," Curt Gowdy says on the transistor. "Someone's coming over from the Franklin Park Zoo. This bird could be famous, Don. Today, Fenway Park…tomorrow, who knows, the Johnny Carson show maybe? Think they need another peacock over at NBC?"

"Right, Curt. An understudy, maybe." Don's chuckle echoes across the field.

Hen lets the binoculars fall as Chickie leaps back up the wide cement steps, two at a time.

"I got Radatz's autograph!" she calls out. "I'm never going to wash this hand again!"

"Your mother may have something to say about that," Nash says.

"Cleanliness…next to godliness," Remi says. "Isn't that what they say?"

"We don't believe in God," Chickie says. "That's why our house is such a pigsty."

"Chickie," Nash warns.

"Well, it's true."

Hen closes his eyes as Chickie bumps down beside him, tugging at his arm. The bird lies still under the net in the corner of the field. His heart beats fast. He wants to go home, brush his teeth, empty his pockets, close his eyes. He feels his breath come short. He knows how that bird feels to have landed on a strange, mocking planet. That bird tricked itself, did itself in, followed the shimmering lights and the sweet smells to what it thought was a safe, green place, crash-landed, maybe even broke its wing. This bird belongs in the book of fables and fools, in a cobweb-covered forest beside the crow that dropped the cheese to sing to the fox and the dog who lost its bone to its own reflection in the water. The moral is, don't be fooled by a father with free baseball tickets, by a grass too green, an ice cream bar too sweet. His belly aches. He missed Yaz's grand slam. The drunk's probably back out on the street now, still soaked in his own piss. Chickie won't leave him alone. And now he's not supposed to touch her anymore. Don't be fooled by a game that is only a game, or a cousin who puts her hands around your neck, pretending to be a vampire when she's really a…

Chickie edges closer, smelling still of gum and now of the rosin from the pitcher's hand. As she presses her fingers into Hen's arm, the tips of her hair brush his knee through the hole in his jeans. "Come on, creep," she whispers. "Tell me. What did Uncle Remi say to you down there? Was it a cozy little father-son moment or what?"

"Buzz off, Chickie," Hen says. "Just leave me alone."

"Fine. Be that way."

"Quarter says Conigliaro will lift his right foot before his left." Remi puts a quarter down on the bleacher.

"I'll take some of that action." Nash digs in his pocket for more change. "I say left before right. How 'bout you, Hen? You want in?"

"Who even cares?" Chickie asks, starting to braid her hair.

"He won't move either foot before the end of the count," Hen says. "Double the bet. Fifty cents." He slaps down two quarters. Chickie cracks the knuckles on both hands and gives him the evil eye. Conigliaro stands still out in right field, as Malone hits one foul ball after another. The man on the Marlboro sign waits, gloved hand poised. With un-blinking eyes, Hen wills Conigliaro not to move. Under the net the bird lies motionless. Hen bets he knows just how that bird feels.

2

When Chickie and Nash get home from the ball game, Violet's sitting on the couch in the living room, darning a white linen tablecloth. They have only one. Violet mends and irons it every year before the Fourth of July picnic on the river. Every year it gets flung over a warped picnic table—stained with ketchup, booze, and grass, ravaged all over again. The tablecloth belonged to a grandmother Violet was made to visit every summer as a child. Part of her still believes she gave her grandmother that stroke the summer she was fourteen, wishing it on her from over a hundred miles away, just so she wouldn't have to board that Greyhound bus one more time, to eat cold, lumpy oatmeal every day, watching the slowest moving clock in the world, the rotary fan creaking in the stifling Iowa heat, flies buzzing around the turning fruit, listening to the litany of her grandmother's ailing friends—failing hearts and stuck bowels, kidney stones, ulcers, varicose veins. Violet will forever see the twisted face of her grandmother after the stroke, the apricot folds under her eye, the slack, drooling mouth. When Violet mends the tablecloth, she's mending that tangled, rubbery mask of a face, that limp body she still half-believes she cursed with her dread.

"How was the game?" Violet asks. She's stopped going to the beauty parlor every week, does her own hair now in a beer and egg wash. Tight curls slowly unwind.

"Sox creamed 'em." Chickie throws her jacket on the couch.

"No contest." Nash pours himself a brandy from the liquor caddy on wheels. "Yaz got a grand slam, and Lonborg was sizzling."

"Sizzling." Violet feels the word dance in her mouth. *Cream, slam, soar.* Maybe if they talked in onomatopoeia, or sports headlines, they'd do better—*Violet mashes potatoes! Fish finally frying. Tub gets scrubbed! Chickie and Nash slide home. Vi seizes socks! Match. Set. Sizzle. Score!*

Violet pricks her finger with the needle. "Damn," she says softly.

"You okay?" Nash says.

"I'll live," Violet says, sucking the blood from her finger.

"'Night, girls." Nash heads for the stairs, brandy sloshing, gleaming orange in a jelly jar. "Sleep tight—"

"Yeah, yeah, don't let the bedbugs bite," Chickie calls back, as she swings into the kitchen and back out again with a slice of Sara Lee pound cake, dipping it into a glass of milk.

"'Night, Mom," she says.

"Sweet dreams," Violet says.

Upstairs, Chickie sits on the edge of her bed. Her room's a junk-yard—chewed-up teddy bears, jigsaw puzzles, cotton candy holders, ticket stubs. On the bedside wall is a poster of Marlon Brando sitting on a motorcycle, below it a color photo of the 1966 Red Sox team. Chickie kicks off her sneakers at the heel, peels off the mismatched socks, and sticks them over the bedposts. Lying back, she studies her hand. Radatz's autograph is starting to smudge. She should've had him sign a piece of paper, something that would last. But she wanted to touch him, see what a ball player felt like—flesh on flesh. She wanted Dick Radatz to touch her back. Taking the team picture off the wall, she kisses his paper lips.

Springing off the bed, Chickie rummages in her top bureau drawer. Behind a mess of underwear and socks, she finds a blue long-sleeved leotard she wore in the sixth grade when she played the part of a wave in a Boston Tea Party skit. Slipping out of her clothes, she catches her reflection in the mirror on the back of the door. When Chickie looks at herself after the ball game at fourteen, she catches a sharp-edged, quick-eyed stranger. She has to twist and turn to find a self that's famil-iar, that's whole. Her neck's too long; her rib cage sticks out in a V. She's softer now, all stretched out. Her bones rattle and her joints crack; her face turns odd shades of pink and green. Her shape's not permanent anymore, not hers to keep. She yanks the leotard up over her shoulders, turns her baseball cap around, pulls pretend pistols out of the holsters of her hipbones, and shoots at the nipple of each breast.

On her way down the hallway, Chickie peers into her parents' bed-room, where Nash sits on the edge of the bed with his brandy, watching the sports roundup on the eleven o'clock news. Used to be she'd fling herself across the bed and they'd watch to see if they could find them-selves in the crowd shots. Now she steers clear of this dark and moldy room. It only smells of her father now—of booze and stale popcorn and newspapers and sweat. Gone are the mother smells of perfume, lilac, baby powder, silk, new paperbacks, and damp wool. Chickie twirls down the hallway, bumping up against the wall in her blue leotard, hugging her shadow as she creeps. Her sisters' old rooms lie empty, untouched—Frankie Avalon posters, disconnected princess phones, Shirelles records, pink chenille bedspreads with dangling balls, sports banners and twisted paper clips, locked and dusty diaries. Doo-wahs, whispers, threats, and swear words sneak out of the doors and pounce as she passes by, holding her breath the way she does passing graveyards in the car. Her sisters' rooms hold Chickie's future hostage. In the closets are brown saddle shoes lined up in a tidy row, scuffed and scrunched at the heel, under the winter loden coats hung in cellophane that she'll have to wear as she grows into them, olive green, old-lady coats with barrel-shaped buttons. Mothballed hats and scratchy woolen scarves. Ugly, spinster, hope-chest hand-me-downs. Only when Seph and Janie really grow up, Chickie knows—when they get real jobs, marry real husbands, make real babies, only then will Violet clean out their rooms and throw the windows open wide. Only then will Chickie be free.

Chickie stands at the top of the rounded staircase in her blue leotard and looks down at her mother on the couch, tablecloth still draped over her legs. Violet's strangely still, the darning needle raised in one hand. A cigarette burns in the ashtray beside her. The living room is filled with things made of glass, leather, and black metal, praying mantis tables, spidery hanging lamps, enamel cratered ashtrays the colors of wet earth and dried blood. Styles from an era not long gone but already lost—everything scratched and dull. Nash's lumpy green armchair is the only soft and homey object in the room.

"Mom?" Chickie calls out, halfway down the stairs.

"Chickie!" Violet's hand flies up to her collarbone. "You startled me. We already said goodnight, didn't we?"

"So?" Chickie reaches the bottom of the stairs.

"So how was the game?"

"You already asked me that."

"I didn't get any details, though," Violet says. "I never get any details anymore."

"This bird flew into the ballpark and broke its wing. A peacock or something, with a beautiful tail."

"How strange."

"I ate too much." Chickie lifts up her fingers to count. "Two ice cream bars, one hot dog, a popcorn, two Cokes."

"Ouch. Time to start watching the scale." Violet snaps the thread with her teeth. "Why do you have that old leotard on, Chickie?"

"I want to be a dancer."

"Why not be a baseball player?" Violet smiles. "They make a lot more money."

"Girls can't play pro ball," Chickie says. "Anyway, I don't care about the money."

"Of course you don't care about the money," Violet says.

"I don't *care* about the *money*, Mom."

"Lots of girls want to be ballerinas." Violet scans the tablecloth for more holes. "That's fine, Chickie. Although I'd say you're starting about ten years too late."

"A modern dancer. Not a ballerina."

"Like Isadora Duncan?" Violet's eyes rise. "The one who was strangled by her own scarf?"

Chickie pauses, hands on hips. "It was an accident," she says.

"Was it?"

The heat rushes up into Chickie's face as she reaches deep down for words that will cut into her mother's steely calm. She takes off her baseball cap and pushes the coffee table up against the wall. "Just watch me, Mom." She turns on the stereo and places the needle on the record's last black ridge. "Just watch me dance."

It's a frightening thing when a child leaps ahead in time before a parent is ready, as children sometimes do in photographs or dreams, caught in a certain pose, a point of reflection, a gesture half-made. Violet remembers looking at Chickie when she was about two years old—disheveled, nearly bald, reckless—and having a flash of worry that as a mother, careless in the making of this child, she'd been irresponsible. She straightens up on the couch, steeling herself against the rush of feelings that spills over her with such force as Chickie begins to dance, coming out of a spin and leaping clear across the room to the edge of the patio door. The muscles in her legs burst to the surface as she leans into a split, bends backwards, and arches herself up into a bridge. On her feet again, she floats across the room, slender arms flung high. Violet breathes deeply. Some part of her has always known this was coming. She's been trying to stop it, without even knowing what it was. On her mind's jagged edge, she's always believed that in some strange way, the rise of Chickie must inevitably mean her fall. More acrobat than dancer, still, there's a new look in this child's eye, a ferocious grace. Gone, suddenly, irrevocably, is the gawky tomboy. This is what Chickie will do, and no one will stop her, though Lord knows Violet will try; why she's started to ride this last daughter so close and so hard, she'll never understand. Some days in the name of protection or pride, some days practicality, some days maybe out of sheer spite. She sees it all now for what it might well be—the last child nearly grown, troubled times and a stale marriage, the mother left in a puddle of loss, the fear of growing older and no better in a changing world, settling for vicarious triumphs and pleasure, giving up, giving in. Now, as she watches Chickie dance, Violet feels the senselessness of the struggle with something between relief and despair. There'll be no keeping Chickie from dancing, or dancing from Chickie. It will feed her and gnaw away at her, and in the end it will pull her away. For once a child has an obsession, she no longer has need of a mother.

The music washes over Violet like a chilling stream—Beethoven's Symphony no. 3. Chickie's no fool. This is the record Nash plays every year on their anniversary. She knows this music makes Violet come undone, spikes her like a wobbly arrow from a drunk Cupid's bow. She knows how this music sends her parents upstairs to the bedroom each year after the family party, tipsy, singing off-key and laughing. Violet rubs the worn tablecloth against her cheek. Chickie's no fool. She comes toward her in a series of fluttering spins. Landing at Violet's feet, she sinks gracefully onto bony knees. "Are you watching?" she says, as she turns.

"I'm watching." Violet reaches out to touch her, but Chickie's already gone, twirled halfway back across the room in a blurry spin. Violet lets the tablecloth fall. Just recently she had a vision of Chickie grown, a teacher with a nice husband and a couple of sturdy kids, a year-round tan and wraparound skirt, a cottage and a rowboat in Maine, a garden forever in need of weeding. She thought she'd come a long way to want the simple things for her last child. Priorities in order. Happiness over success. She'd pushed her first two daughters too hard, too far, too fast, past rebellion into what seems to be a perpetual state of passive-aggressive limbo. She can see now the mistakes she may have made. She thought she'd gotten over the feeling that her children owed her something, the way she thought she owed her mother college and a husband. Such debts are best left unpaid; time always evens the score. One day a granddaughter of hers may come to visit on a bus from a faraway place and put a silent stroke of a curse on her—planting soft lips on withering cheeks with a dark and secret smile.

Next to the framed Ben Shahn print, Chickie does a deep plié, thigh muscles tensing, chin tilted upward. Her head sits regal on her long neck, strong nose pointing upward. She's straight from head to toe, no roundness yet, no true curves—no excess flesh, no swoony smiles, no pretty pleases. Suddenly Violet sees Chickie grown another way—thin and haggard in a loft in SoHo, alone and liking it that way, wiry, explosive lovers and sour milk in a dark fridge, cheap wine and gnarled feet on a wooden stage, bare light bulbs and a ring in the toilet bowl, bills piled high, no breasts to speak of, no children and no money, not much in need of a garden, or a rowboat, or a fond, regretful mother. The music falls into adagio. Chickie sweeps low to the ground, hair trailing the dusty floor. Violet sees herself grown old—fat, bitter, ravenous, substituting lemon drops and cheesecake for sex. An anger sweeps up from her center, searing and powerless. How dare Chickie be so bold, so clever about the music and the timing of things, on this night when she's mending the damn tablecloth, missing the ballpark, remembering the nameless man in the crowd? How dare Chickie have kept this secret for so long? How did this graceful child ever spring from her body, and what did she drag from Violet as she came? How dare Chickie be so impossibly sensual, so impossibly…young?

The music ends and Chickie lands on the floor in a split. The needle of the record player scratches back and forth. Wiggling her toes, she waits. The dishwater-gray cat on the sofa licks its outstretched paw.

"Well. That was quite a performance," Violet says, finally.

"So, can I take dance lessons?" Chickie says.

Violet holds up her palms. "I don't see how I can refuse."

Chickie groans. "Don't say it like that."

"Like what?"

"Like I'm going to screw it up and it's all going to be a big disaster."

"It's a lot of money, Chickie. A big commitment. You'd have to—"

"You just think I'm going to quit. Or be bored or be lousy at it."

"I just told you, Chickie. You can take the lessons. You win."

She collapses on her knees. "Je-sus. I wasn't trying to *win* anything."

"Maybe not." Violet picks up her darning needle again. "Nevertheless, Minerva," she says, "you did."

Chickie goes over to her mother, thinking maybe to hug her, but Violet's all wrapped up in the tablecloth again, holding the needle with the blackened tip pointing upward.

"Thanks, Mom." She heads for the stairs. "I'm going upstairs to tell Dad."

"Go ahead," Violet says. "Tell him you're going to be the next Isadora

Duncan. And, Chickie?" Her voice catches Chickie on the second step.

"What?"

"Don't mention the scarf." The corners of Chickie's mouth rise in a grateful smile. This is as close to praise, as close to apology and affection, as Violet can come. As Chickie pounds up the stairs, she pulls the tablecloth around her shoulders, suddenly cold, seeing it for what it is, a once-fine thing, now shoddy and ruined—beyond full repair. Still, she picks up a frayed corner and starts to mend, pulling the needle in and out, in and out.

"Hey, Da-ad!" Chickie calls out as she hits the top of the stairs.

"Hey, wha-at?"

Violet looks up. She didn't even think to consult Nash before she said yes to Chickie. She rarely does. She plans the meals, the wardrobes, the decor—haircuts, guest lists, vacations, parties. She balances the checkbook, buys the towels, arranges for the gutters to be cleaned and the house to be painted. All her business. The business of house and home. She orders the bulbs for the garden and the winter boots, makes the doctor's appointments, the excuses, all the moves. Nash never questions her, rarely offers a suggestion. "Green might be a good color for those cabinets or pork chops would be nice. We can't afford this." Or, "I don't want to go. It's up to you, Vi. Whatever you want, whatever you think best." Even in bed, she calls the shots—Nash is happy, up, down, beside, behind. He can always get it up, even when he's down. Do we have enough money, Vi? Is it time yet? Does that feel good? Will I be sorry? Can I come yet? Where do we keep the stapler, Vi? *Vi? Vi? Vi?* You won't be sorry. Trust me. Do it this way. Touch me there. Trust me. Again. No. Wait. Now. The stapler's on the desk, Nash, where it's been for the last twenty years. Do it now. Harder. Faster. Trust me, Nash. Twenty goddamned years. Touch me there, again.

Two years ago, when she first told him about her idea to open a stationery store, voicing her worries—the time commitment, the double mortgage, the incredible risk—all he said was, "Go for it, Vi." Just like that. Go for it. Violet saw this as naivete and not encouragement.

"But we can't possibly afford it." She played her own devil's advocate, paced and fretted and fumed. "It's a huge risk. I have no experience in retail. The rent alone. Pott's Pro's a leaky ship. This could be the end of us."

"We'll manage," Nash said. "Life's short. You're a born businesswoman, Vi. Go ahead and give it a shot."

"Bourgeois bravado," she'd snapped, impatient, grumpy, finally giving up trying to shake Nash into a panic and plunging ahead with her plans for the store. But he'd been right. She was ready; she was a natural. She'd done the books at Potts Pro for years, gotten an accounting degree at Northeastern in the years after Chickie was born. She had good people skills, a knack for organization, a flair for design. Nash was right. Life was short; nothing ventured, nothing gained. Even if he'd put his foot down, she would've gone ahead. It was just his relentless optimism she couldn't bear.

The only thing that seems to get Nash out of his armchair these days—besides baseball and his daughters—the only thing that shakes his heart and his soul is the war in Vietnam. He reads the papers, watches the news, mutters, paces, and swears. He writes letters to the president, to his congressmen, to *The Boston Globe*; goes to rallies in the Square and on the Common; rants and raves at the dinner table, at taxi drivers, at the newscasters on TV. "What the hell does Johnson think he's doing? Does he realize these are human beings he's sending over there, not chess pieces?" When Nash is angry, he comes alive, handsome and vital, like the old Nash. When he's drunk, he's not much more than a passive, aging jock. Funny thing, Violet thinks, to be jealous of a whiskey bottle all these years, and now, possibly, a war.

Violet looks over at the empty armchair, the indented cushion of its seat. She sometimes thinks of herself as a widow with a pension and Nash a harmless ghost who shares their house, drinks the liquor, and rumples the sheets, asks for sex every couple of nights, watches TV, tells dumb jokes—Why was Six afraid of Seven? Because Seven ate Nine. He laughs easily, cries at the drop of a soft hat. A ghost who leaves the appliances on but is harmless enough and surely entitled. After all, it's his lineage, his town, his home. She married him. To love, honor and—she refused to say the last word—obey. It was only a symbolic act, a pagan ritual, an archaic word. Grown-up people didn't obey one another anymore. In her family, power had been a man's legacy. Her father worked the farm with her brothers, brought home the bacon, made the rules. And as the bacon sizzled and spat in the pan, her mother quietly enforced them. But Nash never wanted to take the helm of this family. Power makes him uncomfortable; he's always pushed it her way. She didn't set out to oust him from his patriarchal throne. Secretly she may have wanted the power, but no one could ever claim she stole it. So why, then, after all these years, does she feel guilty?

Violet swore when she left Iowa that she'd freed herself forever from the windswept wasteland of her Midwestern home, where a girl had but two choices: to be a wife and mother or an old maid. She swore she'd marry a good man, a fair man, a fun man; swore that her children would never have such a father as hers—humorless, hard, and narrow; swore that any daughter of hers would never feel as she often had, like a piece of cattle, raised to cook and breed. She vowed that her daughters would understand that they could do anything in this world—*anything*—if they wanted to, if they really tried. The awful thought occurs to Violet, as Chickie flies off to tell Nash about the dancing lessons, that she, Violet, is slowly turning into her father—weary, bitter, controlling. She's even molded a waxen father image for her children. She's reinvented Nash over the years, shaped him, put words in his mouth, ideas in his head. Dad will do this. What Dad means is…Nash made it easy. He bowed out early. Do whatever you want, Vi. You care more than I do. Whatever you say. Mom says this. If Mom says. I don't want a scene. I don't want to hurt anyone. No hard choices. Don't leave me alone. Don't take away my children. Baseball or booze. Sunday dinner. Sex. Beethoven. Bar stools. Bridge. Some people hunt change. Some fear it; some flee it like a plague. But change simply hurt Nash's feelings.

Violet hears thumping upstairs and knows that Nash and Chickie are dancing, not the kind Chickie did for her in the living room, but a made-up dance of celebration and affection—part jig, part tango, part twist. Violet closes her eyes as Nash's voice rises in silly song— *"I dream of Chickie, with a tutu on."* She hears Chickie laugh and then groan. In the dark, behind closed eyes, Violet pictures her new stationery store on Putnam Avenue, the tidy, swept aisles, shelves neatly stocked, a world where order reigns, where she feels the wash of power, cool and clean, a world where she is truly queen. She pictures herself there, alone, unclothed in the darkness, a tall shadow lurking in the aisle, breathing hard—the man in the trench coat from the baseball stands—who after all these years, would never have aged, who would've kept her in mink and diamonds, the man whose children wouldn't have caused stretch marks or worry, whose hairline never would have receded, the man with no apparent name, no apparent past, the man who will play with her weaknesses, forgive them, the man whose lure she has resisted all these years. *Resisted*, by god.

Violet wraps the tablecloth tightly around her. She's done all right; she's done the best she could. It hasn't been easy. She's kept the fever inside. It could've ruined her. All these years she's been faithful. When she married Nash, she thought she was headed down Easy Street, not this bumpy, twisted road. Someone had to keep this family glued together. At times it's been a thankless job. But it's not much of a father she's drummed up for her children—a hapless, shuffling, drunken ghost. And in the end, as Chickie and Nash dance together in the TV-lit room above her, it's her own feet that are left itching.

On the Fourth of July, the Potts family gathers upriver in the late afternoon, near the Brighton line, across from the stadium and the AM radio station, where the grass is lush and the water just short of foul, where children swing and splash in an aqua wading pool and gardeners putter in tangled plots, picnickers toss burgers on the grill. On the Coppertone billboard, the pigtailed girl's white bottom is laid bare by the teeth of a friendly dog. The modern theater angles sharklike out of the weeping willows. On a wooden bridge, men stand for hours casting fishing lines which bring up bits of trash or metal, an occasional gasping carp. On this hot afternoon, the wind blows strong from the southwest and the river doesn't smell too bad. Chickie drives over to the picnic in the Ford Falcon with her parents, her back and arms sunburned from a day at Crane Beach the weekend before. She sits in the sweltering silence at a red light, peeling bits of crackling, translucent skin from her shoulders. Nash and Violet sit silently in the front seat, reminding Chickie of days gone by, when she was the sulky rider and her parents still spoke to each other in the car.

Violet and Nash tumble out into the parking lot, slumped puppets brought to life by the pulling of old family strings. They start to speak of ordinary things, make plans, even touch each other in passing.

"Gotta get some air in that back tire," Nash says.

"Damn it," says Violet. "I left the bug stuff at home. They'll eat me alive."

"I'll get the charcoal going. Vi, you ready for a drink?"

"Scotch and soda." Violet slaps at a mosquito. "There's the first bite. They just love me. I always forget how pretty it is down here."

The lines of old July Fourths tumble forth. Chickie guides her toes in between the thongs of her flip-flops and steps out onto the parking lot. She feels an odd comfort, wrapped in the warm tangle of the warped familiar. Nash takes her three-speed bike off the car rack and swings it down with a bump of its tires. She waits for the echo of the déjà vu—Nash grumbling she better ride the damn thing after he lugged it all the way down here. "You hear me, Chickie? *Chickadee? Chickadee?*" She wheels the bike over onto the grass and leans it up against a tree. Her uncle Remi and aunt Faye stroll over, hands in the pockets of their matching madras shorts. Faye pats Chickie's arm hello.

"Where's Hen?" Chickie says.

"Down there." Faye smiles and points toward the riverbank. "He's been waiting for you."

Remi bends over and opens the cooler to grab a beer. Violet spreads her grandmother's tablecloth over the picnic table and runs her fingers over the darned patches admiringly. Nash lugs over the charcoal bri-quets and wipes the black grit from his palms. Chickie's sister Janie is there already, sitting alone, reading the newspaper at a picnic table. Her oldest sister, Seph, the birthday girl, arrives soon after, loaded down with bags, breathless, rumpled, an unannounced guest at her side.

"Hi, guys," Seph says. "Sorry I'm late. This is Meadow."

"You're always late, Persephone." Violet barely kisses Seph's cheek. "We depend on you to be late. Hello, Meadow. Seph didn't mention she was bringing a friend."

Nash gazes fondly at his oldest daughter. Despite Vi's relentless crit-icism, Seph is still nothing less than perfect in his eyes. Solid, smart, real in every way. It seems to infuriate Vi that he so steadfastly holds their eldest child in such high regard, as if he's not paying attention, not being a good father, by refusing to acknowledge her limitations, her flaws. Weren't they supposed to love and champion their children uncondi-tionally? Wasn't that the idea? he once asked her. Yes. Exactly. Vi was furious, defensive, insisting her disappointment was a measure of how much she *did* love Seph, how highly she thought of her. Seph could do anything she set her mind to. *Anything. That* was unconditional love, Vi said. Above all else in the quagmire of family life, the rift between Seph and Violet bewilders Nash the most. He can't convince Vi, doesn't even bother to try anymore, that it's not denial, or stubborn refusal, the way he feels about Seph, about all of his daughters. Whoever and whatever they turn out to be, to him they'll always be exquisite, shining stars. It's simply the truth of the way he feels.

Seph was the oldest of all the cousins, though not by much, with Buzz arriving right on her heels. Nash remembers his first little girl so well, born in the spring of '44, sturdy and impossibly sweet, so easy with a hug it made his heart ache and made Vi worry that later she wouldn't use caution with strangers. What odd notions Vi had, how skewed sometimes, perverse almost, imagining Seph as sexual prey for pedophiles, even as she chattered away in her playpen with a toothless smile. A talker at ten months, three syllable words—*everything, invited, marmalade,* prepositions by a year, compound verb tenses by sixteen months. *Actually Mom, I'd rather have Rice Krispies.* Before her first tooth fell out, Seph was reading the morning paper. An exalted, high-minded child, Vi declared, and how was Nash to do anything but agree? A keen ear and sharp mind, playing Beethoven sonatas at six and writing play-scripts with parts for each family member by seven.

Whatever in god's name happened? It's been Violet's outcry, her lament now, for so many years. Since Seph turned twelve and became suddenly, bewilderingly, sullen and hostile, as insular and depressed as she'd once been affectionate and outgoing, as intellectually passive as she'd once been bold. Adolescence. It was a rough ride—everyone consoled them—teachers, relatives, friends. She'd pull out of it, come around. Vi voiced her worries openly, her disappointment, her dashed hopes. "Oh my god, have you seen all the weight she's gained? A C+ in calculus? That's it; Radcliffe will never take her now. She's turning into a slug. Remember how beautifully she used to swim? And do you think she might ever actually pick up a book about someone who hasn't entirely given up on the human race?" Nash sighs. Vi's love was exhausting sometimes.

Problem is, he *does* remember, and yet he forgets so much. Vi would say he remembered selectively, only what made him feel good, that he was too much of a coward to face the tough facts, the realities. But what Vi's never realized, still so blinded by that first rush of betrayal, is that Seph *did* come out of that adolescent funk, did turn back into that frighteningly intelligent girl with a ferocious heart. She did go to college and she did thrive, just not in the way Violet had planned. Middlebury, not Radcliffe. The outdoor club, not the debate team. Three languages. But none of them Latin. A solid, good-looking girl, if not a beauty. Her fierce love of people took a political turn and she took on the causes of the underfed, the underappreciated, the unrepresented. Turned out she didn't want to rule the world, only try to help make it a little better.

"Hey, Dad," Seph says suddenly from across the picnic table. "What are you thinking about? You're a million miles away."

"You, kiddo."

"What about me?"

"I was just thinking how terrific you are," he says.

Seph rolls her eyes and laughs. "Jeepers, Dad," she says.

Violet spins a three-quarter turn to face her sister-in law. "Faye." The Iowa in her voice always rises when she talks to Faye. "How are you?"

"I'm fine," Faye says. Their eyes race up and down each other's bodies. "Have you lost weight, Vi? You look—"

"Just got over the flu," Violet says. "Lucky me. Couldn't keep down a thing."

"It suits you," Faye says. "How's business at the store?"

"Steady. That's as much as I can hope for, I guess," Violet says. "They say the first year of owning a business is a killer and I've survived. It's been a challenge, I'll say that much. I'm exhausted. At night I dream about drowning in vats of ink, being smothered by truckloads of paper."

Faye laughs. "I love your shirt." She blurts out the lie before the truth beats it to the punch.

"You like it?" Violet sucks in her stomach, pulls the shirt away from her skin. "I bought it on a whim. A girl was selling them on the street. Tie-dye, she called it." Until Faye's remark, Violet had thought the shirt one of the boldest, most beautiful things she'd ever worn, but now, glancing down, it looks like nothing more than a mess in a child's paintbox let loose in a white load of wash.

"It's not like anything I've ever seen before." Faye comes around to seeing the shirt's beauty just as Violet loses sight of it. "It's quite gorgeous, actually."

"I don't know," Violet says. "I don't really think it's me."

"Maybe with some black slacks."

"I'm really too old for this sort of thing," Violet says. "I should give it to Chickie. It's more her style."

"What's style, anyway?" Faye says softly. This is how she and Violet talk, after all these years, all these picnics, in the ebb and flow of innuendo and flattery, gibe and suggestion—half in cahoots, half for the kill—this, their very tense and fragile version of friendship.

Nash and Remi sling off their shirts, collars faded, alligators peeling snout to tail's end. Hen's brother, Buzz, pulls up in his beat-up Mustang and throws a football from the parking lot out onto the field.

"Hey, Buzz, old man!" Remi calls out.

"Who you calling an old man?" Buzz calls back to his father. Making *hut-hut* noises, he joins the twins on the grass. The three of them run around in lumbering circles, marking end zones and goalposts with shoes and discarded clothes, tossing the spinning ball back and forth. On the river boats glide by, bare-chested boys astride their bows, beer cans in hand. On the way down to the riverbank, Chickie passes Hen's sister, Tory, walking with her new boyfriend, John.

"So what do you think, John?" Tory stops him by a tree and digs her chin into the ridge of his shoulder. "Move over Addams Family or what?"

"They're not so strange, Tor," Adam says. "From the way you described your family, I expected a bunch of borderline psychotics. They seem very nice—quite conventional, actually."

"Yeah, but behind all that convention is a whole lot of WASPy neurosis. You're the shrink, Johnnie. Tell me all about it."

"I'm not a shrink yet."

"Close enough." She wraps her arms around his neck. "Go ahead. Analyze me, delve, interpret, explain. How do I fit into this wacko crowd?"

"You're the jewel, Tor." John brushes her cheek with his hand. "The uncut diamond, the—"

"Seriously."

"We all feel critical of our families." John's hand slips away from Tory's face. "Especially when we see them through a new pair of eyes."

"You know almost everything, don't you?" Tory kisses him on the mouth.

John half-catches Tory's lips before they pull away, never sure when she's teasing him. "You know the rest," he says.

Unpacking the picnic stuff, Faye watches Tory, so full of herself and this boy, surprised to see a softness in her daughter's dark eyes. This one is different—calm, self-assured, a blusher but no fool. Tory seems to really like him. Maybe this boy matters. If he does, it's reason enough for Faye to take note, to watch him carefully. If he's the one who can keep Tory from her own self, then there's reason to be grateful.

Remi jogs down to the riverbank. "Come on, Hen," he calls out. "Game time. Forty yard line. Up and at 'em. Go out long, man. Reach!" Running backwards, Remi spirals the football high into the air. Hen shuffles a few steps to his left, dives for the ball, and misses. Buzz swoops in and scoops up the bouncing ball at the edge of the brackish water. "Got it, bro!" he calls out. "Comin' back at you, Dad!"

Remi catches the ball and runs, slams it down on the ground near the goalpost shoe, and does the age-old touchdown dance. Hen stands still by the water, hands stuffed into his pockets, waiting to see if anything else is expected of him. From across the field, still breathing hard, Remi gives him a distant look. *It was a good throw, son,* the look says. *You should've caught it. It's a good game. Why don't you want to play?* Hen catches his father's look as neatly as Buzz caught the fumbled ball and sits back down by the water's edge.

Back at the picnic table, Faye breathes deeply. At least Remi doesn't torture Hen anymore. In years past, he's sneered at him—army-general-style, made him try another catch, punched his shoulder hard and told him to go out long for the ball—again and again. Faye's worries about Hen haven't changed much since he was small—that he's too fair, too fragile, too fey. She never worried this way about Buzz. Buzz was just, well...Buzz. As if in answer, he jogs by and plants a clumsy kiss on her cheek. "Hello, Mader," he says with a grin. Her fingers rise to touch the cheek when he's gone. Maybe it's the job of the firstborn to humble and ennoble a mother this way. When she was first pregnant and people asked her what she wanted—boy or girl—she'd spout the usual answer, that she didn't care, as long as the baby was healthy, had all ten fingers and toes. Buzz was born healthy but, as if in jest, without the thumb on his left hand. The tiny hand unfurled, incomplete, no trick of the pain or the weary eye. No one's fault, the doctors assured her, maybe a fluke, maybe the medicine she'd taken for the flu in her second month. She should feel lucky. In the room next door, a baby was missing part of his brain. They did terrific things these days with reconstructive surgery—a bit of buttock for an ear, a chunk of thigh for a thumb. Lucky, they said. But try as she might, Faye couldn't feel lucky. She felt guilty, inadequate; worst of all, she felt cheated. Buzz wasn't the baby she'd imagined. He didn't babble or coo; he kicked and cried. Even in sleep he wasn't peaceful; he whimpered and tossed and fussed. She didn't love him enough, she was sure. Buzz wanted to be held endlessly, walked on her shoulder, sung to, no matter what the time or tune. If she stopped even for a minute, to reach for the phone or open the refrigerator door, to clear her throat or shake her shoulder free of a cramp, he'd arch his back and start to wail. And every time she thought to hold her ground and put the baby firmly down, his thumbless hand would clutch at her, not as well as it might have had the hand been complete.

When Buzz was eight months old, he broke the handle off Faye's favorite coffee mug. She'd carelessly left it on a low coffee table. He was learning to walk, cruising along the table's edge, babbling happily for once—that was the irony. She'd let down her guard, relaxed for maybe the first time since he'd been born, for maybe all of thirty seconds. She remembers the mug so well, a flock of penguins diving off an ice floe, the handle a perfect fit for the curve of her small hand. As Buzz's chubby fingers reached out and grabbed the mug, the coffee spilled all over the just-cleaned Oriental rug. Faye wasn't prepared for the rage, for the first clear feeling she'd felt for her baby besides a kind of bewildered responsibility. She plopped him down roughly in the playpen, afraid of what she might do next. For the first time in her adult life, as she mopped up the coffee and listened to Buzz howl, Faye wept. She somehow felt that with one thumb missing on her first child and the handle broken off her favorite coffee mug, she had no grasp left on her life. She glued the handle back on with Duco Cement and let it set for two days.

The next time Faye rocked a fretful Buzz to sleep, humming him a lullaby, sipping from the penguin mug, the glued handle came off and the hot coffee scalded Buzz's leg. Faye put butter on the burns. He cried for an hour before dropping into a restless sleep. She kept watch in a chair next to his crib all night, drinking in his pain and outrage, begging forgiveness, vowing to be a better mother from that moment on, to do whatever it took. But the day Buzz got burned, he changed. When he woke up the next morning, he smiled at Faye, held out his arms without malice or fear, his leg still raw and bandaged. He still wanted to be rocked in the same chair, with the same song, the same mother. He stopped crying except for when he needed something. He started to sleep through the night, to let other people hold him, to smile a roguish smile. It was as if the burn had clarified something, dislodged some huge rock of uncertainty wedged between them.

Buzz still bears a scar from the burn, but no grudge it seems, never any grudges. He's never even minded the oddly shaped thumb they made for him when he was six, a doughy stub with no knuckle or nail, the resulting dent in his thigh. Another child might have felt angry, withered, self-conscious. What separated man from the apes, after all, but the jointed thumb? Children with disabilities often overcompensated, the doctors said—the ice skater with the mangled toes, the ballplayer with one arm. Some people found ways to rise above it all, and Buzz had done just that. It was on the day he got burned that Faye started to love Buzz. And ever since, she's been sorting out how much love has to do with gratitude, how much guilt has to do with fear. Faye is truly fond of Buzz, grateful, and proud of the well-placed feelings. So gentle, consistent, loyal. Her earnest, lumbering, firstborn son.

Down by the river now, slumped against a birch tree, is Hen. Another son. Another matter. Faye watches the back of his shaggy, Beatle-cut head, motionless, on level with the passing boats on the water. She wishes she weren't the one to know his secrets. She can't tell him it's okay for a Potts to hate football, or to cry, to want to spend a day just leaning against a tree. He's so much like her. She's helpless before him; she knows him far too well. But she can't let on; she must play dumb. All these years she's been the mother in the apron who makes him French toast and drives him to the dentist, who takes out his splinters and sees to it that his homework's done. In days gone by she changed his diapers and made him eat his peas. The job of mother doesn't change much in nature—provider, protector, promoter, saint. She's never felt quite real as a mother—a good imposter, to be sure—adept at the pat, the speech, the ready, reassuring smile. But children get used to the mothers they're given, rely on them to stay the same. Faye can't all of a sudden be Hen's confidante, his philosopher, or his critic. She can't let down that brave smile, or take back all the things she's said all along to protect him and make him thrive—that one plus one is always two, that as long as I am here and you are mine, nothing will hurt you, that it will all get better when you're older. If Faye says to Hen, I understand a little bit what it's like to be you, she will betray him. There's nothing she can do to help Hen except leave him alone.

As Hen turns away and sits back down on the grass, Remi shakes his head and throws the football to Nash, who, in the end, catches all of his twin brother's disappointments. Nash tosses the ball back to Buzz, but Chickie appears out of nowhere to intercept the pass.

"Thatta girl," Nash says. "Nice steal!"

"Chickie!" Violet calls out.

"What!" She throws the ball underhand back to Buzz.

"Tuck in your shirt. Your navel's showing."

"What's the big deal?" Chickie yells back. "It's just a hole."

The men laugh. "Gotta keep those holes covered, Chickadee," Nash calls out, tossing the ball back to Remi.

"Nash!" Violet yells.

Nash jogs over to the picnic table, pulled to Violet's side by the edge in her voice. Chickie joins the huddle, clutching the ball. "What's the matter?" she says.

"Why do you always do that?" Violet hisses.

"Do what?" Nash says.

"Make a joke. Drag things into the gutter that way."

"Relax," Nash says, breathing hard. "It just slipped out. I couldn't resist."

"You don't even try, Nash. You don't even goddamned try."

"Ah, come on, Vi." Nash wipes his sweaty brow with his forearm. "No need to make such a big deal."

"I'm not making such a big deal," Violet says. "You're the one who—"

Janie looks up from her newspaper. "Just leave Chickie alone, Ma."

"Yeah, Ma," Seph says. "Why is that so hard for you?"

"Yeah, Ma," Chickie says. "No one cares what I'm wearing."

"Or not wearing," Janie says.

"You see, Nash," Violet says. "She's missed the point completely. And, as usual, I'm the villain here."

"Okay, okay," Nash says. "No need to spoil the party. Just tuck in your shirt, Chick. No big deal, right?" He holds up two fingers in a *V*. "Peace?"

"You just said it didn't matter," Chickie said.

"For god's sake, Nash, at least stand your ground," Violet says.

"Listen," Nash sputters. "I was just trying—"

"Je-sus." Chickie pulls away from her mother. "Do you guys have to fight everywhere?"

"Chickie, please." Violet holds out a barrette. "Put this in your hair and tuck in your shirt. You look like the unmade bed."

"I *am* the unmade bed!" Chickie says, running off.

"It's so absurd, making the bed every day," Seph says. "Only to rumple it back up every night."

"Yeah," Janie says. "Doing laundry I can see. Washing dishes. Keeping the mold and the cockroaches away. But making the bed? Forget it. I've just let it fall into the existentialist abyss."

Meadow nods her head and smiles.

"Why don't you two try taking a dive into the existentialist abyss," Violet says to her two older daughters, draining her glass of the last drops of scotch. "Who knows. You might find husbands there."

"Hardy, har, har," Seph says.

Chickie runs hard and fast, the football tucked under one arm. Headbands. Hairy legs. Hassles. Holes. Her mother's afraid for her. Her body's changing; she keeps having to learn to move all over again. In dance class, she's off center, tips in a plié, falls out of her spins. She's clumsy, out of sync, out of whack. Her nose has grown longer; her eyes are no longer green, but gray, *rain eyes*, Hen calls them. Full of mud. People look differently at her, too closely or not at all, or, like her uncle Remi at the ball game, out of the corner of one eye. Her heart flips and flops. She's too hot. Too cold. Tired. Restless. What's wrong with her? As Chickie gathers speed by the wooden bridge, a fisherman winks. When she fumbles the ball, he laughs. Her heart trips over itself; her legs can't stop. She's never run so fast in her life.

"Honestly," Violet says to Faye, embarrassed by the row, dumping more potato chips into a plastic bowl. "I don't remember them rebelling this early."

"Sign of the times." Faye mixes up a batch of onion dip with dried soup mix and sour cream in an empty margarine tub. "They grow up sooner these days, I think."

"I guess so." The heat slowly recedes from Violet's face. She doesn't like getting ruffled in front of the ever-calm Faye, but she often does.

"How are Chickie's dance lessons going?"

"She lives for them," Violet says. "Her teacher says she's got talent. For what, I'm not sure. This Irena's an odd duck, but I guess she ought to know. They say she used to dance with Martha Graham." Violet keeps dipping chips into Faye's dip, on her way to being unable to stop, feeling her hard-won flat belly begin to swell under the tie-dye shirt, and not giving half a damn. "Still, I don't know what Chickie will ever be able to *do* with dance."

"Do with it?" Faye dips a chip into the bowl, just barely.

"I mean let's face it, Faye. Dancing is no life. It's close to an obsession with Chickie, though. I worry. High school next year and all." Faye's cool silence fuels Violet's tongue, her abstinence, Vi's hunger. Like a leaky faucet, she drips steadily on. "But I might as well cut off Chickie's legs as make her quit. She's got her first recital next week, three nights in a row. I hope you'll all come."

"We wouldn't miss it," Faye says quietly, already thinking of the excuse she'll make for Remi, who'll refuse to go, what she'll say to Hen, who'll want to go all three nights, how she'll put it to Violet if Chickie's no good.

The twins come off the field and start mixing drinks. They've brought ice crackers, tonic and bitters, lemons, maraschino cherries, and limes. Nash wipes the sweat from his neck with his shirt. His eyes land on Faye as she molds the pink hamburger meat into patties with her delicate hands. He still fills with a satisfied pride every time he sees his sister-in-law. He found her for Remi in college, noticed her browsing one day in a bookstore in the Square. He'd already met Violet by then; Vi was bossy, energetic, flirtatious, more his type. But the girl with soft hair reading *The Rise of Silas Lapham* in the aisle of Reading International was for Remi. Nash knew it right away. He struck up a conversation, got her phone number, and set out to court her for his brother. As he watches Faye stack hamburger patties on a paper plate, he remembers kissing her on the roller coaster all those years ago, her hands on the back of his neck, her thin lips. He remembers feeling too big, too sloppy, too rough. He remembers a tenderness he felt for her that frightened him down to his core, how he worried he might hurt her, how that turned him on.

"Come and get it, girls!" Nash calls out. He hands Faye her drink—bubbly, iridescent green—a lemon peel floating on top—a pretty, deadly concoction that will turn her first sentimental and then mean.

"Thanks, Nash," Faye says quietly. As she sprinkles garlic salt on the hamburger patties, she is thinking about clay. She has a secret, the first one for as long as she can remember. She feels slightly giddy with it, slightly foolish, slightly brave. Perhaps given courage by Violet, with her new stationery store up and running, Faye is thinking about opening a pottery school. She's got her eye on a vacant storefront in Inman Square. She went to the bank to test the waters. They were encouraging; she thinks she could get a loan. She'll tell Remi soon—tonight, maybe, after the picnic, if the mood is right—give him plenty of time. Remi always needs time. He won't like the idea at first. He'll balk about the money, the risk, the commitment. All along he's thought of pottery as her hobby, was sure the brick kiln he built in the backyard would keep her busy, content for a hundred years. But it's frighteningly, deliciously too late to be afraid of what Remi will think or do, what she can or cannot say to sway him. The idea's taken hold, rooted in the spongy bottom of her brain, and tonight the vodka's like sweet rain on a newly planted seed.

Faye feels the booze lurch down her throat. After all these years, it still does a twisted tango in her stomach. She's never acquired a taste for alcohol, still has to drown it in sweet bubbly drinks—ginger ale, Tom Collins mix, grenadine—like a giddy college girl. She watches Chickie run toward Hen down by the water's edge. She'd like to make a sculpture of her niece in flight. Hen's other half, more like a sister, really, and so, in a way, almost a daughter to her. Chickie's not strictly pretty, like Tory. Tory was never soft, never a little girl. Tory was, before anything else, a beauty—a perfect, polished stone. Her looks have always taken care of her in a certain way—defined her, distanced her, armored her, anointed her—early putting Faye out of a job. Sometimes, in a strange lapse of thought, she thinks of herself as a mother of only sons, and then is startled to remember Tory—guilty to have forgotten Tory. But Chickie's a mysterious, feral child. Had she been born to Faye's family in Michigan, she would've been considered odd. They would've tidied her up, trimmed her hair and her sails, tried to make the best of her, without having any idea what the best of her was. Everyone in Faye's family could've hopscotched out of a Norman Rockwell painting—square-jawed and worn, pinned-back ears, strong teeth, good bones—dull, passionless, beyond reproach. But Faye hasn't come so far from home for nothing. She sees the fire in Chickie's eye as she breaks free from Violet, sees the fisherman wink as Chickie runs by. She knows what Hen's eyes seek, what Remi's eyes avoid.

"Chickie's all Potts, isn't she?" Faye says as Violet sits down in a lounge chair and slides her sunglasses down onto her nose.

"All Potts?" Violet says, thinking *fat*.

"Big-boned," Faye tries to explain as she unfolds her chair. She always seems to say the wrong thing with Violet. "Statuesque. Regal, almost."

"Your kids are so slender," Violet says.

"Maybe too much so. Hen may never grow. And I'm afraid Tory's gone overboard." Faye is torn, as always, with Violet, between the urge to confide and conceal. She watches Tory wrap her arms around the beefy, handsome boy she's brought home with her, as he sets up a chessboard at an empty picnic table. "I think she may be too thin."

"No such thing," Violet says, dipping a chip, following Faye's eyes. "Seems like a nice boy."

"First one she's ever really brought home," Faye says. "I guess that counts for something."

Faye's never comfortable when Tory comes home to visit. She makes the house feel shabby, spends her time cleaning, picking at her food, taking endless showers. Earlier that afternoon, through the bathroom door, as she handed Tory a clean towel, Faye saw Tory's hip bones slicing up through her stomach, the lumps of her spine poking through her skin as she turned, the pointed elbows, chicken wings in back, the spare rise of her meager breast. Faye wonders, perversely, as she leans back in her lawn chair and begins her second vodka Collins, what the hulking young man thinks of such a phantom body, how easily it would crush under his weight. Faye wonders, perversely, what happened behind the closed door of Tory's room that afternoon, how far the two of them have gone, what John would look like naked in the steam through the crack in the bathroom door, when the towel dropped from his thick middle, when he turned, how far under his flesh his hip bone could be found.

"I wonder what they live on sometimes," Faye says to Violet, shutting down the image.

"Spite," Violet says. "It's filling enough, heaven knows." Violet has an old, unsatisfied longing that feels almost sexual in its urgency, to spill her guts to Faye. All these years, they've lived so closely together, yet kept such a distance. They have so much to offer each other yet keep endlessly on their guards. It's an unspoken rule. They don't cross certain lines, and the boundaries have always been Faye's. Faye's so much better at caution and tact than she is. For Violet, such restraint is exhausting. She'd like to ask Faye straight out how it's turned out, life with Remi—how many times they have sex a week, what passes between them at the breakfast table, if she remembers what drew her to the man in the first place, what led the four of them down the daisy-strewn aisle of the church for better or for worse, to the big, old houses on Hemlock Street, and how much of the better she's seen.

If Violet would only ask her any of these questions, Faye might try to answer on this restless summer night. She's always admired Violet. Over the years, she's tried to borrow bits of her savvy, her boldness. Faye, too, is looking deep into the murky waters of middle age to find the shiny coin of an explanation that has sunk to the silty bottom of their lives about the events that led to this moment on the riverbank, how the roller coaster ride led to the wedding to the first child to the last, just why it was that she married Remi. At the time, she was so sure about its being a good idea. Good as in sound. Sensible. Faye was nothing if not sensible. There was something about Remi's being a twin, Faye remembers, something both mystical and safe, safe for a person cursed with a dread of touch, remembering the jolt on her bed when her parents came to give her goodnight kisses, when she'd turn her face in the pillow and pretend to be asleep. She can't remember being that little girl, whose only wish was not to be an only child. A baby brother or a sister. The wish never changed, never came true. Faye shakes the memory free. It's all water under the bridge now. She tries not to dwell on the past. What bothers her most is that she can hardly remember what made that little girl so much stronger of purpose and will than the woman she's turned out to be.

Faye somehow knew that what she couldn't give Remi in the way of intimacy he'd get from Nash. Her hunches about sex had been right, too. For Remi, sex was more a goal than a passion. He was only set on having some, rightfully, his own, in the privacy of their dark bedroom, sex that would give him children, relieve his urges, and never shame him. She knew about Remi's being a fractured man. She wasn't surprised the first time he couldn't perform in bed. All that pressure; it wasn't fair. She didn't blame or judge or pity him. If she'd been a man, she, too, would have been afraid to fail. As it was, all she had to do was lie still beneath him and pretend. Being soft was a passive act; as a woman, she was not required to turn hard. Her own sexual disappointments and inadequacies have been private, her own. And for all this, she's grateful. Faye's never been one to think that men have any less of a claim to weakness or fear than women, any more than she thinks that power and prowess are the exclusive domains of men. From the start, Faye looked at sex practically, philosophically. Sex wasn't so bad, if you were prepared for it, if you recited poetry all the while, if you had enough booze in you, if you balanced the minutes it took against all the time it didn't, if you set out to make a baby. She'd been ready for infidelity, too, thinking that in their case, it wouldn't be so much a crime as a salve. But Remi's turned out to be nothing more than a half-hearted, middle-aged flirt, a man whose eyes burn while his tongue gets tied. As if on cue, a young woman rides by on the river path on her bicycle, a floating vision in fluttering purple, long black hair streaming behind her. Faye watches Remi's head turn, his hand spanning the football, staring open-mouthed as she passes by.

"So. What are your plans for the rest of the summer?" she asks Violet.

"Have to stay pretty much put," Violet says. "Can't really leave the store yet. And I did the stupidest thing. Agreed to be treasurer over at the tennis club. Meetings every Tuesday and Thursday nights. Kind of kills the week." Violet smiles. Stupidest, wildest, luckiest thing she ever did, it turned out. She met Charlie at a meeting a few weeks ago at the club, Charlie the ex-tennis pro with the monkey arms, come to Cambridge with secrets of a shady past, come to teach tennis, the whispers buzzing around him—curly-haired Charlie, thighs thick as tree trunks, hungry, hungry Charlie. He drove Violet home one night after she'd arranged to be stranded at the club. At a red light, he took his hand off the gear shift and put it on her thigh.

"So," he said. "Where should I take you, Mrs. Potts?"

"It's Violet," she said. "And you can take me anywhere you like, Charlie. As long as you bring me back again."

"What if you don't want to come back?" His hand slid up under her skirt.

"Get one thing straight, Charlie," she said, already wet and willing. "I will."

Violet shifts in her lounge chair. It makes her uncomfortable, how simple it all was, how easily she's become an adulteress. After all these years, she'd thought, maybe even hoped, that she'd changed, that when push came to shove, Nash's face would loom up and steer her home, that a stranger's voice and hands would leave her cold. But she'd let Charlie drive her away that first night, her belly pulsing, to some cheap motel on Route 1, next to the Hilltop Steak House. She wanted him to take her inside and strip her bare, let him do whatever he wanted with her, and all it felt was good. Charlie's hands have made her say, do, submit to things she used to read about in her brother's trashy paperbacks in the soft dirt under the porch in the summer dusk. A few nights ago, she and Charlie got going right out on the open clay court at the tennis club under the full moon, the police cars cruising by, the crickets chirping in frantic chorus. Charlie fucked her through the center net, his erection straining its threads, her back nearly bent in half. She got home at midnight, her legs still damp and crisscrossed, trembling from the strange positions they'd been in, long after the courts had closed and the tennis balls had settled in their cans. The drunk, sleepy Nash looked up from his sports page and said, "Long meeting tonight, Vi?"

Violet looked him straight in the eye and said, "We had a lot of ground to cover," loving the danger and the utter safety of the deception, the play of words on deaf ears, loving both the man in the armchair who'd never leave her and the man she'd left laughing on the service line who would, a cigarette dangling from the corner of his mouth. She's got it all figured out; it's under control. If she's careful, no one's heart will be broken. Nash is all heart, and Charlie, well, the good thing about Charlie...apparently, he has no heart.

"How 'bout you and Remi?" Violet says. "What are your plans?"

"The usual," Faye says. "Cambridge in July. Nantucket in August."

Sharing the cottage in Nantucket has always been a strain, the old and tired confusion about whose nooks and crannies are whose, whose peanut butter and blue cheese on a rusty shelf of the refrigerator, whose driftwood and whose wet towels, which husband will fix the ancient plumbing or the deck steps, who's better at pulling out splinters and whose moods will rule or spoil the day. Some years, the two families have tried to stagger their visits, but Chickie and Hen no longer go willingly, one without the other. And as the years go on, isolation seems a worse fate than a crowd. This summer, Faye would welcome the company. She's dreading the trip. She doesn't want to have to go to the gray shingled house on the dunes, to spend the long, silken days with the dust of the dirt roads and the restless ocean, with her salty brooding self, her salty brooding younger son. Buzz and Tory don't come much anymore, a weekend here or there. Faye can't bear the thought of meeting Remi at the ferry dock every Friday evening, wishing him already gone. Nantucket makes her feel idle, arid, ungrateful. And what about her clay school? Clay City. She's already picked out a name. Her secret might melt or fade in the island sun. Without Violet's synergy, she might lose her courage; without Remi's resistance, her resolve; without the city as cradle, her vision of brick and clay might crack and fall. Maybe she should tell Violet, ask her advice. Why would that be so hard?

"You guys coming to the Island this year?" she says.

"Last two weeks in August, maybe," Violet says. "When the tennis club closes, if I can get someone to cover the store. If Chickie doesn't grumble too much. I hate not to go. A summer just wouldn't be a summer without Nantucket."

But Violet, too, feels a lurch thinking about those long, idle days on the island, meeting Nash at the ferry dock with his bottle of whiskey and the smells of city still on him, his four-day beard which he'll shave at her behest, coming to the breakfast table with bloody bits of toilet paper stuck cheerfully to his face. She'll have to get used to it all over again, to his body lumbering into bed beside her, the boozy breath, to the bad jokes, to the groans. Chickie will brood. The older girls don't even bother to make excuses anymore. Violet sighs. She doesn't have to go to Nantucket this year. Her reasons are legitimate. Work at the new store. Duties at the club. Nobody would question her. No one would care. But Violet feels not so much guilty as beholden to all that is hers, obliged to prove that her family is still intact, that she has control over her own deception, and not it over her, that her life has an order, a rhythm, a right that's thicker in its blood than the wrong. She's having an affair. It's true. She's an infidel, a low-down adulteress. Why call a dark rose by any other name? But she's not desperate and she's hurt no one. She doesn't plan to. She doesn't need Charlie, or the sex. She'll banish herself in August. Nantucket will be her confession booth, the Hail Mary days for her delicious urban crime. She'll suffer luxuriously—those long, lazy days away from Charlie, away from temptation, packing picnic lunches, drifting in the salty, buoyant waves, sweeping endless grains of sand from the wood-planked floor, sleeping still and alone, finding the cool spots in the sheets with her toes, counting the flowers on the wallpaper and then what's left of her blessings. She'll paint the cottage, lose some weight, take a hike up the cliffs, spend some real time with Chickie, try to really get to know Faye for the umpteenth time. Or maybe…

Violet shifts again in her chair. Island dreams turn wild in the heat. There'll be too much time for dalliance and good deeds, sleeping, strolling, repentance. Fever unleashed, it might run wild. Her dreams will be full of twisted sex, sex that makes even what she and Charlie did on the tennis court look tame. She'll let the wicker shades unfurl, undress, oil her body, lay herself down. And the day may come when she rises up to comb the island of a summer's day, when she sidles into a cheery seaside bar with dark glasses and a tight skirt and turns it seedy with her wicked, middle-aged ways, picks up a tan, lanky kid and lures him behind a dune…

"But then again," Violet says to Faye. "We may not make it at all this year."

"That's too bad," Faye says quietly. "Hen will be disappointed."

Violet lifts her sunglasses from the bridge of her nose, studies Faye beside her in the lawn chair, eyes closed, neck tilted up to the setting sun. At such a moment, when all is calm, and some small things have been said, Violet can almost love Faye, as she might a sister who left home in a blaze of glory and returned home simply subdued. At such a moment, Violet can admit that Faye is pretty, prettier than she is as time goes on, better preserved, no longer mousy but sexy in a hungry, lean cat kind of way. Delicate features, thin wrists, shoulder-length hair, with only a crinkled neon strand or two of gray, short, crooked bangs. The look's in vogue now—hipless, flat, and pale. Faye wears her hair pulled back in a careless ponytail, tied with a piece of colorful rag, a clay-spattered oversized work shirt buttoned low and hanging at the knee.

"Funny, isn't it, Vi?" Faye waves an idle hand. "How this day never changes? How it's almost like an echo."

"It is," Violet says, surprised, for a moment, speechless. This, for Faye, is almost chatty. She looks different today, as if she's let loose some old, blackmailing secret into the murky river. She wriggles her toes, runs a finger down her neck, lets half a smile rise. Maybe Faye has a lover, too, Violet thinks, draining her second drink, hoping secrecy and deception look as good on her.

Faye opens her eyes and stretches. "Nash is looking well," she says.

"Oh, come on, Faye," Violet says. "He's overweight and drinks like a fish. He still thinks he's a goddamned kid. Some days I look at him and think, my god, what a waste of a perfectly good man."

"Remi, too," Faye says with a sigh. They watch as the twins collapse on the grass, huffing and puffing, their stomachs folding up like puppy skin, sipping their drinks, lighting up filtered, menthol Kents. "Sometimes it's frightening," she says. "They're even aging alike."

"Yeah." Violet reaches down to scratch a mosquito bite on her ankle. "Like a coupla old Saint Bernards."

3

Down on the riverbank, Hen's doing nothing, as he does so gracefully and so well, when Chickie tackles him from behind. The blood rushes up through his neck to his face before he flings her off, looking over at his father, who's still playing football on the grass. Chickie lands on her back and jumps up to pounce on him again, this time pinning his arms to the ground.

"Tell me what you're thinking," she says as they wrestle.

"Nothing." Hen struggles to push her away, palm to palm.

"That's impossible." Chickie bears down, her arm muscles flexing. "Even nothing is something."

"Not necessarily." He finally topples her with a mighty shove.

Chickie flops down on her back, lifts her legs up high and starts to pedal.

"Hey, you're bleeding," Hen says.

"Where?" A trickle of blood runs down the inside of Chickie's thigh. "Oh, crap," she says. "Not again."

"What is it?" The answer comes to Hen just as he asks the question. He's seen the ads, mysterious women in silky dresses riding horseback on the beach.

"It's the curse." Chickie goes into vampire mode, fangs bared. "Blood and guts. Aaggghhh! Another egg bites the dust."

"What kills it?" Hen yanks up a blade of grass low to its stem.

"Nothing kills it." Chickie hooks her fingers into the back of her bathing suit, hikes it down. "The egg just dies unless you make a baby out of it, spaz. I don't have to explain all that to you, do I?"

"No, you don't." Hen pulls the blade of grass tight between his thumbs. Guys all talk about it, banging up girls, what happens if you don't pull out quick. But guys get these things wrong sometimes, make it up if they aren't sure. Chickie knows. She'll tell him everything, but no way he's going to look at her while she does. He bends his head, puts his lips to the hole between his thumbs and blows a feeble squeak. Chickie comes closer.

"It's amazing, isn't it?" she says. "How people fit together that way?" The words swirl around his face like fireflies. "It's disgusting. But kind of amazing, too. We're like the factories; the eggs drop every month and wait for the sperm. And you guys are like the cannons." Chickie's thumb and finger spring out of her hand. She fires at his temple. "Shooting out millions of little tadpoles, all pushing and shoving, trying to win the race."

"Male seahorses lay the eggs," Hen says.

"Jealous?" Chickie licks her finger and smears the blood into her skin.

"Yeah, right," Hen says. "I'm jealous of a seahorse."

"It's supposed to feel good," Chickie says. "Some people get addicted."

"Seahorses mate once a year."

"Whoa. Sex maniacs." She grins. "Just like my mother."

"She is not."

"So why do they keep doing it?" Chickie jerks her chin toward the grown-ups. "Up to the bedroom. Slam bam thank you, ma'am. Over and over again. They're so *old*!"

"Mine don't." Hen finally gets the tension right between his thumbs and blows an elephant blast from the blade of grass.

Chickie stares at the crotch of Hen's shorts. "Hey, have you—"

"Shut up, Chickie." Hen takes off toward the pool.

"Come on," she calls out, running after him. "What's the big deal? How am I supposed to know? I don't have one. And I don't have a brother either."

"Good lord," Violet says to Faye as Chickie and Hen run by, handing her drink glass to Nash for a refill. "Now it's a brother she wants."

Remi squirts lighter fluid onto the coals and drops in a lighted match, which explodes instantly into a burst of purple and orange flame.

Overtaking Hen on the grass, Chickie does a cartwheel which lands her in the wading pool, climbs up onto the back of a cement tortoise, and wraps her arms around its neck. Hen stands in the piss-warm pool, fists shoved into his armpits. A little boy stands shivering at his side. Hen remembers being that little kid, watching everything while his teeth chattered and his lips turned blue. Chickie splashes him and laughs. He imagines blood spurting out of all the holes in her body, just as water does from the tortoise—eyes, nose, mouth, and the spout at the center of its back. He imagines her falling off the tortoise, weak and bled, gray like the underbelly of a dead dogfish, the water stained crimson, floating face down and bumping up against the side of the pool.

"You're always trying to get me wet," he says.

"And you're always trying to stay dry," Chickie says. "Is that like a guy thing or something? Once you start getting hard-ons, you can't get wet or they'll shrivel up and you won't be a real man?"

"Give it a rest, Chickie." Hen turns his head away. Who the hell knows? Chickie's three inches taller than he is. He hasn't even used a razor yet. There's nothing to shave. At school he's a weed in a forest of pimply, croaking trees. Late bloomers, his mother says, end up being the rarest of flowers. What the hell is that supposed to mean? No way he'll join the jack-off parties in the gym. There's a stash of *Playboys* hidden in the locker room. Mr. Keifer prowls around with a wet towel slung over his shoulder, whacks you on the butt if he catches you looking at the centerfold, laughing his head off like a crazed hyena. Hen closes his eyes. Better to make it happen yourself than have it rise up like a snake out of a basket for a picture of some strange naked girl, better to be in control of your horniness, your own goddamned hard-on. Andrea Marswell would look great stretched out on a pool table. Vickie Schuler with that purple sweater…without that purple sweater.

"Stay dry," Chickie hisses into his ear. "Shrivel up. Turn into dust. See if I care. I was a fish in another life and I'll be a sea urchin in my next. Or an octopus, maybe, a six-legged crab." Chickie jumps off the turtle's back. Hen's eyes blink clear from his steamy fantasy as Chickie leaps out of the water. She's the toughest, most beautiful thing he's ever seen.

"I stole some of my dad's beer," she says, as they head back to the picnic table. "I'll ride you double on my bike. Let's go down to the bridge and get plastered."

"I don't want to get plastered," Hen says.

"You don't want to do anything anymore," Chickie says.

"I do so."

"Name one thing."

"Go up into space."

"They'll never let you. Besides that."

"Nothing."

"See? You're such a spaz."

"You don't even know what a spaz is, Chickie."

"I do, too. A boy who smells girls' bicycle seats."

"What? That's crazy. Why would anyone want to do that?"

"Hell, I don't know," Chickie says.

Hen stands knee deep in the pool, arms crossed, eyes squinting to the sun. "Are you going to let someone do it to you, Chickie?"

"Do what?"

"You know what."

Chickie looks over at their parents, all four sprawled now in the lawn chairs with their drinks. "Sooner or later," she says with a shrug, rubbing the strip of bare belly between the two parts of her bathing suit. The smells of burning briquettes and lighter fluid float their way. Remi moves his chair out of the line of smoke, swats at a mosquito hovering near his leg. Nash tells the joke about the deaf hawk and the blind dove, gesturing with his hands. Violet looks over at Faye and rolls her eyes. Chickie, dripping wet, and now with another trickle of blood running down the inside of her leg, turns back to Hen. "We're probably going to end up just like them," she says.

The hamburger patties land sizzling on the grill. Chickie takes off down the bike path, standing up to pedal, three cans of beer wrapped in a shirt in her bike basket with the plastic daisies. Grabbing a handful of potato chips, Hen strolls over to the picnic table where Tory's playing chess with John. Her other boyfriends have been prickly, nervous. Some have tried to bribe him; most have just ignored him. John taps his Hush-Puppied foot on the grass. Tory studies her fingernails, the girls' way, fingers flexed out straight. Hen tries to crunch a potato chip quietly.

"Hey, little brother." Tory reaches up to stroke the hair out of his eyes. "I was beginning to think you were glued to that tree down there. Did you meet John?"

"Hey, John," Hen says.

"Hey." John looks up, nods his head, moves his knight. "Check," he says to Tory.

Her fingers brush his thigh as she studies the board. "Trap my queen with your bishop, will you, sire?"

"You left her hanging there unprotected, Tor. She was asking for trouble."

"Maybe she wanted it." Tory moves her queen.

John topples Tory's king with his. "Mate," he says.

"Damn. Maybe later, big guy."

John looks over at Hen. "You play?" he says.

"A little."

"Have a seat." John starts to set up the board again. "You're white."

Tory gets up from the picnic bench, tugs her jeans down at the crotch, and flips her hair over her shoulders. "I hope you'll acquit the family honor better than I did, Henny," she says.

"Yeah, sure, Tor," Hen says. "Whatever you say."

"Nice game, Tory," John says, looking up.

"If you say for a girl, I'll strangle you." She circles his neck with her hands.

"I wasn't going to say that." John rolls his head against her hands like a cat. Hen sits down and John scoops up one of his black pieces and places it at Hen's elbow. "I'll give you a rook odds," he says.

"Just one piece?" Hen asks.

"Let me show you what a rook can do on the seventh rank," John says. He shows Hen the Nimzowitsch Defense and a position from a game played by Capablanca in 1922, then pushes out the first pawn as they begin a game. John talks quietly as they play, pointing out strengths, weaknesses, patterns, possibilities. Everything he says makes sense. Hen sees why taking John's knight is tempting, at first glance a must move, but really only a temporary gain, how it will set him up a few moves down the line for an attack on his queen. Better to get his pieces out, concentrate on the center. There's no one piece, one strategy, no one idea that can pull off the win. It's a complex web of memory, stamina, ideas. Did he see, in the game with Tory, how an idle queen could be crushed by a watchful, patient pawn?

Remi strolls by and leans over Hen's shoulder, puts his drink glass down next to his captured pieces. "How's he doing, John?" he says.

"Holding his own," John says. "Hen's solid in his thinking, creative but not rash. His mind doesn't wander, sir, like your daughter's." John looks over at Tory as if he'd do anything in the world for her except lie, as if he knows already that integrity will come between them. "If Hen has half Tory's competitive edge," John says, "he could be good."

"I'd say Victoria has most of the killer instinct in the family," Remi says.

"Behave, Dad," Tory says. "Hey, aren't you wearing Uncle Nash's shirt?"

"Am I?" Remi lifts the hem of the shirt, looks over at Nash, who's now wearing his. "Guess so," he says.

As the sun drops, the salmon sky is suddenly peppered with thin gray clouds. For a while Hen feels his father's shadow looming. He forfeits a rook but gets some compensation. His pieces are well-positioned, most of them on solid squares. The fishermen on the bridge lay their poles down on the grass and unpack their dinners. The outside of Remi's drink glass glistens with gin sweat. Time and material. Hen's in no rush. He has ideas two or three moves ahead, but he's not committed. He could sacrifice his knight or try to hold on with a locked position. He sees intrigue, mazes, traps, and lines. It's okay. He'll lose the game, but this day's a gift. Anything's possible. Ali floored Liston in a single round and Ryun's about to break the four-minute mile. The hamburgers are grilling. The salad's being tossed, Wishbone-style. Chickie's out of sight, out of mind. His father's not on his case today. The ice cubes in his martini have melted. For now, the drink is dead. Remi's hand squeezes Hen's shoulder as he takes one of John's pawns. The last touch of that hand Hen can remember was when Remi gave him handshake lessons the year before—firm, fingers extended, no dead fish, son. Really put it to 'em. Show them who you *are*.

John corners Hen's knight and scoops it up with one hand. Hen moves his bishop to watch over the long diagonal. Tory strokes the back of John's neck. Slowly, Hen's pieces collect at John's side. He's getting creamed, but it doesn't matter. It all makes sense. Something finally makes sense. This is just one game. There'll be another. And another. As many chess games as his brain can hold, as he can cram into a life-time. All he needs is a board and thirty-two pieces, however crude. Hen moves his knight. Check. John saves his queen with a tricky move Hen might not have seen in a hundred more games. But it's okay. John taps his foot on the grass. Chickie comes back wobbly on her bike, kicks the kickstand down. She's talking loudly, causing a commotion. Hen tries to shut out her voice. An hour's passed, maybe two. It's okay. He's fourteen years old, pale and liquid, an invisible fairy boy. He was worried, because he's always felt so small, so weightless, as if he had nothing to anchor him. Now he's got chess.

"Check." John moves his bishop to threaten Hen's king. "Take your time, Hen," he says. "This is a critical point in the game. You have to de-cide what's really at stake." Tory whispers in his ear. John slowly shakes his head. From a faraway place, Chickie keeps calling Hen's name. He studies the board for a long time before finding his only move.

As the sun shuts down on the horizon, they gather around the picnic ta-ble to celebrate Seph's twenty-second birthday. Violet asks Seph to come over to the next table to help with dessert, which is usually forbidden,

family tradition holding that the birthday child sit like the Queen of
Sheba and be waited on hand and foot. Seph follows Violet, looking
back at her friend. Meadow flashes her the peace sign and smiles. She
has a boy's haircut, wears black nail polish and no bra. All evening, she's
spoken only to Seph and nibbled sparingly on the Pillsbury rolls.

"Twenty-two years ago today, our little pipsqueak landed on the
planet," Nash says. "Hard to believe."

"You can't be over twenty-one and still be a pipsqueak," Janie says.

"Oh, I think the pipsqueak label's good for a lifetime." Nash makes
a funny face. "Hey, look at me."

They all do and laugh.

At the neighboring picnic table, Violet slides the Pepperidge Farm
cake out of its box, scraping off a hunk of chocolate frosting as it
comes. "Damn," she says. "I do that every time."

"What's the matter, Ma?" Seph asks. "Why are you in such a lousy
mood?"

"I am not in a lousy mood. I've always done everything I could to
make this a special day for you, Seph."

"Well, whatever it is, please don't take it out on my cake." Seph steals
a lick of frosting with her finger. "Oh, by the way, Meadow doesn't eat
white sugar."

Violet's hands stop short. "What color sugar does she eat? Purple?
Should I have gotten neon green?"

Seph throws up her hands. "I'm not going to bring people here if
you act this way. I warned her—"

"Warned her about what?"

"About you being so uptight."

"This girl is strange, Seph. She's downright rude. Tell me, if she
didn't plan on eating anything, or talking to anyone, why on earth did
she even bother to come?"

"She came because I invited her. She's a friend of mine, Ma. Not
everyone's a nice fucking Talbots girl. People are individuals. It's a good
thing, by the way."

"Does it make you feel very grown-up, Persephone, to swear like
that?"

"I'm twenty-two years old, Ma." Seph's laugh sputters before it dies.
"I *am* grown up. But I didn't do it the way you wanted, and so you
just pretend it hasn't happened yet. You're even more infuriating than
usual. What is going on? You know what Freud says, or someone who's

supposed to know, although why it's always some uptight white guy who gets to play God, I'll never understand." She twirls her hands in the air. "Let's see if I can regurgitate some pablum from Psych 101—something about how people who constantly feel the need to criticize and lash out at others are often unconsciously expressing their own sense of personal inadequacy or guilt. Think any of that might apply to you here, Ma?"

"Well, thank you for the ten second analysis, Doctor Potts." Violet's voice dips low as she avoids Seph's blazing stare. Inside, her heart clutches. This one never did miss a trick, this first born, all-knowing child, who always had some sort of sixth sense about what made people tick, what could make them explode, too close to clairvoyance—in which Violet places not a whit of stock—for comfort.

"Why don't you just come right out and say why I piss you off so mightily, Ma?"

"It's your birthday, Seph. Don't push me."

"Come on, Violet. Out with it. What is it about my life that's such a tragedy? Why don't you just stop the suffering martyr act and tell me?"

"You want the truth?" Violet lights the first candle.

Back at the other table, listening to the fray, Chickie stares at a mole on the side of Meadow's cheek. It blurs and wobbles; with every spin of her head, it disappears. Chickie uses it to spot herself, the way she does in dance class, to keep centered, balanced. She's drunk from the beer she drank down on the riverbank. Drunk. As a skunk. *As a skunk.* She's got to keep it together, keep from falling over, apart. The déjà vus are piling up on top of each other—endless old arguments, songs, and angry words. She feels numb and jumbled. High as a kite. Everyone keeps telling her to pipe down, but no one's even listening. Faye scrapes and stacks the paper plates. Janie reads the financial page of the newspaper. Hen studies a problem John's given him on the chessboard. Nash empties his third martini and folds his napkin. "Twenty-two years," he says. "Hard to believe."

"You already said that," Chickie says. *You've already said everything you're ever going to say in your whole fucking life. Over and over again.* She wants to scream at him.

"He likes to repeat himself, your father," Remi says.

"Echo, echo, echo." Tory hoots like an owl.

Janie lifts her head from the newspaper. "What are we talking about?" she says.

"Are you fucking deaf?" Chickie says.

"Whoa," Nash admonishes her. "What's gotten into you tonight, Chick?"

"Mom and Seph are having a humongous fight, Janie. How can you just sit there and pretend it isn't happening?"

"It's easy," Janie says. "I sit here dutifully. Daughter number two. Cleaned and pressed and accounted for. Get it? I'm an accountant? I make bad jokes. Listen selectively. Speak when I'm spoken to. I'm sitting right here."

"So young." Nash sighs. "Such a cynic."

"Who, *moi?*" Janie's fingers spring flexed to her cheek.

Meadow chews on her Pillsbury roll and smiles.

"And another thing," Violet says, the angry voices riding the breeze between the picnic tables. "Nobody has a name like Meadow."

"Coming from someone who named her daughters Persephone and Minerva," Seph says. "That is truly a laugh."

"Those are old family names. Mythical names. Persephone was the daughter of Zeus and Hera, the king and queen of the gods."

"Yeah," Seph says. "Talk about the classic dysfunctional family. She was kidnapped by Hades to be his wife in Hell. How screwed up is that?" She groans as she makes her way back to the table. "Sorry for the bad theater over there, Meadow. You'll have to forgive my mother."

Meadow nods agreeably and holds up two fingers. "Peace," she says.

Violet's eyes burn purple by the light of the candles as she follows Seph with the cake. With a waving fork, Nash strikes up an out of tune "Happy Birthday to You."

"We live in a zoo," Chickie mumbles along.

Oh, man. Chickie squeezes her eyes shut tight as another wave of nausea rolls over her. She's dizzy and sick from the beer, from the fighting, from all the déjà vus. She thinks of the monkey that rode the knife sharpener's shoulder as he roamed the streets with his cart when she was young, watches her mother's tight, angry face as she marches over with the cake, her father scratching his armpits with the ending lines of the song. "We lo-ok like monkeys!"

And man, Chickie thinks, as her brain swirls round and round—we act like them, too.

Back on Hemlock Street, Chickie lies in bed in her attic room. The pounding at her temple is just out of sync with the chirping of the crickets. *Thump*. Chirp. *Thump*. Chirp. Every seventh beat, they collide.

"Ribbit." Chickie tries to burp and discovers she's lost the knack. The lump in her throat lodges more deeply as the night goes on. When she got to the bridge, she dropped her bike to the ground and leaned up against a tree. Slowly, she drained the first can of beer, sour and bubbly. Slowly her tongue grew numb. After the second can, the taste grew sweeter, less strange. The good feeling came out of nowhere and left as soon as she got back to the picnic table where Hen and John were playing chess. She shouldn't have drunk all three cans. Hen was supposed to have shared it with her, but then he chickened out.

Getting up from her bed, Chickie straightens her twisted nightshirt, one of her father's old button-downs, opens the door of the widow's walk, and steps outside. She and Hen used to camp out here on summer nights with Ritz crackers, Fresca, and flashlights, searching for the constellations. The night's still muggy, under a bank of heavy clouds. The shirttails tickle as a lazy breeze steals through Chickie's legs. She feels the sanitary pad resting in the sling of her underwear, catching the spurting blood. Across the fence, Hen's light comes on in his room. Chickie lifts her hand in a wave, but the blind stays in place, lapping gently against the windowsill. The sky is still, no sign of the fireworks yet, only the distant lights across the river.

Across the way, Hen's shadow floats by on the window shade, topped by an enormous Silly Putty head. It comforts Chickie, that distorted, monster noggin, those skinny elastic arms. The rusty pulley lies near, sagging on the rope. They haven't sent any messages in a long time. Used to be they'd trade secrets, tell jokes, make plans. The night's still tense, unfinished. Her parents are quiet below her, too tired to unpack the picnic stuff, too tired to flirt or fight. The dirty tablecloth's been stuffed back into the hamper, another year when the vote went against going to the fireworks down on the Esplanade, the crowds too big, the wait too long. The firecrackers set off by Violet and Seph's blowup are slowly disappearing into some unknown reach of the sky. Chickie lifts her arms high, feeling every one of her five foot seven inches. She's fourteen years old. Fifteen, actually. Babies in China start out being one, not zero, Hen told her. It's the kind of thing he always knows, like the seahorse thing. A collector of facts, Hen is. She collects feelings, fantasies, now, more and more, fears. They wrap around her, trip her, strangle her, take her breath away. Standing out on the widow's walk, Chickie imagines jumping off the railing into the night. If you drank three hundred beers, she wonders, would you actually believe you could fly?

The only way to get undrunk, Chickie figures, is to dance. Working from the first plié, she goes through the moves of a solo she's working on in class—a one and a two, a *piqué* and *tombé pas de bourrée*, and a five and a six, *coupé* and *rond de jambe*. The moon flickers and dims. Hen's shadow bounces by again on the shade. Chickie comes to the end of the dance, folding herself up small. And when she unwraps herself to begin the dance again, the shadow is gone.

Next door, Hen's feet creak on the second and seventh stairs as he goes down to find the chess set in his father's study, although Remi has never been known to study much of anything in this room, despite the stately mahogany desk and all the books, the leather armchair in the corner. The chess set's there on the shelf where it's always been, pieces perched on the board like forgotten characters in a dusty Oz. Clear circles appear when Hen lifts up the velvet-padded pieces, one by one—bishop, rook, queen. He wraps them up in his T-shirt and blows the dust off the board.

Out in the living room, Remi's asleep in the armchair. The TV screen fills with a bulls-eye, testing the emergency broadcast system with a high-pitched hum. At school, a rumor's been going around the eighth grade that all the fourteen-year-olds are going to be taken to another planet by aliens in a spaceship, lifted up out of themselves and replaced on earth by clones. Some kids got all freaked out and cried; some even called their parents. Some went around joking, "Take me! Take me!!" or walked around with their arms stretched out, saying robotically, "I-am-an-a-li-en!" Hen felt a strange disappointment to know none of it could be true, that there were no other worlds as far as anyone knew, no other ways out. The humming, ice-blue living room would be the perfect target for an alien invasion and Remi the perfect hostage, half asleep, blotto from all the booze. Hen walks over to the chair. The heavy wooden chessboard under his arm gives him the courage to look closely at his sleeping human father, a dash of drool hovering on the corner of his lip, just zapped by the alien's gun and lifted up out of himself, the last human smile sliding off the edge of his mouth. In the end, all of the melted smiles will be tossed in a pile, headed for a museum hanging in a moonless galaxy, where human relics lie in a glass case next to humongous dinosaur bones.

The bulls-eye disappears and *The FBI* comes back on the TV screen. Hen edges forward and turns off the sound. Efrem Zimbalist, Jr.'s tie blows in the wind as he flashes his badge with one hand and points the gun with the other. He blows the bad guy away in the alleyway, once, twice, three times in the gut. The guy crumples against a trash can with a silent grimace, a graceful forward slump of his well-groomed head. Hen goes back upstairs to his room and opens his window a crack before he gets into bed, a habit of long ago, when he used to dare the night demons to come in, to keep him from sleeping. Pulling the shade aside, he sees Chickie out on the widow's walk next door, dancing in one of her father's old shirts. Her hair wraps around her as she moves, hiding the new curves of her body. He can't make out her face. All winter long, she was covered up; she just started dancing in the spring. He was shocked by what he saw on the riverbank that night, the blood running down her leg, the changes in her body. It's Chickie who's the alien. They *did* come to get her, lifted her up out of herself, left a clone in her place, a clone with curves and claws, beer-drinking lips and tits, strong arms, a two-piece bathing suit, dripping swear words and blood. This Chickie has new powers, makes him blush and stammer against his will, turn dumb as if she'd pushed the OFF button in his brain. Maybe his father was right. He'll have to be careful with this new Chickie, be on his guard, get out his zapping gun…Name. Rank. Serial Number. Ah, hell, what's the use? Chickie knows him too well. Hen climbs into bed with the chessboard and lifts it up against his chest. From where he sits, he can still see Chickie's bottom half dancing out of the corner of his eye. He gets up and pulls the shade down all the way.

Out on the widow's walk, Chickie sees the shade fall. Goddamn Hen. Why's he acting so weird? Ever since the Yankees game, he's been such a jerk. She starts her solo all over again. This time when she lifts her leg and spins, it's one fluid motion the way it's supposed to be. She gets that hard part—*tombé, pas de bourrée, pirouette en dedans.* Hen doesn't want to talk to her, doesn't want her around anymore. Fine. Two can play that game. Man, can she move. But it's not a good thing, to have to feel this way to dance. You can't just pull anger out of a hat and make it work for you. You have to feel bad first. You always have to suffer.

Chickie goes back inside and sits down at her desk and pulls out the article she saved about the Quaker guy who burned himself up in front of the Pentagon to protest the war in Vietnam. She knows the details by heart now, how he poured gasoline over his arms and legs and finally his head, puffing out his cheeks so he wouldn't swallow, how he lit the match and burst into flames. For the thousandth time she tries to read between the lines, to make the man speak to her out of the blurry, fiery photograph, to find out if he screamed and flailed or tried to roll himself out, if he called out anyone's name, if he had a last, hopeless split-second change of heart. But there's nothing else—just a few more sentences about how his charred body was covered up and taken away.

Chickie finds a candle from an old Halloween pumpkin in the mess of her top desk drawer, a pack of matches she and a friend used the winter before to light the Newports they'd stolen from Violet's purse, an experience at once so putrid and glorious she swore in the same breath, after the first two killer drags, that she'd never smoke again, knowing full well she would. She looks at the matchbook cover, offering a treasure trove of foreign stamps for a song, still and always magical to her. She wants to slip inside the worlds of those white-fringed stamps—the hot, red triangle of loping-antelope Tunisia, the cool, turquoise rectangle of Greece with the cream-colored sky. She lights the candle, watches the flame form its wobbly teardrop shape. She swings her finger through it, then back again. On the third swing, she lets it linger. "Ouch!" As she blows out the candle, the smoke whooshes up in a swirl. She feels the crisp pad of her fingertip, smells her singed flesh. *OUCH. Ouch. Ouch.* Such a strange word, after you said it so many times, not a word anymore but a sound—crunchy and sharp. She looks down again at the picture of the burning man. "How could you *do* that?" she says.

Chickie finds a pencil and writes notes to Hen to send over on the clothesline pulley, ripping sheet after sheet off the pad as the messages keep coming out wrong.

> *So what did you think of Tory's new boyfriend?*
> *You should have come on that bike ride with me. You should've had some beer.*
> *I'm still drunk. Headache city. Man, Violet's a bitch.*
> *Maybe seahorses have the right idea. Are you coming to my dance recital next week?*
> *You never say what you mean anymore, Hen. You never mean what you say.*
> *Are you mad at me, Hen, or what?*

Chickie clips the last message to the rope with the clothespin and gets it halfway across the yard before she reels it back in and throws it away. She leaves the balled-up papers in the wastebasket, knowing who'll empty it, who'll uncrumple the papers and read them with her X-ray eyes. And maybe, if Violet's so smart, she'll be able to figure out what's making Chickie feel so lousy these days. So lousy and breathless and beautiful and scared.

Later that summer, as part of Violet's Family Improvement Program, they recite poetry at the dinner table. Chickie chooses Carl Sandburg's "Fog," the shortest poem she can find. Violet reads Whittier's "Snowbound," an endless, dreary rhyme. Nash rounds things off with a recitation of "The Raven," in vampire cape and wax candy fangs. *"Darkness there and nothing more."*

"Honestly, Nash," Violet says. "You're not exactly helping the literary cause."

"Awk, awk," says Nash, with a flap of his caped wings. "Nevermore!"

After dinner, the three of them move to the living room, where Violet finishes reading *A Tale of Two Cities* out loud. Nash falls asleep in the armchair with the newspaper open in his lap. As his head falls back, he starts to snore. Chickie chews her middle fingernail, all tangled up in the lotus position on one end of the couch, waiting to find out what happens in the end. Violet sits on the other end in an Indian T-shirt and bell bottom jeans, a cigarette burning in the ashtray beside her.

"'Woman imbecile and pig-like!' said Madame Defarge.'" Violet's voice rises dramatically. "'I take no answer from you. I demand to see her. Either tell her that I demand to see her, or stand out of the way of the door!'" After each page, she picks up her cigarette and takes a drag.

As Violet's face emerges from a cloud of smoke, Chickie imagines her mother as Madame Defarge—wild-eyed and cunning, knitting secret messages into scarves with a smile as she plots the revolution. Violet's that smart, that tough—she would have been running all of Paris back in the day. She starts in on the last paragraph of the book. "'I see Barsad, and Cly, Defarge, The Vengeance, the Juryman, the Judge...I see the lives...a sanctuary...I see that child, a man winning his way up in that path of life which once was mine...It is a far, far better thing...'" She closes the book with a flourish. "'Than I have ever known.'"

"Man," Chickie says, stretching out her legs. "That Madame Defarge was one cool chick."

"Yes," Violet says. "I don't imagine you could get much cooler than Madame Defarge."

"Vi?" Nash lifts his head, roused by the reading's end. "We done?"

"Yes, Count Dracula. The revolution's over. We're done."

"We've got our own revolution brewing right here in this country." Nash straightens up in his chair with a yawn, snaps the paper open. "This week the U.S. death toll exceeded the Vietcong's. Ninety-five to sixty-seven. And this is what Johnson calls winning?"

"So, don't just sit there grousing, Nevermore. Go out and do something about it." Violet gets up from her chair. "I'm off, you two. I still have to take care of some stuff at the tennis club."

"You're leaving me with the peacenik again?" Chickie points to her father. "Do you know what happens here when you leave, Mom? Last night we ate a whole package of onion dip for dinner."

"Don't be giving away all our cooking secrets now, Chick," Nash says.

"It was disgusting." Chickie puts her hands to her throat, slides down off the couch onto the hardwood floor. "I had a killer stomachache. I almost bought the farm."

Violet just smiles. "No one ever died of eating onion dip that I know of," she says. "Anyway, it's high time you two learned to fend for yourselves."

Chickie picks herself up from the floor and flops down on the couch again. She doesn't know whether to feel freed or abandoned. Used to be she felt sorry for her mother, always the one at home, cleaning, cooking, worrying, left out, it seemed, a prisoner in her own home. *Plus ça change...* Some stupid French proverb. The more Chickie changes, the more she needs Violet to stay the same. Irony. *A Tale of Two Cities* is full of it.

Violet pulls the arms of her sweater over her shoulders and reaches for the door. *"Au revoir, mes amours,"* she says, blowing them a kiss.

Nash raises his head. *"Amour?"*

"Love, Dad," Chickie says. "It means love." A phone rings in the distance and they both start in their chairs before realizing it's not theirs.

"Ah, love." Nash nods his head and goes back to his paper.

The summer of sixty-six wears thickly on.

4

SUMMER 1969

The game they play is called "the Game," a Square-wide hide-and-seek. They hide in back alleyways, restaurant bathrooms and booths, the aisles of bookstores, body-wide cracks between buildings, fire escapes, dumpsters, tree limbs, unguarded manholes. The Game begins in the cobblestone courtyard at Holyoke Center, where the chess master hangs his sign, where musicians strum guitars and pass the hat, where a woman draws pastel chalk designs on the sidewalk—swirls and zigzags and stars. The right-to-life man paces with his placard and bulbous nose, and a tall bearded man sells the "Old Mole" and "Avatar," a full front page of swirling psychedelic obscenities. The Hari Krishnas dance and chant in a circle in the courtyard, tambourines keeping measured time, Creamsicle robes and pigtails bouncing. A Weatherman shouts from a bullhorn; a Gray Panther stalks the bent and white-haired. On the weekend's cusp, dusk rises and quivers. Offices empty, traffic snarls, dinner smells start to simmer. The cop who got in trouble with his fists walks the traffic beat up near the Wursthaus, nightstick in hand, ducking in and out of The Tasty for endless cups of coffee. The cobbled courtyard in the center of the Square is where the night twitches, where twilight waits, where the Game begins.

The players start drifting to the Square—Chickie, Hen, other kids from high school; people from around town, the Common, underground, Club 47, Hazens, Elsie's; from the riverbank or the street. It's a melting pot game. Anyone can play. One degree of separation, anyone who's ever crossed your shadow, passed you a joint on a subway bench, put a quarter in the jukebox at Tommy's Lunch and played a tune you could dance to, the girl lighting up through the window of Hayes Bickford. When enough people have gathered in the courtyard, the "it" waves a tie-dyed flag and the players scatter, bearing lumpy joints and cubes of crusty hash, rolling papers and matches tucked into their sleeves, nips of coffee brandy or vodka slid into their back pockets. After a while, the "it" sets off to seek, cruising the hidden reaches of the Square. The hiders are found one by one, crouched under the ticket booth at Nini's Corner, up in a tree on Dunster reading *Mad Magazine*, on the grate of the Lampoon fire escape with the *I Ching*. Once caught, the captives drift back to the courtyard, no telling how much time has passed. Those never found simply split and wander. No beginning, no end, no winners or losers in this game, no rules that can't be bent or broken.

Hiding in the alleyway behind the Casablanca, Chickie and Hen lean up against a poster on the brick wall of the bar—two dead soldiers, one no more than a blur in the background, arms flung behind his head like a jointless toy. The other soldier is close-up, a mud-spattered body sprawled on an open road, rifle by his side, one bug eye open, the other socket a deep black hole. Hen searches the picture for the other eye. It could be any of the pieces of rubble lying on the ground, any of the flaws in the poster's print. WHO? is written in bold red letters on top, and below one soldier's rifle, WHY?

"My dad says it's premeditated murder," Chickie says.

"They can make you go," Hen says. "But they can't make you pull the trigger."

"You turn into a different person in a war," Chickie says. "I read an article about it in *Life*."

"So that makes you an expert?"

Chickie shrugs. "If someone was going to shoot you, you'd shoot first. Self-defense. It's a natural instinct."

"I'd drop the gun." Hen pantomimes, walking slowly, one foot planted carefully in front of the other. "Raise my hands. Just keep on walking."

"Yeah, and you'd get blown to bits and your mother would *not* be happy," Chickie says.

"If they saw me put down my gun—"

"It's not Monopoly, Hen. It's a really sick game. Whichever side kills the most people wins. You're not allowed to pass go or skip your turn. You have no choice; you have to fight."

"I'd walk toward them...slowly..." He drops his hands, crouches low and turns. "I'd talk to them, explain."

"In what language, Pig Latin?" Chickie says. "You'd try to say 'peace, man,' and they'd think you were saying 'pig man' and they'd blow your head off."

Hen winces. "I could never shoot anyone."

"You would if you had to."

"I wouldn't." Hen takes a squished and nearly empty pack of Remi's Lucky Strikes out of his back pocket. He taps one out, tamps it down on the back of his hand and lights up. The tobacco's stale, the smoke harsh. He coughs out the first drag, takes another.

"Hey," Chickie says softly. "You don't smoke."

"I do now." Hen inhales, looks over again at the poster of the soldiers sprawled dead on the road, trying to keep the cigarette lit, swallowing hard to keep from coughing.

"Give me one then," Chickie says.

Hen hands her a cigarette. "I'd drop the gun and run like hell, Chick. I swear."

"Yeah, you and Superman," she says as she lights up. "Faster than a speeding bullet—"

"Faster than the fucking speed of light," Hen says in a hoarse whisper.

"Gotcha!" a voice yells down from the rooftop. It's over. They've been found by the "it."

Back in a shaded corner of the courtyard, Chickie and Hen settle in with the other captives, perched like lizards on city ledges, belted, bearded, ears pierced, long hair spent at its tips, army jackets, navy bells, stripes, zigzags, polka dots, watching time and the world pass by in a smoky haze. Most of them are on the safe side of young, strong of limb and spirit, comfortable on this hot night, equal enough for a time, by the rules of this game, anyway, no better, no worse, no faster or slower, higher, lower. The smells of Chinese food and dope and coffee fill the air. The laughter's thick and full of possibility, brain swell, imploding sex. The last person to be found becomes the "it." And when the tie-dyed flag waves again, as darkness settles deep, the lizards raise their sleepy eyelids, crush out their cigarettes with their curled-up leather sandals, dust off their jeans of city dirt, and are off and running again.

Hen slams the back screen door of Chickie's kitchen. First day back. Senior year of high school. Red Sox down six games to the Yankees. Another restless, muggy September.

"Hey, preppie." Chickie sprinkles cinnamon sugar from a plastic bear onto her toast.

"New school clothes." Hen's dressed in straight-leg Levi's, a blue shirt with three buttons down at the neck, hiking boots, a bookbag slung over his shoulder. "What can I say?"

"Well, you look really swell, Wally." Chickie takes a swig of orange juice from the carton and wipes her mouth with the back of her hand. She wears a blue and orange Marimekko miniskirt and a red silk T-shirt with tiny breast pockets, *fabriqué en* France. Her tights have clocks on them, all striking midnight. Black Converse All-Stars still ride her ankles high.

"Summer's over, eh, kids?" Nash watches the little TV on the kitchen table. Woodstock's still in the news; almost a month later, the mess still hasn't been cleaned up.

"Brilliant, Dad," Chickie says. "450,000 people at Woodstock and I was stuck working at Vita Mart all summer."

"Two guys got to walk on the moon," Hen says. "And I was stuck here on Earth."

The TV flashes footage of the rock festival, fields full of barefoot, painted hippies, smoke, flowers, guitars. "Half a million people," Nash says. "That's how many kids are over in Vietnam fighting right now. Eighty college presidents tell Nixon to pull out and he's not the least bit swayed. Who the hell's going to knock some sense into him? He's withdrawing troops but resuming bombing at the same time. What kind of twisted logic is that?"

"It's twisted," Hen says.

"Looks like they're bringing back the draft, Hen."

"I know."

"Don't *talk* about that, Dad," Chickie says.

Violet swings through the door from the hallway, slipping her arms through the sleeves of a tan, belted raincoat. "Don't you look nice, Hen," she says.

"Thanks," he says. "How are you, Aunt Vi?"

"I'm fine. And thank you for asking." She gives Chickie a pointed look. "You two want a ride to school?"

"You don't get *driven* to high school," Chickie says.

"Is that right?" Violet turns to Hen.

He shrugs. "It's a nice day for a walk."

"You don't have to pull an Eddie Haskell on her, Hen." Chickie finishes off the last crust of toast. "She's always like this in the morning. June Cleaver, Cambridge style."

"June who?" Violet pours hot coffee into a thermos. "Did this June person have a stationery store to run, a house to clean, bills to pay? Did this June person have such a wiseass, ungrateful daughter?"

"No such luck," Chickie says. "Just two really psycho sons."

"Be good," Violet calls back as she heads for the door—but not with much conviction.

The old high school sits like a fortress next to the public library, a structure of dull gold brick and cement, pieced together over the years, small barred windows, and massive steel doors, not so much a building as a hulking mass. Chickie and Hen cut down a diagonal path intersecting what was once a green, but is now a wasteland of cracked sidewalks, broken benches, litter, and dirt. At the far end of the green, a man plays the saxophone while a pigeon jitterbugs at his feet.

"Back to prison," Hen says.

Chickie stops at a bench and lights up a Camel. "Have you ever thought about what people *do* in prison, Hen?"

"Count the cracks in the ceiling?" he says. "Beat each other to a bloody pulp?"

Chickie French-inhales. "They think about getting *out*, Hen. Ways to escape. Use your imagination."

"It's dead," he says, starting to walk toward the school. *Dead. Dead. DEAD.*

"Hey there, Goldilocks." A skateboard slips out of nowhere and presses up hard against Hen's chest. Two boys appear, both in satin maroon jackets, one with a Fu Manchu mustache and sideburns, the other's face shaven clean.

"Who, me?" Hen can't believe it. Finally a senior and he's still a target for goons, a shrimpy, baby-faced, hairless freak.

"That's right, Goldilocks. We mean you." One boy sits down on the broken bench while the taller one slings his arm around Hen. "Listen, Goldie, Cozmo and I have a little something we'd like you to do."

"What's that?" The tall boy's arm lies like a concrete slab across Hen's shoulder. Chickie stands frozen at his side.

"The thing is—it's something you really have to do with your shirt off." The tall boy looks over at his friend. "Isn't that right, Coz?"

"That's right, Fitz." Cozmo zips and unzips his jacket on the bench. Hen looks over at Chickie. She shakes her head.

"Maybe he needs some help, Coz."

"Maybe he does."

"Gee, it's a shame." Fitz pulls Hen's collar up around his neck. "It's such a swell shirt, with a nice little lizard on it and all." He flicks the logo with his fingers.

"It's an alligator," Hen says.

"Did you hear that, Coz?" Fitz laughs. "My mistake. It's a fucking alligator." A knife blade pops suddenly out of one hand.

"What the—"

Fitz grabs the front of Hen's shirt and bunches it up into a fist, yanks him up into his face. "One thing Coz can't stand, Goldie, is reptiles." Hen's breath stops cold as the knife snags his shirt at the neck and rips it clear to his waist. "Now, take it off," Fitz says. "You know, like that Noxzema ad says. 'Take it all off.'"

Hen peels what's left of the shirt over his head.

"Excellent," Fitz says. "Now there's one last thing, Goldie. Coz's feet have to be kissed once a day by a naked prince or he turns back into a toad."

"What the hell?" Coz's back springs away from the slats of the bench.

"Hey, Coz." Chickie steps forward. "Why don't you tell your friend here to leave us alone."

Fitz's hand flies up to his mouth in mock surprise. "Who's this, Goldilocks. Your bodyguard?"

"She's my cousin," Hen says. "Leave her alone."

"Ooh, his cousin!" Fitz makes two fists, pretends to shiver. "Don't mess with her, Coz. She looks like a mean hippie bitch."

"Don't call her that."

"Let's go, Hen." As Chickie starts to walk away, Fitz jams the skateboard up under her chin, stops her in her tracks. "Jerk," she hisses.

The knife of Fitz's blade tilts toward her. "What did you say?"

"She didn't say anything. And will you put that knife away?" Hen pushes the board down. "Shut up, Chickie. You're only making this worse."

"I can't believe you're letting them do this to you, Hen."

"Chickie? And Hen?" Fitz starts to howl. "Looks like we got the whole barnyard here, Coz."

"Looks like."

"You're actually going to kiss this moron's feet?" Chickie says.

"Ooh, cat fight, Coz," Fitz says. "I bet on the bitch. She's tough."

"Don't *call* her that, I said."

Fitz raps one of Coz's sneakers with his stick. "Just be a good little faggot, Goldie, and we can wrap this up in no time."

"Don't do it, Hen," Chickie says.

Hen looks over at Fitz, at Coz squirming on the bench, at Chickie standing pale and furious beside him. He lets out a breath he's held for so long, since the beginning of time it seems. And when he realizes that Chickie's fought his last battle for him, a strange calm passes over him like a warm wind. "You really want me to kiss your feet, man?" he says to Cozmo.

Cozmo shrugs, twisting his neck uncomfortably from side to side.

"You heard him, Goldilocks," Fitz says.

"He didn't say anything, It's you who's been doing all the talking, man. Now, I'm talking to him."

"Kiss his fucking feet."

"Why?" Hen says. "Why should I kiss his fucking feet?"

Fitz hefts the knife in his hand. "I told you, Goldie. The toad thing."

"Ah. The toad thing." Hen lifts his arms in mock surrender, as the sax music loops and slides. The voice of sarcasm parches his mouth, burns his cheeks, but still, miraculously, it speaks. "Can't argue with that. I get it." Kneeling down, bare to the waist, he slowly lowers his head. The journey downward is endless, surreal; it may be the first truly intentional act of his life. "Cozmo doesn't want to turn back into a toad. Can't blame him. Who really would?" Cozmo's enormous feet loom suddenly before him as he purses his lips.

"Jesus Christ!" Cozmo pulls his legs away and jumps up from the bench, kicking Hen square in the face. "You're sick, kid, you know that?" He shuffles nervously as the blood starts to spew from Hen's nose. "Now look what you did, Fitz. He's bleeding."

"Boys! Boys!" Down the cracked cement path comes a woman in a turquoise suit, tipping from side to side like the biggest of the wooden dolls that fit inside one another and break apart at the waist, waving wildly with her arms.

"Fat Ass Prentiss!" Fitz flicks the knife closed and grabs Cozmo by the arm. "Time to go now, Coz."

"Stop it right there, boys!" the woman cries as the boys fly across the green. "You hear me? Stop it right there!"

Hen spits out a mouthful of blood, holding the rag of his new shirt up to his nose. Fat Ass Prentiss arrives breathless at the bench, bracelets jangling, hair the color of a copper penny, flipped up at the ends like fishhooks. She takes over the dabbing of Hen's face with a hunk of Kleenex produced magically from the folds of her sleeve. The smell of perfume swirls up his nose and nearly makes him gag. "Hooligans!" Fat Ass Prentiss's voice slips out in a hiss as the two boys disappear around the side of the school. "Jesus, Mary, mother of God. In the end, they'll get what's coming to them. I swear that they'll get theirs."

Crashing one fleshy arm against the steel bar of the high school door, Fat Ass Prentiss leads the way. The corridors are dark and endless, the walls pale green and peeling; track lighting casts an eerie glow. The swishing of panty hose against thigh is the loudest sound to be heard. The smells are old, familiar—warm milk, chalk, mimeograph ink, ammonia. A cackling voice, half human, half chicken cluck, breaks the silence over a loudspeaker on the wall.

"The following students will report immediately to the main office: Diane Downing, Linda Fantini, Geraldo Haber, Tina Jackson..."

Fat Ass Prentiss leads Chickie and Hen to an office on the first floor.

"A few more stragglers, Mrs. Lugbout," she says to a woman sitting at a broad wooden desk. Thick glasses, turned-up nose lost in a moonscape of bumpy flesh, ringed fingers, heavy makeup—these are the glories of Mrs. Lugbout, the senior dean.

"Late note?" Mrs. Lugbout sticks out the hand that's not busy scribbling.

"You'd better look, Mary," Fat Ass Prentiss says from the door. "I'm afraid there's blood."

Mrs. Lugbout lifts her head. "Oh, good lord, Eileen, call the nurse." Heaving herself up from her chair, she makes her way around to the other side of the desk. Her hips are gargantuan; her glasses slide low on her nose. She plants one hand on the top of Hen's head and tilts it back, eyes running over the naked parts of him under his ripped shirt. "Any loose teeth? Lacerations? Broken bones?"

Hen's lip has swollen to the size of a wad of Bazooka. His nose is swollen, still dripping blood. "It's just a fat lip," he says. "I'm fine."

"You most certainly are *not* fine."

Chickie feels an old twinge as Hen is pawed and examined—a twisted wire scraping the underside of her belly, the end of the feeling she had when Fitz's knife clicked open, when Hen told her to shut up and the board pressed hard up under her chin. Hen flings Chickie a look as Mrs. Lugbout's fingers brush his naked shoulder. *Help me, please*, it says. She laughs, turns hard on her heel. Mrs. Lugbout leads them out into the hallway, points Chickie upstairs toward her history class, and beckons to Hen, the nail-polished spear of her index finger leading the charge. "And you, young man, to the nurse!"

Chickie hits the stairway running, starts down the halls she'll roam in her dreams for years to come. As she opens the door of the social studies room, her stomach flutters. The smells of old ruins and battles float her way. She feels her hair go limp, her breath come hard and fast. When the door slams shut, they all laugh. Chickie shoves her fists into the pockets of her miniskirt. The laughter dies down. Big deal, she thinks. They're half an hour wiser to all this than she is, had time to sharpen their pencils, tell each other what they did over their summer vacations. She sizes up the class. A new kid with a ponytail wearing motorcycle boots in the second row, prettiest girl off by the window, slackers in back, ass kissers up front. Mr. Hurlehee's no more than five foot two, with a harelip and pea-green eyes. His twangy voice comes at her from the front of the room—half East Cambridge, half *Gone with the Wind*.

"Do you belong here, miss?" he says.

"Who knows?" Chickie says. "I think so."

Mr. Hurlehee grins like a forest gnome that gives children treats by day and roasts them on a spit at night. "Well, thinking is an admirable start. We encourage that here in Mr. Hurlehee's class." His hand waves over the sea of scattered chairs. "Have a seat, Miss-Who-Knows-I-Think-So. And we will try to determine just exactly who you are and where you belong."

"Good luck," Chickie says, leaning into one hip.

A few half-hearted laughs roll up from the back of the room. The pretty girl looks up and the boy in the motorcycle boots does nothing, which is just as it should be. Mr. Hurlehee peers over his bifocals, not sure who's to have the last laugh. Chickie feels the ripple flow back into her hair, her breath start to pace evenly. The biker boy's eyes shift as she passes by. She chooses the last seat, last row, by the window, and catches sight of the end of an airplane's trail as it swells and blurs in the sky. She crosses her legs at the ankle and finds a point in the back of the biker boy's head to use as her center, as her spinning brain winds down.

Holy shit, check it out.

I heard about this dude.

What a freak.

The whispers start from the back of the room and zigzag forward. Chickie looks up at the blackboard, where Mr. Hurlehee has slid a Civil War cap onto his head and taken a sword out of his desk drawer. "Now that we're all assembled," he announces, his voice taking on new strength and more of the Southern drawl. "My name is Charles Anderson Hurlehee. Commander Seventh Battalion, Twelfth Regiment." He adjusts his cap and cocks his head. "But under the circumstances of our capture and imprisonment here during the present siege, you may all feel free in the coming months"—he takes off his hat and bows—"to address me as Colonel."

And it's at that odd, karmic moment that the loudspeaker comes on again to announce that the first Cambridge High and Latin School graduate has been killed in combat in Vietnam. Andrew Gardner. Former varsity football player and glee club member. Class of 1969. May he rest forever, the cackling voice says, in peace.

The sound of the ice tray cracking has always meant the coming of darkness. It's a sound Hen can remember from the beginning of time, a sound that means his father's home from work and everything will change. After the ice tray cracks and darkness falls, the plum house slips out of order and grace. Remi retreats with his whiskey to the armchair. Faye becomes silent and hard, mad if it takes more than a few words to explain something or answer a question. She jerks things around with claps and bangs, tight lines springing spiderlike to her face. The day loses softness, all reason and rhyme. Little messes crop up in odd places, open spaces. Pictures fall off their hooks on the wall; dust rises in ragged, swirling balls from the floor. The dishes get half-washed, a body half-dried by a wet towel, homework half-done. It's at this time, at dusk, after the ice has cracked, when the leaky faucet goes from a drip to a trickle, when the last spotted banana in the fruit bowl sends out its thick, pungent smell.

Pressing his back up to the side of the house, Hen edges slowly toward the back screen door. When he hears the ice cubes clink into a glass, he peers inside. Remi takes off his sports jacket and throws it over a chair. Turning on the radio, he swivels the dial to *AM Sports Talk*, lights himself a Lucky Strike, takes two drags, and places it on the kitchen table, smoking end hanging over the edge. After he dumps the ice tray into the chipped gold ice bucket, he reaches for the gallon of Jim Beam.

"Let's get real, callah." The King of Boston Sports's voice grazes through the holes of the screen door. *"Benson's been snoozing at the plate since April."*

"But you got to admit, Eddie, the guy's been rock solid on second," the caller says.

"Who the heck needs rock solid on second?" the Sports King brays. *"Give me Ross Merlot any day. Let's talk rock solid on first."*

Hen comes into the kitchen, naked to the waist, belly hard, knees square. Eighteen in twenty-five days. So somewhere along the line, he must have become a man. He watches his father uncap the Jim Beam. It's hard to feel like a man in this house where he's always been a boy, where a sentence rarely gets finished, where the ice never hardens all the way through.

"Damn this freezer," Remi says, closing the door. "Jesus Christ, Hen. What happened to your face?"

"I had a run-in on the basketball court."

"Ouch. There go your Cary Grant credentials."

"How was your trip, Dad?" Remi's been away on business for two weeks. They still don't talk often. But this is the best moment to catch his father, the only moment, really, when he's about to pour his first drink, as relaxed, as close to happy as he gets.

"Not half bad." As the whiskey splashes over the ice cubes, Hen's eyes lock to the flow. It's beautiful to watch, like a pretty girl playing with her hair, but the smell, even from a distance, nearly makes him gag. "Got some new sponsors for the store." Remi takes a swig from the glass, curls his lips up over his teeth and draws in air as he swallows. "How 'bout you, Mussolini," he says. "How're the wife and kids?"

"Mezza-mezza." They run through the old jokes, shared between the two of them since before Hen got any of their parts. "Bam, slam, to the moon, Alice." Hen grins feebly, feeling foolish to be bribing his father with these old jokes for a moment of his time.

"To the moon." Remi laughs and reaches for his drink again. Hen makes a fist by his side and wills his father's arm to stop lifting the glass. For a second, it does, to shoo a nearby fly. The arm lifts high in a toast; the lips make contact with the glass's rim. Third swallow. The throat constricts. The voice pulls back. "How's school going, Hen. What are you now, son. Junior?"

Son. The word presses Hen back against the screen door. "I'm a senior," he says.

"Oh, right. What're they teaching you these days?"

"The usual." Hen unclenches his fists as his father's glass comes back down to the tabletop. "Same old shit," he says.

Remi nods, half in reprimand, half with approval. After the fourth swallow, he yanks loose the knot of his tie, leans back in his chair. "It's a bore. God knows, Hen, I remember. Still, bottom line, you can't run Potts Pro without an education."

"Buzz is going to run Potts Pro, Dad."

"I'm planning on the two of you running it together," Remi says. "You and Buzz will make a good team."

"Do yourself a favor, Dad. Let Buzz run Potts Pro. He's the pro in this family. He'll do a great job."

"Oh, Christ, Hen, you'll learn. It takes time, that's all. You kids have no patience, no sense of responsibility. In my day—"

"Yeah, kids these days. I know." Hen pulls at the tape on his hockey stick. "Look, Dad, sports just isn't my thing."

"And so the question arises, just what *is* your *thing*?" Remi twists the words in whiskey-laced mockery, bringing out the same hard voice in Hen.

"Oh, I don't know." He'd say chess but Remi would only joke that you can't take a checkmate to the bank. "Selling dope. maybe. Joining the circus. Getting blown away in some jungle with an M-16—"

"Translation," Remi interrupts. "You have no plans."

"That's right." Hen counts the cigarette burns on the edge of the table. Three. Four. Five… "I have no plans."

"Well…"

Sixth swallow. Seven burn marks on the edge of the table. It's a miracle the house hasn't burned to the ground. Eighth swallow. Remi's voice lets go its grip, starts to ooze. "Well, if I were you, Hen. I'd consider making some. Plans, that is."

"Right." Hen tries to say something with his hands, but they fail him. He should leave now, just get the hell out of there, but he's come this far and it's always so hard to scrounge up what it takes to try again. "Did you hear about Andy Gardner, Dad?"

"Phil's son? The one who got into Princeton?"

"Yeah, he got into Princeton, but he enlisted instead. And he just got blown away in Vietnam."

Remi winces with the ninth sip. "Oh, Jesus, no," he says.

"They're bringing back the draft, Dad. I have to register within five days of my eighteenth birthday. That's next week."

"Jesus, you're that old?"

"You don't even know how old I am?"

"When you get to be my age—"

"I don't want to go," Hen says.

"Aren't you jumping the gun a bit?" Remi rubs his forehead. "Sorry, bad pun. Let's not panic here, Hen."

"I'm not panicking," Hen says. "But I want to be ready. Uncle Nash says I should keep ahead of them, know my own mind before they come after me. I want to know what I'm going to do, and I want to be able to say why. I don't want to come back in a frickin' box, like Andy Gardner."

"Jesus. What a tough break." Remi hasn't heard the rest. "I'll have to give Phil Gardner a call. He must be crushed. He was going to take that kid into the law firm with him. What a damn shame." Remi collapses with the tenth swallow, reaches for the whiskey bottle as tears well up in his eyes. "Poor old Phil. I remember that kid when he—"

"Oobleck." The word slides out of Hen's mouth.

"Oobleck?" Remi spits it back. "What the hell is that?"

"Nothing." Hen turns his head away. He can't tell his father that he's like oobleck now, after the whiskey's gotten to him—a mixture of cornstarch and just the right amount of water, sliding through your fingers if you let it flow, a thick creamy liquid, hardened instantly with the squeeze of a hand like a chunk of clay. A nasty word from Faye can do it, a pressing, bitter word that shuts Remi up tight again. Hen could do it now. He could say, "There's no point in having this conversation anymore. It's going nowhere and you're at least halfway drunk. And even if it were, and you weren't, you wouldn't remember any of it in the morning." But he's not that quick, that mean, that stupid, not anywhere near that brave.

"Phil used to be quite the prankster. I remember the time when he and Nash and I…"

Hen turns away. The moment's passed, the window of chance slammed shut with his father's teary collapse. He's got to get out of there, before all hell breaks loose in his brain, before… "I'll catch you later, Dad," he says.

As the front door opens and shuts in the distance, Remi's teary eyes rise. They hear footsteps on the stairs. Faye doesn't announce herself anymore.

"It's Mom," Hen says.

"Mom," Remi echoes, his jaw falling slack on the last *m*. He gets up from the table, picks up his drink glass, and swings through the door to the living room.

Hen kicks the bottom of the refrigerator to drown out the echo of the last spoken word. *Momomomomomomom.* The rusty enamel panel clatters to the dingy floor.

On the other side of the swinging door, Remi settles in the armchair and waits to prove himself right. He knows Faye won't come back downstairs. For it's clear. She's leaving him, not in body, maybe, but in spirit. Was it just three years ago that she announced she was going to open a pottery school? Just like that. She told him at a clambake in Nantucket in August, under a cockeyed moon, a beach fire crackling seaweed and driftwood, her face ablaze in the dark. She really wanted to do this, she said. She'd been thinking about it for a long, long while. The time was right. It seemed important. Maybe it would make her happy. This last thought had been his, not hers. Remi wanted Faye's happiness. It was worth a great deal to him. He listened carefully, softened and turned on by the light in her eyes, the flicker of the flames on her rising breast, her legs tucked underneath her in the sand. The kids were finally grown, she said. She had the energy now, the time. There was a clear demand. Art was "in" these days, the wave of the future, as good as gold. And the beauty of it was, clay was cheap. She'd start slowly, test the waters, wouldn't bite off more than she could chew. After a while, who knew? He could hear the excitement build in her voice with each proverb flung. She might even start pulling in some revenue.

What could he possibly have said or done? Back in Cambridge in the fall, he cosigned the lease on a storefront in Inman Square, helped Faye paint the place, and made the rounds of old furniture shops looking for countertops and sturdy wooden stools. He put fliers under the windshield wipers of a thousand cars, unloaded a literal ton of clay from a smelly dump truck. He did everything she asked of him, everything she wanted. Helped her build her goddamned city of clay. But just as Remi had feared, it didn't end there, couldn't end there. Clay City was greedy, and now, so too is Faye. She isn't grateful, or content. She wants more of everything—more rugs, more stools, more pottery wheels, more students, another ton of clay. Her school has been a huge success. There are waiting lists for classes, people lined up at the door. A local TV news show did a feature on the place a few weeks ago. Faye looked young and sexy on TV. The cameraman flirted with her, told her she had Greta Garbo eyes. Everyone tells Remi how proud he must be, how lucky he should feel. Everyone says, "Good for Faye; that Faye is really something"—as if she'd been nothing before and that were somehow his fault.

"You old dog, you." A friend poked him in the ribs on the tennis court the other day. "How does it feel to be slipping under the sheets with a local celebrity? Damn, she looked good on TV, Remi. *Damn.*"

Damn. Remi takes another sip of his drink. They'll never know. And he'll never tell. That Faye comes home at night silent and spent, flops onto the couch, sometimes doesn't come to bed at all, and when she does, turns her back to him, curling up into a tight ball. It's his secret—theirs—and he'll take it to his grave, that sex in the plum house is co-matose, all but dead. Remi can't feel proud, or lucky. It's not something he could ever say out loud or try to explain. How furious he feels, how humiliated, cheated, worst of all, again…abandoned. Call him a spoiled, chauvinistic prick of a man…Jesus, poor old Phil Gardner, losing his kid like that. He couldn't bear it. But goddamned son of a bitch. He doesn't want Faye to be successful or sexy or strong. He doesn't want her to work, to test the waters, to start bringing in some cash. He doesn't want her to be out of the house so much, to turn her back on him in bed. God knows, he's not a tyrant, or a sex maniac or really even much of a judge. Remi closes his eyes and leans his head back in the chair. But one thing he just can't stand is sleeping alone.

Dis donc, ou est la bibliothèque?

Mademoiselle Gladstone's chest swells as she begins the French dialogue for the day. She pulls her hair back tightly in a bun, trying to look French, Chickie supposes, but looking more like one of the stuffed grizzly bears in the Peabody Museum.

C'est tout droit. Tu y vas tout de suite? The class answers in dull refrain, a few voices rising clear above the mumble. Chickie sits in the back row, doodling on her paper-bag book cover—slowly her name appears in busty, three-dimensional letters. She adds some accents, a circumflex, a cedilla under the C. ÇHICKIE. Good name for a rock star. Of course, she'd have to ditch the Potts.

Monkey Man Ackerman raises his hand. "I feel sick, Miss G.," he says. "I think I better go home."

Mademoiselle Gladstone looks up at the clock. "It's almost two-thirty, Reginald. *Deux heures et demi.* I'm sure you'll feel better then. *Meilleur.*"

"I might croak before then." Reginald slides low in his chair, grabs his throat with his hands and gags. "You know, like *croquer.*"

"We will all pray"—she raises her palms in mock prayer—"that you will make it safely through the end of the school day. *Prier, Reginald. Prier.*"

"Il faut que j'aille chercher un livre," Chickie murmurs along. It is necessary that I go look for a book. I need a book. I need something. *Quelque
chose.* Eighteen years old. In French, you *have* years. After you've lived
them, they belong to you. That seems only fair.

"I'm telling you, Miss G...." Monkey Man Ackerman won't quit. "I
got a wicked headache."

Mademoiselle Gladstone sighs. "At least say it in French, Reginald.
Au moins en français."

"*Ma tête* hurts. *Très* bad." Reginald slaps the side of his head. "I gotta
go *a la* home. Tooty-sweetie."

A few titters rise.

"*Chez moi.*" Mademoiselle Gladstone coaxes patiently. "Literally,
it means 'to the house of me.' In French, there really is no word for
home."

"Yeah, I gotta go to the house of me," he says. "*Vite. Vite.* Let me
outta here, Miss G."

"Give it up, Monkey Man," Chickie mumbles.

Mr. Harrington, the biology teacher from across the hall, sticks his
head inside the door. His mustache is waxed, shoes two-toned, suit
polyester, blue plaid. "A moment please, Miss Gladstone?" he says.

"*Certainement,*" she says. "I'll be right with you, Mr. Harrington. Class,
please study the *chez* idiom on page ninety-two. *Etudiez. A la page quatre-
vingt-douze.*"

"No hanky-panky, you two!" Monkey Man calls out.

As Mademoiselle Gladstone steps out into the hall, the snickers rise.
Someone taps Chickie on the shoulder. She lifts her head. It's Elvis Donahue, two seats over, the kid with the motorcycle boots and ponytail
she noticed in the colonel's class on the first day of school. He rides a
motorcycle to school, just moved to Cambridge from Pittsburgh, the
armpit of the nation, she heard him tell some kid during the hygiene
movie a few weeks back. Everyone was pretending to pop their zits in
the "danger zone" around their noses, yelling, "Splat! Ah, you got me!
Now you die!"

"Mind if I copy your history homework?" Elvis Donahue says.

"Stayed late at your Boy Scout meeting last night?" Chickie says.

"That's exactly right." He grins. "Very busy helping old ladies cross
the street. Hey, you want to hang out sometime?"

"Sure." Chickie takes out her homework and hands it to him. "So
what do you think of the colonel?" she says.

"Hurlehee?" Elvis shakes his head. "I can't believe they let a crazed old fossil like that teach history."

"He actually believes he was in the Civil War. In another life, he says."

"The dude may need another life soon," Elvis lifts his boots onto the back of an empty chair. "He was nodding off yesterday while we were taking that test. Everyone was cheating their tails off."

"He can't help it," Chickie says. "He's old."

Elvis's boots drop to the floor as Mademoiselle Gladstone comes back into the classroom. Her face is flushed. Her pointer rises. "*Maintenant, classe. Ou étions-nous?* Where were we?"

"You were telling us about the quiz we're going to have tomorrow," Diane Downing pipes up. *"Notre examen. Demain."*

"Merci beaucoup, Diane. What would we do without you. *Que ferions nous?"*

"Celebrate," Hen says under his breath.

Chickie looks up at Hen, who's sitting in front of her. The back of his T-shirt reads WYMAN WINGNUTS—the name of his street hockey team. His hair sticks up in crooked shoots; he's a funky, messed-up Ken doll. He's finally starting to grow; it's like he ate some freaky magic mushroom. Every week, it seems like he's another inch taller. His nose healed crooked from Coz's kick and he likes it that way. Chickie wants to neaten Hen up, turn his shirt right side out, stretch the legs of his pants to meet his socks at the ankle. If she didn't know him better, she'd think he was perpetually stoned. They saw another film about pot in the auditorium. It kills your brain cells, the movie said, turns you into a zombie, someone your own mother wouldn't recognize. It leads to harder stuff, stuff you shoot up with a needle and it slowly kills you. They'll find you in the snow, under the wheel of a car, in rags, on a park bench panhandling, nodding out, having an argument with a tree. It's all a big hype; what a waste of time. Still, this is the kind of movie that scares Chickie these days and only makes Hen laugh.

It used to be the other way around.

"Revisions." Mademoiselle Gladstone taps the board with her pointer. "Let's review the *chez* idiom, which means house or home. My house. *Chez moi.* Your house. *Chez toi. Chez vous.* His house…*chez lui*, and…"

Chickie puts her homework back in her history book. Randy Purlow shoots something out of a straw and hits Regina Cremons in the neck. Regina rises up in her chair, throws a dark look around the room as she chews on a clump of hair, then eases back down into her slump.

Hen's French book is open on the desktop, while a chess book rides his thighs—*Think Like a Grandmaster*. Chickie leans forward and pokes him in the back with a pencil.

"Ow!" Hen's whisper loses it in midair as he arches his back in pain.

"*Comment, Henri?*" Mademoiselle Gladstone lifts her chin. "Did you say something, *Monsieur Potts? Vous avez dit quelque chose?*"

Hen looks up, runs a hand through his hair. "Who, *moi?*" he says. "You talking to me, Miss G.?"

"Indeed." Mademoiselle Gladstone beams. "*Je parle à vous, Monsieur Potts.* Tell me, how would one say, *par exemple, comment on dit,* 'at the house of the lazy boy'?"

"Say what?" Hen cups his ear and gets a laugh. Chickie wishes he'd leave the wise-ass stuff to Monkey Man Ackerman, who's been at it longer, who's bigger, stronger, thicker in the skull. Hen closes the chess book on his lap and shoves it into his desk, sits up straight and scratches his head.

"*Chez le garçon paresseux,*" Chickie whispers.

"*Chez le garçon paresseux.*" Hen's voice sounds like a donkey's bray.

"*Bravo, Henri,*" Mademoiselle Gladstone says. "Correct. *La réponse est correcte.*"

The clapping begins slowly and rises to a dull roar. Monkey Man Ackerman whistles loudly through his two front teeth. Books bang against wooden desktops. Another spitball barrels toward Regina Cremons's leg. "Way to go, Pottsie!" someone yells.

"Thank you. Thank you. *Merci beaucoup.*" Hen raises a palm and dips his head. "It was nothing, really. No applause, *see voo play,* I mean really, it was nothing."

"Yes, we all know, *Henri. On sait bien,*" Mademoiselle Gladstone looks over at Chickie. "That it was nothing. *Absoluement rien.*"

5

As Charlie motions for the check, Violet gazes out the window of the Pewter Pot Restaurant. It's a dull October Friday, a day that began with a muted longing and will end up honing her senses to a nearly unbearable pitch. For the first time, after three years of sneaking around, she agreed to meet Charlie in the Square for lunch, out in the open, not worrying about who might be watching, who might see. Free love—it's on everyone's lips these days—why shouldn't she savor the taste? The old mores are crumbling—modesty, prudence, fidelity—now considered archaic, throwback virtues to an uptight, Victorian past. It's both freeing and troubling, this slow cracking of the age-old moral code. Violet once thought such a brazen rendezvous with Charlie might be exhilarating, a thrill. But now that she's sitting here with a stomach full of bad chicken salad, with Charlie sprawled across from her in a booth, working a toothpick in the corner of his mouth, she feels not so much a sense of forbidden excitement as dull resignation. This, she thinks half-heartedly, and with some relief, cannot be liberation, cannot be love.

Violet looks at her watch, then out the window at the street: 12:08. The Square's full of the usual suspects—hippies, college kids, cops, street vendors, office people. High school truants. She can tell them a mile away, laced through the crowd, neon fish in a murky sea—an afroed girl at Nini's Corner, a wisp of a boy bouncing on his heels in front of the Coop. They travel in fast-moving, fleet-footed groups, heads bent together at a conspiratorial tilt, eyes darting full circle, cigarette smoke swirling, ready at any given moment to flee. As Charlie cranes his neck to find the waitress, the blue truancy van pulls up in front of the Coop and the bouncing boy darts inside.

"All set, sexpot?" Charlie takes out his wallet. "Where the hell is our girl?"

"Don't call me that." Violet keeps her eyes trained on the window. "And don't call her that. It's demeaning, Charlie. Vulgar."

He laughs. "No point in being a hypocrite," he says. "Vulgar is..." he twirls his coffee spoon in one hand. "As vulgar does. And you, cheese-cake—"

"Enough, Charlie," she says.

"Damn it, where is our girl? And what the hell are you staring out the window for? You've hardly said a word the whole meal." Charlie looks at his watch. "I've got a lesson at one thirty, but I saved time for dessert. You still hungry, baby? You got a little room left for me?" He licks his coffee spoon and with a sleight of hand that always amazes Violet, graceful as a cat sometimes, this lummox Charlie, he flips it from one hand above the table to the other below. The edge of the spoon snakes its way up her calf, trailing the inside of her leg.

Her leg twitches. "Good god, Charlie, what—"

"I've got my car." His voice is steady as he navigates the spoon up her inner thigh. "I know a nice little graveyard on the other side of town. Very private." The tip of the spoon pulls one edge of her underwear aside and she gasps. Charlie's lewdness, his boldness will never cease to shock her, to arouse her. How dare you and don't stop—both thoughts barrel through her brain as she opens her legs wider to give the spoon more room to play. Dirty. Filthy. Hungry Charlie.

"What do you say?" Charlie leans forward, works the spoon as if it were a puppet, makes it dance, stops abruptly, wriggles it again, flattens it, drags it, eggs it on. "You up for a little graveyard romp?"

"No," she says.

He's whispering now. "Getting slammed on a headstone? Leaving a little love juice for the angels?"

"Charlie, stop!"

Violet stifles a groan, squeezes her legs together, raises her chin. Charlie slides out the spoon and lets it fall clattering to the floor. She looks down in horror, bends down to retrieve it.

"Leave it, sexpot." He slaps a ten down on the table. "To the grave-yard," he says.

Violet slides her coat over her shoulders, hot now, breathless and defeated, ready to hit the car, hit the graveyard, let Charlie do what he will. "Jesus Christ, Charlie," she says. "Can't you even let the dead rest in peace?"

It begins as a shimmering in the corner of her eye, and for the longest time, no more than a second probably, Violet's sure that she *is* seeing things—the long hair rippling down over the shoulders of a girl waiting for the walk sign to change, the graceful tilt of her head, the swing of her arms as she starts across the street, a ponytailed boy at her side—just a coincidence, she thinks, the stripe on the ratty shirt, the jean jacket's too dark, isn't it? They walk with such a sexual swagger, the girl's hand slid carelessly into the boy's back pocket, his arm slung snakelike along the line of her hips. It's not so much a crossing as a declaration. The girl's hips pull up as she leaps, one foot landing on the sidewalk in front of the restaurant window. The leap clinches it. Just as the button of her coat slides into its hole, Violet sees. It *is* Chickie, Chickie no more than a few feet away, looking in through the plate-glass window, hand straightening over her brow for confirmation. Five seconds, no more than ten, before a gust of wind grabs her hair from behind and sends it billowing back over her face. As the boy pulls Chickie on impatiently, Violet hopelessly waves.

In bed later that night, Nash snoring beside her, Violet drifts back in time, to the farm in Iowa where she was born, where body parts lay hidden behind denim and cheap flannel, all just part of the plumbing, sex no more exotic than what the chickens did in the barnyard, walking in frantic, idiotic circles, bumping up against each other in broad daylight. Hers was a decent, hardworking family and Violet knew no shame to be part of it. But by the time she went East for college, all she'd been able to see was the dung on all of the soles of her brothers' boots, their clumsy, calloused fingers and dull farmer eyes, their easily satisfied bellies, her mother's heavy breasts and dime-store clothes, her father's stooped back and lowered eyes. By the time Violet left her family behind, all she'd been able to see and smell and taste was the barnyard on all of them. And it is still and always like a barnyard animal that Violet feels with men—that first boy in a hayloft, several more in college before she met Nash, boys found on bar stools and basketball courts, lanky, muscled, doughy boys, breathless fumbling in musty dormitory rooms, the cracked leather seats of cars, the riverbank on steamy nights. "You gotta have it, don't you," one of them once said to her. It wasn't even a question. Now there's Charlie. And a few...insignificant...scattered... others.

Violet's earliest memories are visceral—a puddle of rainwater closing in on her toe, sunlight soaking the underside of a pale arm, febrile breath on her cheek. She remembers playing in the barnyard mud, rubbing it over her neck and arms and legs, chasing the baby pigs, grabbing the bristly hair on their spines. Violet remembers the feel of her brothers' backs and necks, as she held on for dear life when they played bucking bronco. She remembers the look of their genitals as they dressed by the kitchen stove on winter mornings, the gray long underwear that barely held it all in place, the hair and pimples as they grew, the veins and paunch and muscle of them. When her body started changing, she took to her own room, got a job after school at the grocery store, spent precious, hoarded money on bath powders and sexy underwear from a clandestine catalog, forgoing the pleasures of other girls her age— shakes at the malt shop, movies, cheap jewelry from the five-and-dime.

After her bath, Violet would rub oil on the rough spots on her elbows and heels, low on her belly and down in between her legs. She'd put on the fancy underwear and then take it off, unlatching the lace bra and letting her breasts fall with a shudder that turned instantly to heat. She'd flick her nipples, watch them turn hard as diamonds. She'd lay herself down on a towel and explore herself with her fingers, teaching herself how to feel good. Sex was no different than any other body of knowledge she'd ever tackled. She would master her own desire before she entrusted it to anyone else. Violet was nothing if not practical. Early on, she'd intellectualized what she intuitively sensed—that the sexual urge might as well endow rather than rob you of self-control.

Violet looks over at the sleeping, unshaven Nash sprawled out in bed beside her. She'd like to touch him now, make him stir, watch his libido slither ahead of his brain. It's an exotic dance, an awakening she'll never tire of, the rousing of a still male body to passion. So many times, so many… She honestly misses every one of those boys, those men. Each one of them made her feel good and she made each one of them feel good back. What on earth was wrong with that? If you really thought about it, love *was* free—sex, anyway—one of life's greatest pleasures, and it didn't cost a goddamned cent. She pulls the blanket up over Nash's chest. When she first met him, her junior year of college, she didn't blink an eye. There was something more than money, security, a handsome face, and ready smile—a loyalty, a tenderness for his brother and all children, a ferocious will to be well and happy, a strength in his belief that life should be good, if it couldn't always be fair. When she said, "I do," she had only one fleeting second of panic, entrapment. But she'd made no false promises, to herself or anyone else. The marriage vows were ceremonial, rhetoric at best. She'd married Nash with a clear eye, the sexual fever in check, the best of intentions. She'd made the important values count. Family. Work. Home. She has no regrets, no guilt. Or is she only kidding herself? What the hell about Charlie?

Violet turns away from Nash. Where does she go from here? What does she owe her family, Chickie, the other girls, Nash? How much power does she have over their collective happiness? Who the hell does she think she is? And what do they want from her after all these years? Violet looks at the photo of her three daughters on the bedside table and sighs. She should stop this thing with Charlie, she knows, take the bull by the horns, confess, atone, redeem herself. But in the end, will it even matter? Fidelity, too, is just a word, an old-fashioned notion, no longer the bedrock on which love was once thought to depend. Love is nothing so static or true. It's slippery, wet and tough like an eel, writhing in constant, exhausting motion. What an unlikely idea, really—given the complexity of human nature and physical attraction—and six billion people on the planet—that one person was only ever meant to love one other.

Closing her eyes, Violet replays the rickety reel of her strange afternoon, foreplay with a battered cafeteria spoon—she'll probably get some dreadful disease—and sex with Charlie in the graveyard on a fallen headstone, the raised letters of a dead man's name pressing through her blouse onto her back. HOMER WINSLOW—strangely, the artist's name reversed. Charlie'd never heard of him, he said, when she tried to explain. Who cared, he said. Another snobby WASP artist who'd made a fortune painting everything in the world that was boring—rowboats, dandelions, lobster buoys, watering cans, plain-faced, frigid women. He ranted on and on. Funny. Vi looks over at the sleeping Nash. On the other hand, a Winslow Homer painting had been known to put a lump in this guy's throat. The dancing coffee spoon spins out of nowhere to tease and taunt her. She runs her hand over Nash's stomach. Groggily, he reaches out one arm.

"Fuck me, Nash," she whispers. "Fuck me now and fuck me hard."

Nash brings his hands up to her breasts. "Mmm…" he says drowsily, starting slowly down her body. Kissing, stroking, licking. Inwardly, Violet groans. Maybe she is insatiable. Maybe she'll never be able to get enough—from Nash, from her children, from Charlie, from herself. And somehow it doesn't seem like a good enough excuse anymore, that she's only human.

After all, so is everyone else.

As Remi pushes through the turnstile at the racetrack, he feels more flab than muscle in his stomach as it pounds against the metal bar. This so infuriates him, this treachery of once firm flesh, that he exits and reenters, sucking in his gut and tensing, breath drawn up tight. He goes at the snickering bar again, pushing headlong and hard, this time feeling the clenching resistance of muscle, an exultant wave of nausea as he bursts through the gate. Satisfied, he makes his way to the ticket window. Whistling. He can actually hear himself whistling. That's how good he feels. He can't wait to pull out his money and throw it at the grim reaper teller behind window number six. He always goes to this teller, and it's true, his loss column's longer than his win. Anyone else might consider the surly, shriveled-up old man in the houndstooth jacket a jinx. But to Remi, he's just a crusty old-timer behind a rusty set of bars who holds no sway. And only a fool would bet against loyalty having something to do with luck.

The crisp new bills just sprung from a bank drawer burn a hole in Remi's fraying khaki pocket. This time, nothing can go wrong. This tip comes from a place so high, so invincible, it's as if he's snatched an egg from a bald eagle's nest. He's putting down big money on this horse. None of the small stuff he's been throwing around like confetti for years. He's always played the horses for a pastime, a lark—that's how it started out. Lately, it's been a once-a-week thing, more of a mission. He can admit this freely. No guilt. Maybe because Faye's out on her own now, Nash so preoccupied with politics and the war. The track must be his *thing*—isn't that what the kids call it these days? And the horse's name—that's just a bonus, a fluke. Remi's not overly superstitious or sentimental, doesn't usually attach any meaning to such trivial things. But how could he possibly ignore this omen, along with this grace-of-god tip? This is *his* race, *his* horse. He's a winner. Fourteen-to-one odds be damned; they'll only make him richer. It's not a feeling Remi's had often. That he just can't lose.

"Five hundred on *Remington Steel* in the third." Remi slaps down five one-hundred-dollar bills. "To win," he says. *To win. Twin. To win.* A woman comes up behind him. He smells her perfume, the boozy, chewing-gum breath. She brushes his arm as he turns away.

"I'll take whatever he had," she says, sliding a five under the window. "I feel the luck rolling right off his back." The woman takes her ticket and follows after Remi, balancing expertly on high heels. "You wouldn't steer me wrong now, mister, would you?" she says.

Remi stops in his tracks, scratches his head and turns. "Are you speaking to me?" he says.

"That's right," she says. "I'm speaking to you."

"And what was it you said?" Puzzled, Remi loosens the knot of his tie, takes in the look of the woman, her tight black pants and low-cut blouse, the enormous purple bag slung over her shoulder.

"My bookie turned on me," she said. "And I don't like losing, you know?"

"I do." Remi looks at her pretty, open face, the rouge and heavy eye makeup, blood-red lips and high, spun hair. She's not a woman of the times, not one of these skinny, bell-bottomed, barefoot hippie chicks you see everywhere these days. There's something different, something off. "Oh, I see," he says finally. "You're a prostitute."

"Dawn breaks over Marblehead." The woman laughs, her Boston accent drowning out the Rs. "This is a big moment for you, isn't it, governor?"

Governor. He doesn't get it, doesn't get it. He's infuriated; she's laughing at him; he's repulsed, confused, turned on. He doesn't want the moment to continue but couldn't possibly be the one to end it. It's the same old, same old song. A hot and teasing girl. The red-faced boy flailing in the quicksand of inadequacy and shame. "I'm Remi," he says, extending his hand. "Remington Potts, from across the river. Cambridge."

"Of course you are." The woman gives him a firm handshake. "And I'm Cammie Cahaley. From down the beach. Revere."

"Pretty name," Remi says.

"So, about your horse, Remi. You sure he's going to win?"

Remi shrugs. "Call it a hunch," he says. "Come on up and watch."

They make their way up through the vault of Suffolk Downs and into the stands. On a listless gray day, the crowd is languid and scattered. Remi experiences more of the wilting *déjà vu* as he and Cammie sit down, a thousand-fold deep, so many times he's been here, in these stands, with a girl, a woman, sliding in beside him, tempting, teasing, trapping him. The tension of a race, a contest, a win-or-lose proposition. The scent, the touch, the heat of female, his terror of it all, his longing mixing now with nervousness and excitement and the smell of dirt and horse manure and sweat. And money. That's what makes this all so different, how much cash he's put down. It's breathtaking, terrifying, sexy as hell.

The horses take their places in the gates for the start of the third race. Their names boom rapid-fire from the PA system—*Apse's Way, Brillo Pad, Remington Steel, Corolla, Betsy's Hope*. In the tense seconds before the gates open, Cammie puts her hand on Remi's leg. He glances over at her. He can't be distracted; he's got to focus. The fact that a hooker's hand has slid onto his thigh is not important, only something to keep shored up in the back of his mind. Remi's plan is to win. Quietly. Today. And then again. Win big. He's hit the mother lode with this bookie. He'll win big and spring it on them all. Nash, Faye, Violet, the kids. He'll put the dignity back into the old family name, raise them all back up to the higher place they inhabited before the old man pulled them crashing down, pathetic lech of a drunk that he was. All the backsliding, the secrecy, the struggle. He'll set it right. Make it up to his poor mother in the grave, show his dead bastard of a father that he's finally amounted to something. This will be his legacy, his gift. He doesn't know why he didn't think of it before. He—of all people—will be the family savior.

As the horses lunge out of the starting gate, Cammie's hand tightens on Remi's leg. *Remington Steel* gets a slow start, edged out on the outside lane by *Apse's Way*, running wild and sloppy, to kill. A shot of anger shoots up into his throat like a spurt of hot oil.

"Don't let him squeeze you, damn it," Remi says. "Keep focused. Bear down. Stay low. Find your opening." The horses come thundering around the curve and head into the second lap in a cloud of dust. *Remington Steel* moves up into fourth place, then third. "Okay. That's it. Steady. Ease up. Slowly. Veer into the curve. LEAN." Remi coaxes, exhorts, pleads with the horse, the jockey, the horse. "Push. Rein in. Watch *Old Spice* on your back. Don't look around. Okay. Edge in. Start to make your move. Now!" Cammie squeals as the horses head into the final lap. *Remington Steel* surges to catch up with the front-runner, *Apse's Way*. They dance neck and neck, legs reaching, heads bobbing furiously. The image dances on Remi's retina as *Remington Steel* inches forward, bit by tiny bit by bit—just the way he's supposed to, just the way he's planned—crossing the finish line no more than half a head in front of *Apse's Way*. Remi jumps up from his seat, his whole body surging with the heat that rushes back up to his temples from his groin. He feels Cammie's hand on his shoulder, turns his head slowly, looks into her bloodshot eyes. He's trembling all over, can't get hold of his breath. He's just won seven goddamned thousand dollars.

"Well, well, governor," she says. "I see you're a man of your word."

"He was magnificent," Remi says. "The jockey gauged it perfectly. He came out of nowhere."

"He won," Cammie says. "We won. You were right. You called it,

Remi. We're rich. You are anyway. You want to go celebrate some-where?"

Remi looks at her hard, then softens. "Oh no, you don't understand," he says. "I don't want to have sex with you. I'm married—"

"Hey, no problem." Cammie is suddenly brisk, tucking her winning ticket into her purse. "No skin off my back, Remi. No harm, no foul."

"No, you've got me wrong, that's all." He laughs, reminded of Faye, her sudden defensiveness, the proverbs and platitudes she spills. "I'm not even really much of a gambler," he says. "I'm doing all this." He motions out to the track. "For my family. Not for me. It's for my family."

"Sure, I get it," Cammie says. "It's for your family. You're a good guy. You love your family. You're doing all this for them."

Remi nods, suddenly feeling the importance of making her under-stand. "Everything I do is for them. For her."

"Lucky girl." Cammie slings her purse over her shoulder. "You sure you don't want to do something for yourself today, Remi? You probably heard, all work and no play…"

"*This*…" He slaps his winning ticket against his palm. "*This* is what I did for myself. This right here."

"All right then." Cammie takes out her lipstick. "It was nice meeting you, Remi. And thanks for the tip. I could use the extra seventy bucks. Listen. You ever change your mind, I'm here Tuesdays. I'm always here Tuesdays. If you ever change your mind."

"Wait." A sweat breaks out across Remi's brow. He grabs her at the wrist, pulls her close. "Did you change my luck, Cammie Cahaley? Did you turn everything around for me today? Tell me. Because if you did, then I'll come back again. I'll come back Tuesdays."

"You got money, Remi?" Cammie asks, steely-eyed now, all business. "Are you rich?"

"I'm supposed to be," Remi says, at that moment knowing it to be the most ragged, indisputable truth of his life.

When he gets home, Remi swings through the door to the kitchen for a nightcap. Seeing flickering lights in the backyard, he opens the screen door and steps outside. Over the sagging fence, Chickie sits at the picnic table, reading a book. In front of her are six lit candles, teardrop flames flickering in the dark.

"Whatcha reading, kiddo?"

"*On the Road.*"

"Ah, young heart. Got enough light?"

Chickie points up to the sky. "Full moon," she says.

"Ah," Remi says. "Young eyes."

"Where're you coming from, Uncle Remi?"

"Out and about." Remi reaches for the wad of cash in his back pocket. Chickie's simple question unnerves him, as if her sharp eyes were somehow drinking in the sordid details of his strange day, first the trip to the racetrack and then to the motel on the Lynnway with Cammie, a cheap place where the rooms cost twelve bucks and smelled of old suitcases and hairspray and toilets not cleaned quite well enough. He made a point of not looking at her body when they had sex, covering her up with a sheet, kissing all the luck from her, pumping her, draining her. He had no trouble getting it up—his cock was hard and stayed that way—the money sliding into the hand of the teller behind window number six, coming back at him fourteen-fold...fucking seven grand, *fuck* money.

"Aunt Faye was looking for you." Chickie wets her fingers and snuffs out one of the candles. "She pulled out of the driveway a while ago. She went over to Clay City."

"Clay City," Remi says. "Where else? You be careful with those candles, kiddo, you hear?"

Chickie nods as she extinguishes the last flame. "Aunt Faye was worried," she says, as the smoke shoots up in a swirl. "Next time you should give her a call."

"Right, I will." Remi turns around and walks back to his car. He can't turn over the ignition fast enough, can't get quickly enough to the bar.

Faye knocks on the open door of the olive house, finds Nash alone in his armchair in front of the TV.

"Faye!" Nash says, his face warming. "Come on in."

"I just stopped by to give you a message, Nash. I ran into Vi in the Square. At a red light, actually. We were side by side in our cars. I rolled down my window. She wanted you to know she might be late."

Nash gestures around the empty room. "She already is," he says.

"I'm not sure why." Faye might lie for Violet's sake, but she's no good at it. "She was with someone," she stammers softly. "I didn't know...I'm sure they'll...she'll be back soon."

"I'm more than capable of spending an evening alone." Nash senses her discomfort and smiles. "Will you sit for a while, Faye, have a drink?"

"Now?" she says.

He lifts his arms and shrugs. "Why not?" he says.

Faye looks around, suddenly aware the two of them are alone. "Where's Remi?" she says.

"No idea." Nash laughs. "This is my house, remember? And I'm not always my brother's keeper." He heads for the liquor cabinet. "Vodka, vodka. You're the vodka girl, right?" He rummages through the bottles. "What'll you have it with, Faye?"

"Do you have anything lighter?" she asks. "I never really could take the hard stuff. It undoes me."

"Glass of wine?" Nash says. "I think I've got some Almaden." He pours her a glass of wine.

"Great, thanks." She takes a sip, grimaces.

"No good?" Nash laughs.

"It's not the wine, Nash," she says. "It's me. Truth is, I don't really like alcohol. It doesn't agree with me." She puts the glass down. "Feeling's mutual, I guess."

"Why drink it then?"

"It's something to think about." She looks over at a card table strewn with cards. "Aren't those Remi's poker chips?"

"Yeah, I borrowed them last night for a game." Nash sits down on the couch next to her. "So, how are you, Faye? Everything okay next door?"

"Not *everything.*" Faye smiles, crosses her arms across her chest. "How could it be, Nash?"

"But you're okay."

"Sure. I'm okay." She turns to him. "How 'bout you?"

"I'm surviving. It's the world that's in trouble." He takes a sip of his drink. "The war." He shakes his head. "Over forty thousand dead, and that's just our side. It's probably twice that for the Vietcong. The numbers are staggering."

"It's a terrible thing," Faye says.

"You have your boys to think about," Nash says. "Nixon's about to sign the draft bill into law. It's official. No more student deferments."

Faye turns her head away. "I try not to dwell on it," she says. "Stay positive, keep my fingers crossed, all that jazz. I'm sure Buzz is safe, with his thumb, and Hen, well..." Faye's drink hand trembles slightly. "We'll just have to cross that bridge when we come to it."

"I didn't mean to upset you," Nash says.

"You didn't," she says. "You can't very well upset the apple cart, you know, if it's already been overturned."

"You sure you're all right?"

Faye laughs. "Pretty sure."

"Don't take this the wrong way," Nash says. "What I'm about to say."

"I'll take it literally," Faye says. "I don't have much imagination, so that's what I tend to do. So be careful."

"You're a beautiful woman, Faye. Do you even know that?"

"Maybe a little," she says, lifting a hand to her face. "Maybe a little I'm beginning to see."

"Good." Nash takes a sip of his drink. "Because you are. Remi's a lucky guy, you know? He knows it. He tells me all the time..."

Faye reaches over and puts her hand on his arm. "It's okay, Nash," she says, realizing what an odd gesture that is for her, the spontaneous thrust of the arm, the uncalculated touch. The warmth of Nash's arm burns through his sleeve and fills her palm. She floods with affection for him, wonders if this is how she might have felt for a brother, or even another man. "You're a good brother," she says, picking up the cards from the table and starting to shuffle. "But the question is, can you play cards?"

"Phillips Exeter Crazy Eights Champ, 1935," Nash says. "Deal 'em and weep."

The cards mingle effortlessly as Faye shuffles, her thumbs releasing them into the shooting arch of a bridge. She slaps the deck down on the table, pushes it toward Nash. "Cut," she says. And when he's done, she whips neatly into the deal.

On the evening of Chickie's fall dance recital, Hen walks alone to Sanders Theatre from the Square. People love to argue about Memorial Hall—how ugly it is, how beautiful—with its steeples and stained glass windows, bright-colored fish scale shingles. This building has always been to Hen what he imagines churches are for people who believe in God. Fate keeps bringing him back here; he's not sure why. Last year he was one of fifty people Bobby Fischer played simultaneously on this stage, the grandmaster circling the arc of his opponents, round and round, barely glancing at the boards, beating every last one of them with time to spare. When he and Chickie were ten, they played the part of a camel together in the Revels Christmas Pageant on this stage. The first time Hen can remember coming to Sanders Theater was when he was eight. Tory and Buzz were teenagers, still living at home. Faye left dinner cold and dragged them all out to hear Robert Frost recite his poems. He was getting so old, she said. They might never have another chance. The poet was short and bent, with a thatch of pearl-white hair. He cleared his throat at the podium and let loose his thick and ragged voice. He read about the snowy woods, the death of a hired man, the road not taken, a mending wall. When he was done, the audience rose and clapped until the rafters shook. Not long after that, he died. Something about this place—the smells of old wood and wax, the watery light in the eyes of the dead men in the portraits that line the halls—men with names like Ambrose, Hezekiah, Nathaniel—names Hen's seen on his own family tree, the echoes and lights, the swift precision of Fischer's every move, the feel of Chickie's sweaty body next to his in the camel costume—something about this building makes Hen feel small, but not unimportant. He opens the door and walks inside.

Chickie pulls aside the curtain backstage and looks out over the audience. Her family's taken over the entire third row. Such a motley crew, they might as well be painted in neon green. There's her father on the left, smiling at nothing, at everything, as if she were already taking her bows and he were already so proud. And Violet sitting beside him, though she might as well be a million miles away, frowning, fidgeting, filled with all of her doubts about dancing, all that could go wrong. There's her aunt Faye, sitting prim and still, so out of place among the rest of them, and Hen, head bent low over something in his lap—his chess set probably. Janie's there with her new boyfriend, Warren, one of only a few Black faces in the crowd. Seph sits quietly in the aisle seat. Even Buzz is there tonight, good old lumpy, handsome Buzz, with his girlfriend, good old, handsome, horsey Lainey. Nash taps the rolled-up program on his leg. Hen scratches his ear. Violet files her nails and Buzz yawns as he scrunches Lainey's shoulders in a clumsy hug.

Not exactly the dancing types, Chickie thinks, as she lets the curtain fall.

Chickie and two other dancers take their places on the stage. The music starts and the curtain opens with a steady creak. The surging ripple of applause takes her by surprise, knocks her momentarily off balance. She rights herself, pulls herself up tall, takes one quick look out to see if Hen's head has lifted. As the music builds, the *pas de trois* unfolds. The three dancers converge at the center and then disperse in waves. Chickie's gauzy skirt rises and swirls as she moves. She catches a glimpse of her outstretched arm, the flex of her wrist and the swell of her bicep, and in that one jagged second, she admires them. She feels her left leg accept the weight of her body as she circles her right in a *ronde de jambe*, feels the strength build inside her, the power to keep herself upright, to bend and stretch in such fantastic ways. And with a drop of her heart, as she catches a quick glimpse of her family coming out of a spin, she sees suddenly how far that strength must take her—to keep her head up, her spirits strong, her mother and father together, her sisters from exploding, Hen from going up into space or to the war. Chickie's head tilts upward into the stage light as she steps into an *arabesque*.

As the music slows, the two other dancers leave the stage and the light slowly dims. Chickie stands alone, in a twisted fifth position, arms held high, and waits—one, two, three—for the cue to start her solo. But what reaches her ear instead is the distant roar of a wave as it pops out of the horizon and races toward you on the shore, the sand giving way below your heels, the tumultuous silence that follows as the wave takes you under, tosses you to and fro, drags you along the sandy bottom of the ocean floor by the cusp of your upper lip. Standing frozen in the column of blinding light that suddenly encases her, it comes to Chickie, in fifth position, in front of a whole roomful of people—in that one roaring split second that uncoils into a lifetime—that she's going to die. Right then and there. She's so completely sure of it. The rushing silence fills the walls of her chest, presses hard against her lungs. Her heart prepares itself to stop, not because it's sick or broken, but because it's just so tired, because she can't keep it going anymore. She suddenly feels so old. Ancient. Exhausted from the struggles of a million previous lives. Arms circled above her head, her legs kick out from under her as she leaps into the shimmering column of light, disappearing into a billow of dust. Landing back down, she *chassés* into her ending position and looks out over the audience as the curtain starts to close. And there is Hen, holding her gaze, holding her steady, as she takes a final bow.

Later that night, Chickie goes next door. Hen's sitting at his desk by the window, doing his homework.

"Hey, Chick," he says, looking up. "Your dance was fantastic."

"Liar." She puts her arms around his neck from behind. "I was in a trance or something at the end. Didn't you see?"

"You were incredible," he says.

"Whatever. I saw Violet in the Pewter Pot the other day with some guy. I think she's fucking him."

Hen winces. "Ah, Chick, come on."

"She looked guilty as hell," Chickie says. "And this Neanderthal creep—"

"It was probably just a friend."

"Violet doesn't really have any friends," Chickie says, flopping down on the bed. "Except the martini freaks and the bridge boozers, and they don't come around much anymore."

"Your mom's a straight shooter. Just ask her who he was."

Chickie plays with the edge of Hen's bedspread. "Not so sure I want to know."

"The truth will set you free."

"Says who?"

"John Lennon. Or Jesus or someone. What's wrong, Chickie? Why are you so freaked out?"

"I'm not freaked out," she says. "I'm just afraid sometimes."

"Of what?"

"Everything," she says.

Later, in bed, Chickie remembers the first time she thought she was going to die. One winter afternoon, at the outdoor skating rink, when she was nine, some kid on hockey skates told her, right in the middle of a wobbly figure eight, that the world was going to end at six-thirty that night. Her heart nearly leapt out of her chest to think she might die alone in her holey Fair Isle sweater and black figure skates, with only some stupid boy to know. She walked across the street to the drugstore in her skates, without the guards, crunching bits of gravel and glass, and called home on the pay phone. Violet picked up on the first ring. Chickie loved her mother more at that moment than she ever had before, for being home, for saying, "No, Chickie, of course the world's not going to end, just like that. It took a long time to get started, and it's going to take a long time to go down the drain, despite what your father says. He'll be there to pick you up in half an hour." It was about this time that Chickie began having nightmares, about the world exploding and being the only one left alive, searching the charred earth for her family, for Hen, and finding only the knife-sharpening man, who used to push his cart around the busted-up streets with his monkey on his back, calling

out, *ooh-la, ooh-la-lay*. She started to be afraid at odd, unexpected times—
of strangers and spiders and death lurking in dark corners, her thoughts
rolling in circles until she was dizzy on her feet. But then it got better.
She forgot about the end of the world for a while.

Mrs. Pfeffer, her fourth-grade teacher, used to say that if Chickie
weren't careful, she'd let her imagination run away with her and the
two of them might never come back. Violet, when she told her, had
laughed. But the world really *is* spinning beneath her. Chickie can feel
it now—the dizziness, the sweat-filled palms, the thumping heart, even
as she lies perfectly still in bed. Clenching her fists, she makes a deal
with her racing heart and damp palms. It's all right to be petrified, deep
down, of anyone, anything at all. No one has to know. All around her,
people have dark secrets locked away in tight-lidded boxes, the ground
around them kept tidy and swept. A heart can't simply explode. A voice
can always speak, a mind reason, a body dance. If you're not afraid, you
take away fear's power. Some rock star said that. Or maybe it was the
colonel.

She raises one arm and tenses her muscles. She's young and smart
and strong. And she's probably not going to die, not for a long, long
time. She'll bluff fear if she has to, scare it back, yell at the knife-sharpening man in her dreams to go away, or at least to really talk to her,
instead of chanting that creepy chant. Chickie closes her eyes. She'll
fight the demons in her brain and then some on earth, her mother,
the chameleon, all the Cozmos of the world, her calculus teacher who
humiliates the smelly kid in the front row by sniffing in his direction, the
knife-sharpening man who roams her dreams, snobby Ross Treadlow in
physics class who thinks she's dying to do it with him. She'll jump off
the bridge to save the leaper, rescue the dog from a burning building,
outwit Lugbout, listen to the colonel's war stories, keep Hen from going
to Vietnam, keep her distance from her mother and forgive her father
his weaknesses…or maybe the other way around. Turning over on her
back, she watches the rise and fall of her belly as her body slowly calms.
And she'll have sex. Soon. She's eighteen years old, for god's sake. Hardly anyone she knows is a virgin anymore. Everyone's doing it. Anything
goes. It's way past high time, Chickie knows, that she got fucked.

6

In late October, the twins change the window display at Potts Pro from an autumn panorama to a winter wonderland. Remi stands on a ladder, profile to profile with a mannequin in a snowflake sweater and matching headband, plastic arm reaching out to trim a fake tree. A passerby stops to wonder at the man grown out of the dummy—older, more rumpled, but still a remarkable likeness. Inside, from the floor of the store, Nash hands Remi the ornaments, frosted balls plucked from an age-old carton. Remi hooks them, one by one, to the glistening branches of the tree.

"A whole village, Rem." Nash starts up about the war. "Obliterated from the face of the earth. Most of them women and children. They're right to call My Lai a massacre."

"Bad things happen," Remi says. "Mistakes. Especially in wartime. You don't like it. But they do."

"A massacre's not a mistake," Nash says. "It's an atrocity. Unconscionable. It's madness."

"Madness," Remi says quietly. He swings a silver ball back and forth on its hook, tries to drown out his brother's angry words. The ornaments remind Remi of Faye. Everything does today—anyone or anything of any delicacy or beauty—the light rain falling outside, the perfect lemon Danish he plucked from the Sages Bakery tray, a whiff somewhere, of the last autumn leaves. Remi leans forward to hook the ornament onto an overlooked, far branch of the tree. The ball, not well secured, falls to the floor and smashes into glittering pieces.

"Damn." Remi looks down at the shattered ball, feeling the weight of his head on his neck and shoulders. Faye's not so fragile anymore. Maybe that's why it happened. Maybe he was testing her, to see how tough she really is, how breakable, how far away she's gone. *Damn.* He climbs down off the ladder and bends to pick up the ornament shards from the floor, while Nash goes off to answer the ringing phone. Remi feels like crying, for something old, something lost. In the beginning, Faye was like a delicate spinning ball. He knows why he loved her instantly, why he married her, for better or worse. A woman like Faye, he knew, would never spill. A woman like Faye—shy, steady, contained—would harbor all his secrets. A woman like Faye would never drive a man wild, and wild was a place Remi knew he couldn't go. A place like wild might put him out of his mind, literally, the way he got sometimes, without warning, without permission, as he does sometimes with Cammie at the motel, like last night with Faye—Remi looks over at Nash talking on the phone—or that first time, with the knife, when they were kids.

He and Nash had just turned nine. Their father had recently died, wiped from the earth with a mysterious wave of a heavenly hand, suddenly giving Remi an excuse for everything that had ever been hard in his life and he grabbed at the chance, eating greedily through the red licorice string of his lucky misfortune. All that summer he and Nash were pampered and indulged, forgiven all their boyish crimes. He became greedier, more emboldened. Remi can see now how he let down his guard. It was a hot summer night, a few days after their birthday. He was angry at his mother for giving Nash a red pocketknife as a gift, with two blades and a can opener and an ivory toothpick. Remi had wanted a knife too, but instead was given a book about pirates. Nash had been flashing and bragging about the knife all day, and Remi was beside himself with envy. That's how it felt sometimes, as if the heat of his fury melted him into a puddle and he'd rise up out of it, re-formed, as another, monstrous boy. He was angry at everything, really, his mother because she made his world turn and he couldn't make it stop, the cross-eyed kid next door, the *k* in knife, which, if forgotten, took points off his grade on his spelling test. That summer, people came to believe that Remi behaved badly because he'd lost his father so tragically and so young. But it wasn't true. He'd always been that way, for as long as he could remember. His father's death only meant he didn't have to pretend anymore.

That night, Remi stole Nash's knife while he slept and went into their mother's empty bedroom. Since their father had died, she'd been sleeping downstairs on the couch. He remembers most of all the excruciating silence, the silence of his fury, his loneliness, his desire. Going over to her bed, he slashed the pillows and the quilt until they were no more than a pile of shreds. He took the clothes from her closet and tore them to pieces—dresses, blouses, hats. A blizzard of cloth and feathers floated to the floor. He stood still afterward, feeling the pulse in his neck beating wildly. He looked at the knife in his hand, the storm still swirling around him, the piles of shredded clothes. He knew he'd done it. There was no one else in the room, no one else to blame. But he didn't remember doing it, or even thinking about doing it, only the ache of wanting the knife to be his, wanting all that Nash had, to be all that Nash was. Nash still carries that red knife in his pocket to this day, used no more than ten minutes ago to open the taped-up box of Christmas decorations. And Remi still has a dream where he comes into his mother's room with the knife, not the boy Remi, but the man, and slashes not just a pillow, or the quilt, but a dangling, unidentified hand.

"Remi!"

Nash tosses a clump of tinsel down on his brother's head to get his attention.

"What?" Remi pulls a strand from his cheek.

"Hand me that star, bro," Nash says. "Where were you, anyway? The moon?"

Remi hands the tin star up to Nash and watches him attach it to the spindly, plastic spire. He feels a sudden, helpless rush of love for his twin brother, for the forgiveness he'll soon receive. Sweat pools in his closed palm; he closes his eyes. "I hit her, Nash," he says.

Nash's eyes snap downward from his perch on the ladder, draining of all their softness, their give.

"What did you say?" he says.

"I hit Faye," Remi says again. "Last night. I hit my wife."

"You hit your wife?" Nash says steadily. "You hit Faye?"

Remi takes a deep, convulsing breath. "I did," he says.

"Oh my god, it was an accident, right?" Nash rakes a hand through his hair. "Tell me it was an accident, Rem."

"It was…" Remi raises his arms and lets them fall. "A mistake."

"Jesus Christ." Nash flings the last clump of tinsel onto the tree and comes down off the ladder. "What the hell were you thinking?"

Remi shakes his head back and forth, waiting for the answer to come to him. *What were you thinking? Remi! Remi! Remi!* It's his mother's voice, his teachers', his friends', the voices of past outrages, past betrayals. Most people confess to their priests, to their lawyers, to their wives. And having done so, they're on their own. They must mount their defenses, offer apologies, make amends. But for Remi, confessing to Nash is like confessing to a conscience, which, because it's partly responsible, cannot truly lay blame. Nash will share his guilt and his pain, rationalize, help to make it right. And in the end, Nash will forgive him. It's part of the twin pact. Nash always has to forgive him.

"I wasn't thinking about anything." Remi finally answers the question. "It was the damnedest thing, Nash. By the time I hit her, I was done being mad. I felt completely…empty."

"So what the hell happened? Before that?"

Remi drags the splintered answer from his brain, piece by jagged piece, slicing the air with the edge of his palm with each point. "I was so damn tired. She came home late. Again. She's never around anymore. That damn clay school of hers." He speaks carefully, pushes Cammie and the gambling away, his big loss at the track the week before, the parts of the story that keep intruding, that ones he can't reveal. "I hadn't eaten any dinner. She hadn't made any. I was hungry. Starving, Nash. She came in and sat down. She wanted to move the lamp."

"What lamp?"

"The lamp by the couch. She wanted to move it over to the corner. That was the only thing she had to say to me all night. That she wanted to move the lamp. And I said no."

"Why?" Nash asks carefully. "What was the problem, Rem? You were using it? You were reading? You needed the lamp where it was?"

"No, I wasn't using it. And I didn't need it." Remi's hand stops in midair. "But that lamp's been there since we bought the house, Nash. I was hungry. And tired. I just couldn't stand for one more thing to change. But she wouldn't listen." His hand stills in the air. "She just… doesn't…*listen* anymore."

"Oh my god." Nash rubs his forehead. He feels the sting on Faye's cheek, the anguish in Remi's heart. He is responsible. He miscalculated, about his brother, about Faye. She was lying when she said she was okay. There was so much more to her than he knew, so much more to Remi. He comes right up into his brother's face. "Tell me one thing and tell me the truth," he says. "Has this ever happened before?"

"Never."

"First time you ever raised your hand to her? You swear?"

"I swear."

"Okay." Nash backs away. "Good. That's good. Thank god. Okay." He lets out a ragged breath. "We're all human, Rem. These things happen. Jesus. I spanked Chickie once. She dropped my watch in the toilet. On purpose. Did I ever tell you that story? God, was I mad. But this, this was an accident, right?"

Remi wraps the shawl of makeshift truth around him. "This was an accident," he says.

Calmer now, Nash grabs Remi's gaze and holds it. "You've got to give her some room, Rem. The girls have been cooped up a long time, all these years, at home, with the kids, with us. They need to spread their wings. You know. Women's lib and all that. If you think about it, it makes sense. We had our chance. Now it's their turn. They need some space. Some support."

"I never stood in her way," Remi says.

"I know you didn't."

"I did exactly what she wanted, Nash. I didn't try to stop her. I even helped. She's the goddamned Queen of Clay now, isn't she? I didn't punch that drooling idiot with the TV camera, did I?"

"Okay, okay," Nash says. "So what else have you done, big brother? What have you done to make it right?"

"I said I was sorry." Remi drops the handful of broken ornament pieces into an overflowing wastebasket, shakes his head back and forth. "A thousand times. What the hell else can I do?"

Nash plants his foot on top of the overflowing wastebasket and shoves it down, the shards crunching beneath his size-twelve foot. "Take forgiveness, Remi. Walk on it like eggshells. Don't blow it, brother. Whatever else you do, don't blow it. I don't need to tell you. You don't pick up a woman like Faye at the five-and-dime."

"No." Remi peels a last squiggle of tinsel from his shirt. "You pick her up in a bookstore. And bring her home to meet your brother."

"She was perfect for you, Rem." Nash raises his arms in surrender. "What the hell else could I do?"

Remi runs his hand through what's left of his hair, looks out the plate-glass window onto the bustling street. It's a question that for the life of him, no matter how many times it's been asked, he can't even begin to answer.

Faye stands trembling in the cellar at Clay City. She tells herself it's because she's just finished carrying six heavy loads of clay upstairs, because she's never asked such drastic feats of her body before, because she's so damn tired. And all of these things are true. But in fact, it's been happening since daybreak, after only a few restless hours of sleep on the couch at Hemlock Street. All day, without warning, random parts of her body have started to twitch and quake—her top lip, the bottom of her left foot, a spot near the tendon on the right side of her neck. All day she's been on the verge of spilling tears, like a child awaiting punishment, still unsure of her crime. She's had this feeling before, the strange, shameful sense of anticipation mixed with fear. In truth, she's been trembling ever since Remi hit her the night before. All day she kept it together, gave Hen his breakfast, came to Clay City, taught her classes, threw some pots, cleaned up, signed the delivery slip, lugged the clay up from the basement to the studio. All day she thought calm and rational thoughts. Remi wasn't a bad guy. He hadn't meant to hit her. He was tired too, on edge. She'd been neglecting him lately, the family, the house, their *home*. It was true. She'd grown distant; Clay City *was* taking up a lot of her time. And she loved it here. Maybe she hadn't realized how much. And maybe Remi had. If she were fair, she could admit to all this, give him his resentment, his due. Bottom line, he'd never once raised his hand to her before. That had to be considered. Everyone was entitled to a bad day, a bad night. Heaven knows, she was no saint.

All day she's kept these rational thoughts in check, running them with the whip of cool logic like trained circus horses circling her brain. They steered her from point to point, steered her carefully, steered her clear. But now her thoughts lunge out from the back corners of her brain and break through the fence of her brow in a thundering head-ache. And the trembling starts all over again, creeping down through her legs and invading the soles of her feet, as she replays it all another way. She remembers Remi's face when she first reached for the lamp, bruise-like purple in its rage. She realizes with a strange mix of pity and admiration how hard it must have been for him to have kept that monster face hidden from her, a secret for so long. How dense she must have been never to have caught even a glimpse of it before, a darkening flush in the smooth, pale flesh. She remembers his voice warning her—ordering her, even—not to move the lamp, her sudden exploding fury that he should have the nerve, the right to tell her *not* to do something. Or, for that matter, *to* do something. Was this the way it had always gone between them? Was this the crooked balance of power in their marriage? The simple, profound clarity of this realization floors her. How dare he. How had he ever dared? And how on earth could she have let this happen?

Faye remembers the feel of the lamp's cool, ridged column as she gripped it, the calm force of her hand, the stunned look on Remi's face as she lifted the lamp off the floor. How simple, how deliberate an action—in a flash she understands what a triumph of will over fear that was. She remembers his hand coming at her and realizing with a start that she'd had the very same urge, just a split second after he did, the thought to up and smack him. She remembers the shame caving in on Remi's face, after his hand made contact and before it withdrew, and a sudden warped surge of power. She remembers how relieved she was that he'd beaten her to it, literally beaten her to the punch, how her outrage crumpled then in exhaustion, even sympathy, how Remi's voice wobbled toward her, hopeless and ragged as her cheek started to burn. "Oh my god, Faye. I'm sorry." And she remembers how glad she was that this had happened now, not before, now when she had a reason to rise up and fight back, when there was something at stake besides her dignity, her marriage. Nothing, no one, would stand in her way at Clay City. She'd already barricaded those doors.

Faye rubs the ache that's now spread across the lower band of her back. What bothers her most is, it all felt so familiar somehow—the mixed feelings of fascination and fear, as she watched Remi start to boil, revulsion and longing, pity and fury and the odd, empty feeling of vindication that came afterward, as the steady, droning voices took over and worked to calm her—it was okay, she was fine, no big deal, he loved her, didn't he? In a way, maybe it showed how *much* he loved her. In his clumsy way, wasn't he just trying to get her attention? It wouldn't happen again, would it? The questions spin in floppy, lasso fashion in her mind. And in counterpoint dances the tentative, whispering refrain of a smaller voice that keeps asking, *but if then…why, but if then…why?* Remi, after all, is only a man. The phrase is odd, almost sacrilege in this paternalistic culture, but, taken literally, strangely true. Is she to blame for his paranoia, his shortcomings, his moods? If she has in fact provoked him, what then are her crimes? Ambition? Independence? Working too hard? Coming in late? Wanting to read? Being a bad cook and a lousy housekeeper? Starting the clay school? Being on TV? Turning her back on him in bed? All of these acts have been selfishly motivated, yet he takes all of them so personally, so hard. Faye's surprised to understand at that moment how little her thoughts and actions have to do with her husband anymore. Is she to blame, then, for knowing that although she's never been the perfect wife, Remi still imagines she is, still wants her to be? Is it her fault for understanding that she's hurt him—hurt his pride, his manhood, his simplistic sense of order? In the end, is she to blame for knowing her husband too well?

Faye goes over to the deep, rusty sink to wash up. She rubs her clay-caked hands together under the running faucet and splashes water on her face and neck, relishing the cool, wet flow as it streams down into the pools of her collarbone, under her shirt and down her belly, catching in the waistband of her jeans. Slowly, the trembling subsides. Damp and finally still, Faye listens to the last drips from the tap, feels a dull heat well up inside her. She brings one hand up to her stung cheek, still blotchy from the slap. She unsnaps her jeans and lets the ring of water at her waistband run down her pant legs, starts to rub her stomach in circles with her palm the way her mother used to do when her belly ached, or was it her father? Her breath quickens. She slides off her pants, runs her hand down the length of her thigh. Sliding her hand up under her damp shirt, she feels the soft contours of her breasts and the sudden clench of her nipples, remembers a time not so long ago when she would have felt naked and scandalous without a bra. She remembers when her belly was flat, not stretched and dimpled from childbirth, her chest punctuated by two flat dots, when the place between her legs was as smooth as the pleated underside of a baby's arm.

Faye slides off her underwear and sits down on a crate of clay. Tilting her body backwards, she spreads her legs. Her hand finds its way down to the mass of dark hair and pulpy skin beneath, a place she's never touched before, never really considered *hers*. Her fingers work clumsily, urgently, until the warmth gathered in her toes climbs up through her legs into her thighs and belly and up through her neck, a quiet, steady hum building in her ears, a warm wetness released from her center. The muscles inside start to spasm, and the trembling starts again, different now—urgent, arhythmic. Her hips rise up from the box of clay. She hears the raw scrape of a voice she's still not ready yet to acknowledge as her own. The shudder builds speed and strength. Faye is horrified in that instant to picture Remi's hand coming at her, the whispering voice just as she stiffens, reminding her that for every pleasure, there's pain. "Oh god," Faye groans as she comes. *Ohgodohgodohgodohgod.* Anything to drown out that voice. That voice—which keeps telling her that for everything that's not right or explicable or sane in the world, she is somehow to blame.

"We must work harder on our irregular verbs," Mademoiselle Gladstone announces as she passes back the French midterm. *"Il faut travailler plus sérieusement."*

Monkey Man Ackerman raises his hand. "Why are they *our* verbs,

Miss G.? We don't actually own them, do we? I mean it's not like we picked them up down the Coop."

"They are *our* verbs, Reginald, *nos verbes…*" Midway through the semester, Mademoiselle Gladstone still rises tall to this kind of question. "Because we are learning them, embracing them, *les embrassons*, if you will."

"Hope we don't get any nasty diseases," Monkey Man Ackerman says, getting a few feeble laughs.

"*Ne t'inquiète pas*, Reginald." Mademoiselle Gladstone's French voice is sweet cream, her Boston accent battery acid. "Not to worry your pretty little, empty head. *La petite tête de Reginald. Complètement vide.*"

"Hey, you can't say that to me." Reginald straightens up in his chair.

"*Mais oui, Reginald,*" she says with a smile. "*Enfin, je peux.* I can."

"Thirty-two?" Violet starts sputtering like the three-horsepower motor on the skiff in Nantucket when she sees the grade on Chickie's French midterm that afternoon. "How on earth did you manage that, Minerva?"

"I didn't *manage* it, Mom. And why did you give me that name if all you planned to do with it was yell at me?"

"Minerva was—" Violet begins the old refrain as she collects the dirty dishes from the kitchen table.

"I know, I know," Chickie says. "Minerva was the goddess of wisdom, and an actual great-great somebody to boot. And I had such a wise look in my eye when I was born."

"You did," Violet says. The dishes clatter in the sink. "I often wonder what happened."

"I got stupid." Chickie opens the refrigerator door. "What can I say?" A chicken lies thawing on the countertop by the sink. Her stomach rumbles. It isn't often that Violet cooks a real meal anymore. "Roast chicken, Mom? Tres cool. Will you make stuffing, too?"

"Imagine my surprise," Violet says, "to get a call from Mrs. Lugbout today."

"Lugbout called here?" Chickie bites into a dill pickle, the crunch long since gone. "Gross." She tosses it into the trash, dripping green juice. "What'd the old buzzard want?"

"She called to say that you've missed the last three Fridays of school." Violet peels the shrink-wrap from the chicken. Out comes the bumpy carcass, yellow and wrinkled, legs springing downward. "Mrs. Lugbout was confused, Chickie, because the first and last of your absence notes—but not the second—said that you had the German measles, and she wasn't aware that measles came and went that way. Enlighten me please, Dr. Potts."

"Hen's not always so swift," Chickie mumbles.

"Hen? What does Hen… Oh my god, Chickie, *forgery* too?"

"I love roast chicken, Mom."

Violet picks the chicken up by its legs, thrusts her hand inside and slides out its innards. "All right, let's have it," she says. "What's going on in French class, Chickie? Or should I ask, what *isn't* going on?"

"The reviews are on Fridays. I missed a couple, so I messed up on the midterm. It doesn't mean I'm stupid."

"And you actually find logic in that argument?"

Chickie thinks for a minute. "Yes," she says. "I actually do."

"Well, in that case," Violet flops down into a kitchen chair, "I really am worried."

"Don't make a federal case out of this, Mom. So I missed a few days of school, blew an exam. I'll make it up. What's the big deal?"

Violet swings around in her chair. "The big deal is, Chickie, if you don't apply yourself in high school, you won't get into a decent college—and by the way, you should be starting on your applications—and if you don't go to college, you'll be marking down clothes at Filene's Basement for the rest of your life."

"Someone's gotta do it." Chickie shoots up onto her toes, spins herself full circle. "Anyway, I keep telling you. I'll be all right. I'm going to be a dancer."

"Okay, so you're going to be a dancer, so you're going to be all right. Couldn't you just give your brain a do-si-do every once in a while?"

"Do-si-do?" Chickie collapses into a chair. "Oh, man, Ma. Give me a break."

"Ma? Good lord." Violet's hands rise to her temples as she wails. "That's what your sisters call me."

"So?"

"So, it makes me feel like some toothless old hick mama, out in the hills, holding a jug of moonshine in one hand and a shotgun in the other." Violet sighs the sigh that means she's floating back in time. "Which is basically what I am. Let's face it. I was raised on a farm. I fed the pigs slop, cut off a chicken's head. I've held a shotgun in my time. I had to shoot a lame horse once."

"Oh god," Chickie groans. "Don't go back to Iowa on me. Please."

"Who am I to be so righteous?" Violet says. "I grew up in the corn-fields. I'm a mother. What's the difference? I'm lucky to have all my teeth. It's all so… Set the table, Chickie, will you, please?"

Chickie pulls out the silverware drawer, filled with the tips of broken plastic forks, crumbs from the toaster. She feels oddly comforted by her mother's distress, oddly calmed.

"Don't freak out, Mom. Everything's cool."

Violet rubs oil on the naked chicken. "I just don't want you to make my mistakes, Chickie."

"What were they?" The face of the man through the window of the Pewter Pot rises up before Chickie as she gathers up three forks, three knives, three spoons.

"In my day, girls played dumb." Violet's talking more to herself by then, sitting in a slump of swirling memory, sprinkling paprika on the glistening chicken. "It was fashionable to have no brain. But that was no excuse. I knew it. I played along. We all did. Mostly, I suppose, because we were scared."

"Scared of what?" Chickie places the silverware around the kitchen table.

"Of not being proper enough, not being approved of, never being able to find a husband. Although, you know, sometimes I wonder if what we were really riled up about in those days was not *being* men."

"You wanted to be a man?"

"Not literally." Violet lights up a cigarette. "But we wanted the free-dom and the choices that men were allowed to have. Why were we so excluded, so caged in all the time? Why did we have to toe the line so closely, repress ourselves, play by all the rules? It didn't seem fair."

"That's my point." Chickie folds three napkins. "If I were a boy, you wouldn't be freaking out about the thirty-two, because you'd have faith that I'd do better next time, that I'd land on my feet. You wouldn't be so scared all the time that I'd fuck up. Sorry, *screw* up." She looks up at her mother. "You'd say, 'boys will be boys.' Well, how about 'girls will be girls'?"

"Never heard that one before."

"Who was that guy, Mom?"

"What guy?" Violet's heart clenches.

"The one in the Pewter Pot. That day you waved."

"Just a friend."

"What kind of friend?"

"Not a very good one, I'm afraid." Violet closes the lid of the paprika. "And who was that boy you were walking with? Someone from school?"

"Just some kid named Elvis."

"You two looked pretty chummy."

"So did you," Chickie says.

A thump and a clank from above signal that Nash has turned on the shower upstairs. Chickie and Violet's eyes rise to the ceiling as the water rushes through the pipes. Violet looks up at the clock and jerks up in her chair. "Oh good lord. What happened to the time? I had no idea it was so late. I have a meeting at the club at 7:30." She opens the freezer door and disappears into a swirl of cold smoke. Out come the beef patties, potato puffs, and frozen succotash. She takes another drag of her Turkish cigarette as she balances the stack of ice-crusted packages in one hand. The naked chicken lies untouched on the counter; dripping water mixes with the bloody cellophane on which it lies.

Chickie sighs. Here she is again, the mother with no answers, no faith—opinions tangled, voice shaky, hair mussed, cigarette perched on the edge of the table, smoking end dropping ash, one minute righteous and opinionated, the next frazzled and sunk. This mother is needy, unpredictable; this mother has come undone. She smokes and slinks and swears. She sits in restaurants with strange men in broad daylight. This mother has gotten darker, but has lightened up, is more in your face, yet has floated so much farther away. This mother may or may not know it all, may or may not be real. Her sisters were wrong about Violet. The rules that got made a few years back never got enforced. The Rules of Violet were like clouds—floating and wispy and blurred. One failing grade is the kiss of death for her future, but Chickie hasn't heard one reprimand about belching or good manners for as long as she can remember, the irony being, she can't even burp anymore. And since she started dancing, her back's as straight and strong as an arrow. Good posture for a sloucher like her? It almost feels like a betrayal.

Chickie gets down three faded plastic Woody Woodpecker cups, the ones she ordered from the back of the Rice Krispies package when she was nine. "Don't worry, Mom," she says. "I won't make your mistakes. I'll make my own."

"Well, that's a great comfort." Violet cracks a weary smile.

"And just for your information, no one actually eats succotash anymore. It's not even considered a real food. After they sell what's left in the supermarkets, that's it…succotash will be officially dead."

Violet smiles.

"It's kind of funny, isn't it?" Chickie straddles the chair backwards. "If it were someone else's kid, you wouldn't think it was such a big deal. You'd tell Dad later and say how the school system sucked and you'd let it go and laugh. Wouldn't you?"

Violet heaves another deep sigh. "You're not someone else's kid, Chickie." She pounds her chest for emphasis. "You're *mine*. And I *want* you to go to school. I *want* you to pass French. I wouldn't even mind if you won the Nobel Prize." Pulling the sticky rolls of Pillsbury dough apart, she places them one by one on a warped and rusty cookie sheet. "God help me, or whoever else is listening out there. And I know I'm not one to throw stones, Chickie. But I just want you to be good."

"I'm good." Chickie curls her hands into fists inside the pockets of her jeans. "I *am* good, Mom," she says.

Nash sticks his head into the kitchen then, clean-shaven and showered, hair parted on one side, hiking up his khaki pants and rubbing his palms together. "So, when's that roast chicken going to be ready?" He sniffs the air, which reeks only now of pickle juice and stale Chesterfields.

"Never," Chickie says.

"I can't roast a chicken tonight, Nash." Violet measures out a quarter cup of water for the frozen succotash. "This old oven is so damned slow. There's no time. I have a meeting in an hour at the tennis club. We have all these things in the freezer. We might as well use them. Anyway, you probably haven't heard. Succotash is almost dead."

"What?" Confusion washes over Nash's face. "I thought we were having roast chicken." He turns to Chickie. "What happened?" he says.

"Let's just say," Violet says, looking over at Chickie. "That it had to do with French."

"Still on that *Tale of Two Cities* kick?" Nash bites into a limp pickle. "That was one hell of a story, I have to say."

"How would you know?" Chickie says. "You slept through most of it."

"Don't speak that way to your father," Violet says.

"He doesn't care."

"Well, he should."

"Hey, what's going on?" Nash says. "All I asked was—"

"I got a thirty-two on my French midterm," Chickie says. "And Mom's having a conniption fit because I'll never win the Nobel Prize."

"A thirty-two?" Nash looks at Chickie and then over at Violet. "Is that a joke?"

"Hardly," Violet says.

"I thought it was kind of funny," Chickie says.

"That's not all, Nash," Violet says. "There's more."

The uncooked chicken gets covered in tinfoil and put back in the refrigerator. No one speaks at dinner. They eat the warmed-up frozen food. The succotash lies untouched. There's no dessert, not even a piece of bruised fruit, not even a single, solitary Fig Newton.

Chickie jumps in her skin every time the alarm starts to wail. "*Levez-vous, classe,*" Mademoiselle Gladstone says calmly. "Rise and file." She takes her belted raincoat from the hook and applies lipstick by the light of her compact mirror. They straggle through the door out into the hallway. Three bomb scares this month and it's not even Thanksgiving yet. School's a joke. They come every day, take out their books, go through the motions, but no one's really there. There've been racial "incidents," school-wide assemblies, political rallies, TV news cameras, canceled classes, delayed days. They say Mrs. Lugbout gets the calls in the office, muffled voices telling her to check the lavatories and the locker rooms for bombs. So far, it's been all talk.

"*Vite! Vite!*" Mademoiselle Gladstone herds them down the stairs and out into the schoolyard. No one's really afraid. It's old hat, a bluff, a lark. Everyone knows that Monkey Man Ackerman made at least one of those calls from the phone booth across the street in front of the Ellery Spa. They're safe out here on the grass. And even if it were true, what a trip it would be to see the school being blown to pieces. It's a late Indian summer day, more like August than November. In front of the public library, a group from the Students for a Democratic Society clusters—talking, smoking, handing out pamphlets to students, drinking coffee in Styrofoam cups, always talking. The teachers watch and stir, waddle and pounce, pushing their straying chicks back into the milling flock, tossing the SDS papers into the trash, shooting looks to kill. Mademoiselle Gladstone and Mr. Harrington meet up on a clump of grass. Mr. H. looks sharp in a green plaid suit, rocking on his wing-tipped shoes. Miss G. smiles her stuffed-bear smile. Chickie watches them, careful and shy, trading words like kids do candy, afraid of what they might lose in the deal. What would they do differently, Chickie wonders, if the rules could be bent, if they were alone in a dark, forgiving place, if they didn't have to face each other in school the next day?

Chickie's eyes swing back to the SDS group. A man with a scruffy beard comes up to Hen and hands him a pamphlet. *"Make love not war,"* reads a button on his shirt. Mr. Harrington laughs at something Mademoiselle Gladstone's just said. Chickie watches her blush, watches the SDS man battering Hen with words. "Pigs! Facists!" the man says. "Do you know what they're doing to you here, kid? They're stuffing you with propaganda, literally washing out your brains!"

The fire engines pull up and two men in suits with metal suitcases disappear into the school with two policemen.

"Bomb squad," Hen says to Chickie.

"Good timing," Chickie says. "One more irregular verb and I might have croaked."

"You coming out tonight?" Hen asks. "The Chambers Brothers are at Club 47 and there's a big demo in the Square."

"Another one?"

"This is a big one, Chick. Half a million people are on their way to Washington. We've got to keep things going on the home front."

"You're beginning to sound like my father," she says. "All jazzed up. Excited. Like you're going to the circus or something."

"Chambers Brothers, Chick."

"Can't go," Chickie says. "I've got Driver's Ed tonight. Observation."

"What a waste of time," Hen says. "Driving around with some idiot who can't drive any better than you can. I've got tear gas, Chick. Monkey Man had a few extra canisters."

Chickie sees the rare light in Hen's eyes and it scares her. "What do you need tear gas for?"

"Fun," he says with a shrug.

"Fun?" Chickie says. "Forget it. I don't want to have fun."

"Paul Revere wouldn't have missed the Tea Party to go to Driver's Ed, man."

"Paul Revere didn't even go to the fucking Tea Party, *man,*" she says. "He rode to Concord to spread the alarm. Etcetera, etcetera. And he probably didn't have his mother on his case. Women died early in those days. They got mysterious fevers, croaked right and left during childbirth."

"What's that got to do with it?"

"I have to be good," Chickie says. "Or Violet's going to take away my Christmas vacation."

"She can't do that."

Chickie lowers her eyebrows and whips out an invisible cigarette, doing her best Violet imitation. "Just watch me, Minerva."

A warm wind blows in fits and starts. The men from the bomb squad emerge from opposite doors of the school. The outer fringe of students scatters. Some head across Broadway to the sub shop. Some take off down Quincy Street toward the Square. The teachers linger, stroll, confer. Mr. Harrington walks with Mademoiselle Gladstone, hands clasped behind his back, head bent to her left ear. A loud blast stops all but the farthest flung in their tracks. Only the quickest eyes see the door of the gym fly off its hinges and crash down the steps, the billowing smoke that follows in swirls. The silence draws the last wisps of smoke from the dark hole. Mr. Bunratee, the gym teacher, kicks the gym door as if it were a wounded animal that still might rise and strike. Lifting the whistle from his belly on its string, he blows hard and yells, "Freeze!"

As the bomb squad disappears into the gym, the statues retreat into clusters. The lights of the police cars flash and spin. Distorted, ragged voices break on the police radios and then abruptly cut off. For a long time, they all stand huddled out on the grass. And after a time, because the school day's ended and no one knows what else to do, they all dismiss themselves. Chickie heads down Broadway, past the supermarket and the laundromat, past the Fogg Museum and through the gates of Harvard Yard, the irregular verb *être* pouding in her brain. *Je suis.* I am. *Tu es. Il est.* You are. He, she, it, *is.* She is dead. *Elle est morte. Ils.* Masculine, plural. *Ils sont.* Dead. Martin Luther King. Two Kennedys. Malcolm X. Andy Gardner. Thousands of people in Vietnam she's never met. All dead. *Tous morts.* She looks behind her at the Widener Library steps, suddenly spooked, but the tidy pathway is empty. What happened to Hen? Did he go home? I want to go home. I have to go home. *Il faut que j'aille...chez moi, chez lui, chez nous, chez le garçon paresseux...* to the house of the lazy boy. I'm afraid and I don't know why. *J'ai peur.* I have fear. Another thing you *have* in French but just plain *is* in English. This day will grow dim sooner than Chickie will know, more grist for strange and scary dreams, a day when she may change more than on any other of her life. But from then, she'll be able to recite all of the forms of the irregular verb *être* in her sleep—*à jamais*—forevermore.

7

Back at home in the early evening, Chickie eats Hamburger Helper out of the pan and watches *The Dating Game* on TV. "Let's start with Bachelor Number Two," Sharon from Amarillo says, cocking her head to one side. "If you were a fruit, what would it be and why?"

Bachelor Number Two laughs.

"Don't try to be cute, Number Two," Chickie warns. "Sharon won't go for cute."

"A fruit, you say?" Bachelor Number Two buys time.

"You heard her, bozo," Chickie says. "Man, I must be losing it. I'm talking to the bachelors."

She's home alone. Again. Violet's note on the kitchen table is dashed off in three letters. O-U-T. No explanations anymore—no dinner on the stove, a meeting at the club, time of return, how was your day, XX-OOXX, Mom. Just O-U-T and a sloppy heart, followed by a slapdash V. Chickie leans her head back in her father's armchair. There's a smell that won't leave the front of her nose, the harsh, sulfury odor that lingered at the gym door after the bomb exploded. The smell was everywhere, in the maple trees as she walked to the Square, after she stopped in at Potts Pro, in her bed where she tried to read *Jude the Obscure*, seeping up from the copper-bottomed pan she now scrapes clean with a spoon. She'd hoped she might have dinner with her father somewhere in the Square, but Nash said he was going to grab a pizza with some friends before the demo started. He was one of the organizers of the march and they still had work to do. Anyway, he wasn't really hungry, he said. "How about a rain check, Chickadee?" *Chickadee. Chickadee.*

"Well, I can say this much, Sharon…" Bachelor Number Two finally comes up with an answer. "These two other guys up here look pretty fruity, but if you go out with me, we'd sure make a good *pear*."

"Oh my god," Chickie groans. Sharon smiles a weak, knowing smile. The canned laughter rolls as she fiddles with her stiff hair.

"You blew it, Number Two," Chickie says. "You went for the lame joke. You put down the comp. And now you're dead meat."

"How 'bout you, Bachelor Number Three?" Sharon's mascaraed

eyes turn toward the psychedelic dividing wall. "What kind of fruit would *you* be?"

"Banana," Bachelor Number Three answers too soon, too smug, arms crossed confidently, foot tapping on the rim of the stool. "No question about it, Sharon. I'd definitely be a banana."

"A banana?" Sharon raises her painted eyebrows. "Would you like to tell me why?"

"I don't really think we can go into it on TV, Sharon," says Bachelor Number Three. "But if you pick me, Sharon, we can talk about it over a candlelight dinner. Sharon."

"Why do you keep saying her name?" Chickie says. "Is that supposed to mean you really care?"

"Dinner sounds nice." Sharon's cool as a cucumber. "I'm not sure about the banana though."

"Ah, give me a chance, Sharon." Bachelor Number Three's face turns a horrible shade of magenta on the new color TV. "I'm sure I could change your mind."

"Don't grovel, Number Three." Chickie lurches out of the armchair. "It's pathetic."

Chickie fills the burned pot with hot water, as hot as it gets these days, and grabs her army jacket from one of the elephant hooks out in the hall. Leaving Sharon and a bewildered Bachelor Number One in a slight embrace, she heads out the door to Driver's Ed. Brattle Street's quiet and empty. On the Common, people gather in clusters, lighting off smoke bombs. Marchers gather at the Lincoln Statue with a banner that reads WITHDRAW NOW. Chickie sees Nash in the crowd, passing out leaflets, giving directions, testing a bullhorn. She waves but he doesn't see her. Nash stands in his khakis and corduroy jacket next to the tree she crashed into when she was learning to ride a two-wheeler and lost one of her top teeth, the tree under which George Washington first took command. She barely recognizes her father here—mouth to megaphone, barking orders, so strong and in charge, a strange twin to the slack-jawed, good-hearted father who watched helplessly as she wobbled off on her rusty bike toward the looming tree, who bends to Violet's will at home.

Chickie leapfrogs up onto one of the black Revolutionary War cannons, feels its bumpy trunk slide cool beneath her thighs. The Gray Panthers walk in circles kitty-corner to the dancing Hare Krishnas. A man practices Tai Chi on the edge of the green. Another in face paint juggles three red balls, hair dangling in his eyes. Chickie slides off the cannon onto the cobblestones. Passing the juggler, she wraps a smile around the spinning balls; miraculously, they don't fall. In the Square, the stores are closing up early and the streetlights are on before their time. Sidewalks and storefronts are strangely empty. Only the street people hold their posts—on the kiosk and the grates, in the Brigham's doorway, the entryway of the Coop. A cop comes galloping on horseback around the arc of Brattle Street as Chickie heads down Mass Ave., a beefy Lone Ranger without the mask. As the reins pull tight, the horse rears, causing Chickie to stumble. The cop caresses the hot neck of the skittish horse and bends down as it snorts and prances. "Where you supposed to be, young lady?" he asks.

"Driver's ed." Chickie points down Mass Ave. "Down near the church."

"Get there quickly. Then, afterward, hightail it back home." The cop reins in the horse as a firecracker lands nearby and spooks it. "Tell your friends to stay off the streets tonight."

The cop takes off at a gallop toward the river. Chickie heads down the straightaway of Mass Ave., past the leather and jewelry shops and the Baptist church where protestors gather to burn their draft cards. The driving school at the corner of Bow and Arrow is dark and locked. CLASS CANCELED says a sign on the door. Darkness has fallen and she finds herself in a wispy fog. She wipes her stinging, watery eyes. The streets are empty. Police cars cruise the Square like sharks; voices boom out of distant bullhorns. Streetlights cast a garish glow. Small piles of trash swirl in the wind—candy wrappers and sheets of newspaper and the shells of the things that keep exploding. Chickie heads back toward the center of the Square. The Old Mole Man has moved his pile of newspapers up near Bartley's Burger Cottage. Her stomach rumbles as she passes by. In the window of Krackerjacks hangs a display of striped bell-bottoms and hanging crushed soup cans. Antoine the string-and-tin-foil man stands beside a shopping cart in front of the tobacco store. Holding court at the entrance to Cardells, Plato, the street poet, recites his war poems, dressed all in red.

"Hey, Chickie!"

As she crosses the street to the kiosk, someone grabs her arm. Elvis Donahue and two other boys are crouched low by the Out of Town ticket window.

"Hi, Elvis." She ducks down with the boys. Without looking, she stops to remember what she's wearing. Miniskirt made from sailor pants, thirteen buttons at the waist, a peasant blouse with dangling strings at the neck. Stupid high-tops. Time to ditch them, save up for those purple clogs in the window of Capezio. Her army jacket's tied around her waist. Like a stupid kid.

"Where you coming from?" Elvis asks.

"Driver's ed. It got canceled," Chickie says. "What's happening here?"

"You just missed it," Elvis says. "The protestors came marching up from the Common. The cops were waiting in a line at the Coop. They just kept on walking. People got hauled away. The tear gas was flying. The handcuffs were clicking. Must have been five, six paddy wagons. It was far out." He hands her a lit joint. "Those people in the front line had balls."

"My father."

"What?"

"Never mind." Chickie takes the joint between her thumb and middle finger and takes a drag. "Isn't this kind of stupid? There are cops all over the place."

"Pigs don't have time for jailbait like us tonight," Elvis says.

"It's an insult to the animal," one of the boys says. "Pigs are cleaner, smarter, and have a social conscience."

"How the hell do you know, Kramer?" the other one says. "You ever hung out with a pig?"

Chickie crouches low with the boys. The pot tastes different than the nickel bag she bought with Wanda Melrose and toked in the girls' room at school. Stronger. More bitter. Smoke curls up into the air. The boys talk baseball and dope. They had some Colombian Red the night before. It was so good, it was like tripping. Chickie rocks in her crouch, takes another drag. The Celtics are looking fine. And the Bruins. With Cheesie in goal, and the Habs in a semi-slump, this could definitely be the year. The boys keep looking at her, as if they want something, as if she's keeping them from saying what they really want to say. Chickie feels more than ever before like a girl. But what does she really know about being a girl, a woman? Can the boys tell how much she feels like an imposter, despite the breasts and curves and blood? She doesn't feel kind or brave or good enough to be a girl. She thinks of her sisters, how it might've been different if they'd been closer in age, if she'd had someone to grow up with besides Hen. She thinks how she's never really had any close girlfriends. And how maybe that's strange. "Thanks for the pot," she says, handing the joint back to Elvis. "I'll see you tomorrow at school."

"Wait." Elvis takes a quick toke and passes on the joint. "Where you going?"

"Club 47. I'm meeting my cousin there. The Chambers Brothers are playing."

"No way," Elvis says. "Everything's been canceled. Because of all the demos. They've taken over the Mall in Washington. The Stones are doing a concert on TV. To keep people off the streets. The cops made an announcement through the bullhorn."

Chickie shrugs. "I guess I'll head home then."

"Want a ride?" Elvis says. "My bike's parked over by the graveyard."

The other boys snicker. "Why don't you take her up to see your etchings, Donahue."

"Shut up," Elvis says. "Don't listen to these morons, Chickie."

"What morons?" she says, turning away.

Chickie swings her leg over the leather seat of Elvis's bike and puts her arms around his waist. The silver chrome plate reads *Norton 750* in slanted silver script. It's such a pretty thing, with its wheels and pipes and bars, steel and black rubber, such a beautiful, ugly thing. As Chickie rests her feet on the footrests, her mother's face comes into focus. Violet says: *Riding on motorcycles may be hazardous to your health. Stay off them, Minerva.* Chickie says: *Every cigarette takes a second off your life, Ma. Put it out.* She thinks of her father leading the march into the Square. "Those guys in the front lines had balls," Elvis says. He kicks the bike started with the crumpled toe of his boot and they take off with a lurch, tilting low to the ground, picking up speed as they near the bend of the Common, Chickie's hair whipping straight back in the wind.

On the Common the crowds are beginning to break apart. Hen sits on the Lincoln statue in the middle of the green, roosting with a band of pigeons. On the back of Lincoln's greatcoat someone has spray painted, *Oink, oink, Abe.* A circle of protestors chants down below. A riff from a saxophone drifts by, a Chick Corea tune, meandering and slow. As Hen's eyes swing toward the Square, a motorcycle bombs around the corner down Garden Street. "It's them," he says under his breath. Two things Hen would never miss—a Commando and Chickie's hair. He takes out the canister of tear gas and squirts some into the air. The pigeons scatter, all but one. "Get lost," he says, giving the last pigeon a gentle push. "Get lost, you stupid bird. This stuff will kill you if you hang around too long." He presses his finger down on the button and empties half the can. Slowly his eyes fill until the whole scene's nothing but a stinging blur. The Norton disappears out of sight. The last pigeon flaps gracelessly to the ground, leaving Hen alone on the statue of Lincoln, who stares straight ahead, ever still, ever noble, with a splat of bird crap on his marble beard.

Nash is the last one into the paddy wagon and the cop pushes him hard. "Whoa, there, easy, fellow," he says. "No need to exercise undue force."

"Just doing my job," the cop says. "You can save the rest for the judge."

"I'm cooperating," Nash says. "I'm not resisting."

"Have a seat, pal," the cop says.

"What's your name?" Nash asks.

"Palmer. Lieutenant Frank Palmer."

"Hi, Frank. I'm Nash. Nash Potts. Nice to meet you."

Nash takes his seat alongside his co-protestors, a boisterous, energized group bolstered by the strength of the night's turnout, the strong speeches made, the voices heard.

Good work.

I'd say we made a statement.

TV cameras were everywhere. We'll be front-page news.

Nash has been vaguely aware of the guy in the corner, sitting quietly, nondescript, wearing an Orioles cap and a Jim Morrison T-shirt. He's never seen him on the protest circuit before. They're a pretty tight group. Must be a newbie or an out-of-towner. The cop closes the door of the paddy wagon and sits down next to Nash.

"You riding with us, Frank?" Nash says.

"Someone's got to keep an eye on you peaceniks." By now, Frank is more relaxed, his work for the night almost done.

"Yeah," Nash says. "We're a pretty dangerous bunch."

"What do you do for a living, Nash? Besides disturb the peace."

"My brother and I own a sporting goods store in the Square. Potts Pro."

"Oh sure," Frank says. "I got my kid a baseball glove there. Years ago, now."

"He still have it?"

"I bet he does." Frank smiles. "So what do you want to get mixed up with a bunch of kooks like this for, Nash."

"This bunch of kooks has something important on its mind."

"So don't the rest of us," Frank says.

The quiet guy in the corner has good timing, catching them all off guard. No one is quick enough to stop him from lunging at the cop. Nash tries to pull him off.

"Fucking pig!" The man starts to pound Frank with his fists. "Fascist murdering pig. Who the hell do you think you are?"

"I'm an officer of the law." Frank pulls out his nightstick and begins swinging, trying to get the guy under the knees.

"Whoa, easy, Frank." Nash pulls at the cop's arm. "Put down the club. We can take him. The two of us. We can take him."

"Get out of the way," Frank says.

"How can you sleep at night?" the man yells.

"I sleep just fine." Frank starts to hit the man harder and harder, wailing on him without mercy.

"Stop it, Frank!" Nash says. "You're going to kill him."

But Frank is a big guy, enraged now, beyond all reason, beyond all senses. The nightstick rises, hitting higher, the guy's chest and arms. "I sleep like a goddamned baby," he says.

"Go ahead, kill me!" the man says, fending off Frank's blows. "Have that on your fucking conscience too."

Nash tries to grab the nightstick and falls into the fray. The three of them wrestle as the paddy wagon heads down Mass Ave. Nash lands flat on his back, sees the nightstick coming at him. He tries to move out of the way—out of the way—he tells himself. *Get out of the way!* In the funny way that the brain works, or doesn't work, in such extreme moments, it will be years before Nash realizes that the cracking noise he hears just before the light goes out in his head, the sound that will wake him from many nightmares to come, is not some external noise, a gunshot or a clap of thunder or a car crashing into a wall, but the sound of Frank's nightstick cracking open his skull.

As the Norton zooms down Brattle, Chickie leans into the leathery arc of Elvis's broad back. He smells good, like motorcycle grease and pot and burnt coffee. They curl around the dump road out onto Fresh Pond Parkway and across the wooden bridge at the reservoir. Elvis plunges down the walking path into the darkness and rides along the fence at the water's edge. Moonlight glistens on the water. Chickie's eyes start to tear. She ducks the branches of trees, looming shadows, zapping bugs. Without warning, they leap back into the open, darkness giving way to the neon green of the golf course. Elvis drives the bike up onto one of the mounds next to a weeping willow tree. The moon is almost full. No one else is in sight. The chrome on the motorcycle gleams.

"Fourth hole," Elvis says, turning off the bike. "Good place to get high."

"Aren't you high enough?" Chickie asks.

"Never," Elvis says, unstrapping his helmet.

"I think I'm *too* thigh." Chickie swings her leg up and over the seat.

"Far out. Are you a contortionist or something?"

"I'm a dancer. Sort of," Chickie says.

Elvis props the bike up on its kickstand and sits down next to Chickie on the ground. "You like golf?" he says.

"Never played it," Chickie says.

"My grandfather's a golf fanatic," Elvis says. A slit of white underwear shows through the split in the crotch of his jeans. "He'd sleep on the links if they let him."

"Does he live around here?"

"No, down in Florida. He pays my way down there every February vacation. I lug his golf clubs around for him, make him scrambled eggs and stuff, read him his horoscope. He keeps his teeth in a jar, plays the dogs. The senior set. It's that kind of deal." Elvis's arms stay locked around his legs. "He can't stand my old man," he says. "He pretty much disowned my mother when she married him. But for some reason, he digs me."

"You're lucky," Chickie says. "I never knew any of my grandparents."

"Yeah, he's a cool old dude." Elvis takes another joint from his shirt pocket and lights up. "Crazy, though. He's into guns and he's got this thing about long hair. When I go down there, I have to cram it all under a hat. If he sees any hanging out, he takes out his shotgun and threatens to shoot it all off. Sometimes the look in his eye is so crazed, I almost believe him." He takes a clump of Chickie's hair and lets it slide through his fingers. "People get so uptight about hair," he says.

"So, are you named after Elvis Presley?"

"Nah. He wasn't even famous when I was born." Elvis sucks on the joint to get it going. "Now the joke's on me."

"Do *you* like golf?" Chickie says.

"Nah." Elvis draws on the joint slowly, speaks on the inhale. "But I like golf courses."

"Dig it," Chickie says. "I don't like airplanes, but I like airports. Hen and I go out to Logan sometimes on the subway."

"Who's Hen?"

"My cousin?"

"The chess freak?"

"Yeah, he plays a lot of chess."

"What do you do out there?"

"Watch the passengers," Chickie says. "I like it when they come off the plane and the people are waiting for them. At first, they don't see each other and then when they do, they all have to turn back into whoever they were before they left. I like watching that moment."

"Yeah, that's a cool moment." Elvis nods, talking on the exhale. "Kind of like when Johnny and Ed come back from a commercial break."

"Kind of."

Elvis fishes in his pockets for his roach clip. "Hey, what was that joke you told the other day in French class?" he asks. "I need that joke for my repertoire."

Chickie takes the roach clip from Elvis's hand. "Well, see, this rich oil baron guy from Texas comes to Harvard Square and he goes up to this professorly type and says, 'Howdy, pardner, where's the post office at?'" She takes a drag, inhales slowly. "The professor's lip gets all stiff and shit and he says to the guy, 'Here at Harvard, sir, we never end a sentence with a preposition,' and so the Texas guy tips his ten-gallon hat and says, 'Okay, then...'" Chickie lets out what's left of the last toke. "Where's the post office at, *asshole?*'"

Elvis laughs, leans forward, kisses Chickie on the lips. "I dig that joke," he says. "You want to fuck?"

"What?" Chickie pulls away.

"If you don't want to, that's cool," Elvis says. "I'm no rapist."

"I didn't say I didn't want to."

"Either way." Elvis lies back on the grass, hands clasped behind his head. As his T-shirt rides up, Chickie sees the line of hair that starts at his navel and disappears under his jeans. He's bigger than she is, softer, a blond dragon boy in black motorcycle boots. Chickie stares at Elvis Donahue, at the stubble on his chin, the veiny bulge of his biceps, the rise in his jeans. She can't answer the voice that asks why, only the one that asks why not. She breathes in deeply, grateful for what the night's given her—this freaky warm night, this breeze, this ride, this dope, this grass-covered hill, this freedom, this soft, stoned boy. Maybe it's the pot. But she doesn't care. Elvis Donahue wants to fuck her and she's going to let him. All he's waiting for is a sign. She reaches out to touch his arm; he pulls her toward him. She straddles him, knees pressing in against his sides. When she leans down, her hair falls forward. He pushes it behind her ears and it slips back out again, brushing across his face. Elvis slides his hands under her shirt up her back. Chickie runs her hand over his stomach and unsnaps his jeans.

"Whoa." Elvis rises up on his elbows, stomach muscles tightening, chin pushing down into his chest.

"I thought you wanted to." Chickie pulls her hand away.

"I did. I do. I just didn't know…"

"What?"

"That you'd be so *into* it."

"I'm not so *into* it." Chickie stands up and turns away toward the reservoir. "I'm just as into it as you are," she says, wrapping her arms around her chest.

Elvis reaches out to touch her leg. "Don't be mad," he says. "I'm sorry."

"What are you sorry about?" Chickie looks down at him. "It's supposed to be this great, mind-blowing experience, right? If we don't want to do it, then we shouldn't do it."

"I just don't want to push you into anything," Elvis says.

"I don't want to push you into anything either."

"You couldn't push me into anything. No way."

"If we both want to do it, then nobody's pushing anybody. I'm no rapist either, Elvis."

"Girls can't be rapists," Elvis says, standing up next to her.

"Why not?"

"Man, it's a good thing, Chickie. I'm not trying to be a jerk. You're just not strong enough, You're…" Elvis pulls her around by the arm, kisses her on the mouth, steers her back against the willow tree. Chickie kisses him back, rolling her tongue around the smooth inside walls of his cheeks. "You're soft," he says as his hand slides down under her skirt.

"Wait," she says, pulling away.

"Jesus," Elvis groans. "You're the one who was in such a rush."

"I'm not anymore," Chickie says.

"Past a certain point, it's not so easy for a guy to slow down."

"What point?"

"Let's just say I'm about to pass it."

"You are? Cool. What does it feel like?"

"Oh, man." Elvis runs his hand through his hair. "We're not exactly moving heaven and earth here, Chickie."

"I wonder what the big deal is," Chickie says, "what it's going to feel like."

"Christ, how should I know?"

"You mean you're a virgin, too?"

Elvis rubs his forehead with his palm. "What can I say?" he says. "What can I possibly say?"

"Let's start over again." Chickie puts a hand on his arm. "Let's take off all our clothes."

"What?"

"Strip for each other. Come on, Elvis. You first."

He shakes his head. "I don't know, Chickie. Man, I just don't know about this whole thing." He takes another joint from his T-shirt pocket and lights up.

"I've never seen a boy naked," Chickie says. "I mean up close. Not since Hen and I were kids. I don't have any brothers."

"You should hang out over at my house. My parents are into nudity. It's sick."

"Who isn't *into* it?" Chickie says. "It's not a religion or anything. It's just the way we're born. When I was little I used to think babies came out with their clothes on. That's how uptight my family was about sex."

"Yeah, well, a little modesty doesn't hurt. Either way, it's no big deal."

"So if it's no big deal," Chickie grins on the dare, "then take your clothes off."

"It's no big deal," Elvis mutters, handing her the lit joint. He kicks off his boots, slides his belt out of his belt loops. Off comes his T-shirt, then his socks. Chickie puffs away. The smoke starts to go down smooth and easy. She smokes and smokes, as Elvis's body is slowly revealed—arms, belly, legs. It comes to her, as Elvis undresses, that besides keeping people warm, clothes make them look older. As Elvis sheds his clothes, her body starts to feel lighter. The moon seems to grow and grow. Elvis slides off his pants, stands in his underwear. "You seen enough?" he says.

Chickie shakes her head. "Not yet," she says.

"What am I doing here?" Elvis looks up to the sky. "What the fuck am I doing here?" He slides off his underwear, looks down over his body, holds up his hands in naked surrender. Chickie takes in all of his parts as he fidgets and wriggles. She keeps on toking at the joint until she feels the heat of its tip near her fingers, a warmth rising up from her toes.

"What are you smiling at?" Elvis asks.

"You look good," she murmurs. "You look nice."

"Nice?" Elvis sits back down beside her and wraps his arms around his knees. "Man, you're bold, Chickie. You really rattle me. Give me the last bit of that joint, will you?"

Chickie hands him the roach clip and lies back down on the grass. Digging the small of her back into the ground, she kicks one leg up high, bends it to her chest and laughs out loud. Everything that's come before this moment seems dim and dreamlike. French class. The bomb in the gym. *The Dating Game*. The demo in the Square. The cop on horseback. Her father with the bullhorn. The dark night and the fog. The crouching boys. The dope. The motorcycle ride. A kiss. It's all come to this—a naked boy on one side of her, a motorcycle and a willow tree on the other. The day will end as it was meant to. She isn't afraid, doesn't care anymore what comes of this night, what she and Elvis Donahue do or don't do. He's just a boy, with a toothless grandfather, a boy who hates his name, just the way she hates hers, who's embarrassed to be naked in front of her, even though he's stoned out of his mind. In the end, it won't really matter who she fucked first. She rolls on her side, props her ear on her hand. She feels how her hip dips, how her breasts fall together, how good she looks in Elvis's eyes.

"Your turn now," Elvis says. Chickie feels his nervousness, his excitement, like cricket chirps in the night air. The lights of the houses in the distance flicker. On the parkway, the neon dots of Big Ed's used-car sign roll around in frantic, blinking circles. She probably only imagines she can smell the wontons and moo shu pork from the Pagoda Restaurant, but still, she could swear. Across the reservoir, the muffled sounds of night rise in a muted blare. Somewhere from afar, the Stones belt out a song, hoarse and raw from a radio. A car horn is stuck somewhere, beeping endlessly. Chickie unbuttons her peasant blouse and slides it off her shoulders. Standing up, she slips the thirteen buttons of her sailor pant skirt through their holes one by one, up, over and down.

Stepping out of her underwear, she drops them, a white puddle on the green. Elvis watches, knees clasped in arms, hazy in a tangle of smoke, ponytail reaching halfway down his back over his hunched shoulders. Chickie stands finally as Elvis did for her, arms dangling and naked on the fourth hole. She points her toe, raises her arms, pliés and twirls. "Ta da," she says.

"Dance some more," Elvis says.

"I'm naked."

"So am I," Elvis says. "Dance, Chickie. It's fantastic. No one's watching. No one's out here tonight. We're the only ones, the only ones left on the whole fucking planet. Doesn't it feel that way?"

"Don't say that," Chickies says, falling to her knees. Elvis pulls her down beside him. They lie side by side on the grass. He climbs on top of her, shimmies his body down, and brings his mouth to her breast. She buries her hands in his hair and feels what the sucking does, the shiver that moves like a marble that falls down a pipe and hits a bell which flips the marble up and sends it down into a pool where the water swirls. The warm feeling in her breasts moves into her stomach and shoots up into her armpits and down in between her legs. Elvis feels heavy, solid. He moves his mouth up to hers. It trembles. With one knee, he pushes her legs apart. Chickie hangs on to his hair as he struggles to get centered, his mouth locked to hers all the while, reminding Chickie of the Dutch kissing magnets on the refrigerator. A pulsing laugh rises up from her middle and she moves her tongue back to keep it from exploding, from betraying her. Elvis pushes against her, searching for the right place. And when he finds it, he stops, hands propped up on the grass. He looks down at Chickie for the first time, really, all night, moving his hips back and forth, breathing fast. "You sure this is okay?" he whispers.

"I'm sure," Chickie says.

"You won't be a virgin anymore."

"Neither will you," she says.

Elvis pushes silently, hard. A bird screeches and a breeze sweeps the shadows of the willow trees across the green. After that first jab, it's not painful, or anything, really, except hard to imagine, surreal. Elvis keeps pushing, rocking. Chickie feels the motion. It seems to last such a long, long time. Her mind floats; her thoughts are so strange. She thinks of a day long ago in Nantucket with Hen on a beach and a horseshoe crab, Bachelor Number Two smiling sheepishly after he didn't get picked by Sharon. Chickie feels Elvis's stomach flat on hers. He starts to move back and forth, his face buried to the side in her hair. He murmurs. He pushes. *God*'s lost somewhere in his words. She pulls her muscles tight and arches her back to let Elvis reach as deep as he can. She waits for what she's supposed to feel and when he stops short in something like a groan, she knows she's missed it. Her fingers sketch figure eights on his back, as his breathing slowly eases. They lie still and silent that way for a while, top to bottom. Elvis gives one last push, one last groan. Chickie smooths the hair from his damp forehead, strokes the back of his neck, sings him "ooh-la, ooh-la-lay."

By the time the car horn's stopped beeping and the nightbird's finished its screech, by the time Hen's put away his chessboard and closed his burning, tear-gassed eyes, by the time the protestors have been booked at the police station, and Nash has been lifted into the ambulance as the lights flash and the sirens start to wail—Chickie and Elvis Donahue have gone all the way.

8

JANUARY 1970

The new decade slips in quietly, bringing with it a stretch of bitterly cold days. On Hemlock Street, in the olive-green house, Nash recovers slowly from a grade-three concussion. He slips in and out of sleep or consciousness; he's never sure. The pain's not bad, and he can live with the ringing in his ears. The worst part is the confusion—who, what, when, where, and most of all how. He's been all sorts of things in his life—weak, scared, lazy, but rarely confused. The faces of his life come and go, peering at him as if through the rim of a glass jar.

After her initial hysterical response to the accident, Violet has slowly grown more exasperated than concerned. "Honestly, Nash," she's said more than once. "When will you ever learn?" Learn what, he keeps reminding himself to ask her later.

Chickie talks as if he'd been deafened, not wacked on the head. "Dad, can you hear me? Are you going to be okay? Do you have amnesia? Are you going to forget all of us? Dad?"

"Hi, Uncle Nash. This is Hen. They had the first draft lottery. Got up to #191. Chickie and I…"

The touch of a feminine hand. "Is that you, Vi?" No, the hand is too cool, too tentative. A whisper in his ear. "Crazy Eights. Rematch." *Rematch.* It must be Faye.

Nash wakes up one morning in a sweat and sees the strangest thing. He sees himself sitting in the chair beside his bed. One of a few dividends of getting clobbered, he thinks, is having an out-of-body experience, the chance to take a good hard look at the man you are, the man you've been. He looks at himself curiously, dispassionately. Broad faced, slumped shoulders, not bad looking, in familiar old khakis and frayed pink shirt. This looks like a good sort of guy, a guy you could shoot the shit with, a guy you could trust.

"Hey," a voice comes suddenly out of the vision's mouth. "It's about time you woke up, brother," it says.

"Remi." It's when Nash reaches out to touch his brother's arm with his own hand that the confusion starts to clear.

"Goddamned cop." Remi gets to his feet and paces. "Nearly killed you, Nash. We've got a lawsuit on our hands."

"Ah, what's the point, Rem? I'm not going to press charges. I'm just going to let it go."

"Let it go? You've got to be kidding me, Nash. That cop nearly killed you."

"He didn't, though."

"He might have."

"He was doing his job. The guy attacked him, viciously, without provocation. I'm a witness. Self-defense. Okay, so maybe Frank took it a bit too far."

"Frank? You're on a first-name basis with the guy?"

Violet came into the room just then.

"Hey, Vi," Remi says. "Talk some sense into this guy, will you? He wants to let the cop off the hook."

"So let him," Vi says.

"Really?" Nash says, his newfound clarity suddenly in doubt. This isn't the Violet he knows, the one who seeks justice at any cost, like Remi, who always needs an answer, atonement, closure. This is another Violet, a preoccupied Violet, a changing Violet, a Violet who might surprise you.

By late January, the school ground looks like a prison yard—cracked cement, windblown trash, chain-link fences, junior dean lingering at one corner of the school building with shuffling feet and a turned-up collar. Chickie lights up a Camel at the kissing bench, where Hen kissed Cozmo's feet. Since the fall she's taken up smoking, and Hen's given it up. She wears a hacked-off fake fur coat, satin pockets rendered useless by the cut, bell bottoms, an Indian print T-shirt that barely covers her belly. Everything Hen has on is gray. Looking up from his seat on the bench, he feels the first few flakes of snow.

Dear Mrs. Lugbout, he writes. *Please excuse Minerva for being tardy...* He looks over at Chickie. "What'll it be, Chick? Another relative bite the dust? Dentist appointment number sixty-three?"

"Broken alarm clock." Chickie takes a bite of a chocolate chip cookie, one of three wrapped in cellophane. "Technical difficulties at home." She snorts. "And that's no lie. Since my father got home from the hospital, Violet's even more psycho than ever."

Hen slants the script backwards. *Her alarm clock broke and she slept late…*

"Write overslept," Chickie says. "It sounds better."

Hen crosses out *slept late* and writes *overslept*. "Very truley, yours, etcetera, etcetera."

Chickie leans over Hen's shoulder. "No *e* in truly, Einstein," she says. "Now copy it over. It's a mess."

"Man, it's not easy being your mother." Hen sets up the pieces on his magnetic chess set. "How's your dad, by the way?"

Chickie lights up a Camel. "He's better, I guess. But the accident's made him kind of loopy, even more of a wimp, if that's possible."

"He's not a wimp," Hen says. "Compared to my father, that bastard—"

"What?" Chickie leans closer. What's true of Hen's father might be true of her own.

"He hit my mother."

"No way. When?"

"A few months ago."

"Why didn't you tell me?"

"I'm telling you now," Hen says. "He smacked her right across the face. I was at the top of the stairs. I saw him."

"Oh my god. Why?" Chickie smushes out her cigarette with her heel.

"She wanted to move a lamp and he went berserk. He started yelling, 'That lamp's been there for the last twenty-five years and it's going to stay there, damn it!' like some raving lunatic."

"Why did he even care?"

"He didn't care, Chick. It wasn't about the lamp. It was about power. About him having to be in control. He just kept saying, 'Don't move that lamp, don't move, that lamp,' as if just by saying it over and over again, he could stop her."

"What'd she do?"

"She said it was just a lamp and it didn't matter where it was. And then she picked it up and moved it." Hen shakes his head. "So he up and belted her right across the mouth."

"Man, our family is so fucked up," Chickie says.

"She walked out the door, Chick," Hen says. "She didn't come back until the next night."

"I'd never come back," Chickie says.

"But where would you go?" Hen remembers the Robert Frost poem about home—the place that when you go there, they have to take you in.

"Anywhere else," Chickie says.

"Did Uncle Nash ever—"

"Hit the warden? Nah, he never does anything unless she tells him to. That would be irony for you—Violet telling Nash to hit her. And then him doing it. Even though he's such a pacifist. And her being a masochist, even though she wears the pants in the family. He doesn't stick up for himself." Chickie picks up a twig and starts to trace the letters of her mother's name in the dirt. V-I-O..."She tells him how to butter his toast and when to brush his teeth. She makes him crazy and he just takes it. She's cheating on him, and he doesn't do anything about it."

"You don't know that for sure. Anyway, what's he supposed to do?"

"Tell her off. Give her an ultimatum." Chickie finishes writing her mother's name in the dirt. L-E-T. "He should get off his ass and fight back."

"What if he doesn't want to fight back?"

"Then he's chicken."

"He's not chicken. He tried to help that cop with that psycho."

"Yeah, and look what happened."

"Anyway, it's a different thing...with your mom," Hen says. "Maybe he just doesn't see the point."

"So what are you saying? That your mother shouldn't have moved the lamp?" Chickie taps a fresh cigarette out of the pack. "Just because your dad was in some kind of weird mood? Are you saying she should've backed down, just because she didn't want a fight, that she should've just walked away? Are you saying that because my mother's a nymphomaniac, my father should just sit back and take it?"

"No," Hen says. "But you don't always have to duke it out. Ali didn't slug his way out of the draft. He just refused to go."

"Ali's the freakin' heavyweight champion of the world. He can do whatever he wants," Chickie says. "God, poor Aunt Faye. I'd be scared to come home now, scared to eat dinner with him, scared to sleep in the same bed."

"They don't sleep in the same bed anymore," Hen says. "They haven't for a long time." He takes Chickie's stick and slides an *N* between the *E* and the *T* in his aunt's name in the dirt. "He was crying, Chick. Do you believe it? When she left the house, he was actually crying, as if someone had hit him."

"He worships her," Chickie says. "I bet he'll never do it again."

Hen looks down at the word etched in the dirt—VIOLENT. "If he does, I may have to do something."

Chickie looks up. "Like what?"

"Like never talk to him again. Or help my mother get away. Or punch him or something."

Chickie smushes out her mother's name in the dirt with her shoe. "You've never punched anyone in your whole life, Hen."

"I've never had a reason to," he says.

"Come on, Henry." Chickie pulls him up from the bench, takes him by the arm. "The colonel's waiting. It's Reenactment Day."

"Let's not go, Chick. I don't know if I can hack it today."

"Five more months and we're free." Chickie starts down the path to school. "This is no time to quit, Hen. It's the end game. Let's go."

The groundhog sees its shadow in the morning, and it starts snowing at three. By six, there's a good five inches on the ground. Remi closes up Potts Pro, locks the door, and goes into the back room to go over the numbers. Check, calibrate, slip, and slide them. Fudge them if he has to. He'd like to think he's about even—that he's put back in as much as he's taken from the till. He tries to go over it all, piece by piece. In the fall, he slipped that first seven thousand into the bank fast, tried to make it work for itself, but he needed a bit here and there to cover a few bum bets, and before he knew it, it was down to four grand and then two and then five hundred. And then there was that disaster at the track. He got overconfident, fell for some outside sucker bets, got cocky, went to a different ticket window, shot a big wad. Cammie was sick. She didn't come for two weeks. Turned out she had the mumps. Nearly killed her, she said. Never had them as a kid. And she'd done him a favor, she said, by staying away. Mumps could make a man sterile. He was furious when she told him. He was forty-seven years old, for Christ sake. Did she honestly think he was planning on having any more kids? He'd lost big that second week and gotten angry, almost took a slug at Cammie the next Tuesday when she finally reappeared, before she worked him over and calmed him back down.

Remi rubs his bleary eyes at the office desk, tries to reconfigure. So after that whopping loss, he was dead even from his first big win, and he had to take a little bit from the store till, just to get back on track. Five hundred that one time, just two last week. Then he won a solid wad on that skinny horse in the fifth, *Hang Ten Hans*. No one else could have seen it coming. But then that skittish roan let him down right after Nash's accident, gave up after the first lap and finished dead last. Remi crunches the numbers, pushes, pulls, and prods them. Down about three thousand all told. He breathes a sigh of relief. Not as bad as it could be, not enough to outwardly rock the cradle. The business can absorb both—the dip in capital and a few white lies. He'll make the money back the next week. Or the next. It's not the worst luck that Nash is out of commission for a while. He never would have wished such a terrible thing on his brother, but if this deal with the cop had to happen, the timing couldn't have been better. Remi's always wanted the upper hand; now that he has it, he's got to keep it steady. He's got to be careful. No more outside bets. Keep tapping the mother lode; stick to the original source. He got careless, impatient. He always does when things start going well. Greed, it's a character flaw, one of his umpteen deadly sins. He's got to stay focused and alert, stay grounded. He's got to keep his eye keen, his palms dry, his luck hot. He's got to keep his hands on Cammie.

Cammie haunts Remi, not the whole of her but just a floating, disembodied head, the searing eyes and full mouth, the square, dimpled chin. He still won't look at her body when they have sex, keeps them covered with a sheet at the motel the whole time. But he's studied her face so closely—skin soft and pinched under all the makeup, which he makes her wash off before they start, high cheekbones, creases at the brow and a layer of fine down at the temples. Stripped clean, it's a beautiful, noble face, the face of an angel, a warrior. And then there's that thing he makes her do, on her knees, with her tongue, three times, from behind, before they start. Three times. No more. No less. As kinky rituals go, it's pathetic, he knows, but it gets him going every time; it works. It's crazy, sick even, Remi knows, to think of Cammie as his talisman, their trips to the motel part of the chain of his good fortune. But luck is capricious; it doesn't play by any logical rules, so in a way, why the hell not? It's puzzling, though a huge relief, that he feels so little guilt over Cammie—he is usually the first to succumb to its pull. He sees her clearly for what she is—a means to protect all that he has and loves. In that sense, she's a guardian angel rather than an evil temptress. He's just taking care of business. And Cammie can take care of herself.

It's after nine by the time Remi closes up Potts Pro. The wind's picked up and the Square's deserted, snow blowing in gusts down Brattle Street to the river. He heads for the Blarney Stone, which was Cronin's back in the day. No point in going home. No one's ever home anymore. And in February a man needs company and warmth. The wind sweeps him down Brattle; already he's knee deep in snow. By the time he opens the door of the bar, his eyebrows are encrusted. Chilled to the bone, he slides his leg over a stool at the bar and orders a double scotch on the rocks. And then another. He can't seem to drink them, feel them, fast enough. He looks around the bar, remembers the night he and Nash made their drunken pact here years ago. He smiles, remembering the baby Hen, the beautiful baby boy.

A noisy crowd of young men comes in, stomping the snow from their feet, swooping their hats from their tousled heads.

"Man, it's a real honest-to-goodness blizzard."

"Subway's out. The whole street's dark."

"They're going to have to shut the whole town down."

Remi looks up from his drink, annoyed. The Blarney Stone isn't a hip place. Never was and isn't meant to be. It's dark and scuzzy and off the beaten path, an old geezer bar, one of the few places in the Square that hasn't changed. He can usually count on coming in here and sitting peacefully, undisturbed. Why can't these clowns take their act down to the Ale House or the Plough and Stars? The boys make their way noisily over to the bar, talking, laughing, flushed from the cold. Remi turns his head away.

"One for the road at the Blarney. A venerable institution in my family." A brash, familiar voice sails out of the crowd. "This is where my old man's been coming to get plowed for the past thirty years." An embarrassed fury rises inside Remi as his eyes turn toward Buzz. Buzz, at twenty-five, still living like a college kid in a crummy apartment in Allston with a bunch of transient apes, working occasional afternoons at Potts Pro, taking business classes at night at Northeastern, classes he never bothered to take at Harvard. Still hanging out, still wearing the same preppy clothes and loafers, still carousing with the boys. Buzz, a Harvard graduate, but just barely, groundless, ambitionless Buzz. It's a wonder that sweet girlfriend of his sticks with him, Remi thinks.

"Dad." Buzz catches sight of him, sobers instantly. "What are you doing here?"

Remi raises his glass. "Said it yourself, Buzz. My home away from home. What about you? What are you boys up to?"

"Swillathon, sir." Remi recognizes Roy Clarion's voice, a college friend of Buzz's, his father an occasional tennis partner, though never Remi's first choice. The boy extends his hand. "How are you, Mr. Potts?"

"Roy." Remi shakes his hand. "Good to see you. Say hi to your old man for me, will you? Tell him the old tennis elbow's been acting up but I'll give him a call. What'd you say you fellows are up to?"

"Swillathon," Roy says again. "A class of 1963 tradition. Our own variation on Groundhog Day. One beer at every bar on Mass Ave from MIT to the Arlington Line. If we're still standing at the end of the night, winter's over. This is just a little detour. Buzz wanted to come here. In your honor, I guess, sir."

"In my honor," Remi says with a laugh. "How thoughtful."

"This is our eighth stop," Roy says. "We're taking notes—the darkness of the beer, number of pisses—"

"Quite an ambitious mission." Remi looks over at Buzz. "Worthy of the finest Harvard alum." He raises his glass. "Well, boys. Here's to your swillathon. Here's to your success."

"Thanks, Mr. Potts." Roy backs away, embarrassed. "Good to see you again, sir. Really great seeing you."

Buzz hangs back while his friends grab a table and order a pitcher of beer. "So how are you, Dad?" He glances at the two empty glasses on the bar.

"I'm holding up quite well, actually," Remi says. "How those business classes going, Buzz?"

"They're fine. I'm learning a lot."

"I need you this weekend, Buzz," Remi says. "With Nash out of the picture. Can I count on you Saturday morning for inventory, seven o'clock sharp?"

"I'll be there." Buzz puts his hand on his father's arm. "You heading home now, Dad? You had enough?"

Remi gives him a hard look. "How many bars you been to tonight, Buzz? Eight was it? And how many more to go?"

Buzz shrugs and turns away. "Okay, then. I'll see you later," he says quietly.

"Hey, don't be a stranger at the house. Your mother misses you, Buzz. Stop by and visit sometime, when you don't have dirty laundry. You don't need an invitation. The door's always open. Your mother misses you. So does your brother."

"Okay, Dad. I'll stop by soon. For a visit. No dirty laundry, I promise. Okay?"

Remi sits at the bar with his back to the boys, listening to their laughter, their careless banter, remembering these sounds of ribbing and revelry as the most rousing, comforting noises of his life. He should get up, he knows, slap a few bucks on the counter, buy the boys another round, and wave to Buzz as he heads for the door. He shouldn't embarrass himself any further, embarrass his son. Any good father would get the hell out of there, take his cue along with his dignity and skedaddle. But Remi's never been versed in the graceful exit, adept at the mindful swing of fate. He feels Buzz's eyes burning holes in his back. And yet it's all he can do to keep himself from going over to ask if he can join the boys on their swillathon, go on to the next bar, the next beer, and the next. It would be all he could do not to tell a dirty joke or punch one of them in the gut if he got looked at the wrong way. He keeps his eyes straight ahead, his back straight, his ears tuned, listening to the boys, to the music, to the clink of glasses and the scraping of chairs, long after they've gone, until he's the only one left in the bar.

"One last scotch on the rocks," he says steadily to the bartender. "And while you're at it—"

"I know, pal," the bartender says softly. "Make it a double."

"Thanks for coming, Janie," Violet says. "You're a lifesaver. Amy's sick and the new girl didn't work out. It's the Valentine's Day rush. And with your father under my feet, I'm way behind on everything. I knew I could count on you."

"Yeah, you know me." Janie takes off her loden coat. "Good old, cherry-flavored, dependable Jane."

"It's nothing to be ashamed of, you know." Violet slits open a carton of envelopes with a knife. "Being dependable."

"Speaking of being dependable..." Janie hangs up her coat. "I got a promotion at the bank. I'm head teller, now. I matter, Ma. I count. Big word in a bank—count. You get it? Today I was told I have a future in finance. That's what you always wanted for me, wasn't it? A future?"

"That's wonderful!" Violet's face beams. "You always were so good at math, so focused, so organized. I knew you'd pull yourself together, Janie. I knew you'd come around."

"Yeah," Janie says. "Middle child. The striver. The coper. I wear my little pantsuit to work every day and do my little job and smile. Talk about an anachronism. Just when the whole corporate world is crumbling, I'm climbing up the shaky ladder of bourgeois success. Just a matter of time before the whole system collapses and I fall flat on my behind. I never did fit in. I was born into the wrong era, the wrong family. I'm convinced of that."

"Middle children often feel squeezed," Violet says. "Neglected, put upon. They shoulder their own burdens, but believe me, it's a blessing as much as a curse. I was the baby, Janie. You never get over being the baby. No one ever really treats you any other way."

"Like Chickie."

"I'm worried about Chickie. I really am."

"Chickie would be fine if you just left her alone." Janie bends down to straighten up the notepads. "And you can thank me now for never giving you a moment's worry."

"That's not true."

"When did you ever worry about me? And I mean really worry. About *me*. Not about how I looked, or how I was behaving, or reflecting on the family, or—"

"That time your appendix almost burst," Violet says. "We had to rush you to the hospital. You were ten. I was worried sick."

"Best week of my life," Janie says. "I ate ice cream every day. You bought me *Little Lulu* comics and brushed my hair. I was in heaven."

"You gained ten pounds." Vi sighs. "I had to starve you for a month."

"Yeah, you always kept me from falling off the edge, Ma. Of being too lazy, too forward, too fat. Look at the name you gave me. Talk about a self-fulfilling prophecy."

"I was reading Jane Austen at the time. It's such a wonderfully good and simple name."

"Good and simple." Janie starts to organize the photo albums. "I rest my case. Doomed to mediocrity. Right from the start."

"Good and simple in the best sense of those words," Vi says. "Good lord, why must everyone in this family hate her name so much?"

"Let's review here," says Janie. "Minerva, Persephone, and *Jane?*"

"You may not know this," Violet says. "But I saved you from a far worse fate. Your father wanted to name you Esmerelda, after some old maiden aunt of his. Would that have been better?"

"Esmerelda?" Janie considers this. "Sure. Why not? Cinderella. Snow White. Little Lulu. Anything, really. But Jane?"

"Okay, so I doomed you." Violet slaps price tags on stapler boxes with her labeling gun. "So, tell me, Snow White," she says. "How is everything else? How is—"

"Warren? My beau? The man I'm stepping out with?"

"Yes. How is Warren, Janie?"

"Warren, the man I'm dating whose skin is a different color than mine? The man I'm—"

"I was just asking."

"Well, Warren's still Black, I'm afraid." Janie puts the staples on the shelves. "We've tried putting him out in the sun to bleach, but he just keeps getting darker. We can't quite figure it out."

"I never said a word," Violet says quietly.

"You haven't had to," Janie says. "What goes unsaid in this family could fill a whole set of World Book Encyclopedias. I saw how uncomfortable everyone was when I brought Warren to Chickie's dance recital."

"So then, speak up, middle child." Violet's eyes are suddenly clear. "How's Warren?"

"He's great." Janie meets her mother's gaze head on. "You know, he's great at dancing, basketball. All sports, really. And he's such a great kisser. You know what they say—"

"Where all of you get this disgusting strain, this hostility," Violet says.

"Apple doesn't fall far," Janie says, reaching for another pack of staples.

"What's that supposed to mean?" Violet says.

"Oh god, nothing, Ma," Janie says. "It doesn't really mean anything. I'm the middle child, remember? I've got a monster chip on my shoulder. I'm tired, put-upon. I lash out. I'm angry. Resentful. Sarcastic. It's my nature. Warren's just fine."

Violet unpacks a box of felt-tip markers. "I really am worried about Chickie, Janie. She's drifting, she's reckless. She flunked her French midterm and she's been cutting school. I never thought this would be a concern, but she's even missed a few dance classes."

"You have to lighten up, Ma," Janie says. "Be the grown-up. Let Chickie go through her own adolescence. If you've got to relive yours, do it on your own time. Don't play games with her mind."

"I *am* lightening up. God forbid I should have to relive my adolescence. And I am *certainly* not playing games with Chickie's mind."

"Stop trying to make her into the next Joan of Arc. Just accept it, Ma. You've got normal, run-of-the-mill kids. None of us is ever going to save the world."

"Including me, Snow White. Please try and remember that." Violet finishes stacking the accounting pads, catches that shadow again in the corner of her eye, the shadow that tricks her every time, the shadow of the man in the trench coat, the faceless man no more. Now, of course, the face is Charlie's, full-lipped, greedy, always hungry Charlie. It's odd, though. For the first time, the image is blurry and leaves her cold. "So tell me." She looks up at Janie. "Are you seeing anyone else besides Warren?"

"Yeah, actually," Janie says. "His twin brother, Walter."

"What?"

"Just kidding, Ma." Janie raises her hands in surrender, smiles a tired smile. "Sudden, involuntary, middle-child madness. Just can't help myself sometimes."

Hen's barely spoken to his father since that night in October after Andy Gardner died. The logic may not be sound. But after your father hits your mother, what's there really left to say? Who knows what good his vow of silence has done—for his mother, for him, for any of them. Now it's about to be broken. He was on his way over to talk to Nash about the draft when a twist in his stomach bent him over double and turned him around. The more time he spends with his uncle, the more his father seems to fade. Hen's had an eerie sense lately that he's losing his father, and it scares him.

With a heave of his left shoulder, Hen pushes through the swinging door. On the other side, Remi's watching the news. "Hey, Dad," he says. "Can we talk?"

Remi straightens up in his chair. "Sure we can talk, son. Absolutely. What's on your mind?"

"My draft lottery comes up in July," Hen says. "And the war's still out of control."

"No one likes the idea of war, Hen. Nash isn't the only one."

"So why do they exist?"

"It's human nature. We're an aggressive species and our survival instincts are strong. Never underestimate them." He gestures around the room with his sweating drink glass, as if the answers could be found within, in the glare of the glass coffee table, the gloss of the Matisse print. "Wars are usually about something, Hen." He shrugs. "Wars get results."

"What's this one about?"

"South Vietnam's a tiny, helpless country under Communist siege."

Remi leans forward in his chair. "It can't defend itself. It can't survive without our help."

That's what you've always thought about me, Hen thinks to himself but does not say out loud to his father. "But how do we know that?"

"The facts bear it out," Remi says. "The numbers."

"The numbers say they're being decimated. Not to mention our side. Over thirty thousand dead so far."

"Wars have casualties, Hen." Remi leans back in his chair. "It's inevitable. Bottom line, they need our help."

"Did they ask for it?"

"In the beginning?" Remi pauses. "I really don't know. But the point is, we had to step in. We're the biggest superpower on the planet. We've got the money, the manpower, the technology. These people's liberties were being threatened, Hen. It was our responsibility, our moral imperative, to come to their aid."

"But what about the moral imperative of not taking another human life? How do those people feel when they see American soldiers coming into their villages? They don't know if they're going to get fed or bombed. Why can't Nixon just pull out? Stop the killing. Spend the money helping them to organize, rebuild? Bankroll the farmers, build houses and schools. Wouldn't that be the morally responsible thing to do?"

"Nixon inherited one hell of mess, Hen. He's doing the best he can."

"What would Kennedy have done?" Hen says. It's the question his mother always asks, as if the answer were the prism through which all truth shone.

"Kennedy?" For a moment, Remi confuses his son with his brother—the same outrage smoking from his ears, the same relentless, needling questions. He feels the same crumpled way he always does when he talks politics with Nash—battered, defensive, defeated before he's even begun. His brain's not all of a piece; he can't hold his own. His son has important questions, and he has no good answers. Remi relives that November day—the surreal footage on TV, Jackie waving in her pillbox hat, the crowd, the smiling, propped-up hero in the slowly moving car. He remembers trying to track the piece of Kennedy's head as it flew off the convertible, as they replayed the Zapruder tape on the news, over and over and over again. He wraps his hand around his drink glass and looks over at Hen. He's out of answers. He hasn't been much of a father. He's never really known how to take care of them. And so, another side of the imposter is revealed.

Remi runs his hand through his hair, considers his latest failure. When you have sons, you must prepare them to be men, accept the fact that they may have to go to war. The draft board left Buzz alone, the oldest son, with a physical impairment. But there's nothing to stop them from coming for Hen. He's a healthy, all-American, red-blooded boy. If there weren't a war on, the service might actually be a good thing for him, to build his confidence, his manhood. Hen doesn't have a girlfriend yet. Strange. Maybe. Or maybe not so strange in this age of free love and peace or whatever the hell it is. At his age, Remi was fumbling around with girls in the back seats of cars, whether he wanted to or not—call it pleasure, torture, pride. He remembers Marcia Lacey's cool lips and hot hands and shivers. *It doesn't really mean anything,* she said. *You know, about being a man.*

Remi takes another sip of his drink, arranges his words carefully. "Kennedy manned a PT boat in the Pacific, Hen. He was a leader, a damn good soldier. He led his troops into battle with an unflinching eye; he had to make some tough choices."

"The lottery's a crapshoot. I don't get a choice, do I?"

Remi rubs his forehead with the back of his thumb. He doesn't want to answer any more questions with "I don't know." He wants his son to be responsible. He'd like him to be brave. Remi just wants to be the good guy, the good father. Just for once, he'd like his son to look up to him, to trust him. But on this night, drunk too fast and still trembling from what happened at Potts Pro earlier that day, Remi's on edge. He screamed at Brian in the stockroom, the kid who works for them at the store. *Imbecile! You goddamned incompetent idiot!* The echoes, only just now, with the third glass of whiskey, are growing faint in his brain. Brian lost a receipt and Remi felt the old rage swell up inside him, the same fury he felt when Nash got the red pocketknife for his birthday, when Cammie came back to the track after having the mumps, when Faye moved the lamp. He can feel it coming now, but always too late, rushing up from inside him like a hydrant uncapped, love and reason gone terribly askew, muddy, rusty, gushing. Brian looked so scared, a big, easygoing kid. Tears filled his eyes and Remi felt not remorse but disdain, and he knew it was the wrong reaction, but still he'd kept on feeling it as Brian blinked and stammered. He'd scared the kid. No one had ever screamed at him that way. There were no such people left in the world like him, screaming middle-aged madmen in Adidas sweatsuits with pot bellies and thinning hair. Nash just happened to be in the store. It was one of his first days back at work. He came into the stockroom then, the echoes of Remi's outburst beating bat wings in the air.

"Looking for this, Bri?" Nash held up a piece of paper.

"You found it?" Brian's voice shook with relief. "You found the receipt?"

"$8.99. Pair of ski poles. Must have fallen from the register when you took that call," Nash said. "No big deal."

"Thanks." Brian looked back and forth from one twin to another. "Thanks a lot, Mr. Potts. I really appreciate it. I must've—"

"No sweat." Nash slapped Brian on the back. "Listen, why don't you go out back and unpack that crate of swimming goggles, okay?"

"Okay," Brian said. "Sure. Okay. Thanks a lot, Mr. Potts. I'll do that."

"You all right, Rem?" Nash asked, when they were alone.

"Yeah, sure," Remi said. "I'm fine."

"It was nothing, Rem," Nash put his hand on his brother's arm. "$8.99 Men's Active. Ski poles. It fell. Gravity. Never stops. Not on this planet anyway. Happens all the time."

"I know." Remi held Nash's gaze, repeating the calm, steady words. "It was nothing. Ski poles. $8.99. It fell. I know, Nash. Gravity. All the time. I know."

"Brian's a good kid, Rem." Nash's grip tightened. "He does a good job. It's no big deal. These things happen."

"I know, Nash. I know they do, damn it."

"You didn't do anything—"

"No, I didn't." Remi tried to pull his arm free. "Ease up, Nash. Give me a goddamned break. I've been under a lot of pressure lately. With you getting your head cracked open and—"

"The hell with all that," Nash says. "Did you touch the kid or not?"

"I told you, I didn't touch him."

"Good." Nash relaxed his hold. "You could lose it all, brother, you know that, don't you? In one fell swoop, it could all be gone. You know what's at stake here, don't you? And I'm not just talking about Brian."

Remi shook his arm free. "I'm not an idiot, Nash."

Nash nodded, his jaw relaxing. "No problem then. We're going to the Celtics game on Tuesday, right? You get takeoff clearance from Faye? Everything okay between you two?"

"Sure. Why wouldn't it be?"

"Just asking."

"Everything's fine."

"Okay then." Nash slapped Remi on the back. "Knicks, Rem. It's gonna be a hell of a game. Why don't you go on out and tell Brian you're sorry. You're okay. You're fine. Just tell him you didn't mean anything, that you're tired, running a little ragged. You hear me? You listening to me, Rem?"

"I hear you," Remi said. "I goddamned heard you, Nash."

Remi breathes deeply. It *was* okay. He'd made it right. He went out back, apologized to Brian, said he was tired, on edge. He told a story of a similar screwup he'd made at a similar age, threw in a raunchy joke for good measure. Brian laughed, a little tentatively, but still, he'd laughed. Remi'd made it right. It won't happen again. He won't let it. He heard the warning in his brother's voice. And he *does* know what's at stake. It scares him—all of it—the maniacal spurts of anger, the gambling, Cammie—the risks he's been taking lately. He's got to keep his head on straight, keep his cool. It won't happen again. It can't. He'll surround himself with the people he cares about, those who count on him to act a certain way, to be a certain kind of man. They'll keep his fists clenched, the demons in check, the primal roar muffled. Remi's always believed he has it in him to kill someone, but never in front of anyone who thought better of him. The task ahead of him is simple, clear. He must arrange never to be alone. He needs his brother, his wife, his daughter. He needs his sons. And goddamn it, he still needs Cammie; he still needs his goddamned whore.

"Listen, Hen." Remi puts his drink glass down. "Let's not worry until we have to. We've got some time before the draft. Maybe by the summer, this will all be academic."

"And if it's not?"

"If it's not?" Remi repeats. "There are ways, Hen—tactics, loopholes. Maybe you're color-blind. Or maybe you have flat feet. I'll get in touch with Phil Gardner. Jesus, did I ever call him after—"

"You don't even know if I have flat feet?"

Remi takes another sip of whiskey and lifts his chin. The alcohol levels him then, leaving him defenseless, defensive. "Don't make me feel like such a crumb, Hen. Women know these things about their children, for god's sake."

"What do fathers know about their children?" Hen doesn't know which way to send the spike of his fury, into his father's dull eyes or better to shatter the glass in his hand. He doesn't know why he keeps at him this way, why he even bothers.

"Fathers know things like..." Remi waves his hand in the air, wedding ring tight on his finger. "Like when you got your first haircut or how many home runs you hit in Little League."

"I never played Little League."

"Okay. Bad example. Sorry."

"So when did I get my first haircut?" Hen fires out the question.

"I took you to Gino's on Mass Ave," Remi says. "You hopped right up onto that chair—"

"That was Buzz," Hen says. "Mom used to cut my hair with a bowl to save money. I looked like a freak."

"Yeah, you did. Sorry about that, old man. I should've put my foot down." Remi rubs his forehead, suppresses a smile. "Fathers live on the outer rim, Hen, don't you see? They get left out. They're pariahs, really. You think I even know if *I* have flat feet? Believe me, no one ever told me."

Hen stares at his father, the limp wrist stiffening for the last watery gulp of booze, TV news blaring in the background. Faye passes by and squeezes Hen's arm as she heads for the kitchen, dressed in jeans and a blue work shirt. "I'm not really here, honey," she says. "Just home to change and make dinner. Then I'm off to the studio again." Remi turns up the volume on the TV. Hen knows what to expect from here on in. Faye has a ceramics show coming up in a downtown gallery in May. Any time she's not teaching, she'll be working on her own pieces. The house is a mess, dirty laundry piled high, dishes in the sink, petrified flowers on the mantel. Faye will open a few cans for dinner and leave the warm pots on the stove, then disappear back to Clay City, a place that reminds Hen more and more of a morgue, the cold lumps of clay on newspaper, the gaunt potters and spattered stools. And his father will sulk and mutter like a little boy until it's all over.

Hen stands between his father, sunk in the armchair, and his mother, banging pots and pans in the kitchen. The war news on TV isn't good. Another village massacre. Countless civilian casualties. Rampant drug use. Troop morale at an all-time low. A shot of local war protesters flashes on the screen, holding signs and placards and chanting, "Hell, no. We won't go." During an aspirin ad, little white balls of pain tumble from a chute into a man's aching head. Hen looks out the glass patio door into the coming darkness. He'll serve himself dinner and put his dishes in the sink. In the morning, the kitchen will be clean, as clean as Faye gets things these days, and no matter where the night's taken her, she'll be back to make him breakfast before school. Hen feels an ache rise in his own head as the man in the TV ad pops two pills. Slowly, the white balls of pain disappear. "Hell no," Hen says, pushing through the swinging door. "I can't go."

In the olive house, as Nash recovers, he keeps the deck of cards shuffled. He never knows when Faye will slip in for a game of cards. He likes her quiet company. It soothes him. Since the accident he's more sensitive—to noise, to hot and cold, to everything, it seems. He's tired, more tired than he ever used to be. Vi's efficient, nurse-like devotion, her shrill voice and brash stride are just too much sometimes. The girls fussing, trying to make him laugh—monkey imitations and elephant jokes. Remi's pacing and ranting. He needs a break sometimes, from all of them, from their boisterous, sloppy love. "Hey," Faye always says softly when she comes in. The rest is mostly pantomime. She holds up the pack of cards. He nods. She shuffles. And deals. They play. One wins, one loses. They grimace and moan. She shuffles. Wags a warning finger. He pumps his fists. He smiles. "Hey." Sometimes they don't even say another word.

9

A Saturday in April dawns still and gray. Hen wakes up early, lies in bed and plays out a Lasker game on his magnetic chess set. On his way downstairs he can smell his sister, Tory, in the hallway—incense, leather suitcase, perfume. She must have arrived sometime during the night. In the kitchen, his parents clatter around, getting ready to go to Nantucket to open up the summer cottage. Nash and Violet went last year. Now, it's Faye and Remi's turn. Hen goes out to the driveway in his jeans, bare-chested, barefooted. The gravel scrunches under his tender feet. He leans against the rusty Saab as his father closes the trunk. The sun slinks low behind dark clouds. His parents start to argue about the clothes they've packed, the wind chill factor on the ferry, how much wood got left in the woodpile, whether the seagulls like peanut butter sandwiches, which Faye has packed for lunch.

"I made those sandwiches for us, Remi," she says, arranging a paper bag full of food in the front seat. "Not for the darned seagulls."

"Gee, Mom, that's pretty strong language," Hen says. "My virgin ears and all."

"You've got beautiful ears," Faye murmurs, looking over at him fondly. "A sign of good breeding. Be good, honey."

"What else could I be?" Hen motions back to the house with a toss of his head. "The warden's here."

"Such bad timing." Faye sighs. "Tory comes home so rarely now. And she's no sooner here than we have to leave. Try and be civil, will you, Hen? She is your sister, after all."

"I will if she will," Hen says.

"Have some fun, old man." Remi slaps Hen on the back. He turns away from his father's wink, his hopeful smile. He smells the liquor on his breath already, or maybe still. Best way to beat a hangover is to surprise the hell out of it first thing in the morning, Remi claims. Feed it a goddamned beer for breakfast. Hen pats the hood and waves as Faye backs slowly out of the driveway, still afraid, after all these years, of the rude Boston drivers, the rotaries and mazes of potholed, jackknifing streets, still the girl who grew up riding the straight, wide avenues of Lansing, Michigan, in her father's Pontiac. Remi sits sullen beside her on the edge of his seat, hunched up against the window. Hen can almost hear the silence settle in the space between them over the bag of lunch, the smell of brown paper, jelly-saturated bread, over-ripe fruit. He's lived enshrouded in this thick and turning silence for so many years.

"Have fun, kids," he says, as the Saab pulls out onto Hemlock Street.

Hen walks back to the house. He has no underwear on and his jeans chafe at the crotch. A zit on the back of his neck is erupting and something funky lurks between his toes. He's grown almost six inches since the fall. The late bloomer thing. He's ended up tall, how rare is another matter. Laughter comes from the kitchen. Peering in through the screen door, he sees Tory and the back of another girl's head. She arrived late in the night, as she always does, when everybody else was asleep. She lives in New York in what Remi calls the Pillbox Palace, a studio apartment on Riverside Drive, works in a publishing house going through the slush pile, and models raincoats for London Fog on the side. She rides the night train to Boston, not often, without warning, always with a sidekick, a disciple, a friend.

"Hey, little brother," Tory calls out. "Come meet Melody."

Hen stuffs his hands into his pockets and pushes the door open with one shoulder. "Hey, Melody," he says to the girl's back.

"Hey, yourself," Melody says, turning around in her chair.

Hen will forever be able to conjure up that first good look of Melody with a jolt of deep-down, almost frightening pleasure—black curly hair, full lips, bushy eyebrows, an overbite. Her laugh fills the dingy kitchen; she has nothing to hide, including the biggest breasts he's ever seen, braless in a lavender T-shirt.

Hen pours himself some Shredded Wheat and sits down at the table with the girls. Tory picks at her unbuttered toast. She's supposed to be very beautiful, but Hen's reminded of this only when he looks closely at her. Her hair's a true jet black, straight and shiny, parted razor-blade clean on the side. Her face is as smooth and chalky white as the inside of a clam shell, her eyes a stinging blue. One of her top front teeth is twisted ever so slightly, jeans pressed, shirt sleeves folded up over her wrist bones—Tory, just, just so.

"So how's John?" Hen keeps asking, just to bug her, even though he knows they broke up in the fall. He and John played chess by mail for a while. He sent Hen a few chess articles, a few friendly notes. He's been meaning to write John a letter, to thank him for turning him on to chess, to ask for another postal game, but he's not sure John would understand, that he's different, not like Tory.

"John's ancient history, little brother," Tory says. "I keep telling you that." She turns to Melody. "A little bit of denial going on here. You see, long ago, in a faraway land, John was Henny's hero, his knight on a shining chessboard."

"The psych guy?" Melody says. "The one who told you you had sadomasochistic tendencies?"

"You got it. Mr. Holier-than-me. Mr. Stick-up-his—"

"John was the only guy you ever went out with who wasn't a jerk," Hen says.

"This from Casanova himself," Tory says, and Melody laughs.

In that instant, when Tory smiles that chilling smile, her tongue sliding out from behind the one crooked tooth, Hen sees it—the cold, blinding beauty of that face. Even his friends from school whistle low under their breath when they look at her senior picture hanging on the living room wall, speak her name as if they might break it. But when Tory's smile disappears across the kitchen table in the pale green morning light, Hen can only see how she's a part of his family, how they all look like broken-off sea glass pieces of the twins.

"Melody's from Virginia," Tory says. "She's come to Boston to see the sights. Faneuil Hall and the Old North Church. How'd you like to play Paul Revere today, Henny? Show her around the town."

"I can't," Hen says. "Sorry."

"Not in the mood to walk the Freedom Trail?" Melody spears a chunk of canned pineapple with her fork, raises her bushy eyebrows.

"I don't even know where it starts," Hen says, his face reddening. "Or where it goes. Or where the hell it ends."

"Over the river and through the Combat Zone," Tory says. "Just follow the little red bricks. See where John and Mildred Hancock got it on, where Sam Adams powdered his wig. It's a gas."

"Sounds like a lot of fun, Tor," Hen says. "But I'm busy. No offense," he says to Melody.

"None taken." She stabs another piece of pineapple.

"We're having a little get-together tonight," Tory says. "While the cats are away and all that jazz."

"Meow," Melody says, looking over at Hen. There's something rich and almost disgusting about her, like frosting ankle high on a cake.

"If you're around later, I mean if you're not too busy playing Tiddly

Winks or Spin the Bottle," Tory says. "Come on down, brother, and we'll get you high."

Hen looks down into his bowl of soggy Shredded Wheat. He wishes he'd put his T-shirt on. He can't stop looking at Melody's breasts and he knows how red his face must be. He's glad his father isn't here. Remi would've waited until the cocktail hour and then started to make conversation, make eyes at Melody, make a fool of himself.

"Man, it's a mess around here." He gets up from the table and pours his cereal down the disposal. The sink is stained brown; the sponge smells like overripe cheese. He opens the cabinet doors while the disposal whirs and takes out the Ajax. The scouring pad is like a mass of wet cat fur, dripping with bubbly blue detergent. Hen scrubs the sink clean, puts the breakfast things away, wipes the counters clean, squishes dead six milling ants.

"Henny the Homemaker," Tory says. "Someday you'll make some girl a—"

"I'm out of here." Hen grabs his jacket and heads for the door.

"Where you going?" Tory calls out. "Hen. Wait!"

Hen slams the door, stands silent for a moment, back pressed against the house, catches his breath, listens.

"My, oh my, where did he come from, Tor?" Melody's voice slides out through the screen door.

"Venus," Tory says and they laugh again. "Jupiter. The Land of Nod. How the hell do I know? He's our little alien. My parents' last little roll in the hay. Our favorite six-foot martian."

"Beam me up, Scottie," Melody says in a voice low to a groan. "Oh, lordy, beam me right on up."

Later that afternoon, Hen walks home from the basketball court along the river's edge, dribbling a ball. A few warm days have dredged up the river bottom's smell; the shore's lined with oil slicks and rusty metal and trash. Plato, the street poet from the Square, is pushing a shopping cart up the river path. "Doesn't matter, matter." Plato's head jerks rhythmically as he approaches. "No matter what you do to try and stop it, they gonna do it. Do it. Do it Boy-o. Baby. Do it!"

"Do it." Hen hails him as he passes with a raised fist. "Right on, Plato, man."

Back on Hemlock Street, all is quiet. Hen goes upstairs to take a shower, watches the sweat and dirt pour off him in chutes. Thinking of

Melody's tits, he jacks off as the hot water pummels his back. Wrapping a towel around his waist, he goes down the hallway to his room. The window's sash cord is frayed almost to the breaking point. The pulley between his and Chickie's window lies slack. No sign of life across the way. She's hardly ever home anymore, sneaks out of the house at night and disappears with Elvis. He sometimes hears the Norton revving down below in the nether hours and, strangely enough, thinks of Violet, the old nursery rhyme churning round and round in his head. *Are the children in their beds? For now it's eight o'clock.* He dozes off, wakes up to the uneasy dusk, feeling thirsty and little-boy strange. He wonders if his parents are having any fun in Nantucket. He worries for them, wonders how they'll manage overnight without him. This is the first time they've gone away alone together since the slap. Hen's been watching his father carefully—a husband on parole, being tested and proven all over again. His mother's different now, stronger, more distant. But his father's still hopelessly in love.

After Buzz and Tory went off to college, the three of them would go to the cottage in Nantucket on the spur of the moment sometimes, catching the last Friday ferry. He'd get dragged along, but he wouldn't really mind. There was a kind of lonely pleasure in it for him. He'd linger behind his parents as they walked on the beach, picking up shells and seaweed and snatches of their scattered, married conversation. They'd go to the Cliffside Diner for fried clams and soft, swirling ice cream in soggy waffle cones, watch the mango sun slip behind the dunes. He'd go to bed in his clothes with a scratchy layer of salt on him, the smells of the fire and garlic bread and old starfish lingering. He'd feel safe and almost happy, relieved as he lay in bed and heard the door next to his close and then slip open again, the black iron latch slipping out of its groove, as the bedsprings started to creak, for that was love, wasn't it, what went on in that sagging, island bed—the sudden, salty silence, the low, halting groans? Hen rolls over on his back. He can barely remember when his parents used to sleep together. Now his father lies sprawled across the master bed, a body that knows it won't be sharing the space. The bed never gets made; the sheets rarely get changed. His mother moves around the house at night like a vagabond, out into the yard with the old kiln burning, falling into different beds at all hours—the abandoned beds—Buzz's and Tory's—the guest room rollaway, the couch, and back out at dawn to check the kiln. She sleeps in her clothes and changes later in the morning, or the next day, just the shirt maybe, or clean jeans. At meals the three of them sit in lockjaw silence.

On Hemlock Street, love is sick, dying, lost in the crack of the swinging door. A few days ago, Remi tried to find it at the dinner table. Hen remembers with a wince. Remi'd had more whiskey than usual, or maybe more *was* usual now. Out of the blue he leaned over his plate to give Faye a kiss. They'd had a big fight the day before, which started out about the shape of Utah and ended up about trust. Hen watched as his father gathered his courage to try and make things right, held his breath as Remi leaned forward. Just before his lips reached Faye's cheek, she moved just so. He lost his balance and his elbow landed in his plate of mashed potatoes. His mother said, "Honestly, Remi. What was that all about?" Remi dabbed clumsily at his shirt with a frayed linen napkin, embroidered with their curlicued, married initials. Hen can't remember ever feeling so angry at his mother. She had every right to harden the oobleck of his father's leaking heart with those few cruel words. But maybe it wouldn't have killed her to let him kiss her cheek, just that one time. Maybe his father was sorry…has been sorry…long enough. Even if he is a jerk and a drunk and a coward sometimes. Even if he did hit her that one time.

As long as it was only that one time.

Hen saw the look in his father's eyes as he wiped his elbow clean. He knew what his father feared, that he might never kiss Faye again, and where did that leave any of them? He understood how hard it had been for Remi, that clumsy stab at a kiss, how stupid, how brave, what a big risk he'd taken. Now he might never have the courage or the heart to try again. Hen can understand. Love could die as easily in a plate of mashed potatoes as anywhere else.

Slipping on a pair of jeans, Hen goes downstairs and eats all of the odd bits of cereal left in the boxes, which Faye can never throw away until the last crumbling flakes are gone. In the end, only the Grape Nuts box is still half full. Tory and Melody get ready for their party, filling bowls with pretzels and potato chips, arranging pillows on the floor, incense in the ashtrays, sipping Kahlua straight up as they go. Hen makes himself a bowl of Lipton's chicken noodle soup, dunks a stale English muffin, and considers his options for the night. He could go into the Square, cruise the Ale House with his fake ID, play the Game, or chase down a chess game in the courtyard, but he might run into Chickie and Elvis, and he doesn't need that. Or he could stay home and get stoned with Tory, watch the Bruins. With Orr's knees in good shape, this could definitely be the year.

Darkness drops softly into the backyard. The doorbell starts to ring. Tory's guests arrive, drifting into Faye's living room like a straggling ill wind, snooping, settling in, sprawling on the sofa, hefting their sandaled feet onto the chairs, dipping into Remi's Lucky Strikes as if they'd spent the fifty-three cents themselves. They make fun of the furniture, the artwork, Faye's clay pieces on the shelf, the goofy school pictures on the wall. Far out. Funky. Fantastic. Freudian. They examine the clutter—empty matchbooks and egg cartons, oatmeal boxes and ancient travel brochures, an armoire of miniature things—ceramic cats, wheelbarrows, tools, magazines piled high, leaves found in the fall and never pressed between wax paper, an empty tinfoil box, a crushed silver spoon, things once slated for a purpose, now out of work, all come to rest in Faye's gallery of the useless.

"Man." A girl with striped bell-bottoms and a poor-boy T-shirt leafs through a *Life* magazine on the couch. "These people are heavy into things."

Hen feels a rush of dull and fierce love for his mother, for the home she's tried to make, a fury at these people who dare to laugh at someone they don't even know, someone as fine as his mother could be. He wants to say "get the fuck out of here. All of you." He feels his mother's angry gray eyes flash upon this scene, invisible among them, slender hands on slender hips, a how-dare-you look in her eyes that would have driven them all away in stampede style. He sits down on the sofa with a book called *Chess Praxis.* Slowly the room fills, all strangers to Hen, not the friends Tory knew in high school. Where they come from he can't imagine. They must follow her from all the places she's been, like rats trailing a piece of exotic cheese. The gravel driveway fills with VW bugs, a motorcycle, a mail truck, Fords, a rusty Karmann Ghia, a silver XKE, and an old Dodge. A few people come right off the street. Tory greets them at the door in a sleeveless purple minidress, a silver choker, blood red lipstick, a flicking, sharp tongue. "Hello, Adler." She grazes a nervous boy's cheek with thin lips, hair falling in a slanted, razor-straight line. "It's been a while since we knew each other when. Don't squirm. You passed muster." She looks out of place among them, so neat and prim, slithering among them like a painted snake.

Melody mingles, in a low-cut Indian-print blouse and pants that billow from the thigh down, barefooted. Hen's eyes fix on the swell of her breasts, follow the sway of her broad hips as she moves. She dances alone in the living room, singing into the microphone of her fist with her eyes closed to Billie Holiday, her mouth set as if in pain. Next to Melody, the other girls look sexless. They wear hip-hugging bell-bottoms and shirts that ride up over their navels. Their stomachs are flat and creamy, breasts pointy and small, no bras. Slender hands, small wrists, headbands pressing oily bangs against high foreheads, beads hanging heavy on willowy chests. From where Hen sits, Melody's the only 3-D girl in the room.

The boys wear ragged, worn blue jeans, denim stretched and nearly white at the crotch, silken shirts, leather, army fatigues. Greasy hair hangs over the ledges of thick brows. Jeans hang off skinny asses, leather belts with handmade silver buckles, thick-strapped sandals, hairy toes. Hen can suddenly imagine how man evolved from the apes and the apes from the anteaters, how they all used to be nothing more than thumping dots of light in the universe and still aren't really much more. There's hair everywhere. Smoke and sweat. Eyes burn bright; voices drag low. In the end, trying to look different, they all end up looking the same. Placid, stoned, androgenous. Except for Tory and Melody. Tory's the shiny tin princess in this odd, Cambridge fairy tale and she's turned the rest into her toads. And Melody, as she bobs and weaves through the smoke-filled, strobe-lit room, is the pure, unadulterated song.

Purple and green strobes flash against the wall. Tiny pyramids of incense burn orange at the tip, sending up a thick, sweet smell in slow curls that hover at neck level to Hen. The lights dart across the school pictures on the wall on which home movies used to dance, making flickering monsters of them all—Remi raking leaves, Buzz flexing his muscles (which way to Muscle Beach?), Seph getting stabbed by Janie at the end of one of their family plays, Chickie dancing in a tutu, bowing, blowing kisses, sweet baby Hen, wide-eyed, droopy-diapered, chewing on a leaf. A tall, thin guy comes to the door. He has masses of brown curls and wears a leather vest over his bare chest. He has the gaunt, cocky look of a British rock star, a Keith Richards or a Roger Daltrey. Something about the way Tory's hand lingers on his wrist, the pause after the wisecrack, tells Hen that she has plans. The tall guy knows. He sits down with a pack of Players in Remi's armchair and kicks off his pointed boots. One of them lands at Hen's feet.

"You want this back?" Hen says, picking it up.

"Later," the guy says. "I may be here for a while. I'm Ferris, man. Who are you?"

"I'm her brother." Hen gestures to Tory. "I live here."

"No shit," the tall guy says. "I never knew Victoria did the family thing. She always seemed like one of those princesses up in the ivory tower, you know what I mean? A lonely only. Are there more of you?"

"We've got a brother." Hen points to a picture of Buzz on the wall in his Harvard football jersey.

"Wow," the guy says. "A regular, upstanding, up-its-ass, Ivy League family. No offense, man. Three pretty kids all in a row, all gone to pot and beyond. Where're Mom and Pop WASP?"

"Nantucket," Hen says. "Opening up the summer cottage."

"Far out," the guy says. "Cambridge Fucking Family Robinson. Now all you need is the tree house."

"We tried that." Hen gestures outside to the yard. "It never really worked out."

Faye's living room is soon a glass-covered box of smoke. Hen opens the patio door to feel the cool night air, squints to adjust his eyes to the dark. The moon is full and circled by a ring of mist. Across the fence, the unfinished tree house stands as if a hidden skeleton in the oak tree. A plane passes by overhead, red lights flashing. White clouds rush by as the music pounds. The Beatles, Grace Slick, Four Tops, Fugs, Temps, Country Joe, Doors, Smokey Robinson, Janis Joplin, Richie Havens, Animals, Strawberry Alarm Clock, Miracles, Cream, Vanilla Fudge. Remi's KLH stereo is on its last legs, bass broken and the balance way off. Still, it rocks and wails. The phone rings. Hen answers it, hoping it will be his mother, but it's just another one of Tory's friends. "Get your ass over here, Randall," she says, leaning against the kitchen wall where they've all been measured in crooked penciled lines all these years, sucking on a big fat joint. "The good pot's almost gone."

In the living room, the stereo blares. The Supremes come on—"Stop in the Name of Love." Melody starts to dance again, gesturing with her hands. Right palm up and out. Three slow, descending clicks of the thumb and middle finger. Another girl gets up and a third one joins them; they shimmy in a line. Right palms up, three clicks down, hands to broken hearts.

Tory comes and sits down beside Hen on the couch. "Melody's got a Diana Ross thing." She licks the edge of the rolling paper to seal another joint. "Skin's not quite the right color, but—"

"I can see that," Hen says.

"What else can you see, Hennie boy?"

"What do you mean?"

"Look into your future, little brother. What do you see?"

"Smoke," Hen says. "Smoke and guns and fire."

"Are you scared?"

"Of what?"

"The black hole, Henry, the great unknown."

"No point," he says. "No way out of a black hole. It swallows you whole."

"Right. That's wisdom in the making. I applaud you," Tory says. "Now, smoke this, little brother." She hands him the joint. "And prepare to die."

Leaving Tory with the roach, Hen grabs what's left of a bag of chips and goes upstairs with his chess book, bringing the portable TV in from his parents' room to his to watch the Bruins game.

During the third period, Melody's head peeks through the door. "You like hockey?"

Hen jumps up from his bed and wipes the greasy chip crumbs from his chest. She's always catching him half naked. He has no shirt on and the snap above his fly's undone. "Yeah, I like hockey," he says.

"My cousin knows one of the Bruins. The big guy with the Frankenstein eyes."

"Bill Preston?"

"Yeah, Preston." Melody comes into the room. "They went to college together, if you want to call it that. Sports Camps for Amazon Ice Freaks is more like it. VCU."

"Really?" He could snap the snap, but maybe she hasn't noticed.

"I could try to get you tickets to a game sometime."

"Far out," Hen says. "I mean, that would be great. Thanks."

Melody comes over and sits on the edge of the armchair piled high with Hen's dirty clothes. "So what did you think of Tory's dope?" she says.

"Great," Hen says. "Really good. It was dynamite."

"Colombian Red," she says. "Not a bad little high, huh?"

"No. Yeah." Hen moves to the edge of his bed. "It was great," he says again.

Melody plays with the silence before she breaks it, winds a curling strand of hair around her finger, grabs her lower lip with her teeth. "Right now I feel like a snake let out of its skin," she says. "How 'bout you, slugger? How do you feel?"

"I feel okay." Hen's eyes turn back to the TV. "Did you ever make it to the Freedom Trail?" he says.

"Parts of it," she says. "Tory played tour guide. We saw a few sights. Boston's a great little town. How old did you say you were?"

"Eighteen." Hen takes a chip out of a bag.

"So what does a guy who's eighteen do in a place like this?" Melody says.

"Play chess, shoot hoops, keep my head above water in school. Bide my time. Wait to see if I get drafted." He blushes, feeling stupid for what he's said. "I'm fair game now. For the war."

"Bummer," Melody says. "They say it's going to be over soon, though, don't they?"

"They say a lot of things. But they're usually wrong." Hen knows she's bored, that he should change the subject. Ask something personal, a friend once advised him on talking to girls. Pretend you're interested. "Do you have any brothers?" he says.

"No. Just girls in my family," Melody says. "One thing my parents knew how to do was make girls."

"How many are there?" Hen asks.

"Five. There's Dawn, Heather, Rose, Daisy, and me, the baby. I did them in apparently. They gave up trying for that boy. He would've been called Stone or Rock or Flint or something. Hey, bring me a chip, will you, Captain Kirk?"

Hen brings her a potato chip, the best one he can fish out of the bag. She opens her mouth. He slides it in. She bites down on it with a crunch.

"Thanks," she says, smiling up at him. "You did that so very well."

Hen stands in front of the TV set, hands stuffed into the pockets of his jeans. The game starts up again. Beginning of the third period. The Chief passes back to Orr, who takes a wicked slapshot. Giacomin, the lucky stiff, makes the save. The puck slides out and Espo takes a quick wrist shot but the puck goes wide. Damn. Hen makes fists in his pockets. If Orr and Espo can't get one past Giacomin on a power play, what are the odds of his making it up here with this girl? He feels his legs buckle. Where have his muscles gone, the ones that showed those Port rats a mean game of ball that afternoon on the riverside court?

Hen looks over at the half-closed door, back at Melody, who's now slid into the armchair on top of his dirty clothes. Her head tilts back and her breasts rise and fall as she breathes. Her fingers play with a gold chain around her neck. Below them, the Stones pound, *12 x 5*. He knows what she's doing. He's only half a fool. No way she's here to talk about sports.

Hen takes a deep, shaky breath. She doesn't understand. For her it's a little thing. For him, it's huge. He'll do it, of course. He has to. It's high time, like his mother always says. He's lucky; he's been given a break. Already it's half-done. They're here. Alone. He's half-naked. She's stoned. She's pretty, not afraid. He's horny, shy, nearly over the hill, desperate. She's nice; she's willing. And built like the Statue of fucking Liberty. So somewhere out there, there must be a god.

Melody reaches for his belt loop and pulls him closer. She runs a finger along the line of hair that runs from his navel downward. He feels every part of himself go stiff. "Are you in the mood?" she says, sing-song. "Are you that kind of boy? Will I be leading you astray?"

"Yeah," Hen says. "I mean, no, yes. Whatever. Jesus Christ." He runs his hand through his hair. "What the fuck."

"Exactly." Melody laughs. "Got any empty beds around here?" She gestures over to his. "Bigger than that one, Captain?"

A few rooms down the hall, Hen opens the door to his parents' bedroom. Inside is the king-sized bed, unmade, a mess of gray, twisted sheets. For a moment, he wishes this were more of a sacred place, not to be disturbed—bed made up clean and tight, pillows plumped, side by side—so he'd have to leave and find another. But by the time he's turned around, Melody's already slid inside and closed the door.

"The master bedroom, eh?" She smiles. "And me here alone with the master. Fancy that. I feel like such a puritan." She starts to undress, sliding off her pants, unbuttoning her shirt, breasts bouncing gently as she moves, shirttails grazing her thighs. She wears no underwear, top or bottom; she knows how good she was made, how good she looks. She walks around the room, lifting up her hair with one finger, bending down to scratch her knee, fingering knickknacks from his mother's dresser, letting him watch her. He stands frozen at the door.

Melody picks up a photograph of Hen and Chickie in a silver frame, the two of them at seven or eight, eating watermelon on the beach in Nantucket.

"Ah, sweet." She wipes a spot on the glass with her finger. "Who's this with you?"

"My cousin," Hen says.

"Cute kid," Melody says.

"She's not a kid anymore," Hen says. He goes over and takes the picture from her, puts it face down on the dresser. Melody hunches up her shoulders and her shirt rides up over her stomach. Hen takes the end of one of the sleeves and pulls. The shirt drops to the floor. She looks at him as if he's finally done something right, goes over and lies down on the bed on her side, completely naked. Hen stands by the dresser, listening to his heart pound, feeling every inch of his body go hard.

"I believe in almost everything," Melody says. "Evolution, revolution, reincarnation." Her southern drawl weaves through the airspace. "But not the immaculate fuck. This can't be much of a happening with you over there, Captain." Melody runs a hand over her belly. "And me over here. All alone."

Hen picks up the photograph again, rubs his finger over Chickie's face. From under the glass, she dares him. He puts the picture face down, switches off the light, and walks over to the bed. Melody reaches out a hand. Her bracelets jangle at the wrist. He turns away and quickly undresses. When his head touches the pillow, he can smell his father's shaving cream and sweat, stale popcorn from a store-bought bag. He's relieved not to detect any of his mother's old smells, the smells before clay—talcum powder and skin lotion, Noxzema after the sun, lime from the before-bed vodka gimlet. He takes a deep breath, flat on his back. Melody leans on her side, watching him, runs a finger over a vein on the muscled inside of his arm. "What are you thinking about?" she says.

Hen turns his head. It's the question Chickie's always asking him. "I was thinking how I probably got made in this bed."

"Ashes to ashes," Melody says, stroking his shoulder. "Seed to seed. Dust to dust."

"I once heard about this guy," Hen says. "He wanted his ashes dumped out of a plane over the Alps—"

"Hey, Captain." Melody's voice is no longer floating and sweet. Her hand runs hard down his side and caresses the inside of his thigh. Climbing on top of him, she pins his arms back behind his head and bends slowly forward, arching her back, sweeping the tips of her enormous breasts across his chest. "Go ahead," she says, releasing his arms. "Touch them. You've been looking at them all day. It's all right. I don't know why the good lord gave them to me, but I do know he meant for me to share."

Hen does as he's told, gently pressing, kneading. The heat that fills his palms takes his breath away. Melody's mouth comes toward him. He gets ready to kiss her, but her head steers clear of his mouth and burrows down into the crook of his neck. Her soft hair splays across his face. Her breasts press full against his chest. She smells like dope and incense and shampoo, so much like a girl. Gently, he spits some of the hair out of his mouth. He feels her sucking his hot skin. He's not worried about losing…any of it. His cock couldn't be any harder; it must've turned to stone. Melody's tongue slides across the ridge of a muscle in his neck and he's just thinking how incredible it all feels when her teeth sink into his skin.

"Jesus. What the—" Hen tries to raise himself up, but Melody's mouth comes down hard on his. She laughs. While they're kissing, he rocks her over on her back. Trying to center himself, he loses track of her mouth. Melody moves her hips in rhythm to the music downstairs, "House of the Rising Sun." His skin rubs against hers; out of his mouth come strange, involuntary noises. Melody's fingers move low, holding him, pumping, guiding. When her hands come back up to touch his face, he pushes hard, only knowing it's done when he feels his stomach flat against hers.

"You made it," she says. "Welcome to the Casa Melody."

Hen feels Melody below him, restless and tense. She starts to move her hips up and down and he pushes once, twice, hard. "Slow down, Captain," she says. But he can't slow down. His body seizes; he has no time to do anything but ram and reach and come. Melody arches her back and smiles a tired smile, as if she's been watching him unwrap a gift, knowing by the end not to expect one in return. There's more to be done, but Hen doesn't know what it is. He slides his hands under the small of her back, hears the slap of their bellies in colliding sweat, his breath coming hard and fast. When she pushes him away, he pulls out of her and turns on his side, suddenly filled with an unbearable fatigue.

After a while, Melody sits up and strokes his back. Hen watches her rise up in the darkness. She wipes the insides of her legs with her shirt and puts it back on, tying it in a knot above her waist.

"Hey," he whispers. "Thanks."

"Pleasure was all mine," she says.

"No," he says. "I'm sorry, I'm—"

"Ssh!" Melody's finger rises up to her lips. Hen closes his eyes again.

The door opens and closes with a click, not quite catching, and creaks back open a crack.

Downstairs, the party gets louder. Hen slides in and out of fitful sleep. He hears whispers in the hallway, laughter and closing doors. He hears the wail of sirens and sees lights flashing out the window. The doorbell rings long and loud. The cops have low, tired voices. Tory's is silky and strong. She sends them away. The noise trickles into a last slam and the house is finally still. As he dozes off, Hen reminds himself to wash the sheets before his parents get home, to ask Tory how to work the washing machine.

Hen slips into a dream. He's fucking a woman in the swaying aisle of a moving train, partly his mother, partly a stranger, and when he realizes what he's done, he kills her with a gun he's half-mistaken for a toy. The police chase him to Chickie's house, but she won't let him in the door. *You killed her.* She hisses at him, accuses him, cat eyes peering through the mail slot. *So now you have to go to Vietnam. That's the rule, Hen. All the killers have to go to Vietnam. And the motherfuckers go first.*

It wasn't really my mother. He pleads on his knees at the door, begs her to understand. *It wasn't really a gun. I wasn't really fucking her. Come on, Chickie, let me in! Give me some water. I'm so thirsty. I didn't know. I'm burning up. You have to believe me. It wasn't really my mother. It wasn't really me.*

Hen wakes up in the dark of his parents' bedroom, pulls the blanket up to his chin. This is what he was afraid of, this moment when he came out of the dope dream, when it was over and far enough away to see from afar, to make sense of it, to see how it's changed him. He has to stop himself from running out to find Melody again, and yet what a strange idea. He imagines her sleeping somewhere in the house, his cum drying sticky on her thighs. He wonders if he'll see her at the breakfast table, what they'll do or say. Hen reaches up to touch the tender bite mark on his neck. All that's clear is that he'll have to do it again. And again. He sees his father's hand raising the whiskey glass to his lips and understands, suddenly, about addiction. What he did with Melody is no longer private, no longer his to keep. Tory will blab and Chickie will figure it out or force it out of him somehow. There'll be some new look to him, some way his body moves differently now. He saw it in Chickie after Elvis, a swagger in her walk, a velvet coating to the eye, less of a need, for other people and things. But what gets lost in the taking? Now he's just one of a zillion guys who's done it—*do it, do it, do it*—as Plato kept saying on the river path that day. Where's the strength and relief he thought sex would bring? Hen looks up and down the length of his body, eyes resting on his limp, spent self. When he was younger, he believed what Horace Killion told him in the fifth grade, that you grew a tiny bit every time you had sex, that real studs had dicks two feet long, bound them up double, triple, with a rope. The grapevine will spread the word, and Hen doesn't mind. More than one person has called him a faggot. He could definitely use a rep.

Hen tastes the salt of a tear that trails down to the corner of his mouth. He's always been a crier. Like his father. If it would only do him some good now, make him feel cleansed, braver, better, then he wouldn't give a damn. If boys who cried didn't get drafted, then he'd bawl all night in his parents' bed, out on the widow's walk until every army recruiter in the land heard him and cried back through a bullhorn, "Coward, traitor, faggot, baby, weirdo, we wouldn't take you if you crawled to us on your hands and knees! We need men in this man's army—capital M-E-N!" He wouldn't mind. If that's all it took, a few tears shed silently in the dark, admitting how scared he was, how none of it made any sense. He could take it then, take it from there. Take it like a man.

10

The next day Hen sits at the kitchen table eating a bowl of Grape Nuts. Chickie comes in through the back door carrying a paper bag.

"Breakfast or lunch?" she says.

"Just woke up." Hen looks up at the broken clock, lifts a dripping spoon. "So it must be breakfast."

"It's one in the afternoon, Hen." Chickie pushes up her sleeves, sniffs the Ajaxed air. "Where're your parents?" she says. "They're not here. I can tell. It's too something, too calm, too…" She pokes her head through the door into the living room. "Ah, much too clean," she says, swinging back into the kitchen. "I didn't know Tory was in town."

"With a vengeance," Hen says.

"Man." Chickie's eyes land on the empty bottles neatly lined up on the counters, the paper bags full of crushed beer cans. "What happened here last night?"

"Big orgy." Hen tips back in his chair, rubs his bare chest, yawns. "Dancing girls popping out of cakes. Skin flicks. The cops came and raided the joint."

"Really."

"Didn't you hear the sirens?" Hen asks.

"I was out pretty late," Chickie says.

"This was pretty late, Chick," Hen says. "This was so late you could even call it early."

"I was out." Chickie sits down and pours herself a bowl of Grape Nuts. "So shoot me."

Hen aims a cocked finger at her. "Bang," he says, the finger falling limp.

"Who's Miss Va Va Voom out there in the living room with Tory?"

Hen plays with his cereal. "That," he says, "is Melody."

"Melody? Well, tra-la-la." Chickie gets up to peek through the crack in the door again. "God, are those tits real?"

"Shut up, Chickie," Hen says. "Get over here and sit back down."

"No. Wait." Chickie puts her ear to the door.

"Catch this, Mel." Tory's voice rises to falsetto in the other room, as she reads aloud from the paper. *"Dear Abby: You may think you've heard it all,* blah, blah, blah…Okay, here we go. *I have a rather unusual problem. You see, I've been married to a wonderful man for ten years. Let's call him Bob.* No," Tory says, in her own voice. "Let's just call him Dick." Melody laughs.

Hen chews his cereal slowly. Melody's laugh makes his skin tingle; the grit of the cereal feels good on his teeth. He hasn't seen her this morning, hasn't spoken to her since she left him on the bed the night before. He's groggy with sleep. Such a sleep. After-sex sleep. It's like a drug. As he pours the last of the Grape Nuts, the dust at the bottom of the box swirls up his nose. Chickie turns to stare at him as Tory's voice reads on. He tosses the empty cereal box dead-on into the trash can.

"It turns out, Abby, that Bob, I mean Dick," Tory says, *"is not entirely the man I thought he was."*

Da-dee-da-da, da-dee-da-da. Melody's voice chimes in, *Twilight Zone* style.

"So Tory had a big bash?" Chickie asks.

"I guess you could call it that."

"What'd you do?"

"Hung around. Smoked some reefer. Watched the Bruins."

"The other day, I came home early from shopping." Tory's voice gets louder. *"And found Dick dressing up in my underwear. Oh dear god, Abby, it turns out I'm married to a cross dresser. Help me, please. What shall I do?"* Tory's voice resumes its normal tone. "My, my. What a dilemma. A princess married to a closet queen."

"Bitch," Hen says under his breath.

"Okay." Chickie comes away from the door. "I can take a fucking hint."

"Not you," Hen says. "I was talking about Tory, Chickie. And don't swear so much. Why do you do that?"

"I was just trying to make conversation," Chickie says. "You know, like, hey, Hen, what'd you do last night. But you're in some kind of weird mood."

"I watched the Bruins."

"What was the score?"

"I fell asleep," Hen says evenly.

"You never fall asleep during a hockey game," Chickie says.

"Tory had some good pot. It laid waste to me."

"So did the Rangers to the Bruins, Hen. Eight to three."

"I knew that."

"Sure."

"What did *you* do last night?"

Chickie sits back down on the chair. "Me and Elvis went to a Swedish movie," she says.

"You never go to movies with subtitles," Hen says.

Chickie looks over at him. "Why don't you just ask me what's in the fucking paper bag?"

"Okay, what's in the fucking paper bag?"

"Your birthday present." Chickie hands it to him.

Hen takes the gift out of the bag, wrapped in the Sunday funny papers, flat and square. He sniffs it, shakes it, turns it over. "My birthday's not until October," he says.

"You may not make it to your next birthday," Chickie says. "You may be a goner, Hen. So, open it up now."

"Don't talk like that." Hen lifts up the tape from the funny papers, pulling off Andy Capp's face.

Hen unwraps the present, a leather chess set the size of a potholder, brown and white checked squares, slits where the plastic pieces slide in and out. He holds it up, asks her softly, almost accusingly, "How'd you know I wanted this?"

"Oh, it was real tough," Chickie says. "For the past year, every time we passed by the window of Leavitt & Peirce, you said, 'Man, I sure could handle having that leather chess set,' and then you'd look at it some more and say, 'Man, I sure could handle having that chess set.' I had to drag you away from that window every time."

"You did not." Hen cracks a smile.

"Yes, I did. Every single time. And since you lost that piece from your other set—"

"Wow." Hen takes a set of flat white chess pieces out of a plastic bag, breaks them apart, and slides them into the slits, working the leather gently—rooks on the ends, bishops, knights, pawns. Chickie drinks in his smile, swallows it whole and wriggling. After a bummer of a night with Elvis, this is what she came for, in search of the old Hen, who makes her feel whole and real, who blushes and stammers, who'd do anything for her. But something's happened. That Hen's not all here.

"You shouldn't have gotten me this," he says.

Chickie's lip starts to tremble. "I wanted to," she says.

"What's wrong?"

"Nothing."

"You didn't really go to the movies, did you?"

"No. And there was no girl popping out of a cake."

"Who pops out of a cake anymore?" Hen says. "What's the matter, Chick?"

"All I wanted to know"—her voice comes out cracked—"was what you did last night."

"Nothing," Hen says again.

"Yeah, well. Stick to your story. That's cool." Chickie gets up, wipes her nose on the back of her hand. "I've gotta go help Violet clean up the yard." She scrunches up the empty bag and turns toward the door. "She's on my case again. She's going to send me to a nunnery if I—"

"Chickie." Hen leans forward and grabs her by the wrist, his stomach muscles clenching as the chair's front legs hit the floor. Chickie feels the heaviness of her own body, once straight and flat like Hen's, now gone to bumps and indents and curves. She feels the old envy, the old yearning to fling off her shirt and run hard on the beach, that old feeling that something about being a girl just plain wasn't fair. She imagines smooth fingers running over the ridges of Hen's chest, down the line of his back, fingers that aren't bitten raw like hers, girl hands, slender, crescent moons on the fingernails. And then Chickie realizes—that's what's happened to Hen. He's been touched.

"Hey, listen," Hen says softly.

"Hey, what."

"I really did want this chess set." He continues to hold her wrist. "I really love it, Chickie. Thanks."

"It loves you, too," Chickie says, heading for the door. She didn't get what she came for after another wasted night with Elvis. There's not much to the night anymore, not much more than the high and the ramble and the sex. She really did suggest to Elvis that they go to that Swedish movie. It was supposed to be poetic, romantic. What was wrong with a little poetry, a little romance? She'd seen the previews. Two lovers picked strawberries and made love in a field, their backs stained red with juice and pressed with the imprints of the leaves. She wanted to do something corny and ordinary with Elvis, just the two of them—holding hands, eating popcorn at the movies, taking a walk—instead of hanging blotto and cool half the night with half the world. She would've liked to have gone to a quiet room with him and slept in a clean bed, sober, just slept, woken up for bacon and eggs together. But they ended up in the Square, as usual, playing the Game far into the night. Elvis drank rum and smoked a few jays on the UT fire escape.

There was some mescaline floating around and Elvis had to have some. When they ended up down on the river, finally alone, on a boathouse dock, he was too out of it even to get it up. She left him there, bummed a cigarette from the sax player sitting by the MDC pool, and walked all the way back to Hemlock Street. She was just as glad, in the end, to go home, alone, to bed. She slept like a baby, until almost eleven o'clock. *This can't be love. It's too old, too tired, way too fucking stoned.*

"Hey, cuz!" Tory calls out as Chickie hits the patio steps. "Come meet my friend. Melody, this is my cousin, Chickie. Minerva, actually. Goddess of something or other."

"Wisdom," Chickie says. "Hah."

"Chickie's Hen's other half," Tory explains. "They were born the same year, joined at the hip. She's a fantastic dancer, the only person in this family who can really move."

"Hi," Melody says. "I saw a picture of you upstairs."

"Which one?" Chickie feels like anything but a dancer in front of her rail-thin cousin and her sexy friend.

"Eating watermelon on the beach," Melody says. "With little Hen."

"Yeah, that was us. The screwed-up Bobbsey Twins." Chickie pushes up her sleeves. "So, what did Abby have to say about the drag-queen situation?"

"Oh, see a counselor, whisper into a preacher's ear, preferably one with a nice ass," Tory says. "You know. If all else fails, ring up God."

"Yeah, Abby and God." Chickie lays her middle finger on top of her first. "Just like this." She pokes a finger into the ring she makes with her other hand. "Or maybe just like this. Who knows what the old pervert's been up to up there." Tory and Melody laugh.

Back out on the flagstone path, Chickie stands still, waiting for a sudden sharp pain in her left armpit to pass. People with heart murmurs often got such pains, like a needle sticking right through you; they were harmless, the doctor said, the one who gave her birth control pills in the fall. She and Elvis had sex a few times before it sank in that she could actually get pregnant. She went to the clinic at the city hospital, where they only seemed interested in her heart murmur. It was very distinctive, they said, very obtuse. They passed around the stethoscope, asked her what the murmur felt like, how long she'd had it, if it interfered with her activities in any way. She felt nothing, she'd had it since she was born. Could she please just have the pills? Did she ever lose her wind, feel faint, pass out? No way. She smoked Camel non-filters and could hold her breath for fifty-three seconds underwater in the pool. She was a dancer, sort of. They made her jump up and down, squat, breathe in deeply, exhale. They called in some interns to listen. "Hear that?" they said. "That's a...gobbledygook... Have a listen. Take a look."

No one once looked her in the eye and said, what are you doing here, young lady? How old are you? Do your parents know you're having sex and with whom? No one ever told her what the murmur meant or why they all found it so fascinating, and why, because of a simple glitch in the rhythm of her heart, she had stabbing pains in her armpits. No one cared what she did, with Elvis Donahue or anyone else, as long as she didn't bring another snotty-nosed kid into the world to hog up the oxygen and the food supply. If Chickie hadn't been so relieved that they finally gave her the pills without a hassle, she might have been a little bit shocked that they'd let a pipsqueak like her walk away with such a powerful thing as a pack of birth control pills in a baby blue case, marked with the days of the week, pretty little pills all in a row, bitter, grown-up candy. Don't miss more than two days in a row or you'll turn into a—

"Chickie!" Violet's voice vaults over the fence. "Get back over here and help. I'm doing all the work!"

Chickie walks down the flagstone path and around to her own back-yard. Melody's laugh echoes in her ears. She's never seen a body like that, not on a real person, anyway. She once heard Hen talking tits with some kid at school. The guy actually asked him, "Hey, what about your cousin, man. How does she stack up?" Hen got all red in the face and told him to shut up. Later, when Chickie asked him to tell her honestly how her tits rated, even pulling up her shirt for a second, Hen closed his eyes and said, "Jesus, they're fine, Chickie, really nice. Thanks for the show."

"On a scale of one to ten."

"Ten," he said. "Ten, all right? Eleven. A thousand. A mil—"

"Don't bullshit me, Hen. They're not that great." She pressed closer to him, pushed her breasts forward. "Shape-wise they're okay, but size-wise, they could be a little bigger, don't you think?"

"Why do you ask me things like that?" Hen said. "Why did you pull up your shirt, Chickie? What the hell do you expect me to say?"

"Just tell me what you think. I want to know. It's not a fucking test. I'm just curious. You're a boy. And boys are obsessed with tits."

"Curious isn't the word. I'm not the tit expert, okay? And what does it matter anyway?"

"Four? Six?" Hen walked away, his fists rammed into his pockets. "Seven, maybe," Chickie called after him. "Six and a half?"

In the backyard, Violet hands Chickie a rake without a word. All she knows is that Elvis hardly pays attention to her body anymore, let alone her mind. He used to admire them both, almost worship them. Now he goes straight for the hole, straight for the fuck, if he can find it these days. Chickie starts to rake the brown, curled-up leaves, which jam in a tight clump at the neck. She lifts the rake, throws it javelin-style at the oak tree, and slumps down into her pathetic pile of leaves. All she knows is that she and Elvis are going nowhere. And that Hen would never go for a girl with tits like Melody's.

"Every year they break the same goddamned window," Remi says to Faye. He stands on a stepladder in the cottage in Nantucket, looking out over the scalloped ocean, easing the jagged fragments of broken glass out of the window frame. "I leave the door unlocked, a pile of wood near the fireplace. They have the run of the house, and still they break the same goddamned window every year."

"People are creatures of habit." Faye cleans the bay windows, spattered with salt and the drippings from the mulberry trees. She sprays Windex and wipes from left to right, up, down and up again.

"That's not the point," Remi says.

"The point is, Remi, they're trying to tell you something. Or ask you something rather. They want to know why you have so much and they have so little."

"If they only knew." Remi sighs. "Maybe if I published my bank statement in the *Island Gazette*, they'd leave my windows alone."

"*Your* bank statement?" Faye says, raising her eyebrows.

"Our bank statement."

"They want to know why you get to come here to play, Remi."

"Me?"

"We, then." Faye bends her kerchiefed head.

"I was just commenting," Remi says, "on how they break the same goddamned window every year."

"People are creatures of habit." Faye wipes up and down, back up and down again. "They need to repeat themselves."

The breeze from the broken oceanside window brushes Remi's

shaven cheek. He looks over at his wife, standing in the dappled light of the bay window. This is as close to a real conversation as they've had in months. It's a huge relief. The morning before, on the ferry ride over, they didn't speak at all, just hung over the railing and let the sea air wash away some of the weary tension between them. All day they worked on the cottage with hardly a word, scrubbing, sweeping, painting, hammering. They slept in separate rooms; the day dawned red and turned quickly gray. They had omelettes turned scrambled eggs for breakfast, exchanging half a smile across the table. Sunday morning's brought a shaky truce. Under a season's layer of dust and dirt, they've somehow found their voices.

Remi scoops the ashes out of the fireplace with a cast-iron shovel and fills an A&P shopping bag full, grateful for this dusty chore, for this moment of uneasy harmony. Faye sweeps the dead spiders and flies from the window ledges and snags a cobweb with her finger. Both of them have come to love this house, in spite of themselves and all that's happened here—the spare look and feel of it, the warped gray boards, the same few things resting in the same few places year after year: soap in the scallop shell, hard and cracked like tough skin; hand lotion set so long on the sink it smells like blue cheese; sea glass on the window sill, milky and gnarled; spotted red lobster claws; cracked yellow rubber raincoats on ancient hooks; faded children's drawings, corners withered around rusty tacks; wicker chairs peeling curly, sharp strips of banded wood—a place arranged by whim and slowly enshrined by time—sea bordered, salty, spare.

At noon, Faye and Remi scrounge for lunch—baked beans and brown bread with raisins from a can, a bottle of warm Almaden. As they sit on the deck in the faded director chairs, the wind stirs as storm clouds gather.

"I think I'll go for a walk on the beach before it rains," Faye says, slightly drunk and not liking the feeling, uncomfortable to be here with Remi alone, with only the broken window left to fix, a wreck of a marriage to mend. Too far away from home, too close to an edge, too ripe for regret. Memory. Middle-aged. Nearly childless. Enisled. She takes off her watch and sets it on the wicker table. "After you get that window in, we can close up and catch the last boat home."

"Wouldn't mind stretching my legs a bit first," Remi says. "Mind if I come along?"

"Do what you like." Faye's already on her way down the open steps, which land her on the sand. She kicks off her sandals and walks down to the water, looking for sea glass and lucky rocks, black with white stripes encircling—white ends must meet, Hen tells her, for the luck to be true. She sits down by the water's edge, bringing her legs up under her on the wet sand. Meditation is said to cleanse you, make you peaceful. Peace Faye would welcome, but the cleansing part scares her, as if she might be bleached invisible by the sun, as if some part of her might go whirling down the drain, a part as yet undiscovered, but without which she'll never be whole. She feels too scoured, too faded, too soon. Forty-five isn't so old. Why, then, does she feel ancient?

Back in Cambridge, one of Faye's pottery students has been trying to get her to come to the Transcendental Meditation Center on Garden Street. He's a pale, almost alabaster young man with long fingers and a ponytail, a black widow of a boy, pretty and hideous at the same time, named, of all things, Demian. All skin and bone and sharp planes, except for full lips which on such a gaunt face can only be obscene. He's got a thing for her. It isn't hard to tell, even after all these years, the bold, laden glances, the strong hands kneading the clay. Though flattered, maybe even grateful for the attention, Faye feels nothing for this cadaverous boy. He touched her bare shoulder once with a spiny hand, hoisted up the slipped corner of her blouse, without invitation, without warning. The brazen hand lingered longer than it should. She looked him in the eye and threw him back the news of her disdain, of her sudden revulsion, and he recoiled, thrown for a loop, offended, a boy after all, more taken than ever.

Faye closes her eyes and thinks of Demian, using him as a focus, the center for her thoughts. She puts her fingertips to her thighs and cranes her neck upward to the sky. The wind lashes her hair across her face. Part of her wishes she could have felt something at that moment, not for Demian so much, but for the touch, for desire. She's desperate for something, passion, she supposes. It's more than sex. Faye wonders what sex after Nash has done for Violet. She seems well and whole as ever, a robust, well-rounded adulteress. But she, Faye, doesn't have Violet's cunning, her stamina. She's not up to secret rendezvous and woven lies, sex in cramped, kinky, deodorized places. She—Faye—would be a lousy infidel. The only ones she's ever hungered after are her children, and that was in the primordial, oedipal way of mothers, wanting direct and complete access to their souls, wanting to taste their happiness like a slice of ripe pear. What a blow to discover somewhere along the dragging line of parenthood that a mother may lay some claim to a child early on, for having made and borne and nurtured it, but never to its soul. The soul is private, unaccountable, never beholden.

Faye hopes wisdom will find her somehow, that some nameless passion or conviction will steal her away, even someone else's. The horrified pity she feels when she watches the shorn Hari Krishnas dancing in frenzied circles in the Square, ponytails flopping, pale children lingering on the sidelines, is often confused as it mingles with a kind of childlike envy of those who've found, however temporary or false, an answer— be it in dogma, robe, or dance. Maybe it is about sex. She and Remi haven't made love in years. Even long before that, she'd given up sex for dead, given it a decent, if shallow, burial in what she hoped was her rational mind. The only love she makes now is to her clay—pounding, smoothing, shaping, firing. With the clay she's still passionate, fertile. She's tried to convince herself that this is enough in the way of love— or lust—if it has to be.

Thunder rumbles low in the distance. Remi sits high up on the sand, leaning against a rock, and watches Faye, filled with a fierce satisfaction, after all these years, that she's still with him, that she is his. He's finally gotten over being bothered that Nash found her in the bookstore in college and asked her out on his behalf. Over time, he's learned the wisdom of accepting his brother's offerings, silently, gratefully. He knew right away that he'd marry Faye if she'd have him. She was the kind of girl you wanted for a wife, good-looking but not too beautiful, strong but not domineering, proud but not brash, smart but never bold. Faye would cover for him, he knew, might even lift him up out of himself. And best of all, no matter how time eroded him, it had always been clear—Faye would last. He feels a tender stirring. All these years, she's been true. He's sure of it. In some ways, she's changed very little. There've been small things. Somewhere along the line, she gave up the fussy lace shirts and pleated plaid pants, or was it tweed? The thing for French films. The poufy hairdos, made by an egg and beer wash, high heels, alligator handbags. The insistence on "may I please be excused from the table?" by the kids. And sex. Well, they used to have sex. They did have sex. In the end, maybe he's been lucky to have had this much from her. Look at Violet. She does what she damn pleases. When, how, with whom she damn pleases. She's made a fool of his brother. But Faye's stayed true. Maybe it's not the worst tragedy, Remi thinks, to be rivaled by a few lumps of clay. Cammie's face floats by to ask a simple, pointed question, and he orders it away.

Down by the water, Faye searches for something in the dark of her closed eyes. But she has no mantra, and Demian the black widow boy won't stay still in her mind, as a center should. He dances nervously, marionette-style, pale, spindly legs dangling in midair. He fidgets and blushes, reaches and crawls. He clings to her, naked and frail, pleads, cries, and whines. He's the child she never had, the one that got made soon after Tory was born, an accident, the child that fell from her a mass of blood and vein and tissue, her breasts still leaking bluish milk, before she'd even told Remi. God. Faye rubs the back of her neck. How many black holes did the secrets of women fill? Instead of peace, Faye's mind fills with vague longing and bits of long-gone memories, a dim one of an outing with her father to a carnival on Lake Michigan, her first trip to the shore, an early memory she's always thought to be a good one, for she has so few. She was nine. Her father wouldn't let her go on any of the rides—they were dirty and dangerous and God only knew who saw the buck at the end of the day, the Communists or the Mafia, he said. But he bought her cotton candy and won her a stuffed bear by shooting out the buck teeth of jumping tin beavers with a water pistol. Never had she seen such a beautiful thing as the lime-green bear he won for her that day, as the pink spun sugar that crunched blood red as she bit into it, that great body of blue water stretching as far as the eye could see. At the fair, Faye saw a man walk on burning coals in his bare feet. She saw the biggest cow on the face of the earth, the tiniest man, a bearded woman with twelve toes. She saw her father change from a cardboard man to a real man that day. He looked almost happy, shooting at the tin beavers, rolling up his sleeves. *I'm going to get you varmints!* he cried.

Get 'em, Daddy, Faye said. *You can do it. Get 'em!*

And he said he'd do it, by god, he'd do it for God and country and for his little girl. Faye laughed, so happy to have her father come alive, to be someone's little girl, to watch those beavers popping up and down. The spurts of water from the water pistol slapped down the beaver's teeth. She laughed so hard, she almost peed in her pants. Her father was sweating under the arms; his suspenders were twisted. His mustache twitched. He was doing all this for her. She could do magic; she could make him laugh, a little girl with brown hair and a pinwheel blowing in the wind, squeezing her skinny legs together to keep from peeing. They were having so much fun.

"Faye!" Remi's voice catches her knee-deep in the ocean, the bottoms of her scrunched-up jeans soaking wet. She turns around, dazed, not remembering the trek from the sand to the water, how she got to here from there, from being Faye Martin to being Faye Potts. She might have kept on walking if Remi's voice hadn't startled her, walking the shelled and potholed bottom of the sea, in search of something—that lime-green bear, that old memory. "What in hell are you doing?" he yells.

"Wading," Faye calls back. "Just...wading."

"It's fifty degrees. The water's not much warmer. Are you out of your mind?"

"Probably," she says quietly, flatly. She turns and looks back out to where the sky meets the horizon in a line, too straight, too clean, to be real. A wave spirals out of the line, a soft, twisting roll. She's never really believed in the beauty of this island. It ripples and wilts in the heat, crumples in the rain, crystallizes in the winter. So much of what she sees here disappears before she can reach out and grasp it—a slippery, taunting mirage. Faye lifts a hand to her cheek, turns to face Remi again. She feels the softness of that cheek, the roguish power of the hovering wave. She feels suddenly young, like playing, releasing herself from the contracts and burdens of these sexless, mothering years. Her children are grown. No one really needs her anymore. Not desperately. Not absolutely. How terrifying that is, how irrevocably and gravely...liberating. Soon she can resume her life as anything she once was, anything she pleases. But whatever was she, before? Child, daughter, student, girl-friend...lover? She lifts a hand to Remi and waves.

Remi pulls a hand from his crossed arms and waves back, digs his toes into the sand, brooding, the way he used to when he was younger. Faye remembers him when. His hairline creeps back down over the rise of his forehead to form bangs. His belly flattens and his eyes grow nervous and clear, flashing the way they used to when he picked her up at Simmons, thin and jittery, and thanked her shyly for going out with him, even before they'd signed out of the dorm. The puffiness leaves his face, the lurch that lurks in the corners of his eyes, the crusted sorrow. She used to go to the track meets at Harvard Stadium and watch him run like the wind that blows through what's left of his hair. He and Nash were often paired in the same races. Nash usually won, just by a nose, a little bigger, stronger, faster, but Remi was always more beautiful in flight—did she ever tell him so?—graceful and strong, haggard as he crossed the finish line, head thrown back, Adam's apple thumping, a careful, gracious loser in those days.

The first time Faye and Remi made love, the night he proposed, she said yes without much thought, just as she'd said yes, she'd marry him a few hours before. Remi *was* sexy that first night, in the moonlit back seat of a jacked-up Plymouth. He laid his jacket down for them, fumbled gently, then pulled away, agonized, explained how he really loved her, how they could wait if she wanted, how he'd always respect her, always take care of her. She pulled him back down. She'd wanted him to want her, to do what normal, hot-blooded young couples did in the back seats of borrowed cars. She'd let him have his way with her that night, trusting it would be her way, too, in the end. Remi made love as she knew he would—quickly, eyes lowered, alternating apologies with thanks. Afterward, he'd wait patiently for enough time to pass until he felt it was fair to ask her for the favor again, even just after they were married—"The Ravishing Time," *McCall's* magazine called it. She'd let him have her often in those days—*take* her, they used to say. She'd even given him a sign sometimes with her toes as they lay side by side in bed. The article in *McCall's* said the average newlyweds made love five days a week. In those days, Faye had wanted so desperately to be average. She'd lain beneath Remi and suffered his stuttering touch, convinced herself that he was the rigid, sexless one, that with someone else it would have been an act of grace and beauty. She rose up from herself, time and time again, a cold and silent angel, looking down upon the act that had brought her full circle—woman, wife, mother—woman. And when it was done, so stark, so quick, she'd close her eyes and turn away, remembering the man in flight on the track, and not the wet heap of a breathless man beside her.

Faye has never told Remi, and maybe it's high time, she thinks as she watches him brood on his rock, that there was some pleasure in those early days, not a true sexual pleasure, but the pleasure she'd felt in being grown-up, taken in marriage, savoring the love of a decent man. What does she have to lose in telling him such things now? In some ways, she owes Remi a great deal. He rescued her, salvaged her, protected her. She never expected him to please her, never asked him to. And in the end, in those early days with Remi, Faye did feel satisfied and almost happy when the sex was over, the task done, her sense of normalcy renewed, her spirit intact, a child perhaps conceived, her heavy, damp paperweight of a husband on top of her to hold her and keep her from blowing away, as she often worried she might do. Just up and drift away…

Remi waves back to her from his rock, smiling a strange, almost fatherly smile.

After they turned on the lights of the amusement park at Lake Michigan, Faye and her father walked along the boardwalk and climbed down the steps to the beach, on such a day as this one, gloomy and threatening rain. Up close, the water was no longer blue, but gray. The small, mewling waves rolled up onto the sand—a far cry from the bold, lurching green of this cold ocean. She walked out onto a jetty of stones, balancing herself with her arms outstretched, tipping to and fro in the peach light, a tight-rope walker, keeping herself from falling to the sharks below. Turning around, she saw the lights of the Ferris wheel and the rocket ride spinning in circles. She heard the distant voices of the barkers and the crowd, the carousel music. No one else on the beach was in sight.

It's so big! she called back to her father on the sand, looking out over the water.

They don't call 'em the Great Lakes for nothing. Her father followed her out onto the jetty to the last rock. He said how he'd worked himself into a good sweat and why didn't they go for a swim. But they didn't have their bathing suits, she said, how could they? They would just have to make do, her father said. She watched as he undressed before her, her strict, always covered father, keeping the front part of himself hidden with his shirt. He sat down on the last rock and slid into the water, waist deep. When she took off her dress, he held out his arms, even as she told him, *I don't want to go in. There are sharks in there.*

Standing knee-deep in the ocean, the pieces of this old memory begin to add up to some kind of new-felt, twisted pain. Faye wants to say to Remi, "It hasn't been so bad. You were a saint compared to my father," or "I've been no picnic either, I know. There's a reason for the way I am. The way we are. I'm sure of it." She would like to say to Remi, "Let's make love," and she would like to mean it. She sees him clearly up on his rock near the dune—bitter, bruised, and willing—not Nash's twin brother or his father's son or the father of their children, but just a man on a beach who's been counting his losses—his youth, his temper, his dignity, his clay-caked, wading wife. She looks around. There's not a soul in sight for as far as the eye can see. A crime could be committed here. She could be the one to commit it. Acts without victims are not true crimes. Acts that alter, atone, give pleasure, shock, jolt, shake the senses. There haven't been enough of those. The empty beach, the cold mist dare Faye. Not to be bad, but different, outrageous, sexy...generous. She walks out of the water. When she hits the dry sand, she starts taking off her clothes—first her velveteen sweatshirt, then her T-shirt, her damp jeans, and finally once-white cotton underwear gone grisly gray. Remi leans against his rock, his mouth open slightly, and watches her come. Naked by the time she reaches the rock, Faye kneels in front of him. When he kneels down to meet her, she kisses him full on the mouth.

"I'm so sorry, Faye," he says afterward in a whisper.

"Sorry? For what?" Faye leans back onto her knees, crosses her arms over her bare breasts. How like Remi to steal the moment, to collapse this way. He cradles his head in his fingertips. Faye rocks back and forth. "Why are you crying, Remi? What on earth is wrong?"

"I'm such a jerk," he says.

"You're not a jerk," Faye says, impatient with the adolescent sentiment, a word Hen would use. Jerk. She fights the urge to do what Remi's done so often with Hen, to tell him to buck up, pull himself together, to be a man. She tries to get the moment back on track. This is her confession, after all, her catharsis, her seduction, not his. "I haven't been the kind of wife you wanted," she says, not in the sorry, inviting voice she'd planned, but in the clipped tone she's cultivated over the years to get out, to get over, to get by.

Remi looks at her, confused. "What do you mean?" he says. "Of course you have."

"I couldn't be," she starts to explain. "Right from the start." She begins to shiver as the cold takes hold of her. "I think I understand now. My father—"

"You're my *wife*." Remi is suddenly full of the wonder that she's naked and cold before him, repentant, full of something to say, nipples hard, belly soft, blue lips chattering. "No one could have done it better, Faye. No one."

"Remi," Faye says.

"I'm not the easiest guy, I know that." Remi takes her by the arms. "I've been...oh god, you don't even know... And that night, with the lamp…" He reaches out to touch her with just his fingertips, a stroke here, a stroke there. He starts rubbing her hands, her shoulders, her spine. "Let me make it up to you, please, Faye. Let me warm you up. You're freezing."

"I'm not," she says, pulling away.

"What were you going to say?" he murmurs. "When you came up here. It seemed important. Tell me, Faye. What was it?"

"Nothing," she says. "It can wait, Remi. It's nothing."

"*Tell* me." Faye sees Remi's frantic eyes taking her all in again, wanting to warm and please and ravish her all in one fell swoop. Her mind retreats and goes back to pick up the clothes strewn on the sand, to find the words to tell Remi that the walk is over, that they should be getting back to the cottage. But by now, of course, it's too late.

"God, Faye, you still have the body of a twenty-year-old." Remi tugs his shirt over his head, grabs the back of her neck and kisses her hard. A gull squawks mournfully on a rock. Faye pulls her twisted mouth away. Remi's belly bloats and his face goes soft; the hairline slowly recedes. Dorian Gray redux on the sand. He's middle aged again, paunchy, muddy-eyed. It's gotten all fouled up; he's misunderstood. Faye wanted to give herself to him, but she has never wanted to be taken. "You know, you're right," Remi says sloppily, pushing up against her, his lips brushing her shoulder. "It's not so cold. It's all relative, isn't it?"

"No. Yes. It *is* cold." Faye struggles. "It must be fifty degrees, Remi, like you said. I'm wet. I'm freezing. Let go."

"Come on," Remi whispers, unzipping his pants. "I'll make you warm, Faye. We'll go for a run, then maybe take a quick dip, like we used to. We never used to get cold." He presses her to him, both of them naked now, pushing himself up against her. "God, I've missed you. Let's forget the last ferry. Spend another night. Hen can take care of himself."

"No." She looks around, panicky, her breath coming short. "He can't. I'm cold. I want to go back to the house now, Remi. Stop it. I want to go home."

Remi pulls her toward the water. "Let's go for a run, Faye, a swim. Let's—"

"No." She plants her feet in the sand, the way she's learned to do in this ocean, in this life, bending her chin down to her chest to prepare for the crash of the wave and the sand rushing out from under her heels. "I don't want to run," she says quietly. "I don't want to swim." She's nine years old again and the naked man is her father—balding, pot-bellied, beloved, and revolting—pulling her, sliding her into the water.

I don't want to come in, Daddy. There are sharks in there.

She and Remi pull at the wrists, a sorry tug of war. Faye lets go and falls backwards, landing in the sand. It's too late. It's her own fault. It's the woman's fault, isn't it, for being what the man wants, for not having the courage or the strength to be anything except what the man has to have, for being within reach, for being naked, and for being sentimental and guilty and horny and repulsed and grateful and scared all at once? What did she expect? She took off her clothes. *A woman who teases rarely pleases,* her mother used to say, and she wasn't talking about stripping naked on the beach, but just having the top button of your shirt unbuttoned or flirting with a turn of a head, saying maybe when you really meant no, or yes, a too-bright ribbon in your hair, a sassy word, a willing look in your eye.

What was Faye to have made of her only childhood, the things her mother said? What was left, without bright ribbons and the fire in your eye, without lively talk and the feel of the wind on your skin? What was her mother telling her to be but a stuffed bird, beak closed, feathers stilled, crows' feet glued to a wooden stand? Caution, boredom, fear. Things that kept you safe, that dried you up to shriveled flesh and bone. Things that lay forgotten between the layers of crinkling tissue paper, amongst the garters and china and pressed flowers in a spinster's hope chest. How could she *not* have gone to the carnival with her father, *not* eaten that cotton candy, *not* gone for that swim? And what had her mother been trying to tell her all those years? That she was done taking care of her husband, and that now it was Faye's job? *Get your father's slippers, Faye Elizabeth. Take him up some coffee in bed. Go see what your father needs, see what he wants, will you, Faye? Go on now, your father's waiting.*

Are you sure there are no sharks in here? Faye asked her father as he eased her into the water off the jetty as darkness fell.

Not a one, he said. *Just a bunch of friendly minnows. A couple of mermaids, maybe.*

Do you love me, Daddy? Faye wanted more of this gentle, laughing father, the one she'd conjured up with her own magic, with a kiss spun of pink sugar. *More than you love Mommy?*

Don't ask silly questions. Her father tightened his grip on her arms, pulled her down off the rock. *Of course I love you. And I love Mommy too.*

Am I a good girl?

Yes. Ever so.

A brave girl too? She felt the water as it covered her ankles, her knees, then her thighs.

You're a brave girl too. Her father splashed water on her chest, his big hand running down her leg. *Show Daddy what a brave girl you are. Come on in.* He slid her all the way down into the water. *The water's fine.*

Remi tackles her on the sand. Faye struggles, but not for long. He's too strong, perhaps even justified. This can't be rape. A minute before, she was thinking of love. She knows the feel of his stomach too well; she's filled it with pot roast and French toast and spaghetti a thousand times over the years. She knows the square, jabbing knees; she's put ice on them when they swelled after a fall in a touch football game. She knows the scratchy cheek, wondered out loud how a beard might suit him. She knows the taste of the slightly sour breath laced with coffee and booze, the feel of him pushing deep inside her. In this very way they made their children. To all sea creatures' eyes—the gulls and sea urchins and horseshoe crabs, they are making love.

"Stop, Remi." Faye tries to push him off her. "Please stop."

"Stop?" Remi pants. "*Stop*, Faye?"

"Yes. You have to stop." She tries to speak calmly, rationally, the way she hopes she'd handle a mugger in a dark alleyway, appealing to his most human, intelligent side as they wrestle in the sand. "I thought I wanted to do this. But I don't anymore." She tries to push him away, but even her new clay muscles are no match for Remi's. She thinks to say, "You're scaring me," but it isn't really true. She thinks to say, "I'm sorry," but it's neither sorrow nor fear that she feels. It's fury, red hot and glare. "Get *off* me, Remi. Now!"

"I love you, Faye. More than ever." He hasn't heard a word. His fingers rub and prod down low. His hip bones jab into her belly. She falls limp, thinking stillness to be the next best course, to gather strength for the next battle, for this one's already lost. Remi enters her hard, pumps and rocks above her. Faye's arms lie slack at her side, her head rising up off the sand with each thrust. She might as well help him get it over with. Remi thrashes and rubs and pants, the fuck that's been in the works for all of these years and more, the one where he'll warm her up, melt her down, make her happy, make her climax, make it right. Tears form in his unblinking eyes as he shudders and comes. Faye looks out over the ocean, mind never emptier, ever clearer. Rolling off her, Remi lies on his back in the sand, chest rising and falling with shallow breaths, closes his eyes.

Faye gets dressed slowly, putting on each piece of clothing as she retrieves it, finally the sandals by the steps to the deck. She walks back up past the cottage, down the winding road, all two and a half miles to the ferry dock. The three o'clock boat is loading. She speaks to the ticket taker, an old man in uniform, too spiffy for the times. She says there's been a family emergency, that she has to leave the island right away. She has no cash; her husband will follow. She speaks calmly, tells no outright lies. It's too complicated to explain, would he please just let her get on the boat? The ropes get coiled. The car platform retreats with a loud clank. What did she say her name was? Faye. Faye Potts. Remi Potts's wife, that's right. Her clothes are wet. The seagulls gather overhead. She shivers. The ticket taker remembers the twins' grand-father, old man Mercy Potts. Owned the cottage up on Willow Creek Road. Lots of spunk. Lots of character. Yes, lots of spunk, Faye says. Wife of Remington Potts. One of the grandsons. The twins. The horn blows; the children clap their hands over their ears. "Please." Faye puts a hand on the old man's arm. "I can't miss this boat," she says.

"All right, go ahead, ma'am, it'll be our little secret." The old man lends her a shaky arm. "Watch your step, now. Easy does it."

The ferry pulls slowly away from the dock. A fine rain starts to fall as it rounds the corner of the bay at the red nun. The passengers retreat down below. The seagulls do their tricks out of habit, squawking for handout food. A camera comes out from under a poncho. Thunder rumbles low beyond an island covered with nesting gulls and straggly pines. *Our little secret.* Leaning over the ferry railing, Faye's memory folds in on itself, a wet, heaping pile. After they'd gotten dressed again, her fa-ther led her off the jetty and up the steps to the boardwalk. He bought her one more cotton candy, grudgingly this time, telling her not how it was magic spun of sugar, but how it would rot her teeth. He wiped the pink stuff from her cheek with his handkerchief and told her not to dawdle. On the car ride home, he was quiet. Faye sat beside him, chatty, damp, confused. It must've been her fault. He'd been so different at the carnival, so happy, so gentle. But as hard as she tried, she couldn't keep him that way. With each passing white line on the road, the magic slipped away. Looking at himself in the rearview mirror as he pulled up to the curb in front of the house, he scrunched up his eyes, stretched the corners of his mouth, smoothed down his thinning hair. The green bear's ears drooped in Faye's arms. He said it would be our little secret, Faye Elizabeth, our secret day, our secret swim, just between us and the mermaids. They never had to share it with anyone, and hadn't he shot those beavers down and hadn't the cotton candy tasted so good?

Faye followed her father into the house and kissed her mother's blazing cheek. They were two hours late. Soaked to the bone. Where on god's green earth had they been? In god's blue lake, Faye told her mother. It was the biggest, most... Hush, now! her father said. It was late. They'd talk about it all in the morning. When her mother shooed her upstairs to bed, Faye tried to kiss her father goodnight. He turned his face away.

Faye leans over the side, watching the water gush out from beneath the ferry's stern. Her hair gathers the weight of the rain and pushes her chin down to the railing. She doesn't imagine herself leaping overboard and being chewed up by the boat's propeller as she often has before. She hasn't the slightest desire to die. It's a simple, clear feeling, the sky a newly painted wall for the etching. She laughs out loud, the first broad stroke of freedom. She's middle aged, scarred and scared. It's true. All of it, and yet the truth is so vast that all this is but one tiny scrap of her story. She is, among other things, the wife of Remi Potts. But in the end, it's a relatively small matter, despite all the years this fact has ruled her life, the line it's drawn in her own blood. It was a mistake, plain and simple, her fault as much as Remi's and no one's in the end. But it's not too late. She doesn't know why she's never thought of it before. Because of the children, she supposes. That was probably the excuse she made. Faye has an instant, exploding flash of anger at Hen, that's gone as soon as it's doused by the rush of love she feels for her last child, who, by being born on a whim and so late in the game, so troubled and fey, has postponed this moment for so many years, this awakening, just by being another baby who took up so much love, for so long.

The only loss is time. She'll leave Remi. Slowly, gently, as gracefully and respectfully as she knows how. By summer, she'll be gone from the house on Hemlock Street. How simple, how clean. What a gift. For both of them. All of them. In the end there are some blessings. She won't have to blame Remi for this day. For unwittingly, he's helped her to remember another, even more troubling trip to the shore, the day she went swimming with the only shark in Lake Michigan.

11

Sprawled naked on a motel bed, Charlie slithers a rope at Violet's feet, snapping her ankles and her calves, working upward with each flick of the wrist.

"Stop it, Charlie," Violet says. She's gotten up to light a cigarette, jerks her feet up after each strike of the rope, tries to grab it away. She takes a drag of her Chesterfield. "I hate that rope, the way you always carry it around with you, like some perverted pet snake. It's the weirdest goddamned fetish."

"You're insulting my rope, the one that's been so good to you?" Charlie wriggles the frayed whip's tail at her ankles, slithers it up along her shins, then flicks it against her thigh.

"Ouch." This time she's able to grab the rope out of his grasp. "I said stop it, Charlie. You're hurting me."

"Pain is relative, though, isn't it?" he says. "Can't you intellectualize the pain, Miss Violet? That's why I came to this town. Aristocratic sex. I wanted to get stung by a few nasty WASPs."

"I'm not a real WASP." Violet gets back into bed, leans up against the headboard, and takes a drag of her cigarette. "Just the cornfield variety. Iowa born and bred."

"Good enough for me," he says. "Talk to me highbrow dirty, babe. Beg me to undulate your nipples or titillate your g-spot. I'll accommodate your every desire. Absolutely free of charge."

"We're both so pathetic," Violet says. "Really, when I think—"

"Let me demonstrate relativity." Charlie takes back the rope, wraps it tightly around her thigh, squeezing the flesh until it bulges red.

"Ow!" Vi says.

"That might hurt now…" Charlie loosens the rope's noose, pulls it back and forth, front to back, easily, steadily. "But this old rope might start to act mighty adventurous if you trained it right." He works it expertly, like a lasso. Violet raises her hips. "How does it feel now, Miss Violet?" Charlie says, sliding the rope between her legs.

"Good, damn it." She puts her cigarette in the ashtray, catches her breath. "Don't stop. It feels good." She arches her back. Charlie pulls the rope away, wriggles it back down her legs, lets it lie slack at her ankles. Violet tugs on his hand. "Up again," she says. "Higher." The rope begins its climb, grazes and teases and pulls away. All of a sudden, Charlie whips it hard against her crotch.

"Ow! All right, that's it!" Violet bunches up the rope and throws it on the floor. "I have no one but myself to blame for ending up in this sordid little soap opera with you, but you're twisted, Charlie, I'm sure of it."

"Ah, we've found your Achilles heel, Miss Violet. No surprise, it's in your cunt."

Violet picks up her smoking cigarette from the ashtray. "What were you in jail for? I want to know."

"I never told you?" He feigns mock surprise. "First degree something or other. Oh yeah, murder. A nun. I don't know what all the fuss was about. I hacked her up so neatly. Put each piece in a separate locker at the airport, wore her habit to the fireman's ball. That was my big mistake, I guess. That's when they caught on." Violet glares at him, says nothing. "They left my food outside my cell. I pulled it through the bars with the hook of my left hand."

"Tell me the truth, Charlie." Violet gets up and starts to get dressed. "Did it have to do with sex?"

"Doesn't everything?" Charlie leans on his elbows on the bed like a teenaged girl.

"For you, it does."

"You too, farm girl."

"What did you do?" Violet clasps the hook on her bra.

"There was this kid I used to teach tennis to. Man, she had talent."

"She. Of course."

"Her parents put her in my charge." He shrugs.

"And you screwed her. Naturally."

"She was seventeen. Practically an adult. One hundred percent consenting. Oh, man, was that little girl loaded with talent."

"Statutory rape," Violet says, pulling up her stockings. "Great. What else?"

"We went to Florida for a tournament," Charlie says. "She got hold of some bad acid and wrecked herself up in a car crash. And of course they all blamed me."

"Drugs too." She zips up her skirt. "You're a thoroughly vile and disgusting man."

"And you adore me," Charlie says cheerfully.

"Adore you? You must be kidding."

Charlie sits up, on the defensive now. "This kid could take care of herself, Violet, I'm telling you."

"No one can take care of herself when she's seventeen, Charlie. I have a daughter that age. She's just a baby."

"Hey." Charlie's hands fly up in the air. "I didn't do the drugs. I didn't drive the car while I was blitzed. Little Alison did all right. Daddy paid the hospital bills, got her a new face, a new Porsche. She's married now, sitting pretty out in California. Private tennis courts and swimming pools, the whole bit. Daddy's still writing her checks. And I'm teaching fat old broads to hit the ball across the net. I'm on the lam. I'm scum."

"You were the *grown-up*, Charlie," Violet says. "And you *are* scum." She starts to button her blouse. "Oh my god, what an incredible feeling. I think I've finally had enough."

"You don't know the meaning of the word," Charlie says. "You'll be back, sexpot. With your old man on the disabled list. You need it way too bad."

"No, I don't," Violet says. "I've got everything I want. Everything I need."

"Nobody gives it to you like old Charlie and you know it," he says. "You'll never get rid of me."

"Don't threaten me, Charlie. You're in up to your neck already. And I don't give a damn anymore. I'm the Brattle Street slut. Practically a legend. I have nothing left to lose. Even this town's not liberal enough for you. Believe me, I could make your life miserable."

Charlie shrugs, looks her over as she finishes dressing. "Yeah," he says. "Little Alison was stacked. Body like a goddess. Probably the way yours used to be. And the face of an angel to boot."

"What in god's name would I have done with a pretty face?" Violet asks.

"Gone to heaven and fucked the archangels?" Charlie says.

Violet kicks the rope under the bed, slips on her shoes, and bites her tongue. She won't say, "Fuck you" to Charlie. She won't give him the chance to say, "It's already been done."

Hen doesn't have flat feet after all. He asks his mother when she gets home from Nantucket late that afternoon. She comes alone, without Remi or the car or any luggage. She's pale and quiet—damp. How he knows this without touching her, he's not sure. Her face looks drained and tired, but the deepest lines have mysteriously disappeared. Something happened in Nantucket. Good or bad, Hen can't say. He watches her slit open Saturday's mail, pictures his father dead on the floor of the cottage in Nantucket, the silver letter opener sticking out of his back.

"Where's Dad?" he asks.

"On his way."

"Why didn't you guys come back together?"

"Broken window." Faye frowns at the electric bill. "Your father stayed to fix it."

"How'd you get home?" Hen asks.

"I got a ride." Faye looks up, as if suddenly aware of his presence. "I had so much to do, Hen. You know? I felt like I really just needed… to get home."

Faye doesn't tell Hen the particulars of her strange day, what happened with Remi on the beach, the chatty woman on the ferry who offered her a ride back to Boston, the way people feel so free to be crazy these days. The woman wanted to stop in Hyannis Port at the Kennedy compound. She came every week for the Sunday tour. The woman told Faye she looked a bit like young Eunice, patted her on the knee. The Kennedys were cursed, she said, maybe even bewitched. Faye moved to the edge of her seat. The woman—Agnes was her name—prattled on as they made their way north on Route 3 in her old Chevy—a litany of Kennedy names, birthdays, educations. They were Catholic to boot; they cast a spell. She herself had been a witch once, in another life. Did Faye believe in witches? Warlocks? Reincarnation? No? That was too bad.

Agnes pulled off the Mass. Pike at the Coca-Cola sign. She had no immediate destination, she said. She thought she might like to look around, do some Kennedy searching. She'd heard one of the nephews lived nearby, wondered if Faye might like to come. She had charts, magazines, binoculars. She was all alone in the world. She had buckets of money; her dead husband had left her very well off. Did Faye need any money? She pulled out a wad of bills. Faye shudders. She doesn't tell Hen how much the woman scared her, how she got out at the red light at River Street and walked all the way home.

Faye tosses the mail onto the hallway table, opens the closet, gets out the broom. "Time for some cleaning," she says.

Hen gestures into the living room. "The White Tornado already blew through," he says.

"White Tornado?" Faye looks into the tidy, polished room, confused. "Oh, my gosh. You mean Tory. I completely forgot she'd been here. When did she leave?"

"A few hours ago."

"She came with a friend?"

"Yeah."

"Nice girl?" Faye looks up at him. "It was a girl, I hope."

"Yeah, it was a girl, Mom."

"Nice?" Faye says.

"She was nice," Hen says.

"How did Tory look?"

Hen shrugs. "The same."

"Was she thin?" Faye asks. "Too thin?"

"I don't know." Hen thinks suddenly of Melody. "Maybe."

"I worry about your sister," Faye says.

"Why?" It's never occurred to Hen that anyone might worry about Tory.

"Oh, I don't know." Faye starts to sweep. "Maybe because she doesn't worry about herself. Sometimes I think Tory never really had a childhood."

"Maybe she didn't want one," Hen says.

"Still." Faye smiles at Hen. "It was my job to make sure she *could* have had one. My responsibility. Don't you think?" She reaches out her hand. "You and Chickie had a normal childhood, didn't you?"

"Normal?" Hen scratches his head. "How the hell am I supposed to know?"

After a dinner of elbow macaroni and Worcestershire sauce, Hen sits in the kitchen with his mother and does his calculus homework. She's gentle, patient, the way she was when he was sick as a kid—everything forgiven, forgotten. She looks pale, ill even, as if she might keel over if he asked her anything more upsetting than the square root of sixty-four. He keeps waiting for the color to fill her face again, for her eyes to settle, a knuckle to crack, a tendril of hair to fall from her ponytail. The tenderness Hen feels for his mother is so strange. He misses her, even though she's sitting right there across the table from him, maybe the way she'll miss him when he's grown up and gone, the way her parents must have missed her after she left home. He never met his grandparents on her side. When he asked her once what they died of, she answered, "Misery, I suppose." Faye sits at the table with Hen, chewing on a certain fingernail. When she reaches for a Frito-Lay corn chip, he knows for sure something's wrong. His mother never, ever eats corn chips.

"Are you okay, Mom?" he asks.

"I'm fine." The half-eaten corn chip descends in her hand. "Just a little tired, that's all."

The Saab's wheels crunch onto the gravel driveway. Hen looks up from the kitchen table. Faye disappears through the swinging door. Remi comes in the back way and looks around, at the open math book, the bag of corn chips, the abandoned chair.

"Hey, Dad."

"Son." It's a question, a wish, a command. "Where's your mother?"

"Upstairs."

"When did she get home?"

"Few hours ago."

"She all right?" Remi reaches for the whiskey bottle.

"I don't know," Hen says. "Is she?"

Remi says nothing, pours himself a drink.

Hen closes his calculus book. "How was the weekend?"

"Okay."

"What'd you guys do?"

"Just a work weekend mostly." Remi takes a gulp of his drink.

"Did you go to the Cliffside for fried clams?"

"No." Remi heads for the door. "We didn't make it to the Cliffside this time."

"Did you—"

But his father's already pushed himself through to the living room. Hen pounds his forehead on the kitchen table three times—once, twice, harder. It's the last sound he'll hear for a while, the thudding of his head on wood as the door swings slowly to a halt.

Night finds them in familiar, twisted positions—Remi slumped in his armchair reading the Sunday sports pages, Faye rummaging out in the hallway closet, Hen watching TV on the couch. The Flintstones have a new baby, Pebbles, with a bone through her onion-style ponytail. *Yab-ba-dabba-doo.*

"You used to be that cute," Remi says out of the blue in a monotone voice. Nothing after. Nothing more.

During the ads, Hen reads from a stack of old *Mad* magazines which

Faye's unearthed from the hall closet as she cleans—the Lighter Side of Everything—College, Parents, Careers—a boy mushing his food in his highchair, his beaming parents picturing him grown up as a great chef. Cut to twenty years later: the kid-now-man has a cigarette hanging out of the corner of his mouth and tosses garbage into a fly-swarmed truck. Out in the hallway, Faye cleans on into the night, sorting and piling. With a squeaky magic marker, she marks one cardboard box TOSS and another one KEEP. After watching a *The Girl from Uncle* rerun, Hen comes out to help her. They speak in mime. She raises up old hardballs and jackets and boots and he shakes or nods his head, but in the end, everything goes into the TOSS box, even the KEEP box. Only as Faye carts the boxes to the front door does Hen rescue an old Red Sox cap from the top of a pile, suddenly filled with a longing for anything that represents life before this moment, this purge. He hangs on to the hat, the canned laughter from the TV, the dull look in his father's drunken eyes, wakefulness, anything that will hold them all together.

Midnight. The day shuts in on itself and grudgingly turns into the next. No one goes to bed. No one speaks. Remi's crack about Hen's having been as cute as the Flintstone baby echoes loud and foolish in the air, the only thing said in a human voice all night. Something is terribly wrong, only this Hen knows. His mother's so busy, so ashen, so disturbingly calm. His father looks dazed and defeated. For once he has nothing left to say. Hen feels the house slowly caving in over the loaded silence, like cheeks collapsing over toothless gums. He fights to keep his eyes open, stretched out on the floor, watching TV. He has to stay up, to keep them together, keep them apart, keep them from hurting each other anymore, keep the silence from exploding. Big bang. It's how the world began and how a family could end. It's his job. He's the night watchman, the keeper of the silence.

Sometime later, Hen wakes up in the dark. A *Mad* magazine lies open on his chest to a movie spoof, "Star Blecch." The armchair's empty, the hall light's still on. Zigzag lines buzz loudly on the TV. Out in the hallway, Faye's working on the bookshelves—dusting, piling, leafing through old books, still cleaning.

Hen stretches and yawns. "What time is it, Mom?"

"Time?" Faye flips her wrist. "Oh, darn. I must have left my watch at the cottage. I took it off to—"

Hen rubs his eyes. "Where's Dad?"

"In bed, I suppose."

"What's going on, Mom?"

"What do you mean?"

"Why did you come home alone? Why's Dad acting so weird? And why are you throwing everything away?"

Faye plants her hands on her thighs. "We have so much *stuff*, Hen," she says. "So much that we just don't need. I've been meaning to do this for years. I guess cleaning up the cottage got me inspired."

"What happened in Nantucket?"

"What do you mean?"

"You and Dad haven't said a word to each other all night."

"Your father and I had a bit of a misunderstanding. That's all."

"That's nothing new," Hen says.

Faye blows the dust from a thin book, a classic from a college lit course, *Silas Marner*. "It's true," she says. "This one went a bit deeper, I guess." She opens the book. "This was such a wonderful story," she says. "A testament to the resiliency of the human spirit."

Hen rubs the side of his face, feels the layer of soft fuzz, still not enough to shave. "Why are you guys acting this way?"

"What way?"

"Like you can't even stand to be in the same fucking room together."

"You sound angry."

"I don't know what's going on," he says. "I feel like I might wake up tomorrow morning and everyone will be gone, like I'm about to walk off a ledge into the Twilight Zone."

"That won't happen, Hen. Don't worry."

"You don't get it, do you? I have to worry."

Faye labels a new TOSS box with the black magic marker. "Worry if you have to then," she says. "All I can do is reassure you that there's always light at the end of the tunnel." She looks over at him. "That I really am okay."

"You don't look okay. You look sick, Mom. And Dad came home like a walking zombie—"

"I'm not sick, Hen. I promise. And as for your father—"

"I know what happened," Hen says, kneeling down beside her. "I know what happened, Mom. And I'm sorry."

"Whatever for? Heavens, between you and your father—"

"I know Dad hit you. I saw him. I was up at the top of the stairs."

"What? Oh no," she says, finally understanding. "Oh, Hen, honey. The lamp. That was a long time ago. Water under the—"

"Did he hit you again?" Hen asks. "Is that what happened on the island? Did he hurt you?"

"No," Faye says. Above all else, she owes this truth to him and Remi both. "He didn't hurt me, I promise."

"Do you forgive him? For what he did to you? For what he's done?"

"I do." Faye's surprised by the quickness of her answer. "Marriage is a two-way street, Hen. Your father and I have both made more than our share of mistakes. Believe me."

They kneel in the hallway, face to face. The clock ticks on the hallway wall. It's almost two a.m. "Do I have flat feet?" he says finally.

"Flat feet?" Faye suddenly knows what he's asking—about a plan, a way out of the draft, but she can't answer just then as a parent should to a child, right away, soothingly, persuasively, the all-powerful we'll see, don't worry, we'll think of something—a hitch, a shrink, a prayer. She can only answer as a mother does fiercely in defense of a child whose perfection has been challenged. "Your feet are perfect, Hen," she says. "Absolutely perfect."

In a second-floor office in Central Square, a psychiatrist in jeans and a corduroy shirt holds out his hand. "Hi, I'm Paul Dunphy," he says. "You're Henry?"

"Hen, yeah." Hen rubs his hands on his pants. "Henry. Hen."

"Have a seat." They sit face-to-face, in comfortable, overstuffed chairs. Paul Dunphy leans forward, backwards, forward again. "So, Hen. I hear you have a gripe with this war."

Hen shifts in his chair. "I guess you could say that," he says.

Paul Dunphy nods his head. "Why don't we start then, with you telling me why."

Hen listens for sarcasm, waits for the condescending smile. "I just basically believe that war is wrong," he says. "The cost in human life is way too high."

"How long have you felt this way, Hen?"

"Always."

"Always?"

"For as long as I've been thinking about it, anyway," Hen says. "When you're a kid, you don't really sweat that kind of stuff. You think nothing can hurt you. But I've never liked conflict, never been any good at it."

"Was conflict something you were expected to be good at?"

The question takes Hen by surprise. "Yeah," he says. "I guess it was."

Paul Dunphy nods. "Let's backtrack a bit, Hen. You do know that this war began—"

"In the fifties, after Vietnam gained independence from France. The Communists came in and tried to take over." The rehearsed parts of his answers slide out smooth as silk.

Paul Dunphy nods again. "So, you're clear on the fact that this war began a long time ago, that it's not a personal attack on you, or your generation, or a deliberate challenge to any one person's or group's beliefs."

Hen shifts uneasily in his chair. "Yeah," he says. "I know all that."

"I'm not trying to be flip, Hen," Paul Dunphy says. "I just like to start by bringing the discussion out of a personal space into a broader framework."

"You do this with a lot of guys?" Hen stretches out his legs, balances the heels of his hiking boots on the floor.

"A fair number. So, I'm sure you also know, Hen, that is to say, you have an intellectual understanding—right or wrong—that death is an inevitable component of war."

"But that's just it." Hen spins his hand in frustrated circles. "I don't see why it has to be. Maybe my brain's fried, or too small to grasp it. But to me it's so simple. No one should *have* to die, over this war or anything."

"Anything?"

"Anything but sickness, old age, freak accidents. Things you have no control over."

"I think we could certainly classify Vietnam as a problem that's spiraled out of control."

"It didn't start out that way," Hen says.

"True," Paul Dunphy says. "Hindsight is twenty-twenty; it's always easy to second-guess. I just want to establish that some people *do* believe in this war, right or wrong. And some of those people are decent, moral people, people you've grown up with, maybe. Friends, family, even. Would you agree?"

"My father, for instance," Hen says.

"Really," Paul Dunphy says, trying to pin down the word. "Hold that thought, Hen. We'll come back to your father later." He leans forward again in his chair. "Meanwhile, let's say your mother is out on a ledge. Would you try and save her?"

"Of course," Hen says.

"At what risk to yourself? Would you go out there with her?"

"I'd do what I could."

"You're both out there and the going gets rough. There's a critical moment. Only one of you might make it."

"Okay, I'd consider risking my life to save my mother who was about to jump off a ledge," Hen says. "But not dying for a cause, for an idea, even one I believed in. There are other ways to solve problems and it'd be better to put our energy into finding better solutions."

"Such as?" Paul Dunphy asks.

"Talking," Hen says.

"Would you try and talk your mother down off the ledge?"

"Yes, I would."

"For how long?"

"Until I saw that it wasn't working, that she really was going to jump."

"That would be a difficult moment to pinpoint, wouldn't it?" Paul Dunphy leans back again in his chair. "I imagine the powers that be in Washington would argue that they'd tried negotiating as a means of solving the conflict in Southeast Asia."

"Then it might boil down to your definition of trying," Hen says.

Paul Dunphy nods, as if to concede him a point. "Let's switch the scenario a bit," he says.

Hen watches Paul Dunphy. He seems to be enjoying himself, getting into it. He's probably the father of the two little girls in the photograph on his desk, too established, too old now to be called to the war. He's a decent guy, a smart guy. He could sit in that chair and talk to anyone in that same calm, rational voice—Hawk, Dove, crazy man, fool.

"Forgive me for taking these liberties with your mother, Hen," Paul Dunphy says. "But suppose she told you, out on that ledge, that she wanted to die, that she was very sick or in some terrible pain, that she was tired of living, that there was a reason she'd made her way out there. Would that change the situation? Would you feel the need to take the same extreme action, even if she had expressed this wish to you? What if you felt her judgment was impaired, that she was not in a position to know her own mind clearly? Would you try and save her, just to save her, whether she wanted you to or not?"

"I would," Hen says. "But it's still not the same. It's a split-second decision versus one that gets made over time. It's the life of one person versus the future of two countries, the whole world, really. It's like apples…" He twirls his hand again. "…and bombs. It's so much more complicated."

"It is," Paul Dunphy says. "My point is, though, people don't always take action just for the sake of taking action. Sometimes they do so because they've been frustrated in their attempts to solve their problems in other ways. Or because they truly believe that if they don't, the consequences will be even more dire, that all hell will break loose."

"I know what you're trying to say." Hen raises his head. "Wars are usually about something, right?"

"They are," Paul Dunphy says.

"I've heard that before," Hen says. "But that doesn't make them right."

"No, it doesn't." Paul Dunphy's hands join at the fingertips to make a bridge. "Problem is, Hen. *Right* is an abstract. When you come right down to it, *right* is only a matter of opinion."

"But no one ever asked my opinion," Hen says. "If I get a low number in the draft, just because of what day I happened to be born, I have to go. That's not fair."

"It isn't fair," Paul Dunphy says. "And yet the paradox is, it's the only fair way."

"Why?"

"If you start asking opinions, picking and choosing, then favoritism arises, prejudice rears its ugly head. Who goes? Who stays? Who's clever enough, rich enough, to find a way out? And who isn't? The draft lottery's fair because it clears the slate, puts everyone on the same footing. In the end, it's the great equalizer."

"A volunteer army worked in World War II," Hen says. "Plenty of guys want to go over there and fight, and I'm not putting them down. I respect their opinion and I admire their courage. I think it's nuts, but I respect their right to want to go."

"And if those guys go, and die, are their deaths any more justified, any less horrific, than the deaths of those who didn't want to go?"

"No, of course not. But at least it would have been their choice."

"Choice? Mission? Obligation?" The bridge of Paul Dunphy's hands collapses. "That's where these labels get tricky. Let's say the angles changed, the pressures were off—an all-volunteer army, as you suggest. What if nobody chose to go?"

"Great," Hen says. "They'd be forced to find another way. They'd have to deal with the problems of peace instead of the problems of war."

"Give a war, and nobody comes." Paul Dunphy considers this. "Why are you so against this war?" He asks the first question again, abruptly, taking Hen off guard.

Hen twists a paper clip. "What do you mean?" he says. "I've been sitting here telling you why. All this time."

"I know. And you're doing great." Paul Dunphy lights a cigarette. "I'd like to get us on another tack now," he says. "From the general back to the specific. What else do you want to tell me, Hen. What else is on your mind?"

"The big thing for me is…I could never shoot a gun," Hen says. "At another person. Into someone. I couldn't. I know."

"You consider yourself a pacifist?"

"I do."

Strangely, Hen hears the marriage vow in his answer.

"And what does that mean to you, pacifism?"

"Seeking nonviolent ways to solve problems. No matter what." Hen looks over at the picture of the two little girls. "Are those your kids?" he says.

Paul Dunphy nods and smiles. "They are."

"What do you tell them when they fight? To hit each other? Or to turn the other cheek?"

"We teach them to talk things over, try and work it out."

"So what do you tell them if they ask why the people in the war can't work it out, why all the people are dying?"

"The dialogue's on a different level when you're talking to a seven-year-old."

"Why?"

"Because you don't want to scare them. You don't want fear to get in the way."

"Why's it any different when you're eighteen?" Hen says. "Or twenty-five or fifty? Why *shouldn't* fear get in the way? It's *real*, man."

Paul Dunphy's eyebrows rise through a haze of smoke as he leans back in his chair. "Do you have siblings, Hen?"

"A brother and a sister," Hen says.

"You guys ever fight?"

"Not much." Hen shifts in his chair. "They're much older. They left home when I was young. So in a way, I was an only child."

"You don't talk to your brother?"

"Not much."

"He lives far away?"

"Just over in Allston," Hen says. "He's off the hook, draft-wise. He has a fake thumb."

"Fake thumb?"

"He was born without one. They made him a fake one from his thigh. Automatic exemption."

"Lucky him?" Paul Dunphy takes another drag of his cigarette.

"I'm not jealous, if that's what you mean." Hen shakes his head. "I never wanted to be Buzz."

"Actually, that's not what I was getting at," Paul Dunphy says. "I was wondering how problems were generally resolved in your family."

"Not very well," Hen says with a shrug. "Pull down the shade and kick the mess under the bed. My father slaps you on the back and tells you to buck up. And my mother recites proverbs and hopes for the best. Basically, my family just can't deal."

"So, is it fair to say that you don't come from a long line of great problem solvers?"

"Yeah. That's fair." There's something about meeting Paul Dunphy's steady gaze, answering his questions head-on, hearing the sure sound of his own voice that calms him. "But I'm working on it," Hen says. "Being a good problem solver. That's a goal of mine."

"Tell me, Hen." Paul Dunphy puts out his cigarette. "Am I the first person you've expressed these views to, in any direct kind of way?"

Hen shifts in his chair. "My uncle and I have talked a lot about the war. And I've tried to talk to my father, but…" He doesn't know why he blurts this out, because he's talking to a shrink, because he came here to tell the truth, the whole truth, because he's so damn tired. "My father drinks," Hen says.

"Drinks?"

"He's pretty much a drunk. We try to talk. But it never works."

"And your uncle?"

"My uncle's active in the anti-war movement. He's always out there on the front lines."

"Does he drink, too, your uncle?"

Hen nods. "They both do. Like fish."

"Do you?"

"No."

"Not at all?"

"Not at all."

"Good for you," Paul Dunphy says. "Tell me about your uncle."

"He's my father's twin brother."

"Really? And he supports you in your beliefs?"

"Yes."

"But your father doesn't."

"My father just doesn't want me to rock the boat," Hen says. "He just wants me to do the right thing."

"And how do you feel, Hen," Paul Dunphy says, "you know, about doing the right thing?"

"I feel like in this case, it's…wrong." Hen suddenly sees the meeting as a test of fitness, alertness. Whoever yawns first, falters for words, breaks eye contact, loses.

"Morally wrong? Or just wrong wrong?" Paul Dunphy is tireless. "Not right for you wrong? Scary wrong? It's completely natural, Hen, to be scared. Frankly, I'd be concerned if you weren't."

Hen rubs his eyes, feels his mind being led offtrack. He's so easily distracted, so malleable, so small. That's what this guy's trying to prove, that he's not strong or principled, just scared, a weakling, a coward, a follower, a giver-in. *Stand your ground, man,* his father's slurred voice comes at him. *Stand your goddamned ground.* He leans forward. He has to keep talking, keep trying to explain. "Look, I'm no great political activist or anything. I'm just a guy, just a kid. And I *am* scared. Scared shitless. But I'm telling you what I know about myself. They told me to be honest, to come here and say what I really feel. Well, I'm telling you, man, if they put a gun in my hand and one to my head and told me to make a choice, *I'd* be the dead man, man. I'm telling you. I couldn't make myself do it."

Paul Dunphy leafs through the pile of papers before him, and abruptly changes the subject. "Do you consider yourself to be a religious person, Hen?"

"No." Hen rubs his forehead.

"No god at all."

"No."

"No belief in an afterlife?"

"No. Just this one."

"No faith, no—"

"Nothing," Hen says.

"You holding up okay?" Paul Dunphy glances at his watch. "Need a break? Drink of water? Seventh-inning stretch?"

"No. I'm good," Hen says.

"Okay. We're just about done. Hypothetical. How would you feel if you *did* get a psychiatric deferment? Saying out loud to the world. I'm unfit. Loony. Deficient in some way. Because that's how it would come down in the public arena. How would you handle the hostility, the ostracizing? Because I can assure you, there'd be both."

"I wouldn't care about the hostility," Hen says. "That's human nature. And...what was the other thing you said?"

"How would you feel about people being angry, calling you names, treating you badly, because you'd found a way out—copped out, even."

"I wouldn't like it," Hen says. "But I'd try to understand where those feelings came from, and I'd try..." He runs his hand across his forehead. "To stand my ground."

"How would you feel about getting a psychiatric deferment, Hen?" Paul Dunphy asks again.

Hen's head snaps up. "I'd take it."

"Without reservations? Second thoughts? No doubt or misgivings or guilt?"

"I'd take it. I would. I'd take it."

"Gladly? Peacefully?"

"Hey, what do you want from me, man." Hen feels himself getting rattled, hears his voice rising. "There's no glad in any of this. No peace for sure. I said I'd take it, and accept the consequences, and I would. That's why I came here today."

Paul Dunphy pulls out another cigarette. "All I'm trying to run home, Hen, is, that if you want someone to say you're crazy, you have to take responsibility for being crazy."

"I know."

"And you understand that I'm not in the business of calling people crazy when I don't think they are. It goes against my professional grain. I prefer to think that my job is to help people see just how normal most of their problems are, how crazy they *aren't*."

Hen nods. "I know."

"So, let's clear the slate one last time. If there were absolutely nothing at stake, no pressure, no draft, no politics, if you were just telling a fly on the wall how you felt about this whole goddamned mess, in one sentence, what would it be? Answer from the gut, Hen, not from the list of answers you brought with you here today."

"God. What's the question?" Hen dips his head, suddenly exhausted. "*What* did you ask me?" he asks.

"Why are you so against this war?" Paul Dunphy's voice is maddeningly calm, even as he asks the same question for the third goddamned time.

"I just don't see why I—why any of us, anyone," Hen says, "should have to take the rap."

"The rap being?"

"Death," Hen says. "Fighting for something we may not even believe in. Being asked to be sitting ducks and murderers, to put our own lives on the line."

"You—anyone—shouldn't have to take the rap for…" Paul Dunphy pulls the rest of Hen's thought from his brain. "The rap for whom, Hen? For what?"

"For being crazy. *I'm* not crazy. *You're* not crazy. The guy on the street corner's not crazy. It's the war that's crazy. The idea of killing people to help them is crazy."

"But take the rap for whom?" Paul Dunphy says. "Who *should* take the rap, Hen?"

Hen gets up on his feet, starts pacing. "The government! The politicians who make the big decisions, who give the orders to bomb. McNamara! Kissinger! Nixon! They should take the rap for carrying on with a plan that's gone totally berserk, out of control. For playing chicken with people's lives. For the way they've abused their power. It's always about power." He looks Paul Dunphy in the eye. "Isn't it?"

Paul Dunphy leans forward in his chair. "What will you do if you *don't* get a deferment, Hen?"

"Maybe go to Canada," Hen says. "Apply for CO status. I'm not sure yet."

Paul Dunphy nods, jots down some notes on his pad. "Okay, we're almost done. Just a few more questions. Ever thought of suicide?"

"No."

"Any concerns about your sexuality?"

"Concerns? What? No way. What are these questions about?"

"Just routine," Paul Dunphy says. "Any physical ailments, Hen? Allergies, bedwetting, color blindness…" He raises his eyes. "Flat feet?"

"No," Hen says. "No flat feet."

"Okay, then." Paul Dunphy closes his folder. "Anything else you want to ask me, Hen? Anything else you want to say? I'm here now. Now's the time."

Hen shakes his head. He watches Paul Dunphy jot down some notes in his folder, a scribble that might wrap him up in a nutshell. "So that's it?" he says.

"That's it, Hen. I've enjoyed talking with you. You're obviously a fine young man."

"What do I do now?"

"I'll send my report to the draft board. Someone there will be contacting you, probably in a few weeks. Let's hope peace beats us to the punch, that it's all a moot point and we can look back on this as an earnest discussion between two friends."

"You don't make the decision," Hen says.

"No," Paul Dunphy says. "I only write the report."

"You can't tell me anything."

"No," Paul Dunphy says. "I'm not at liberty."

"Liberty." Hen hears the sarcasm creep into his voice. "But I'm a fine young man."

"I think you are."

"But I'm not crazy enough, am I?" Hen says. "I don't really make the grade."

"Thanks for coming, Hen." Paul Dunphy holds out his hand.

Hen pulls the door shut hard on the way out. Goddamned shrink won't answer the only real question he's had for him all day.

12

In the courtyard at Holyoke Center, Hen plays a game with the chess master and wins. Pocketing a dollar, he gets up from the chair and stays to watch the next match. Chickie comes back from her hiding place in the Game, does a few pliés using the spiky rim of the streetside fence as her barre. Elvis is still on the loose.

Hen walks over and sits down next to her on a bench. "Hey, Chick," he says. "Where's the Norton man?"

"Who knows, who cares."

"Who cares?" Hen looks up at her. "Mercy." It's so rare now for him to see her alone. Chickie's surrounded. People watch her again as they used to when she was young, bounding up the slide at the park in her scuffed-up Stride Rite saddle shoes. She cultivates her mystery, likes to be watched. She acts for them, shifts on her hip, leans, stretches, French-inhales, talks tough.

"You heard me right," Chickie says. "Who the fuck cares."

"Not me." Hen swings his legs up and puts his head on her lap. It's been four years since that night at Fenway Park, when Remi told him he shouldn't touch Chickie anymore and the drunk fell on the cement floor. Whatever happened to that man, Hen wonders, to the guy up on the Marlboro sign, to that poor, stupid bird? It was on that night that he started to understand how power was abstract, not absolute, how its lines were imaginary, human-drawn, clumsily, arbitrarily, how the drunk could've been the baseball player could have been… That was the night Hen figured out that his father could never make him do anything against his will, only put the fear of his own weaknesses inside him. He shifts his head on Chickie's thigh. As long as he can think straight, he's his own god. He'll make his own decisions. One thing he knows; he'll never drink alcohol. This is one choice he's made. He's no genius, but the math of no booze is simple. Sobriety equals clarity equals strength equals power. He'll keep his mind open, clear, be responsible for whatever he thinks and does. He can decide to be crazy, or tell the truth as he sees it. But whatever he does, he'll be sober. No one can stop him from being a conscientious objector or going to Canada, or from putting his head in Chickie's lap except Chickie. And she's always been able to take care of herself.

Chickie looks down at him, smooths his hair off his forehead. "Hey, sweetheart," she says.

"What's with all this sweetheart jazz?"

"Sweet...heart." Chickie separates the words, as if to explain.

As his neck takes in the warmth of Chickie's thigh, Hen thinks of Melody. She hasn't called him, dropped him any kind of line; he doesn't even know her last name. No way he'll ask Tory. She'd razz him black and blue. He's not even sure how much he cares; how could he after only fifteen minutes thrashing around with her in his parents' bed? He was inside Melody for one burning, bucking moment, and yet he can barely remember what she looks like, what she felt like. Slowly, the tenor of her southern drawl comes back to him, the first feel of her breasts, the smell of her shampooed hair. She spoke in rhymes and jingles; *Welcome to the Casa Melody,* she purred. Hen doesn't miss Melody, just feels an aching need to see her, feel her again. Face to face, he'd have to get up his courage and try to fuck her again, which of course he'd want to do. God, he's been dying to. He's hardly thought of anything else since. But it was so hard, so good, so...hard to remember.

Hen lifts his head from Chickie's thigh. "Ah, the hell with it," he says.

"The hell with what?"

"Nothing."

"Come on. Lie back down," Chickie says. "I miss you, Hen. Where've you been?"

Hen looks up into her face. "I've been right here," he says. "Right here in the flesh."

She rakes his bangs off his forehead. "I haven't seen you."

"You're a busy lady." Hen brings his chin back down to his chest.

"It may be over soon with Elvis. I'm getting frustrated, and anyways, I think he has the hots for Jamie Menneker."

"Oh, come on, Chickie. He's crazy about you."

"Yeah, right. Crazy is the word. All we ever do is—"

"I don't want to hear about it."

"Anyway, I don't need his shit," Chickie says.

"So don't take it."

"Jamie Menneker's pretty, isn't she?"

"You're pretty," Hen says.

"Yeah, but I have to be *up* for being pretty," Chickie says. "Jamie

Menneker looks like a mannequin in a store window. You know, like the less she cares, the better she looks."

"I'm sick of hearing how ugly you are."

"I didn't say I was ugly," she says. "Who do you think is the prettiest, Hen?" Her fingers rake through his hair, over and over again.

"Marilyn Monroe." Hen closes his eyes. After that night with Melody, he replaced his Janis Joplin poster with one of Marilyn, the whooshing air from the subway blowing up her white dress.

"She probably doesn't look so hot anymore," Chickie says. "All shriveled up, flesh half rotted off her bones—"

Hen winces. "Have a little respect, will you?"

"Who's the prettiest girl alive, Hen. Okay, I'll make it easier. Who's the prettiest girl in Cambridge? At the high school? Who's the prettiest senior? And don't say me."

"I don't know," Hen says. "Alison Conway, maybe."

"Alison Conway? Oh, spare me. The Queen of Space Cadets?"

"Space Cadets don't have queens," Hen says. "They have icons, vulcans, gigolos, doormen, maybe."

Chickie points a finger to Hen's temple. "*M. T.* The abbreviation of mountain, Hen. You catch my drift?"

"You didn't ask me about her brain. You asked me who was prettier."

"You think Alison Conway is prettier than Jamie Menneker?"

Hen starts to sit up again. "I'm not going to do this with you anymore," he says.

"Okay, okay." As Chickie pushes his head back down again, her hand trails over his neck. "Hey, what's this?" she says.

Hen reaches up to feel the tender spot near his birthmark. "Nothing," he says. "Just a bruise."

"No way." Chickie leans closer. "That's not a bruise. It's teeth marks."

Hen rubs the spot again.

"Someone bit you," she says in a loud voice. "Who the hell bit you, Hen?"

"Quiet, Chickie."

"I don't believe it. Actual human teeth marks. A few weeks old, I'd say."

"It's none of your business. Believe it, Chickie."

"Who *was* it?" she says.

"Stop it." As Hen's voice rises, the people around them start to stare.

"Just curious," Chickie says. Seeing an audience form, she jacks up a smile and turns it on, takes a stick of gum from an outstretched hand. "Just wondering which vampires you've been hanging out with lately, Henry."

"Shut up, Chickie," Hen says, trying to quiet her. "I mean it. Leave it alone."

"Who was it?" she teases. "Fat Ass Prentiss catch you alone in the locker room? Or did Alison Conway—prettiest girl on the planet—come over to help you with your homework and turn into a werewolf? Come on, tell me, Hen. I'll find out one way or another. The Grapevine knows all."

"It was just some friend of my sister's, all right?" Chickie won't give up. She could care less about making a scene. Chickie loves making a scene.

"Oh my god. Miss Va Va VOOM?" Chickie makes spilling motions out of her breasts. "Miss Tra-la-la-dee-dah?"

"Melody," Hen says. "Her name is Melody."

"That girl in the living room? She did this to you? How old is she, for god's sake?"

"Twenty-six."

"Twenty-six? And you actually fucked her?" Chickie's voice falls back into a whisper.

Hen's mouth rises in a half-smile. "I was there," he says. "I was definitely there."

"What was it like?"

"You should write for *True Confessions*, Chickie. You've got such a one-track mind."

"I told you about Elvis," Chickie says. "Everything except how big his dick is, and you guys probably get out the ruler in gym class anyway, right?"

Hen winces and shakes his head. "Jesus Christ. Why do you talk like such a scumbag? You do it just to get a rise out of me. I hate it."

"I'm just honest and you can't take it. Anyway, it would take an earthquake to get a rise out of you these days, Mr. Hard Ass. An earthquake, or I guess Miss Va Va Voom with tits the size of Mount Everest."

Hen gets up and pulls Chickie by the arm into the shade of a fragile, caged tree. "Look," he says. "I never asked to hear any of that crap about Elvis, how you made it out on the golf course or on the seat of his bike. I never wanted to hear any of it." He can't tell her the whole truth, that he can't look at Elvis's motorcycle boots without wanting to spit on them, not to mention how he does feel when he sees Elvis naked in the shower in gym. Part of him wants to know everything that goes on between Chickie and Elvis, where he touches her, whether she moans or softens or rises above him, what words get said. But the other part can't stand any of it. The other part might go crazy hearing all the gory details, might have to do something wild, find some wire clippers and take the Norton for a spin, punch Elvis out, push Chickie into a dark closet and lock the door. One part of him might have to act like a jealous brother, like a raving maniac, like…

"Hen, let go."

"Sorry." He lets her arm fall.

"Just need my circulation back, that's all."

"She came up to my room, Chick. I was watching the Bruins. It just happened."

"Hey, you don't have to explain. Congratulations. Join the fucking crowd. Ha, ha."

"It was no big deal."

"Hey, it's great. I'm happy for you. It's high time." She gets up from the bench. "Lucky she didn't have a heart attack on you. I can just see the headlines now: *High school boy smothered by lover's tits*. The *Enquirer* would pay you big bucks."

"I'd take every cent!" Hen calls back.

Chickie waltzes off to bum a cigarette. Elvis comes back to the courtyard, puffing away on a Camel. The unsnapped straps on the shoulders of his leather jacket flap as he walks. His long hair trails over the Norton logo on the back. Chickie winds her arms around his neck, cigarette nearly singeing his hair, slowly turning to ash as the smoky kiss goes on and on. Elvis dips her, Fred to Ginger, pulls her back up, and pushes her away at the waist. Chickie starts dancing in the courtyard. Elvis lights a new cigarette with the stub of his old one, watches her, expressionless, one boot raised up on the bench. Chickie's skirt swirls out around her as she moves. A few people gather to watch. The chess master pockets another dollar. Someone tosses some change down on the jacket Chickie's cast off from around her waist. A guy whistles at her from a car. Elvis's eyes narrow in the smoke as he turns toward the street and shoots up his middle finger. Hen can't watch. He goes home to read how Alekhine pulled himself together to beat Capablanca in the 1927 World Chess Championship match in Buenos Aires. He took on all his vices to make himself invincible, stopped smoking and drinking, walked for miles every day. He was the underdog. He simply decided he was going to win. And he did. Even the best chess minds were amazed.

A few days later, Chickie pushes through the turnstyle of Hazen's Restaurant on Holyoke Street. Creedence Clearwater plays too softly on the wall jukebox, to no one and no purpose. The late breakfast crowd lingers. The Wart Lady wipes the counter, busting out of her waitress uniform. Arthur's working the grill, tossing frost-covered burgers onto the hot metal slab, arranging neat bunches of lettuce, slicing tomatoes. He's a small man, with a bullet-shaped head, snow white hair, pinkish eyes. They say he used to live in the alleyway out back, until the Wart Lady dragged him in one day, cleaned him up, and taught him how to fry an egg.

"Seen Hen today, Arthur?" Chickie says.

"Over there." Arthur gestures with his spatula.

Hen sits at the counter near the kitchen, the heels of his hiking boots hooked over the rim of the stool's legs, playing out a chess game on his new leather set. Chickie slides onto the stool next to him. "Order of English, please," she says. "Jam, no butter, please."

"You need to eat more, Lady Godiva," Arthur says. "You kids are all too thin."

Hen looks up at Chickie. His bangs rise up in a swell.

"God, Hen, what's with your hair?"

"What?" He brings his hand up to his head.

"It's doing kind of a James Brown thing." Chickie gestures in waves with her hand.

"Only my hairdresser knows for sure," Hen says.

Chickie sighs. "You're getting so weird," she says.

"I've always been weird."

"You wish." Chickie will never get out of the habit of defending Hen, even against himself. "Come over to a booth. I have to talk to you."

"I can't tell you all of my beauty secrets." Hen yawns, picks up his chess set and coffee and follows her.

"Stop being such a jerk, Hen. You never used to be so sarcastic."

"Coming from the Queen of Sarcasm—"

"All of a sudden you're so fucking full of yourself," Chickie says. "That was one thing I used to love about you. You were never full of yourself."

"And so the question would be—who *was* I full of?"

"And I know when it happened," Chickie says. "It's ever since you made whoopee with Miss Tra-la-la."

"Melody." Hen puts a dime in the jukebox and reaches to press B.B. King. Chickie beats him to the punch, pushes Richie Havens. "Her name is Melody," he says. "And it happens to the best of us, Chick."

"Right. Zillions of people have sex every day. So why do you think it makes you so special?"

"I don't," Hen says. "If anything, I think it's made me much more ordinary."

Chickie picks up a sugar packet, pushes it all into a lump in one corner, under the picture of a snowy egret. "All I know is you're different," she says.

"The draft lottery's in July, Chick. I could be dead by Christmas. It's a whole new perspective. How could I not be different?"

"You think about dying too much," she says.

"You're the one who gave me my birthday present six months early."

Arthur puts the English muffins on the counter and Hen goes up to get them. When he sits back down, Chickie tugs at the yellow chamois sleeve of his shirt. "Something happened, Hen." Hen feels his stomach drop. "I'm pregnant," she says.

"What?" His coffee cup stops dead at a dangerous tilt.

"I got knocked up."

"Who—"

"Who do you think. I'm not some raving nympho."

"Are you sure?" Hen says.

"The rabbit croaked," Chickie says. "Twice even. I've been puking my brains out for the past two weeks. If I'm not pregnant, I'm dying."

"Jesus Christ, Chickie. Does he know?"

"No."

"What the hell happened?" he says.

"I guess the pills didn't work," she says.

"Pills?"

"Yes. I had pills. One of us had to do something and it sure as hell wasn't going to be Elvis. What'd you and what's-her-face use?"

"Nothing," Hen says. "It all happened so fast."

"Nothing? Great. That's really responsible. Well, I had pills. I went out and got the fucking pills. You're supposed to be safe, as long as you don't miss more than two nights. I swear I didn't. I couldn't have. This happens to two percent of women on the pill. Just my luck. God, I don't know. Maybe I did miss three nights. I can't remember."

"What are we going to do?" Hen says.

"We?" she says.

"You, then," Hen says.

Chickie shakes her head. "What do you think I'm going to do? There's no way I'm ready to have a kid."

"You've got to tell him, Chickie."

"It's none of his business."

"It's his, for Christ's sake."

"No, it isn't *his*. It's nobody's. It isn't anything yet."

"He made it, didn't he?"

"*We* made it, Hen. Completely by accident. Elvis didn't want a baby any more than I did. If he'd wanted a baby, he would've said, 'Hey, Chickie, let's make a baby.' But all he ever said was 'Hey, Chickie, let's get stoned. Hey, Chickie, let's fuck our brains out.'"

Hen winces. "You've got to tell him, Chickie. It's only fair."

"Fair." Chickie throws up her hands. "I love this. How guys stick together, no matter what. It kills me. You can't even stand Elvis but you want to make sure he has his rights. What about my rights, Hen? What about—"

"I never said I couldn't stand him."

"It's obvious," Chickie says.

"It's obvious?"

"It's fucking *obvious*, Hen."

"Pipe down, kids," Arthur says from the grill.

"Look," Hen says, lowering his voice. "All I'm saying is, you shouldn't have to go through this alone."

"What if I want to go through it alone?"

"He should help you, Chickie. He should go with you." Hen runs his hand through his hair. "He should pay for half. He should *do* something."

"Now I know why my father hates that word," Chickie says. "Nothing should or shouldn't happen. And I don't want anything from Elvis. This is happening to me, Hen. It's my life, my body. I'm going to get an abortion."

"An abortion? You can't. It's illegal."

"Not in New York," Chickie says. "They have a van at Planned Parenthood downtown. It leaves at six in the morning and comes back the same night. It's all over in one day."

"How much?" Hen says.

"One hundred fifty dollars."

Hen slaps his back upright against the booth. "Where are we going to get that kind of money?" Forty-one dollars in his bank account. He'll take all the change from Faye's cigarette jar, the money she plunks in every day since she quit, money she would have spent on butts. Probably close to another fifty. No, he'll talk to Remi man to man, ask him for a loan, something private. A handshake and no questions asked. Maybe some collateral to show he's serious, a promise of work around the house, at the store. A man thing. Remi will understand that kind of a hush-hush deal, that it has to do with a girl.

"I have the money," Chickie says. "I won that essay contest in the seventh grade, remember? 'Home: Building Block of the Future.' I wrote some corny bullshit but I had good penmanship, so I won. I was supposed to use the prize money for my education. I guess you could say this counts."

"You can't get that money until you're twenty-one," Hen says.

"Janie will lend it to me," Chickie says. "She's been hoarding cash for years. She's a walking Brink's truck these days."

Hen takes a deep breath. "How do they do it?" he says.

"They drive you in a van—"

"No, I mean how do they *do* it." He bangs his hand on the counter, waits in the dark of his closed eyes for Chickie's answer, just as he's done so many times before.

"It's like a vacuum cleaner." Chickie's voice grows calm. "They just kind of suck it out. It's simple, Hen. The doctor explained it to me. I'm only nine weeks. It's easy. It's safe."

"Man," Hen says. "Man, oh, man, oh man."

"It's just like having your period." She puts her hand on his arm. "Before twelve weeks, it's not a big deal. I'm going on Monday. I have to be at Planned Parenthood at six in the morning. I'll take the subway downtown. I'll be home by seven that night."

Hen opens his eyes. "I'll come on the subway with you."

Chickie suddenly puts her hand up to her mouth and groans.

"What's wrong?" Hen asks.

"I don't feel well," she says.

"Fly away, kids." Arthur's voice slides their way. "Truant officer's coming." The blue van pulls up to the curb. Out the plate-glass window, Chickie sees a man in a suit slam the car door.

"Time to go now, Chick." Hen pulls her up by the arm.

"I'm going to be sick," she says.

"You can't be sick."

"I'm going to be sick," she says again. "Now."

Hen rushes her into the men's room where she vomits into the toilet, once, and then again. He rests one hand on her back as she heaves, keeping her hair pulled back with the other. When she's done, she wipes her mouth on her sleeve, leans back on her heels. Hen rubs her back as they wait, until Arthur knocks on the door. "Coast is clear, kids," he says. "Come on out."

"Thanks, Arthur," Chickie says as they come out of the bathroom.

"You go see a doctor, Lady Godiva. Find out what's wrong with you. You hear me? Get yourself some pills."

"I already went to the doctor," Chickie says. "I already got the pills."

Sunday night the weather turns chilly, more like November than April. After dinner Hen puts on an Irish sweater his mother knit for him years before, pearly white and cabled, the warmest thing he can find in his bureau, too girly to wear in public. Ed Sullivan's guests are the Andrews Sisters, Topo Gigio, and a tutued dancing bear. It's been weeks, and Faye's still spring cleaning. The house is littered with half-filled boxes waiting to make their way out onto the sidewalk. As the house gets emptier, it gets colder. Hen sees now how the mess has always kept it warm. He lies on the living room floor with a chess set and plays out an old Morphy game. The grandmaster opened quickly, as he always did, won decisively with a smothered mate. Remi's armchair is empty. The Oriental rug is worn threadbare, its pattern dimmed to a blur of dull browns and reds. From time to time Hen hears his mother humming. Faye floats silently since Nantucket, speaks softly, has new and endless patience for all creatures and things. His parents speak to each other again now; they make efforts, careful inquiries, but never, Hen notices, any plans. Every day plays out only for itself. There's no future beyond each silent night, no certainty of the next day's existence until it dawns. Hen has never been more consciously aware of living in the present— day by fragile day. His parents treat him gently, as if he were a dying dog. His mother can barely meet his eye. His father constantly seeks it. Hen would like to believe they're falling back in love, but in the thick of his heart he knows they're just finally falling out of it. He clings to the fact that they're doing it civilly, without accusation, threats, cruel words.

Next door, in the olive-green house, Chickie sleeps restlessly. She dreams of tiny, amorphous babies—hers; she gave birth to them in a hospital bed behind a half-closed curtain in blue jeans and a peasant blouse. She knows something went wrong because there's no blood, no pain, no visitors, no crying, because in the end, there is no joy. Guilt stains and spots the bloodless dream. Back home, Chickie forgets what's happened, who she's become. She goes off to ride a Ferris wheel, a stranger's hands roaming her naked back. She forgets about the babies as she spins through the night air, forgets that babies need holding, feeding, rocking, changing. There are three, six, nine of them. They slip down the drain or shrivel up like shed cocoons on a tabletop. While she's out cavorting, they wither and die.

Just after midnight Chickie wakes up in a strange pregnant heat in her bed. Her T-shirt is wrinkled and damp with sweat. The 1966 Red Sox team picture is still taped up on the wall. She pulls it off with the hand that Dick Radatz once signed. Her fingers are swollen at the knuckles, her breasts nearly twice their normal size. She lies on her back and stares down at her belly, still flat and hard, trying to imagine something growing inside of her. She makes circles around her navel with her finger, feels the rise of her swollen breasts, the softness of her skin. She slides her hand down between her legs, where one finger works quickly as she pulls back in a shudder. Chickie curls up on her side. All those drunken nights with Elvis, and it never happened once. The first time she's ever had an orgasm. Alone and pregnant in her bed with one swollen finger. How unromantic, how sick is that. She gets up to splash water on her face and sends a message over to Hen on the pulley: *Puked four times today. New record. Can't wait to stop feeling so sick. Is this really happening to me?* But Hen's not in his room. He's not sleeping. Hen's been walking on eggshells since she told him. He's even more freaked out than she is. She'll have to help him through this, help both of them. The white flag of Chickie's message waves ghostlike on the pulley through the night.

At midnight Hen watches *Attack of the Killer Tomatoes*. He won't sleep now until it's over. He doesn't want Chickie's insides to be sucked out. He doesn't want her to have to ride on the early morning subway, sitting on the dirty seats and lurching around in the dark. A drunk might bump into her. The slightest smell sets her stomach off. Some punk might hold up the train, take them hostage. Some nutzo psychic might try to tell her fortune and freak her out.

Not to worry, ma'am, the sheriff says to the panicky housewife. *We've got those dang vegetables right where we want 'em. And we aim to show 'em who's boss.* Hen snorts a laugh, bites into an apple. They don't have to take the subway downtown. He'll borrow his mother's VW bug, drop Chickie off at Planned Parenthood and be back in time for school. At two-thirty, a religious fanatic comes on to praise the lord, closing the night with a frenetic prayer. The Air Force jets swoop across the screen, which then fills abruptly with zigzag lines and a loud, buzzing hum. "The Star Spangled Banner" is the last jarring tune in Hen's brain. For a short while, he dozes. At four-thirty, he puts on his sneakers and reaches for the VW keys on the nail in the kitchen, grabs the last powdered donut from a store-bought box. He pulls the car up to Chickie's house and waits. The streetlights turn off just as she slips out the front door. He chews his fingernail as she comes down the path, feels his heart beating hard. Her hair's messy, her face blotchy. She's wearing some old jean bell-bottoms, her army jacket, purple clogs.

"Cool," Chickie says, opening the car door. "You got the bug."

"I didn't get it," Hen says. "I took it." Chickie slides onto the seat. "You okay?" he asks. "You don't look so hot."

"Thanks."

"I just meant—"

"I'm not going to the fucking prom," she says.

Hen's heart stills. He has to stop himself from looking Chickie all over, as she takes off her jacket and yanks up the sleeves of a ragged striped shirt she's been wearing since the fifth grade, the flesh of her starting to show, the pale insides of her wrists, the knobs of her spine as she bends to reach for the cigarette lighter, her arm as it reaches to turn on the radio and off the raspy heat, the cheek she scratches with a bitten nail, her ankles as she slips off her clogs and brings her legs up underneath her, her breasts straining the stripes of her shirt. He has to stop himself from touching all the places that show her pain—her puffy eyes, chapped lips, and swollen belly. He has to keep himself from asking what it feels like, being pregnant, surprised to be envious more than anything else he should be—curious, sympathetic, scared. *God, Chickie,* he wants to say. *How could you do this to me? How could you have done this without me?*

Chickie finds MEX on the AM dial, Oldies 1510. "Dirty Water" comes on. Hen heads for the river. The cigarette lighter pops out. Chickie presses the red coil to the end of her Camel non-filter. She takes a drag of her cigarette and sings off-tune. "You know what to tell Violet if she calls, right?"

"You're at the library working on your senior report," Hen says. "She won't believe it, Chick. When was the last time—"

"She'll have to believe it." Chickie scrunches up her face in the rear-view mirror. "God, you're right. I do look like shit."

"You look fine, Chickie."

"Liar," she says.

They drive along the river and turn off at the Boston Common. The gold dome of the State House rises on Beacon Hill. The feeble light flickers on the brick sidewalks and wrought-iron gateways, filtering through the bare branches of the trees. At a red light, Chickie looks down at the wading pool in the Common. The bottom is blackened with leaves and winter crud; pigeons peck and scrounge for food. Hen has trouble with the clutch on the hill. The bug lurches and stalls. As they round the corner of the Common past the dry-docked swan boats, the rusted muffler roars. Chickie stares straight ahead.

"Are you okay?" Hen asks.

She nods.

"Are you hungry?"

"Can't eat until it's over."

"Thirsty?"

She shakes her head, stares out the window. "I think I'll join a convent," she says. "Become a nun."

"Are you hot?" Hen fiddles with the heat. "Are you cold?"

Chickie turns to him. "I should've taken the subway," she says, glaring at him. "A nun would've taken the subway."

"A nun wouldn't have been taking this ride," he says.

On Joy Street, two women sit on the steps of the Planned Parenthood clinic. Hen parks the VW high up on the cobblestone hill and he and Chickie walk back to wait for the van. The group grows to six, then eight, clustered in pairs in the early morning mist. You can tell the pregnant women by their silence, their restlessness, their tired eyes. The companions murmur, pat, and frown. Besides Hen, there's only one other man. Two more women wander in from out of the darkness. Neither Chickie nor Hen has a watch, but still, they, too, tip their wrists with the rest, look up to the lightening sky, pace and stamp their feet. Just after six, a white van pulls up to the curb, shiny and unmarked.

"Okay, this is it." Chickie kisses Hen on the cheek. "Don't look so worried, Ozzie," she says. "I'll be back by seven. We'll go out for pizza. I'll be starving."

"Okay," Hen says. "I'll meet you back here. At seven o'clock."

The women start to board the van. Chickie turns to follow. "Bye, sweetheart," she says.

"Don't call me that," Hen says, as the door slides closed.

In the van, Chickie finds an empty seat, next to a woman with curly red hair.

"Mind if I sit here?" she asks.

"Be my guest." The woman holds out her hand. "I'm Jane," she says.

"That's my sister's name." Chickie tries to get comfortable in the lotus position. "She hates it."

"Not much to like," Jane says, with a laugh. "What's yours?"

"Chickie."

"Chickie?" Jane says.

"Minerva, actually," Chickie says. "You see what I'm up against."

Jane smiles, adjusting a pile of books on her lap. Chickie didn't bring anything with her, just the money in an envelope in her back pocket, her hairbrush, and her cup of pee with the pink screw-on lid, which she didn't even think to put in a bag. Chickie rolls up the papers she got from Planned Parenthood and thumps them against the arm of her seat. Jane writes feverishly in a notebook, the words falling in a rush off one line and onto another with dashes, dots, and swoops.

"What are you working on?" Chickie asks her.

"A journal," Jane says. "I'm writing about all this for posterity—what we're going through, sneaking around like criminals in the dark, some stranger driving us over the border. It's Neanderthal. It may even be a conspiracy. You think if men got pregnant they'd be pulling this shit? No way, Jack. There'd be abortion clinics in every baseball park, every bar. Someday this whole trip will seem like a scene out of the Dark Ages. They won't believe what we had to go through. The men should be riding in this van, going to get vasectomies. *That's* what should be happening."

"Right on," Chickie says. She stares ahead as they head west on the Mass. Pike. As she watches Jane write, she thinks of the senior thesis she's working on for her high school lit class, some bullshit she found in the library about the role of women in Shakespeare. Chickie sighs. Bet Romeo never had to ride Juliet on the old stallion to get a quickie abortion in New York.

Near Framingham, it starts to drizzle. Jane touches Chickie's arm and points out the window. "Hey, isn't that the guy who came to Joy Street with you?" she says.

"Where?" Chickie leans over Jane to look out at the highway, forehead pressed against the cold glass. "Oh my god," she says. "He's out of his mind."

"Now that's true love," Jane says, cracking a smile. "Here, switch seats with me. Give your honey a sign."

"It's not true love." Chickie slides into the window seat, helping Jane rearrange her books. "It's crazy. It's a shit box and he's driving like a maniac. He is a maniac. I'm really beginning to worry about him." She knocks on the window. Hen's head turns. "Are you crazy?" Her finger spins in circles around her temple.

Hen points straight ahead. *I'm coming with you*, he mouths.

"Hey, we've got an escort, folks," Jane calls out. "Chickie's beau is following us."

"He's not my beau," Chickie says. "He's my cousin."

"Sure," one woman says, patting her belly. "The guy who did this was my brother."

"I'm telling you, he's just my cousin."

"Hey, you're lucky to have someone who even cares," Jane says. "I didn't even know the guy's last name. One too many sloe gin fizzes and slam, bam, here I am. My own stupid fault."

"You want a name?" a Black girl says. "Herman." She laughs. "Can you imagine, Herman Matel the Third?"

"Elvis Junior right here," Chickie says, patting her stomach.

"Elvis?" another woman says. "You've got to be kidding."

"I swear it," she says. "Elvis Norton Donahue Jr."

"I guess someone loved *you* tender," Jane says.

The older woman in the back corner seat smiles.

Conversations break out like rashes as they head west on 84. Quick smiles flash on and off, like flickering lights. The van sways gently on the blacktop. The women unbutton their sweaters, take off their shoes, scratch their stomachs, stretch their legs. The walls of caution and silence come tumbling down. They talk about nausea, money, men, mothers, bloating, puking, God, guilt, midnight cravings, strange dreams. The older woman in the back passes around a picture of her three kids. They share all of what's happened, and none of what will, keeping their fears tight inside them. They've all come to do a hard thing. It will be easier now to do it together, in good company. Chickie undoes the top button of her jeans and breathes deeply. Levi's 501. Size 29. For the first time ever, they're too tight.

Hen clutches the wheel of the VW, accelerator pushed all the way down to the rusty floor. The gas gauge bobs ominously toward the *E*, but he doesn't dare stop. No clue where he's going; he can't lose them on the last leg. He'll have to hustle to keep up. Bugs get great mileage, have big reserves, and luckily, Faye always keeps a full tank. All he can do is pray. He turns up the radio and floors it. The Stones roll him over the border into Connecticut. "Under My Thumb." The white lines go crooked as the speedometer hits seventy-five. Shake, rattle, and roll. It's nothing for the van, but it's a death run for the bug. Wind swoops in through the melon-sized hole at Hen's feet. The exit signs fly by. Near New Haven, the ocean comes into view. Drizzle turns to a steady rain. The driver-side wiper gives out and Hen has to drive hunched forward, one hand on the steering wheel, the other out the window, moving the broken windshield wiper as best he can, back and forth with an oil-stained rag. His arm grows numb to the elbow. The rain and grit from the highway spit up through the hole at his feet. The sugar from the powdered donut he had for breakfast has long since swirled up and out through the top of his head. The store of fitful sleep he managed the night before is long gone. And the leak he's got to take is brutal.

The van finally skirts the city and heads over the Throgs Neck Bridge onto Long Island. Hen follows it down a tree-lined parkway, twisting and winding in the van's shadow. Around eleven o'clock, Big Apple AM radio time, the van pulls up to a one-story brick building on a quiet street. Fifty feet behind, Hen pulls over to the sidewalk. The gas needle hovers dangerously below the E. He walks up to meet Chickie as she gets out of the van. His shirt is buttoned wrong, his jeans are covered with spattered mud to the knee, and his windshield-wiping hand is bright red. One sneaker untied, hair wild, eyes as blue as the day he was born. The women watch him come.

Chickie stands tall now, arms crossed across her chest. The sleep's vanished. Her eyes have cleared; her hair's been brushed. Her hand lands on his cold red arm; she tries to rub the length of it warm. "You're out of your mind," she says. She drinks in the feeling of Hen as the women watch them, sees his beauty through their anxious eyes. She sees how they envy her his closeness, the touch of him, the wild look in his eye, his panting breath on her face, his frozen, reaching arm. Each one of these women is here because she's lain in some dark place with a man, one who matters, or one who doesn't; and they all think this is what she's done with Hen.

"Don't be mad, Chick," Hen says. "I had to come."

"I'm not mad," she says. "How could I be mad?"

As they walk into the clinic, she looks back at the van driver, who's eating a sandwich at the wheel. He's taken off his Yankees cap. He's completely bald.

The waiting room of the clinic is clean and bright, with a kelly-green carpet and Toulouse-Lautrec prints on the wall in silver frames—ballerinas, horses, clowns. Hen smells the smells of sickness and medicine, weak coffee and overcooked food. While Chickie fills out forms on a clipboard, Hen ducks into the men's room to take the longest piss of his life. When he gets back, he unfurls the roll of papers from Planned Parenthood and reads. He sees the diagrams of the tadpole fetus in the womb and the picture of the vacuum extractor, faceless women's bellies protruding, legs spread. Doctors and nurses swing through the doors, looking too young and cheerful to do what they do. Chickie scribbles away in a messy scrawl, breaks the lead of the pencil, swears. Hen knows a sudden terror of the powers that are now, at eighteen, theirs—making babies, driving across state lines, stolen cars, draft notices, signing your life away on a dotted line. They're not playing games anymore. They're not making mud cakes in the park, sending what-if messages back and forth on the pulley, building sand forts in the Nantucket dunes. He wants to be back in his living room, safe where he began this long day, in the Irish sweater his mother knitted, watching the killer tomatoes attack the head of the PTA. He wants the difference between reality and fiction to be that clear and clean—the idea of the baby in Chickie's stomach to be as preposterous as gargantuan tomatoes waging war on surburban America.

Hen looks over at Chickie, her legs outstretched in jeans and purple clogs, her cup of pee resting on the arm of the chair, cursing the lengthy forms. The other women cross their legs and clutch their purses, their paper bags. In the end, modesty never really found Chickie. Hen's always envied her that. He reads more of the literature from Planned Parenthood—how the women may feel after the abortion—depressed, anxious, sore—what they should do—take long walks, seek counseling—when they should resume sex. After the bleeding stops. Bleeding. Bleeding. Hen reads about birth control options—pills and rubbers and sponges and coils. He vows he'll never have sex with another girl until he's sure she's safe, that they're safe from the mistakes, the choices they'll make. Chickie plays the piano arm of her chair with the fingers of one hand until a nurse calls out her name. "Minerva Potts?" she says.

Chickie stands up with her forms and the cup of pee, hikes up her jeans, looks over at Hen. "Here goes nothing," she says.

"Wait," Hen whispers. His hands are sweating. The voice that speaks is not his own as he knows it, but still it speaks. "Don't do it, Chickie," he says.

"What do you mean, don't do it?"

"Keep the baby." Hen takes Chickie's arm. "I'll help you take care of it. We'll do it together."

"Are you crazy?" She pulls her arm away. "I can just see it—a little mutant chess freak with a runny nose and bare feet. Get real, Hen. Come on."

"Don't go in there, Chickie," he whispers.

"I'm going," she says. "I just want this all to be over with."

"Wait a while longer. Just think about it a little more."

"I don't want to think about it anymore," Chickie says. "It's all I've been thinking about for the last three weeks."

"Why don't you both come inside my office for a minute," the nurse says. She leads them into a small room. "Now," she says, gently closing the door behind them. "It sounds as if you two need some more time to talk this over."

"He's not even the father," Chickie tells her. "He's just my cousin. Here." She hands the nurse the cup. "Take it. I'm ready."

"No." As Hen grabs the cup, the cap comes off and the pee spills, splattering against a chrome sink and onto the floor.

"I can't believe you did that," Chickie says in a hoarse whisper. "I cannot believe you just did that, Hen."

"I'm sorry." Hen grabs some paper towels and tries to wipe up the spill. "The cap must have been loose. I didn't mean to. I'm sorry."

"I'll just pee again," Chickie says.

"It's got to be the first pee of the morning," Hen says.

"How do you know?" Chickie demands.

"I read the stuff."

"What stuff?"

"The papers, Chickie. Didn't you even read them?"

"I skimmed them."

"Don't you even want to know what's going to happen to you in there?"

"Why should I if it's awful?" Chickie turns to the nurse. "Is that true? Does it have to be the first pee of the morning?"

"It's the most concentrated, the most reliable," the nurse says. "Listen. I'm going to leave you two alone for a while. Take as much time as you need. We'll clean this mess up later. We don't want anyone going through those doors with even the slightest doubts."

"I don't have any doubts," Chickie says. "I'm ready. Let's go."

"Talk to him, Minerva," the nurse says. "At least hear him out."

"All right, talk," Chickie says to Hen after the nurse is gone.

"Once it's done," Hen says. "You'll never be able to change your mind."

"Oh my god, Hen. Why did you come if all you were planning to do was torture me?" Chickie fights back tears. All she's done for weeks is puke and cry. The doctor warned her. Hormones made you do strange things, feel strange ways. But what was so different about that? She's always felt strange ways. She bends down to pick up the plastic cup behind a chair, finds there's still a little bit of urine left in the bottom. She lifts it up triumphantly. Hen hands her the cap. She screws it on, wipes the cup with a paper towel. "Maybe it's still enough," she says. "I'll ask Nurse Nancy. I'm going out there, Hen, I'm—"

"Chickie—"

"This is *real*, Hen. Don't you get it? If I *don't* do this, I'll be a mother by Christmas. I'm too young, too screwed up. I want to go home and dance and sleep in my own bed. I don't want to feel sick anymore."

"I could help you," he says. "After graduation, we could—"

"No! Stop it. You're nuts, you know that?" Chickie's reaches for the door handle and before Hen's finished his thought, she's back out in the waiting room, talking to the nurse, handing her the cup of urine. As he comes out of the office, the nurse looks over at him. He turns away.

The door to the operating room swings itself shut after Chickie and the nurse have passed through. Hen stands in the middle of the waiting room until the door's completely still. Sitting back down, he takes out his old chess set—the one he travels with—and sets up the pieces. He lost a white knight somewhere, one night in the fall when he was playing the Game in the Square. It seems like a million years ago. He cut out a square from a matchbook to replace it. He meant to send away for those postage stamps from all over the world—Tanzania, Indonesia, Madagascar—for Chickie. She always wanted those stamps.

Inside a white room where angels might dance in a movie heaven, Chickie feels brave again. She waits on the edge of a bed with three other women. Given no privacy and no choice, they undress in front of one another, donning the paper robes and shower caps they've been given, and the baby blue slippers that shrivel up like beetles under a log. A nurse comes by with plastic bags to put their clothes in. Chickie rolls everything up in her army jacket, feeling suddenly nearly happy, hopeful, to think she's come this far, that this will all be over soon, that Hen's waiting for her outside with his chess set, even though he's still so upset. She stuffs her hair under the shower cap, jams her toes into the slippers and ties the sash of her paper robe at the waist. Dressed first, she stands up and models the ridiculous outfit, posing and twirling, hands on hips. The others laugh. Even the older woman looks up and smiles.

A young woman doctor comes in to examine them. "And here, on bed number three," she plays along. "Our latest creation for spring, modeled by…"

"Chickie." Chickie says it the French way. "Chickie Minerva Potts the First and Probably the Last."

The young doctor smiles. She's overworked and tired. She feels Chickie's glands and stomach, takes her temperature and blood pressure, checks her heart. "You have a heart murmur," she says, taking the stethoscope out of her ears. "Did you know that?"

"Yeah," Chickie says. "They made a big deal about it when I got the pill."

"The pill?" The doctor's eyes rise.

"Something screwed up," Chickie says. "Me, I guess."

"Take any medication for the murmur?" The doctor jots down notes on her clipboard.

"No."

"Had it for a long time?"

"Since I was born, my mom says."

"Long as it's old news," the doctor says, moving on to the next bed.

The first of the four women to volunteer, Chickie is wheeled into a warm room and transferred onto a hard table. A nurse puts a mask over her face and turns on the overhead lights. She starts to feel woozy. One hundred and fifty dollars will buy her unconsciousness and a backward roll of time, a good use of her essay prize money, the educational experience of a lifetime. *Home: Building Block of the Future.* Hah! Chickie thinks of home, can't focus, sees only Hen's bewildered, anxious face. The echoes of the other women's voices hum in her ears. She feels herself being lifted, shifted. No one will look her in the eye. The lights shimmer like sunlit lily pads above her. Someone sticks some of her hair back into the cap and smooths her forehead, tells her to count backwards from one hundred. She feels her legs being pushed apart, the sudden rush of cold air up through her middle. She says ninety-nine and ninety-eight clearly. Ninety-seven is fuzzy. Somewhere around ninety-five, she begins to talk about Hen, the last familiar face she saw, his voice echoing, *Don't go in there, Chickie. I'll take care of it with you. You'll never be able to change your mind.*

"Everyone thinks it's his," Chickie hears a low, woozy voice she doesn't recognize as her own. "But it isn't. We'd have messed-up babies. Siamese twins, probably, with three eyes or five legs or something. It's a joke. It's supposed to be a joke. Don't you get it? Laugh." *Laugh. Laugh. LAUGH.*

Ninety-four. Ninety-three. The lights are so shiny, so pretty. *No.* They don't get it. They aren't laughing; they're all so serious. All dressed in white. Like ghosts, like angels, they fade in and out. *Whoooo!* They won't laugh. They count with her, for her. Ninety-two, ninety-one. *Ninety.* Hush. *Hush little baby, don't you cry.* Chickie feels the pull of warm darkness, the drug that's making her so sleepy, the lull of the doctors' voices. Who is the baby? Where is the baby? A whirring sound enters Chickie's brain, the sound of a blender mixing up a frappe, a car pulling out of a driveway, a baby crying. Not until she's stopped counting and the doctor says, in case she's still listening, the cold steel of the stirrups on her heels rousing her for one last second, "This may hurt just a bit," not until the second she goes under does she think of Elvis, just a flash of his face, his body lowering down onto hers, Elvis, who at that moment is putting the finishing touches on a drawing in French class with a leaky pen, a circle that turns into a breast and then an eyeball, swirling in a maze of snakes and smoke-plumed flames. The moment that the D & C extractor sucks Chickie's womb empty is the same moment that Mademoiselle Gladstone calls out her name in the roll call, the same moment that Elvis looks up to find her seat empty, and then over into Jamie Menneker's brown eyes.

13

In the recovery room, covered with brick wallpaper and filled with potted geraniums, Chickie sits in an orange vinyl chair. The nurses have had personality changes. They push and cluck now, give orders, avoid eye contact. "Time to get moving," one says to Chickie. "Let's get up and walk around." Chickie stands up, holding on to the arm of the chair. Her legs are shaky; her feet are cold. She walks over to a table covered with open boxes of Dunkin' Donuts, cans of Hawaiian Punch, coffee in a silver urn and tea bags in a plastic bowl. "Eat," a nurse says, turning crisply on her heel. Several women shuffle around in johnnies and slippers. Some of them nibble, some chat. Others wander in dazed, limping circles. Chickie looks for Jane, or anyone else from her van, then spots the older woman sitting in the corner.

"You okay?" she asks her.

The woman nods. "I'm fine," she says. "How 'bout you?"

"I'm okay," Chickie says. "May I ask you a question? I don't even know you, but..."

"Go ahead." The woman nods, knowing what the question will be.

"I saw the picture of your kids in the van," Chickie says. "Why didn't you have this one?"

"We had a test," the woman says, putting her hand on her stomach. "Turns out this one was no good."

"I'm so sorry," she says. A passing nurse gives Chickie her bag of rolled-up clothes, a sanitary napkin and belt, and more papers about how to take care of herself for the next few days. "Aspirin for the cramps. Napkins for the blood. No baths, no tampons. No intercourse for at least six weeks."

In the bathroom, Chickie tears off the paper gown and buries her nose in her clothes, searching for whiffs of home and self—kitchen grease, baby powder, Woodbury shampoo. Bending over gingerly, she slides the satin belt up over her hips to her waist and attaches the pad to the front and back hooks, adjusting it between her legs. She looks for changes in the mirror. Only the big breasts are still foreign, swollen and tight. Elvis noticed a few nights ago. "Hey, they grew," he said. "New improved size. Far out." He got excited, tried to squeeze them, suck them. She was furious, pushed him away. "Don't get used to them," she told him. "They're not for keeps." If he hadn't been so stoned, he might have asked her why. Chickie puts her hand on her aching belly, the worst period cramps she's ever had, a fire burning up from between her legs, up through her belly to her dry throat. She puts on her underwear, her jeans, her striped shirt, and her clogs. It takes so long. Every thought she has, every move she makes. It hurts to bend. To think about anything. To be Chickie, so screwed up, so empty, so far away. *This one was no good.* The older woman's words echo in her ears. When she rises from the toilet seat, she's dizzy. Was hers a good one? A monster or a sweet baby child. Hippie, preppie? Boy or girl? Cramps. Douche. Tampons. The words glare up at her from the papers on the toilet seat, bold, underlined, accusing. *No intercourse for at least six weeks.* Intercourse. What a strange, formal word. If they mean fucking, Chickie thinks, who would want to for the next six million years?

With the sight of Chickie coming toward him, the movie reel of Hen's day, which stopped when she walked through those doors, resumes. The people around him start to move; sluggish voices pick up energy and speed. The chess set shifts in his lap. The voices on the loudspeaker sputter. The sky outside's still gray.

"Is it over?" he asks.

Chickie nods.

"Are you okay?"

"I'm fine," she says.

"Let's get out of here," Hen says. "I told the guy in the van you were coming home with me. He made me sign some paper. I hope we're not breaking the law."

Feeling a rush of blood and dizziness, Chickie eases herself down into one of the red chairs. "Maybe I better sit a bit longer," she says.

"What's wrong?"

"Nothing," she says. "Why don't you go get the car? By the time you get back, I'll be ready. I'll be fine."

"The car." Hen's hand rises to his brow. "Damn, I forgot. It's out of gas. I'll go find a gas station, be right back. Stay right here, Chick. Don't go anywhere. Don't move."

"Where would I go?" She feels another spurt of blood explode from her. "Oh god, I need some stuff at the drugstore, too."

"Stuff?" Hen says. "What stuff?"

"Aspirin. For the cramps," Chickie says. "And sanitary napkins. For the bleeding."

"The bleeding?"

"It's nothing, Hen. Go on. Get the gas. Get the stuff. I'll wait here. I'll be okay. I promise."

Hen starts up the VW, heads down the street of the tidy, tree-lined place where women come to get unpregnant. There's not one ramshackle house, not one hippie or Black person or panhandling bum. Hen lets himself cry, knowing the wind from the open window will blow his face dry. It's all over now. He only wishes... He's got to stop. It wasn't his. Elvis made it with Chickie. And doesn't even know he did. How screwed up is that? Sex turns into some kind of crazy, screwed-up war. There are secrets, casualties, power plays, plots. Chickie and Elvis act like they could care less about each other and he and Melody haven't spoken since the night they had sex. Now Chickie's had her insides scraped out and she's dizzy and bleeding. And all for what? For that one moment in his parents' bed with Melody when he couldn't stop and didn't care what not stopping meant, a feeling so painfully good he'd wanted to save it and suck it and swallow it and smear it all over himself. That moment just before he shot himself into some strange girl with a southern drawl and tits the size of Mount Everest. And then it was all gone, evaporated into the dust of an ordinary day. You tried to do something with the memory, what was left of it, jiggle it, stroke it, shake it up, tried to make it keep feeling electric and alive, but all it did was ache and drift and blur and tease. All that was left was a throbbing silence and a million questions and the hungry tail end of the night. You couldn't get it back in your mind, out of your mind. You had to go out and get it again, get some more. You had to do it again. Fuck her. Fuck them. *Fuck it.* Hen slams his fist down on the horn. A distant car replies.

With three quarters of a tank of gas and six dollars left in his pocket, Hen walks into a drugstore. He gets the aspirin, finds the sanitary napkins, rows and rows of them, women in purple floating dresses with mysterious smiles. A woman in a white coat comes over and hands him a box. "These are good," she says. "Kind of all purpose."

"Thanks," he says.

"Six dollars and seventy-nine cents," the druggist says, ringing up at the counter.

"Damn." Hen fishes in his pockets for change. He's fifty-three cents short. He'll have to run the tolls on the way home. He looks back and forth from the aspirin bottle to the sanitary napkins, wondering which Chickie needs more.

"That all you got?" the druggist asks. He knows what's up the road. He has people in here all the time, buying napkins and aspirin and diaphragms and rubbers, foam and jelly and pills. He'll be able to send his kids to college on the sale of aspirin and maxi pads alone. He's Catholic and doesn't hold with abortion. But he's seen the pain in the eyes of the people who come in here, all ages, shapes, and sizes. "Forget it, kid," the druggist says to Hen, taking the bills and waving away the change. "You can leave the rest to me in your will."

Hen slips into the house just after ten o'clock that night. His mother's cleaning out the spice rack in the kitchen. There's no sign of his father. Faye looks relieved to see him, asks him if he's all right, if he's hungry, all in one breath.

"I'm starving," he says. "I'm fine."

"I missed you." Faye starts to make him a grilled cheese sandwich. The kitchen fills with mingling smells—oregano, mint, cloves, melting butter, and bubbling cheese. "Where've you been all day?" she asks.

"There was something I had to do," he says. "It took a while."

"You took the car," Faye says. "I was worried."

"I'm sorry." Hen looks up at his mother. "Next time I'll ask."

"Do," she says, putting a twist tie around the neck of the bread. "Hen?"

"Yeah?"

"Is everything all right?"

He nods. "I just had to do something, that's all."

As Faye cleans the rim of a spice jar, the smell of ginger floats his way. "It must have been important," she says.

The next night, while playing the Game, Chickie and Elvis climb up the fire escape onto the roof of the National Lampoon Building to hide. As the sun sets, the sky fills with cotton candy swirls. Elvis's leather jacket is cracked, worn thin and gray. Chickie wears loose-fitting corduroy bells and one of her father's old sweaters, maroon and shapeless. They come together near a crumbling chimney. Elvis puts his hands under Chickie's sweater, brings them up to her breasts. "Man," he says. "I do love these new tits."

"Shut up," Chickie says, pulling away.

"Sorry." Elvis takes out a plastic bag of pot. "What's with the hobo getup, Chickie?"

"Nothing's *with* it." Chickie sits down and leans back against the chimney. "I'll wear what I fucking want to."

"That time of the month perhaps?" Elvis pulls out a rolling paper from the slit in the Zig-Zag box.

"No, perhaps not," Chickie says. "Where did that stupid expression come from, anyway? The names they come up with for your period, God. The curse, your friend, on the rag. Why don't they just call it what it is, plain old blood and guts?"

"I think it's time to get high," Elvis says. "Life always looks a little rosier through a purple haze."

"I'm sick of getting high," Chickie says.

"Okay, I'll get high by myself."

"Why don't you just go fuck yourself while you're at it?"

Elvis rocks back on his heels. "You want to tell me what I did to deserve all this kindness?"

"Where were you yesterday?" Chickie says.

"Right here on planet Earth." Elvis sprinkles pot onto the rolling paper. "Just busy being little old me."

"What was yesterday like for you?" She rubs her cramping belly. "What did you do? How were you feeling?"

"Feeling no pain." Elvis licks the paper's sticky edge. "Yesterday—what I can remember of it, anyway, was one mind-blowing, far-out gas of a day."

"Was it?" Chickie gets up and walks to the edge of the roof, looks down over Mt. Auburn Street. "What do you think about us, Elvis?" she asks.

"Us?" Elvis seals the bulging joint.

"Us. As a couple, I mean. Where are we? What are we doing together? Who the hell *are* we?"

Elvis looks up, puzzled. "Is this where I'm supposed to say, 'I love you'?"

"You're not supposed to say anything. I was just trying to have a conversation. I know that's a really strange, fucked-up idea."

"You're making me feel weird."

"You always say that," Chickie says. "How good can it be?"

"Hey, I've got no complaints." Elvis twists the ends of the joint. "Have you heard any complaints?"

Chickie lifts her head up. A cloud drifts by at a crawl. "What was the weather like here yesterday?"

"What do you mean *here?*" Elvis feels for matches in his pockets. "Man, you're acting strange tonight, Chickie. Here as opposed to where, Jupiter?"

"Jupiter." The wind stirs the tips of Chickie's hair. She feels a spurt of blood come out onto the pad. She looks through the flame of Elvis's lit match into his eyes. "Ask me where I was yesterday," she says.

"Okay," he says on the inhale. "Where were you yesterday, grumpy?"

"I was in New York," she says. "Getting an abortion."

"What the—" She watches the smoke curl up into his face, waits for his mind to spin around to the part that makes him sputter and lose his balance. "An abortion?" he says. "Are you... What? *Mine?* Oh my god, what happened?"

"You were there," she says. "We took off our clothes. We—"

"But I thought—"

"No, you didn't think. You never really thought about any of it." She walks back from the edge of the roof. "Don't worry, Elvis. I took care of it. You're off the hook."

"Shit, Chickie. You should've at least told me."

"That's what Hen said."

"You told him and not me?" He kicks the gravel with the toe of his motorcycle boot. "Jesus fucking Christ. That's not fair."

"Fair? Fair again. What the fuck is fair?" Chickie whirls around to face him. "Is it fair that both of us had sex and I'm the one that got pregnant? Is *that* fair?"

Elvis's face crumples. "No, of course not. But man, Chickie, I can't believe you're laying this on me like this, after the fact."

"I'm not laying anything on you. You can be all outraged and tell me what I should or shouldn't have done, now that it's over. But be honest. If I'd told you, you would've been scared shitless, totally bummed out. You would have felt bad, and you would've felt guilty, and you wouldn't have known what to do. Part of you would've wished it had never happened. So that part can thank me. I did you a fucking favor. I took care of it."

Elvis shakes his head back and forth. "Maybe I would've freaked out," he says. "And maybe I would have been scared." He's up on his feet now, near tears. "But it was my right to know, Chickie. And you should've told me."

"Don't tell me you're ready to be a father."

"No way," Elvis says. "But I could've done something. I could've helped."

"I didn't want any help."

"You never do," Elvis says. "Maybe that's part of the problem, Chickie."

"So there *is* a problem."

"Everyone has problems." Elvis paces the rooftop, angry now that the shock's passed through him. He stops suddenly in his tracks. "Did he tell you to get rid of it?" he asks.

"No, he even tried to stop me, if you want to know."

"He *what*?" Elvis runs his hand through his hair, singeing one side with the joint. "He tried to stop you? Who the hell am I here, Chickie? The fucking man in the moon?"

"In a way," she says. "We hardly know each other, Elvis. All we ever do is get high and have sex. We made a baby, but it was just an accident, a mistake. I don't even know who the fuck you really are."

"You swear too much, Chickie. That's another thing."

"Right. It's cool when you swear, but not when I do. You're a real hypocrite, sometimes, just like—"

Elvis stops dead in his tracks. "Did he go with you?"

"I didn't ask him to."

"*What?*" Elvis kicks a loose shingle, sends it flying over the edge of the roof. "He did, didn't he? Shit. *I* should've come, Chickie." His voice trembles. "Goddamn, it should've been *me*."

"He followed me in his mother's car," Chickie says. "I didn't even know until we were halfway to New York. I couldn't stop him."

"If you ask me, the guy's fucking in love with you, and let me tell you something, Chickie, that's sick."

"Oh, right, and what about Jamie Menneker?"

"Jamie Menneker?" Elvis is bewildered. "What the hell does Jamie Menneker have to do with any of this?"

"What've you been doing with Jamie Menneker, lately, Elvis?"

"I smoked one joint with her. So crucify me."

"Was it yesterday?"

Elvis rubs his forehead, scrunches up his eyes, trying to dredge up what used to be simple yesterday, and now will forever be a day he'll remember with a lurch of guilt and confusion. "Yeah," he says in a stunned voice. "Okay, it *was* yesterday. We ran into each other after

French class. Outside. Near the library. I was wondering where you were."

"I hope it was good dope," Chickie says. "So good it felt like tripping."

"Come on, Chickie. How could I have known? You didn't even tell me. So don't make me feel like such a jerk."

"Why not?" Her voice is hoarse. "Why should I have to feel this way all by myself?"

An ambulance wails in the distance. Chickie looks at Elvis over the space that's just opened up between them. He tugs on the trailing sleeve of her sweater. "I'm sorry," he says. "I'm really sorry, Chickie."

She sniffs, wipes her nose on the back of her sleeve. "It was no big deal," she says.

"Yes, it was," he says. "It *was* a big deal. A huge, big deal. Did it hurt?"

"Not much," she says. "No more big tits, though. They're shrinking fast."

"Don't joke," Elvis says, handing her the joint. "Here, smoke this. You'll feel better."

"No, I won't," she says, but she takes it anyway.

A billow of black smoke rises. A fire blazes nearby. Chickie and Elvis crouch low on the rooftop, the thin spiral of smoke from the joint curling up between them. It comes to Chickie that they'll never touch each other again. She pulls out an old thought, one she had that first night on the golf course, that in the end, it wouldn't really matter who she had sex with first. In fifty years she'd remember Elvis's name but not much else, his pale face, the feel of his hands on her back, the confusion in his eyes on this smoky rooftop. But in the end it wouldn't matter much. As she stands up, she feels the pad slide back, too far to catch the blood that's still oozing from her. A cramp grips her belly and she lowers her hand. In a strange way, the pain comforts her. Part of her wishes she'd felt more. She never once agonized over her decision, as some of the other women had in the van. Some prayed to God for the souls of their unborn babies, some cursed themselves, asked for forgiveness, imagined how it might have been, and some of them had cried. But she'd gone in dry-eyed and cocky, leading the charge, never blinking an eye. She borrowed the money from Janie, got on the van, marched through the clinic's swinging door. Only Hen's sad eyes, the spilled cup of pee, his shaky voice, ever gave her pause—not the thought of a baby growing inside of her, or the vacuum sucking it out or the pain or her parents or Elvis or anything else. And after it was over, she felt nothing but relief. She couldn't have stood to have her life cut short that way, her future. But what about the baby's life? Elvis's? How selfish, how screwed up was that?

"Listen, do you need any money?" Elvis says. "I could—"

"No," Chickie says. "I don't need any money."

"Did he give it to you?"

"No," she says. "It was mine."

From a distance comes the roll of Elvis's "Hound Dog," blaring from a radio. "Perfect background music," Chickie says.

Elvis takes a last drag. "You know, the funny thing is, I actually like his music. But how the hell could I ever admit it?" He gets up to his feet. "Come on. Let's get out of here, Chickie. Let's go for a cruise on the bike."

Chickie makes fists and tucks them up inside the dangling sleeves of her father's sweater. "You go ahead," she says. "I'll catch up with you later. Maybe back in the courtyard."

Elvis disappears into the night. Chickie leans back against the chimney. The sirens grow faint. The smoke clears. Alone on the rooftop, she dares to imagine the baby that might have been, with a velvet voice and a curling lip, a swiveling hip, a little Elvis, Janis, Grace, John-Paul-George-Ringo, Jr. For just one moment, she imagines a baby at her breast, her heart filling with a jagged warm rush, the clutch of a tiny hand, wide eyes looking out at her from under the fringe of a carriage. Just for a minute, as the wail of the last siren fades in the distance, before she heads back to the courtyard, Chickie imagines being a mother.

Later in the week, Chickie stops in at the stationery store, where Violet's cashing out at the register, counting up the day's receipts on an adding machine. She looks around this orderly world of clean smells, neat shelves, elegant displays. The sheer monastic splendor of it all soothes her as the door shuts behind her.

"Well, to what do I owe this honor?" Violet asks, pushing the cash register closed with a bang.

"What honor?" Chickie says.

"The pleasure of your company, unrequested," Violet says. "It's been a while."

"Don't exaggerate, Ma," Chickie says. "It hasn't been that long."

"I've missed you," Violet says. "How was school today?"

"Okay." Chickie spins a globe.

"No hot date with Elvis tonight?"

"No one has dates anymore," she says. "Hot or otherwise. They went out with the '50s. You know that, Ma."

"What do you have, then? You kids. Boys. Girls. Together. These days."

"Nothing," Chickie says in a flat voice. "We have nothing, really."

"What's wrong, Chickie?" Violet's hand reaches out to her forehead. "You look pale. You've been acting so strangely lately."

"Aren't you used to me by now?"

Violet smiles. "More strangely than usual, I should say. Ever since..." She stares at Chickie. "Ever since you put on that god-awful sweater of your father's. You haven't taken it off in days."

"It's comfortable," Chickie says.

"You have bags under your eyes." Violet tilts Chickie's chin up into the fluorescent light. "Your skin is actually green. What on earth is wrong?"

"You don't want to know." Chickie scribbles with colored markers on a test pad, circles and more circles, round and round.

"Of course I want to know. What's wrong, Chickie. Is it Elvis?"

"Elvis and I are history," Chickie says. "Or in the language of your day—we broke up."

"Oh, Chickie." Violet reaches out her hand. "I'm sorry. Well, actually, if I'm honest, that's not completely true."

"Elvis wasn't so bad, Ma," Chickie says. "He was a nice guy. Just like Dad."

"Okay, so he was a nice guy, just like Dad." Violet puts the day's cash in a leather bag. "I'll take your word for it, honey."

"Honey?" Chickie rips the sheet of paper off the pad.

"Can't I even call you honey anymore?"

"You never did."

"Didn't I?" Violet says.

Chickie looks up at her mother. "I was pregnant, Mom," she says.

Violet's hands freeze on the zipper of the leather pouch. "*What?* What on earth does that mean, you *were* pregnant?"

"I was pregnant. I went to New York yesterday and had an abortion."

"New York? An abortion?" Violet collapses in a black swivel chair. "Oh my god. Tell me you're not telling me this. Tell me I'm hearing things." Her voice rises to near hysteria. "What are you telling me, Minerva?"

"Don't yell," Chickie whispers, her voice cracking. "Whatever you do, just don't yell."

"Yell?" Violet's voice is hoarse. "How can I yell? I'm speechless. I'm…in shock. What in god's name happened?"

"It's an old story, Ma. You know, boy meets girl, the birds and the bees—"

"Chickie, stop it!"

"Okay, so it was stupid to get pregnant. But wouldn't it have been even stupider… Wait, is that even a word?"

Violet's face pales. The money pouch falls to the floor. "You're telling me that you were actually pregnant, Chickie? And you're telling me that you actually went to New York and had an abortion?"

"Wouldn't it have been stupider…" Chickie tries again. "To have had the baby and quit school, for me and Elvis to settle down in some funky apartment—"

"Chickie!" Violet grips the arms of the chair. "Oh dear god. Was it done properly?"

"By a real doctor," she says. "Masks, stethoscopes, the whole bit."

"You didn't even need my permission?"

Chickie shakes her head.

"Oh my god." Violet retrieves the strewn money, stuffs it back into the leather pouch. "It's all my fault. I've been way too permissive. Ease up on the reins. Give her room, everyone said. Don't strangle her. I didn't know how much freedom to give you. I thought you could handle it. I wanted you to know that I trusted you. I wanted you to be independent, but I lost good judgment. This is all my fault."

"Mom. Mom. Listen." Chickie waves a hand in front of her mother's face. "This had nothing to do with you. Nothing."

"Nothing to do with me? I'm your mother, for god's sake."

"I had sex, Mom. I was using birth control, but something screwed up and I got pregnant. It was an accident. Nothing you could have done would have changed any of that."

Violet stares at her.

"*Nothing*, Mom."

Violet reaches for the phone. "Maybe I can still catch Herb Parsons at his office. I want him to give you a thorough examination."

"Stop." Chickie puts her hand over her mother's on the receiver.

Violet looks over at Chickie, backwards into heartbreak, sees the girl who danced for her at fourteen on the living room floor. "My god, Chickie. You're only eighteen. When I was eighteen—"

"I know, I know. You wore flannel nightgowns and read *Little Women* in bed under the covers with a flashlight."

"Not exactly." Violet shifts in her chair. "But I wasn't roaming the streets, that's for sure. I wasn't wearing miniskirts and leopard-skinned tights. There weren't any boys named Elvis, for god's sake. And we did not go around getting...abortions."

"Was Dad the first one?" Chickie says. "Were you a virgin right up until your wedding day?"

"What a question, Chickie. In those days, nice girls were."

"Were you a nice girl, Mom?"

"I tried," Violet says.

"Not quite nice enough, though, right?"

"What do you mean?"

"That man at the Pewter Pot. You're screwing him, aren't you?"

"Chickie!"

"Come on, Mom. Let it out. The truth will set you free."

Violet is instantly, explosively relieved, oddly grateful. With these few words, Chickie has spared her. All that's left to do now is tell the tail end of the truth. "Whatever you saw, Chickie, whatever you thought, all that, too, is history now. I promise you. But that is *not* what we're talking about here."

"You cheated on Dad. You made a fool out of him."

Violet looks surprised. "Says who?"

"Everyone," Chickie says.

"I love your father, Chickie."

"That makes it even worse," she says. "I didn't love Elvis, but at least I was faithful to him. I didn't screw around."

"I'm glad," Violet says. "That shows integrity and restraint. Those are excellent qualities and I'm glad you have them."

"Maybe that's why you did it."

"Did what?"

"Cheated on Dad. Because you never had any freedom."

"Never had any—"

"Maybe that's why you're always mad at me," Chickie interrupts. "Maybe part of you wishes you were like me, living in this time, in my world. Maybe part of you is jealous."

"That's absurd."

"Jealous of my freedom. I'm lucky, I know that."

"Lucky? To be roaming wild on the streets? To have had an abortion? Why on earth didn't you tell me, Chickie?"

"Because you would've freaked out and then I would've had to deal with that too. I had to think clearly, Mom. I had to do my own thing. Not for you, or for anyone else. Just for me."

"I could've helped you."

"No," Chickie says. "You don't get it. No one could have helped me."

"Please just let me call Dr. Parsons," Violet says. "He brought you into the world, Chickie. He's a very decent man."

"No." Chickie shakes her head. Her lip starts to tremble. "It's all over with, Mom. There's nothing left to do. I told you. It happened and it's over with. I fucking took care of it!"

Violet puts her arms around Chickie. "What is it, Chickie? You're trembling all over. Tell me. It's all right. Say it. Get it out. Come on, you'll feel better if you do. Say what you really want to say."

"Oh my god, Mom." Chickie crumples into Violet's shoulder. "How could you let this happen to me?"

14

JUNE 1970

Nash doesn't have many memories of his father, Jocko Potts, doesn't remember much anymore before Vi came along to sculpt his memories for him. In a certain sense, he turned himself over to her then, at the altar, with a litany of words that remains no more than a jumble in his brain, except for those certain four—*from this day forward.* They had comforted him at the time, a reassurance that in marrying Vi, he was getting a life companion and a soulmate as well as a wife. His own mother had thrown in the towel when he and Remi went off to college, relieved, finally exhausted, after years of taking care of needy boys and men. And as if to absolve herself forever of the task, she'd died soon after. From that day forward, Nash became who Vi made him, who she expected, needed, wanted him to be. "For heaven's sake, you must have been a child who was forced to eat his brussels sprouts," she once said when he balked over some food at the dinner table. And forever after he'd thought of himself as a boy who'd been forced to eat his brussels sprouts, though it wasn't likely true. His father had rarely appeared at the dinner table, let alone headed it, and as the years went by, his mother had little spirit left to raise high the specter of the world's starving children.

His memory's so scattered now, so restless. Even more so since the accident. It's the odd, enisled memory such as this one that Nash retains. Over the years he's had to check with Remi. Where did we go that summer? What was that kid's name, the one who stole my bike? Was that before or after the old man died? Remi remembers everything, the early days, the names and faces, the intricacies, the details. For the most part, Nash is grateful for the pictures Remi's always been able to paint for him at a moment's notice of their past, the stories he can tell. But there's one thing he can never forgive Remi for—Remi remembers their father. Memories of the dead aren't reliable anyway, tinged with sadness or anger or guilt—whatever feelings they leave with the living at the moment of passing. What Nash remembers viscerally about his father was his smoothness—smooth skin, smooth hair, smooth voice. Now Nash can understand what a disgrace his father was—as a husband and a father, a human being, how, even before he was gone, many people thought he'd be better off dead, for all the misery he'd reaped, for all the misery he'd sown. The only child of Mercy Potts, Jocko grew up wealthy and spoiled. He lacked a rooted intelligence, what was referred to in those days as a solid *core*. He came and went as he pleased, studied listlessly, never held a real job. Slowly, he grew into the poor opinion people held of him. He drank too much, but couldn't hold his liquor, as Potts men were known for doing so well. Perhaps this fatal missing link in the genes was at the root of his downfall, his inability to be a lush and a player at the same time.

When Jocko married Beatrice Conrad, a secretary for the family business, gratitude and blessings were heaped upon her. Beatrice wasn't especially pretty or well bred. But the Pottses were pragmatists first, snobs second. In the eyes of Jocko's family, she was an angel dropped from out of the blue to pick Jocko up from a bone-ridden field over which the vultures circled. She fed her husband and kept him clean, sobered him up as best she could, kept his affairs in order and one eye closed to his miserable trespasses and failings. And then, Madonna that she was, after two years of marriage, she gave Jocko children. Twin boys. He had no clue what to do with one son, let alone two. As a father, he played the court jester, making a circus of his family, a freak show of their sameness, their identical pointed ears, their fat baby toes, their lisping Ss. He'd knock their heads together, mix up their names, Rash and Nemi, Tweedledum and Tweedledee. Nash can't remember much, but Remi's told him. Jocko would go off on drinking sprees, the smells of bourbon and strange perfume lingering on his shaven cheek when he stumbled home. He'd march them around the house in their pajamas, leading a chorus of, "Be kind to your web-footed friends. For a duck may be somebody's mother." He'd boast of his virility, his twin-making sperm, flirt with every woman in sight. He'd cry and hug and kiss the twins silly, if he remembered they were there. And most nights, after he'd passed out, Beatrice would put him to bed.

Beatrice raised high the scythe of mothers to carve out the twins' differences—avoided matching clothes, had their hair cut differently, insisted they play different instruments in the school band. Quietly, she cultivated unique identities for each—numbers were Remi's gift and words were Nash's. Nash was the free spirit, Remi the brooder. The one was like vinegar, the other like oil. Nash was the practical one. Remi the dreamer. Remi was the poet, Nash the diplomat. Beatrice fought Jocko's stubborn, drunken ignorance at every turn, his boorish refusal to lend his sons dignity, to tell them apart. All this Nash knows by way of small gifts, bits of memory shored up by Remi's stories, old photographs, dimly lit dreams. Over time, Jocko's story has stretched and softened, grown into burnished legend. On a good day, he had a certain charm, some could give him that—a certain way with the ladies. At best, he was a harmless ne'er-do-well, a feckless crooner, an elegant, floating bum. He frequented downtown hotel barrooms, where piano music tinkled, and the jewelry of well-kept women glinted by the light of the chandeliers. Jocko sipped frosted drinks, always finagled on the house, while finely dressed people drifted in and out of elevators on thick carpets, in swanky leather shoes—businessmen, politicians, visitors from out of town. They may have *belonged* there, but Jocko always felt he owned the joint, because it was his turf, his music, his town. Sometimes, when the piano man played, he'd sing along. And when he was in fine, gentle voice, not too drunk yet, his handsome face only just flushed, they'd let him lean on the piano and finish the song, and he might even get a round of applause, a cry or two of encore, a come-hither look from a woman at the bar. Other times, when Jocko's voice wobbled and his knees started to buckle, when the patrons wrinkled their noses and shifted in their seats, he'd be escorted back out into the night.

And so, when Jocko Potts died a young, squalid death, no one was really surprised. He'd had a weakness for whiskey and women; he'd ended up with the wrong crowd. It was never really clear what had happened, and in the end, no one felt any strong desire to find out. He was found in an alleyway downtown, bleeding from a knife wound to his chest. A brief investigation turned up little. Most said it was for the best—for his wife, for his parents, for those two precious boys. Life without Jocko as their father would perhaps not be happier, but it would surely be easier. Out of sight, out of mind. There had never been any question of his absence making anyone's heart grow fonder. And so there aren't many memories of his father, though Nash isn't so sure that even had Jocko lived longer, there'd have been many more. Nash remembers the bloodstained clothes they returned to his mother—the watch and blue satin bow tie, the gold wedding band. He remembers now that she didn't cry, how she never cried, as if the pool of Jocko's sloppy, drunken tears had been deep enough to drown them all. And he remembers a tree house that Jocko started to build in the backyard, not just before he died, but long before, when the twins were too young even to help. Nash has to adjust the flowering memory on its crooked stalk of truth. The tree house never got finished, not because his father died so young, in such a brutal way, but because he'd been a lazy, good-for-nothing drunk.

Nash opens the back screen door of the kitchen on a hot June day, a week before Chickie and Hen's graduation. The yard's a tangled mess of forsythia, withering lilacs, and sprouting weeds. Across the sagging fence, Faye's garden lies in neat, tilled rows, awaiting the bounties of sun and rain. Next to it, the brick kiln sits cold. Nash walks the perimeter of the yard past piles of old tires, rusty bikes, a leaky canoe, paint cans, broken roller skates and pogo sticks, a netless basketball hoop that once hung above the door of the carriage house. Rooted in the edge of his yard, but jutting over the fence into Remi's, stands the oak tree. When they came house hunting all those years ago, it was the oak tree that sold the place to Nash. He'd been happy to give Faye and Remi the sunnier, roomier house, the one with the greenhouse that she so wanted. As long as in his yard, he'd have the oak tree. Both houses are crumbling now, but the oak's only grown mightier, shooting up from the ground like a petrified geyser. The light filters down through a soft covering of new leaves which reveals the weathered skeleton of a tree house.

The unfinished tree house is now for Nash a symbol of time passing and improbability. He, too, tried and failed to build a refuge in the sky. He likes to think it was because of the kids, not because they were girls, but just because of who they turned out to be. Seph could never bear the idea of hurting the tree—invading it, possessing it, stabbing it with nails. "Just leave the poor old tree alone, Dad," she'd said. "It's happy just the way it is." It occurs to him now how sound this advice was. He hopes, when he's old and bent, that Seph will advocate as well for him. Janie was never the outdoorsy type. She preferred to stay inside with a book and her stuffed animals, making lists, listening to the radio, counting her babysitting money, one dollar at a time. And Chickie, well, Chickie was game. For most of her life, he and Chickie had been talking about building that tree house. They drew sketches one year, bought lumber and hammered up the first beams of the sling the next, ordered shingles and a door and a rope ladder the year after. Sometimes Hen would come over and help. But Chickie was always too busy, making

gum wrapper chains, ordering secret code rings from the backs of cereal boxes, dancing, schoolwork, baseball, brushing her hair, playing with
Hen. And Nash was too busy…doing what, he can't for the life of him
remember—rising up each day to go to work, to play…and shot back
down every night by the booze into oblivion. Nash looks up at the tree.
"Tomorrow," he and Chickie would always say. "We'll work on the old
tree house tomorrow."

Sparrows flit to and fro, coming to rest comfortably on the tree
house's weathered beams. Green mold runs through the grain of the
wood. The heads of the nails are rusted. Lifting his hand, Nash feels
the rough of his unshaven cheek. He's nearly fifty. He and Remi have
outlived their father by over ten years. This fact takes his breath away,
nearly makes him cry. In the carriage house, he finds the pile of two-by-
fours he ordered for the floor and walls of the tree house years before,
brushes the dirt and cobwebs from them. His flagging muscles strain
to carry five in one load. He leans them up against the oak tree, rolls up
his sleeves, takes a deep breath, goes back for another load. *Man's work.*
The phrase floats idly through his brain. One by one, he carries the
boards up the makeshift ladder, sweating, breathless at the top, and one
by one, he hammers them down across the base frame, slowly covering
the tree's middle sling, until he's made himself a place to stand. After
hoisting up the wall boards, Nash stands on the platform and looks out
over the yard.

The air is still, the sky a see-through powder blue. A bird chirps twice,
pauses, and then again. Nash hears the hum of a distant plane. The war
goes on, the protests, the bombing, the death toll spreading like a black
ink spill. Cambodia, My Lai, now Kent State—an endless falling line
of human dominoes. Since he got hit by Frank's nightstick, he's been
sidelined, off the political track for a while, but still the anguish builds in
him every day. Part of what he feels is pure and selfish fear, an irrational
terror that the senseless continuation of this one battle may signal the
literal end of the world. Part of him expects to see the V-formation of
planes swoop out of the heavens and slice the sky with a lightning-bolt
glint, a menacing flock of metal birds. How can the human race possibly be sustained when it's at such constant odds with itself?

Nash works into the afternoon. Up go the walls; in pops a window. He
brings up a box of shingles. He still hasn't gone back to work full time.
But Potts Pro seems to be on a steady course, sailing smoothly. Buzz
is slowly coming around—he's able, patient, a steady learner, a good

complement to his high-strung father. Remi still never misses a day. He's obsessed, a better businessman now than ever, on top of every number, every order, every tiny detail. He insists on doing the books alone; it's easier that way, he says, more efficient. Nash has felt no urge to argue.

"Take the day off, brother." Remi's even been trying to push him away; Nash can feel it. "Give yourself a break. Go home. You're not yourself yet. Make yourself a sandwich. Call the White House. Save the world." It bothers Nash to think he may be losing his grip, his edge. Maybe Remi considers him a liability now, not an asset. Strange how things get twisted. It used to be the other way around. What's happening to him? At work, he's careless and distracted, no longer up on the latest latex suits or fiberglass skis, lightweight rackets. The truth is, he couldn't care less anymore. It all seems so trivial—the business of suiting up the leisure class for sport—a ludicrous, almost obscene mission in a dark, chaotic world. He still chats with the customers, buys the coffee and Danish every morning at Sage's, rings up the merchandise, watches the world go by out the plate-glass window. It's still his job, his livelihood. And he won't let Remi push him out the door any sooner than he's ready to leave. But he'll take the day off now and again, by god. He's earned that. More time for family, contemplation, contribution. He's been toying with the idea of entering city politics, trying to help make some changes for his grandchildren. In a way, maybe the accident has been a sort of fortuitous derailment.

The afternoon slips away. At four, Nash brings out a bottle of vodka and one of gin, a glass of ice, lemons, and a small knife, and nails a bar shelf onto the tree house wall. He sips at a martini as he nails down the roofing shingles, the sun sliding down his back before it slips away. The days are open ended now and drift silently into night. He chews the lemon peel and calls it dinner, not expecting anyone to come home. Chickie flies in and out on teenaged wings. Violet is president of the tennis club now, the PTA, the first lady of her store, her life. Remi's living dangerously. Nash doesn't know the particulars, but he knows. He's afraid for his brother. Remi's not alive unless he's at work, unless he's gambling, unless he's full of whiskey, unless... Remi tosses it all off with a brassy laugh. "Seven-year itch, bro. Twenty-eight-, thirty-five-, forty-two-year itch. What can I say? Nothing a good day's work and a bottle of Jack Daniels can't cure." At dusk, the tree house roof is more than half shingled. Nash slides the weathervane onto its spindle—a portly spouting whale.

Hen watches from his bedroom window as the tree house takes shape. He's been upstairs since he got home from school—reading, playing chess. He watches Nash heft the wood, lumbering up and down the makeshift ladder, hammering, sawing. He swells with a love for his uncle which is confused by other feelings he's recently wanted to have for his father. Hen's been sticking close to home these days, staying away from the Square, from TV and the newspaper, anywhere he might see the reflection of anything unsettling—a strange man bouncing out of his aunt Vi's car in the Square, Chickie and Elvis climbing up to a rooftop, his father dipping into the Blarney Stone, Uncle Sam pointing his finger at him on a billboard—anywhere he might see signs that life as he's always known it is about to come to an end. As dusk settles in, he goes out into the yard and slips through a hole in the fence. "Looking good, Nash," he calls out. Somewhere along the line, they've dispensed with the 'Uncle.' "Need any help?" he says.

"Sure." Nash gestures to the carriage house. "Grab a hammer and come on up."

They work together for a while, hammering, shingling. The air starts to thin and cool.

"Ready for graduation?" Nash asks.

"I'd feel readier if I knew what was going to happen next," Hen says. "With the draft and all."

Nash nods. "How'd it go with the shrink?"

"Okay," Hen says. "Still waiting to hear."

Nash shakes his head, his hammer poised over the head of a nail. "Sargent's legality of war bill fell through and now Nixon's invaded Cambodia, so we're only in deeper. You'd think Kent State would have been the last straw, but—"

"What would you do if you were me, Nash?"

Nash looks hard at his nephew. It seems so simple—to just fold Hen up and stash him in the corner of the tree house. Never mind what he thinks or feels, never mind the consequences. "What would I have done when I was your age?" Nash takes a sip of his drink. "Or what would I do now?"

"Now," Hen says.

"I wouldn't go," Nash says. "I'd march into that draft office waving an American flag and say I loved my country too much to be a party to this war. I'd offer to serve in another way, apply for CO status. Dig ditches, work in a hospital, whatever. The Supreme Court says draft evaders can't be penalized after five years. At least that's something." He raises his empty glass to his lips. "I'd go on record now, Hen, take a stand. Beat them to the punch, before they came to get me. Before they came to get you."

"They'll think I'm stalling, punking out," Hen says. "They won't believe me."

"Make them."

"They'll think I'm scared," Hen says. "Like my father does."

"It doesn't matter what they think," Nash says. "In a certain sense, they're not real. They are the establishment. *You're* the individual. You have to live with what you do. Or don't do."

"And I have to live with my father."

"Not for long." Nash starts on the last row of shingles. "Your father just wants what's best for you, Hen. He just wants you to be safe."

"But most of all," Hen says, "he doesn't want me to be a coward."

"One day he'll get it, your old man," Nash says, as the swell of a breeze catches the tip of the weather vane's arrow. "How much courage it takes to be your own man."

On a Friday night, Remi takes Hen to the Blarney Stone to play pool.

"Whiskey for me, Jim," he says to the bartender, and turns to Hen. "What'll you have, Hen, a beer? You're almost legal now."

"Fresca." Hen racks up the balls on the pool table, leaving a perfect pyramid on the nicked green velvet. The eight ball rolls out of the formation. Hen puts it back in place. "Your break, Dad," he says.

Remi sinks two solids on the break, orange and green, and misses a side pocket shot by a hair. Hen clips his first stripe in the corner pocket and ends a run of three with a combination to the side.

"Nice shooting," Remi says. "Where'd you learn to play pool?"

"Around," Hen says.

"Maybe we should think about putting a pool table in the basement. What do you think, Hen?"

"It's like a dungeon down there." Hen scratches off the five ball in the corner. "Anyway, it's a little late, don't you think?"

Remi nods, misses a shot to the corner.

"So what's new, son?" he says.

"I got a letter from the draft board."

"What? When?"

"Yesterday." Hen reaches into his back pocket and hands Remi the folded letter.

"Dear Mr. Potts," Remi reads out loud. "Based on the report of Dr. Paul Dunphy…we cannot recommend a psychiatric deferment for you at this time… Please report to your local draft board…" When he's finished reading, he folds up the letter and hands it back to Hen. "So that's that," he says. "I knew that guy wouldn't find anything wrong with you. I only went along with this whole damn scheme for your mother."

"You didn't go along with anything," Hen says. "It was my decision, Dad. I made the call. I went to the shrink. I wanted to speak my peace. And I did."

"I paid for it," Remi says.

"Yeah, you did," Hen says quietly. "But it was still my decision."

"Anyway, it's history now. And the guy obviously had some common sense. He saw exactly how normal you are."

"Normal Tough-Guy Potts. That's all you ever wanted for me, wasn't it?"

Remi sinks another solid, a long, tough shot to the corner. "It's new, Hen, this sarcasm." Hen sees the pleased look in his father's eye. "It'll make things a little easier for you," he says. "A tougher skin. And as for that letter," Remi gestures with his drink to Hen's back pocket, "I won't say I'm not relieved."

"Relieved?" Hen lines up a shot to the side. "You want me to get drafted?"

"Of course not. All I'm saying is, this guy must know his stuff." Remi chalks the tip of his stick. "I was worried he might have you in therapy every week, dressing you up in high heels or something. But it says right there in that letter, that you're an intelligent, well-balanced kid with normal apprehensions and fears about being drafted, that you even had a few reservations about a deferment. Is that right?"

"I told him I'd take it," Hen says. "I told him three times."

"But it wouldn't have set right," Remi says. "Is that what you were trying to tell the guy?"

"No, it wasn't." Hen puts down his pool cue. "I wouldn't care if people called me crazy, or a coward, or even queer," he says. "People think what they want. It's not important."

"Ah." Remi balances his drink on the edge of the table. "That's the difference between your generation and mine."

"What?"

"Appearances, protocol. Keeping your head held high. Never letting on that you're anything but just one of the guys."

"Couldn't you have done with being a little less of one of the guys, Dad? Didn't you ever feel like all that pressure was a little hard to take?"

Remi looks at him. "Maybe," he says. He sinks the eight ball in the side pocket to win the game, stands his pool cue on end on the bar floor. "What'd you tell that shrink, Hen? I'd really like to know."

Hen lays his cue on the table. "I told him I was a pacifist, that violence is never the answer. Kennedy said that if we didn't put an end to war, it would put an end to us. And that makes sense to me."

"I know you're Nash's favorite disciple, Hen. But don't you think that viewpoint is a bit naive?"

"Not if you go way back in the argument to the very beginning."

"Which is?"

"Point zero," Hen says. "That intentionally taking another human life is morally wrong."

"There's nothing morally wrong with trying to win." Remi shakes the ice cubes in his empty glass, hands it to the bartender. "It's human nature, Hen. To dig in our heels, fight for what's at stake. It's what we're pushed to sometimes, a last resort, what we have to do to win."

"What were you trying to win, Dad?" Hen watches the bartender fill his father's glass.

"What do you mean?"

"When you hit Mom?"

Remi's face goes pale. "What?"

"I saw you. Last fall. She wanted to move the lamp, and you smacked her. So what was at stake there?"

Remi lowers his eyes, his voice. "Oh, Jesus. That was a terrible mistake, Hen. I'm sorry it happened and I'm sorry you had to see it. But that was an isolated incident. One time, I was pushed too far, I let down my guard. I didn't...I'm not perfect, damn it. I never said I was."

"Doesn't Mom have a right to feel safe in her own home, with her own husband?"

"She is safe, Hen. I swear it."

"How can she be sure?"

"God." Remi shakes his bent head back and forth. "You really hate me, don't you."

"I feel sorry for you," Hen says.

"Even worse," Remi says.

"Mom said it never happened again."

Remi looks up at Hen. "It's true," he says. "I would never intention-ally hurt your mother. Ever."

"You already did."

"Listen—"

Hen stops his father's words with a raised palm. "If it's true, that's all I need to know. The rest is none of my business. I believe you, Dad. I want to believe you." Hen racks up and makes the break with a hard crack of the balls. "But if you ever—"

"It's not going to happen, Hen. I swear."

"All right then. Let's shoot pool."

"Not until I know where we stand."

"We stand right here," Hen says. "We finish this game of pool. And then we go home. I'll graduate from high school. I'll make my own decisions."

"You accept what the letter says?"

"I do."

"Means you're fair game now."

"I know," Hen says.

"You don't want your mother and me to intervene anymore?"

"No," he says. "I'll take it from here."

"Good man." Remi's eyes tear as he slaps Hen on the back.

And because Hen hasn't braced himself, he stumbles.

As Hen opens the door to Clay City, he feels his eyes narrow, his mind close. He's never really trusted this place—the rich, earthy smells, the high, paint-spattered stools lined up along the work surfaces, the hanging plants, the girl with the snake wrapped around her neck, the woven straw mats and the jazz that Faye plays on the old KLH stereo, which moved over from the house on Hemlock Street when Remi got a new one. He never wants to get too familiar with this place or with this mirage of a mother. He's not comfortable here; he feels defensive, envious, tight in the jaw. None of this belongs to him; he has no stake, no claim to any of it. At home, his mother shrinks and smolders. Here she thrives, in worn jeans and work shirts caked with Coltrane, clay, and admiration. She floats, stretches, cracks a smile. There's warmth and feeling; here she is alive. At Hemlock Street, the rooms are bare now, scattered with half-filled boxes. No green thing lives there anymore. At home, there is no jazz.

Faye sits in the corner with a boy about his age—her small hands working a hunk of clay—kneading, stretching, explaining as she goes. Hen's heard her say these things a thousand times before, how clay is like a living thing, made up of molecules that move and breathe and respond to human touch. This is the way his mother used to be with him when he was younger, going over everything patiently, gently, as many times as he needed her to, not presuming his ignorance, but only his desire to learn. The last time she was like this with him was in April, the day she came back like a stunned fish from Nantucket, his father trailing behind, the day after Melody seduced him and left without a word, the day Faye sat with him at the kitchen table and ate half a corn chip, the night the purge on Hemlock Street began and the silence settled in like a wet fog. Since then—it's suddenly clear to Hen—she's just been biding her time.

Hen sees the hungry look in the boy's eyes as he listens to Faye. He knows his mother's brought this look to many a boy's eye, to many a man's eye. He's seen this look in the reflection of his own eyes some-times, he can't think when or where. He believes in this mother's gentle beauty, her quiet strength. He just can't understand how a person can be so different in two separate places. He thinks how his father might feel if he landed here, a fly on the wall, the fury he might feel to see Faye coming back to life here, just as their marriage was dying at home, to see the boy's eyes burning holes in the flesh of his mother's rounded breasts. He stands and waits, hands stuffed in his jean pockets. Faye comes toward him, wiping a stray strand of hair from her face with the inside of one wrist. "Hen," she says. "What a nice surprise."

"I was just cruising by," Hen says. "Thought I'd stop in and say hi."

"I'm glad you did. Did you pick up your cap and gown for graduation?"

"I'm not going to wear a cap and gown, Mom."

"Why not?"

"I can graduate just as well in my own clothes."

Faye's face tightens around the mouth. "I suppose you can," she says. "Maybe you could put on a clean shirt, though, and comb your hair."

"I could do that." Hen nods. He's suddenly aware how far he's look-ing down at her. He hasn't stopped growing yet. He's over six feet tall now, taller than the twins, taller than Mercy or Jocko, an aberration in the mid-sized Potts line. "I can do that," he says.

"Good." Faye looks up at the clock, around at the potters. "You headed back to school?"

"Just cleaned out my locker," Hen says. "That's pretty much all she wrote."

"You been home?"

"Briefly."

"Mail come?"

"Yeah," Hen says. "I got into U Mass."

"That's great, Hen. They'll be lucky to get you."

"May be a moot point."

"Let's not count our chickens," Faye says. "We'll cross that bridge—"

"I'm not counting anything, Mom. There's no bridge. No chickens. And anyway, they're my chickens, so—"

"I only meant—"

"I know what you meant," Hen says, filling with his own unkindness.

Faye smiles. "Want to stick around for a while?" she says. "Throw a pot or two?"

Hen looks around. "I don't think so," he says.

"What's wrong?" she says.

It's a minute before he answers. "Don't you even know?" he says.

"Know what?"

Hen crosses his arms against his chest. "You haven't been home for two days," he says.

Faye looks puzzled, pauses to verify the fact. "It's true," she says. "I had late classes both nights. I was so tired, I just ended up staying here."

"Where?" He gestures around the room.

"I didn't mean to worry you, Hen. I'll call next time. I'm sorry."

"Are you coming home tonight?"

"I'll be back by dinnertime," she says. "Maybe we could catch a movie afterward."

After Hen leaves, after the boy and the girl with the snake and all the others are gone, Faye puts the clay away in airtight tubs, cleans the counters and sweeps the floor. She climbs the crooked stairs to her new apartment, her secret sanctuary, her new *home*. It's an empty, sacred place and she's filling it carefully, sparingly—a few cacti, pale yellow walls, a golden pear in the fruit bowl, a few odd pots she's thrown, not the best or most beautiful ones, which she sells from the studio shelves, but the misfits, for which she holds a fierce and stubborn affection, the ones she's never been able to give or throw away. Faye thinks of all the things she *won't* buy for her new place—no couch or drapes or posters from the Coop, no blender, no TV, only a wooden table and a mattress with a white cotton sheet. She'll be able to count her belongings on her fingers and toes. Three children. One clay school. One vase. One rug. One pair of boots. Remi can have all the rest—the house, the car, the new stereo, the color TV, his share of the house on Nantucket. Hopefully, her willing surrender of the material will assuage his hurt, feed his notion of justice, soothe him for a while, before the rage comes. And it will come, Faye knows. She just prays that when it does, Remi won't hurt anyone, won't hurt himself.

Faye closes her eyes to the steamy heat of Remi's fury. She lifts her hair from the back of her neck, feels the crick, stiff and sore, never the same since the wrestle with Remi on the beach. She lets her hair fall again over her shoulders. She's wanted to cut it for years, but Remi always had this thing about short hair on women being unfeminine. Soon, it will be just her—the mattress on the floor, the golden pear, her misfit pots, bare walls and fava beans, her shorn skull and bare, aching neck. Faye picks up one of the bowls she's made recently, blood red splashed on an India-ink blue, lopsided, useless, really, silent and oddly beautiful, the way Hen began. She runs her fingers over the ridges of the bowl, admiring its wobbly form and its hue, its lines and its rough grace. She feels the heft of it, the satisfaction of having made it, molded it, fired it, what she so wanted to feel a few minutes before with Hen as he stood before her, tall and handsome and troubled, before he started to ask tough questions.

Faye puts the bowl back on the shelf. The pots don't pain her, or accuse her, or ask her for explanations she can't give. They never ask her to justify herself, or comfort them, or change. Sitting still on the shelf, they look simply beautiful, the way Tory and Hen and the gallant Buzz did when they were younger, when she lined them up for Christmas portraits in front of the fireplace in Liberty-print dresses and Brooks Brothers suits, bribing them with candy canes for good posture and holiday smiles held just long enough for the click. People used to say what a handsome family they made—and for that one split second they were shockingly, falsely beautiful. Faye looks at the unpainted door she plucked from a Medford junkyard and hung with brass hinges that morning, and is glad, guiltily glad, that it's her pots and not her grown children she's left with at the end of the day.

Faye rummages through a box for a pair of scissors. She's forty-five years old. Her biggest fear has not been realized; she has not been left alone. Love floods through her and she's surprised at how it flows—cool, clear, unspecific. Love for her kids, for the clay, love now for her impending freedom—for a tenacity of spirit that's kept her going all these years. She's not surprised to find that the feeling resembles all too closely an ancient, dull pain that grew with her from the very start and never really left her. But now at least, when she feels the twinges coming, maybe she'll know the difference.

When Hen gets home, he hears voices in the kitchen.

"Henny!" It's Tory, tan from a week away on business with her boss—Tory, home for the graduation, always with a friend, a sidekick, always with a lit cigarette now in her mouth, a slight tremor to her hands. Her lips brush Hen's cheek. He feels the bones in her fingers press against his bare arm. The friend stands by her side, heavily made up, hair pulled back tight.

"Mom's right," he says. "You are too thin."

"No such thing," Tory says. "You remember Melody, don't you, baby bro?"

Hen looks up in shock, the image hitting his eye like the spring of a mousetrap. The two months between them might as well have been a lifetime. "Melody?" he says.

"Hey, studley." Melody gives him a long, laughing look, fingernails gleaming black. "My lord, you must have grown another foot since I last saw you. Can I take any credit for that?"

All at once, he remembers—the tug of her hand on his belt loop, the smell of her hair, the grain of her soft skin, the curve of her belly, the dent in her neck, those incredible, incredible breasts. Her hair's pulled back in a bun. She's wearing a suit, all bound up, neat and tight. Her lips are painted purple. She looks short, tough, made more beautiful now by all the stuff she's put on, or uglier, Hen isn't sure.

"I didn't recognize you," he says.

"I'm a big shot now," Melody says. "Tory got me a job at her publishing house."

"You look so different," he says. She'll never touch him again. She wouldn't touch him now with a ten-foot pole. She's armored, untouchable. "Congratulations," he says.

Tory smushes her Kool out on a plate. "Associate editor in six weeks.

If I weren't playing horsey with the boss myself, MLD, I'd have to wonder."

"You wouldn't catch me in that guy's stall, Tor," Melody says. They're talking to each other now as if he weren't there, chomping on carrot sticks, speaking their own vulgar lingo. "The man's got hair sprouting out of his ears. Anyway, he's over forty, and I don't do over forty. All that dental work and loose skin." She shudders, looks over at Hen and smiles. "I like 'em long and young and lean."

"Someone's got to do the dirty deed," Tory says. "Someone's got to ride in that Porsche. Someone's got to use that extra plane ticket to the Bahamas." She catches the glance that Melody's tossed to Hen. "Cradle robber," she says.

Hen stands waiting. So Tory does know. It's their little joke now, nothing more. Tory's taken over; she's stripped Melody bare, right down to the consonants in her name, taken everything away that ever made her sing, left her with black claws, powdered cheeks, and a spiked tongue. He waits for Tory to stop talking, for Melody to tell his sister to shut up and leave them alone, for her to come over to him, wipe the purple crap from her lips, touch his cheek, scrape the paint off one black claw, unbutton a button, unloose the strand of hair which he may then pull to let the rest of the armor fall. He waits to see if Melody will ask him to go upstairs with her again, to run away. He waits and waits and waits. Hen's fingernails, bitten too low, start to ache. His father sits out in the living room on the other side of the swinging door. There's no party this time, no loud music, no darkness, no pot, no Bruins game. There's no hope left in this house at all, only the garish light of an overcast day. Tory and Melody talk about their plans for the evening, going down to the Square, hitting the Casablanca. Hen feels his heart race, his palms sweat. Unless he does something now, nothing will ever happen again.

"So, how've you been, Melody?" he says. "Besides work, I mean."

"Gre-a-t." Her southern drawl stretches the word like taffy. "All work may have made Jack a dull boy, but not me, darlin'. I dig being a power hound in an age of free love. I've been a free spirit long enough. Give me client lunches, memos, ultimatums. I love power. It's the ultimate high. Yesterday I actually had to give someone the ax."

"Who?" Hen says.

"The mail boy," Melody says. "He couldn't alphabetize. So he had to go. I did it gently, though, with just the right mix of contempt and compassion. So how've you been, slugger? Oh, wait, you're the hockey freak, right?"

"Right." Hen stands before her, his face a deepening red.

"Hey." All of a sudden she fills with the softness he remembers. "I'll ask my cousin about those tickets next time I see him. I promise."

"Forget it," Hen says. All he wants to do is sink into the linoleum floor.

"Hey, Hen, I saw your buddy John the other day," Tory says. "Turns out he's engaged. Isn't that quaint? Seems the chess king found himself a little queen."

"You blew it, Tory," Hen says. "John was a really good guy."

"Far as I'm concerned," Tory says, lighting up another Kool. "Mr. John can just plain kiss my ass."

"Guess he found somebody else's ass to kiss now," Hen says, and Melody laughs.

Tory turns to Melody. "Hey, whose side are you on, MLD?"

"Nobody's." Melody gets up from the table and heads for the swinging door. "I'm going upstairs to change. All this medieval underwear is killing me. See you later, cutie," she says to Hen.

Got everything you need? Hen hears Remi ask Melody as she passes through the living room.

I'm all set, Mr. Potts. Thanks.

Call me Remi, his father says. *What'd Tory say your last name was?*

Hamilton. Hen closes his eyes to the picture of his father's fool.

Hamilton? From Virginia? Any relation to the Alexander Hamiltons?

No. Melody laughs. *No relation at all.*

"So, where's Mom?" Tory asks Hen back in the kitchen, as she gets up to clear the dishes.

"Clay City," Hen says.

"What, does she live there now or something?"

"She might as well," Hen says. "It's like the morgue around here these days."

"That bad?" Tory says.

"They can't stand each other anymore, Tory."

"Tell me something I don't know, little brother," she says.

Hen stands frozen in the kitchen; he looks left to the screen door, up at the ceiling above which Melody is stripping off her medieval underwear, down at his hiking boots, over at the swinging door, and back to his sister's sorrowful face. He would tell her something she didn't know if he could, but for the life of him, he can't.

In the end, it's the ball boy Violet wants, the ball boy she needs, to lie down beside her, touch her, whisper in her ear. It's Andrew she wants, supple, androgenous Andrew with the sleepy eyes, loping across the tennis courts in his Red Sox cap and denim shorts, reading Tolkien in the shade. An after-school job for a few bucks, a few free tickets to Fenway Park from the club's top brass—he must be about the same age as Chickie. Andrew stays late at the club, hitting balls against the backboard, as if this were as good a place as any to be at seven o'clock on a Thursday night. Vi watches him out the window after a board meeting, his chest bare, arms flailing with the racket, bandana wrapped around his forehead, hair flopping on his neck. In many ways, Andrew resembles Hen—blond, gangly, same build, yet more arbitrarily put together, not with as much care. So much is Violet struck by the likeness, so confused by her desire, that she's surprised when a tennis partner, seeing the object of her gaze, remarks on her way out the door, "Bit of an ugly duckling, isn't he?"

Violet lingers in the ladies' room, brushing her hair until the club is empty, quiet—no slamming doors, no Brahman voices talking cocktails, politics, or serves. She studies her face in the bathroom mirror. Why is she so sure that Andrew will forgive this face everything, that he won't see the wrinkles, or guilt, or fatigue? He'll remind her how smooth skin can feel, how long a thigh bone, how soft a breast or an earlobe, how tender a touch, how hard... Andrew will be anybody she needs him to be—the first boy in the haystack back in Iowa, any one of her brothers, Nash as a young man, the son she never had. With Andrew, she'll have a chance to say her past graces, absolve herself of past sins. To her brothers, she'll say, push me away, cover yourselves, beware the fire in my eyes. To the boy in the haystack, she'll say thank you. To her father, she'll simply say, I forgive you. And to the son she never had, she'll confess, I never needed you, to Charlie she'll say good riddance, and to the young Nash, running up to her breathless on the Harvard track, she will, one day, say—I'm ready.

Violet goes outside, where Andrew hits balls from center court. A leftie. Her stomach lurches as she remembers how many times she and Charlie tussled on this service line, twisted kisses and twisted hose, twisted, drunken nights. Now the dusk hovers over Andrew's head, rising up to the fringes of the maple trees that once belonged to Longfellow.

"I'm off, Andrew," Violet says.

"See you later, Mrs. Potts."

"Need a ride anywhere?"

Andrew jogs over, twirling his racket in his hand. "Where you headed?"

"Nowhere special," she says. "I'd be glad to take you wherever you want to go."

"Cool." Andrew goes to pick up his book and shirt from the grass, runs over to her with a lopsided smile. "Thanks a lot, Mrs. Potts," he says.

They slide into Violet's Honda, a tiny box of a car. Andrew looks straight ahead as she pulls out onto Mount Auburn Street. Like everyone of his era, he feels no need to make conversation.

"I have a daughter about your age," Violet says, as they head toward the Square.

"Oh yeah? That's cool."

"Do you have a girlfriend?"

"Nah," Andrew says with a shrug of his shoulders. "Just friends. We don't really go *out* or anything. We all just hang."

"That's what Chickie tells me," Violet says. "Chickie. Minerva, actually. That's my daughter's name. She'll never forgive me."

"Goddess of Wisdom," Andrew says, stretching out his long legs.

"Right."

"What else is your daughter into?"

"Dancing," Vi says. "She's really...into...dancing. She's very good at it, actually. Very talented, I'm told."

Andrew nods. "That's cool too," he says, nodding his head. "Dancing's cool."

Violet looks over at him. "What are you into, Andrew?"

"Me?" he says. "I like wide open spaces, the country. I like to go hang out in open fields."

"I know of a beautiful field," she says.

"Yeah," Andrew says. "I've been to a lot of really far-out fields."

They drive along the river. "Where shall I take you, Andrew?"

"I can get out anywhere," he says. "Anywhere's cool."

"Meeting someone?"

"Nah, just hanging out."

"Nobody expecting you at home?"

"Nah, long as I'm home by midnight, I'm cool."

"I could take you to this field," Violet says. "Just up Route 2 a ways. It will be beautiful in the moonlight."

"I don't know." Andrew plays with the handle of the car door. "I'm pretty hungry."

"We could stop for a bite." Violet's hands clutch the wheel as she thinks to add. "My treat."

"Far out," he says. They stop at Bartley's Burger Cottage in the Square. Vi stays in the car with the motor running. Andrew comes out with two burgers and a side of fries, devours them as they cruise west on Route 2.

Half an hour later they stand in the middle of Five Moon Fields. "So what do you think of my field, Andrew?" Violet says.

"Far out," he says.

"What makes this field special? Different from others?"

"The grass is thin. Beech trees." Andrew points. "I hear a finch. It's definitely a city field."

"Why?"

"No rare birds. Too close to the road. No small animals live in this grass, or feed on it. If I were a mole, I wouldn't hang out here either. It's beautiful, but it's not safe."

Violet kicks off her shoes and sits down on the grass. "Where *would* you go, Andrew?" she asks. "If you were a mole on the run?"

"Canada," he says. "Way up. Saskatchewan. If I get drafted, I'm going to split, go north. We've got relatives up there."

"You're eighteen?" She looks over at him with a start.

"Next year."

"My nephew's eighteen."

"He must be sweating, with the draft lottery and all."

"He must be. I'm lucky. Having all girls. Have a seat, Andrew," she says.

"No, thanks, Mrs. Potts. I'm cool."

"Call me Violet, please. Sit down."

"Okay." He sits down beside her, hugs his knees, pulls up a few blades of grass. They look up at the stars. A few minutes pass in silence. "Hey, whatever happened to that dude, Charlie?" Andrew says. "It seemed like he just disappeared."

"It did, didn't it?" Violet says. Nothing more.

Andrew's head turns slowly toward her. "Why did you bring me here?" he says.

"I brought you here to show you this field," Violet says. "How beautiful, how peaceful it is."

Andrew nods, his face full of pity and grace, his slender hands at a loss. "I'll do whatever you want me to do, Mrs. Potts," he says. "Whatever it is you want."

15

When Violet gets home, Nash is sitting in his armchair watching the eleven o'clock news, gin bottle nearly emptied. His back aches, the good ache of tasks accomplished—having finally finished the tree house, talked to Hen about the draft, talked to him straight, without worrying what Remi would think or say. At this moment, he's not clear on any state other than his exhausted drunkenness, any haven other than the soft, scalloped pocket of the armchair. He can't imagine having any other desires or goals again, other than one last drink, the end of the eleven o'clock news, a long, uninterrupted sleep. Chickie flew in and flew out again, grabbed a bite to eat, changed her clothes, kissed him on the cheek. Janie called to say Warren had gotten into law school. Some good news. She and Warren seem to be the real thing. She sounded happy. He called Seph at her co-op house, just to check in, say hi. She was on her way out the door to a tenants' rights meeting. Nash shifts in his chair as the front door closes. The weather forecast comes on TV. A storm brewing in the Midwest is headed their way. Vi hangs up her coat in the closet and comes into the living room.

"Hi. How was your evening?" Nash asks, rising up in the armchair.

"Meetings are always the same," she says. "Endless. Boring. Unproductive. I tell you, the wheels of so-called progress are held together with some very funky screws."

"I didn't ask how the meeting was. I asked, how was your evening?"

"I survived." Violet comes over and sits on the edge of Nash's chair. "Chickie in?"

"She was in," Nash says. "And now she's back out again. Kind of like the tide, Chickie is."

"Did you tell her to be home by midnight?"

"I thought curfews were out. I thought we were letting Chickie take more responsibility for her own actions."

"She can't handle it, Nash. Chickie needs more structure in her life. I think she's actually been begging for it."

"I haven't heard a peep," Nash says.

"Of course you haven't," Vi says. "You never listen."

"I listen," he says quietly.

Vi turns her eyes to the TV. "What are you watching?"

"The weather," Nash says. "They say it's going to rain all week. We'll have to bring our rubbers to the graduation."

"They're usually wrong," Vi says.

"I think they do pretty well, considering." Nash hears the slur of booze and fatigue in his voice, in contrast with Violet's, quick and sharp.

"Considering what?"

"The pressure." Nash sits up straight, tries to clear his brain. It's not like Vi to linger this way, dangling her legs, dangling a conversation. "If you think about it," he says, "weathermen are the only so-called scientists held accountable for their hypotheses on a daily basis. And on top of it all, they have to act like clowns." He motions to the TV, where the weatherman grins and gestures as the swirling clouds and frowning sun faces gallop across the Great Plains. He struggles to clear his head, keep talking, keep making sense, to keep Vi on the edge of his armchair, the edge of his words. "We find ourselves in the ridiculous position of having to be grateful for the little that these guys *do* know," he says.

Violet looks over at him quizzically. "How was *your* day, Nash?" she says.

"I finished painting the tree house," he says. "All except the trim."

"Already?" Violet looks over at the glass patio door. "What on earth possessed you?"

Nash shrugs. "It's ironic, isn't it? All those years, all that talk. And I did it in just a few days. Hen's been a big help. It's a beauty, Vi, the Ritz Carlton of tree houses. But now who's going to use it?"

"Looks like none of the girls is going to stray too far. They can all go up there to brood. And maybe someday, there'll be—"

"Grandbrooders?" Nash looks up at her.

Violet laughs, shifts her weight uncomfortably on the edge of the chair. "There's something you should know, Nash."

"I already know," Nash says.

"About Chickie?"

"What about Chickie?" The somber tone in Vi's voice sobers him instantly.

"You better sit down for this."

"I am sitting down."

"Then I better sit down." Violet slides off the arm of his chair and sinks into the couch.

"What's wrong with Chickie?"

"She had an abortion."

Nash springs out of the chair onto his feet. "What? What the hell are you talking about. When?"

"A few weeks ago. She went to New York," Vi says quietly. "It was done legally, properly. Thank god. I suppose you could say Chickie used good judgment, after getting herself into a real jam. I suppose you could call that the silver lining."

Nash slaps the lampshade; the lamp's column rocks back and forth. "What the hell?" he sputters. "Who? What? With that kid? That biker kid? That goddamned...*Elvis* person?" He slams his fist down on the coffee table. "Damn it!" Tears flood his eyes. He didn't see. He saw nothing. Chickie kissed him on the cheek no more than two hours ago, no different than any other kiss. "Bye, Dad," she said. "Catch you later, Dad." *Don't take any wooden nickels.* He made a joke. He always does. Once again, he's the last to see, the last to know. He wipes his eyes, looks up at Vi. "Is she all right, for god's sake?" he asks.

"She claims she's fine. She refuses to let me have Herb Parsons take a look at her."

"God, that stinks." Nash slumps back into the chair, leans back his head. "That really stinks."

"Don't feel guilty," Vi says. "Don't feel left out." She's always been able to read his mind. "Chickie didn't tell me either. She did the whole thing herself. Hen went with her to New York."

"God, poor baby."

"Poor baby?"

"I mean Chickie," Nash says. "I meant *Chickie*, for god's sake, Vi. Why'd she have to go through that? She's too goddamned young."

"She'll never have any stars in her eyes," Vi says.

"Nothing wrong with a few stars in your eyes," Nash says. "There's nothing wrong with innocence, Vi, nothing at all. Kids grow up too goddamned fast these days. It makes me want to cry."

"You *are* crying." She puts her hand on his shoulder. "So, is this the night we talk about innocence?"

"What do you mean?"

"Confession time, Nash. I've been having an affair. More than one, actually."

He lifts his head. "I know," he says. "That's what I meant when I said—"

"How—"

"Come on, Vi," Nash interrupts her. "Let's not play games."

"I'd say I'm sorry if I've hurt you. But I don't really think I have."

"No."

Violet holds out her hands. "You could break my thumbs," she says.

"It's like you," Nash says. "To want to arrange your own punishment."

Vi looks at him for a long time. "What do we do now?"

"We do nothing," Nash says. "I forgive you."

"I'm not asking for forgiveness."

Nash shrugs. "It's all I've got."

"You're not angry?"

"Not especially."

"Jealous?"

"Of what?"

"You mean to tell me you feel nothing?" Violet says. "Good god, Nash. At least acknowledge what's going on here. Let it out. Be angry. Yell. Scream. Let me have it. I'm a dirty, rotten infidel. I've betrayed you."

"Have you?"

"Yes, I have. How does that make you feel?"

"Sad maybe," Nash says. "When I first suspected, I felt sad."

"Nothing else?"

"Emasculated, I guess." Nash considers this for a minute. "But that was a knee-jerk reaction. It didn't last long."

"No ranting and raving?" Vi says. "No ultimatums, recriminations. No speeches?"

Nash looks up at her. "Why don't you just tell me what you want, Vi? Wouldn't that be easier?"

She throws up her hands. "I want a reaction," she says. "I want engagement, I want conviction."

"I am convinced," Nash starts slowly, "that you did what you did... because there was something in you...that needed to."

"That's not conviction. That's denial." Vi gets up and starts to pace. "That's turning the whole damn thing around, as an excuse for not dealing with your own feelings. Let's face it, Nash. You have no personal convictions. You've always been content to borrow mine."

"And yours are no good?"

Violet grits her teeth. "God. You are maddening. What *do* you believe in, then?"

"The cosmic view."

"The cosmic view. Honestly, you're forty-seven years old."

"Never too old to believe in the cosmic view."

"Okay, then, tell me. I'm really trying to understand. What on earth is the cosmic view?"

"The big picture," Nash says.

"As in?"

"As in if screwing around for the past few years has kept you happy, kept you here, then in the larger picture, it's a small thing."

"That makes me feel pretty worthless."

"I'm not trying to make you feel worthless." Nash reaches out his hand, exhausted all over again. "I'm just trying to tell you, Vi, that I have faith in our marriage, that I think we can get through this. Infidelity is a blip on the screen, a smudge. The larger picture is—"

Vi raises her hand. "Don't," she says. "Please don't say it."

Nash's hand falls away. "You look pretty, Vi," he says. "You've let yourself go."

"Please don't flatter me," she says, her voice cracking. "Or put me down. Whatever it is you're doing. I'm trying to make a confession here. I'm trying to make it right. You have the strangest way, Nash, of trying to say what you mean sometimes."

"I'm just trying to tell you what you don't seem to want to hear." Nash closes his eyes, leans back in his chair, the liquor washing back over him, the ache stealing into his back. "I'm just trying to tell you that I still love you."

Both families gather out back one afternoon to get ready for the graduation party. Buzz comes over to help Remi tear down the fence between the two yards. They strip bare to the waist and get some old tools from the carriage house—saws, sledgehammer, shovels. Throughout the afternoon, they do what they've always done best together, father and son—pound and sweat, swing the hammer and heft the wood, swig beer, talk sports, talk shop. Hen comes home from playing chess in the Square to find the two yards opened wide to one, moored at the center by the towering oak, and now the tree house, the old fence no more than a pile of rotting lumber spiked with rusty nails. Faye works in her garden. Remi sets up two doors on sawhorses for a makeshift bar. Nash paints the trim of the tree house red, whistling "Fox Went Out on a Chilly Night," trilling on the *town-o's*. The yard is tilled and tidy.

Someone's done some raking and thrown all the rusted scraps into one corner, covered it all up with a bright blue tarp. Standing with his hands stuffed in his pockets, Hen sees uncertain life in the backyard. He sees his mother's back rounded to the sun as she weeds, the muscles flexing in his brother's arms. He sees his father wrestling with the sawhorses, Nash's painting hand pivoting at the wrist. He sees the struggling grass and the sky swirling blue and white above him. He sees the oak in bloom and the birds rushing to and fro, cackling, displaced, their age-old perches disturbed. And the more he looks, the more Hen sees, not the people so much as the land.

"Need any help?" he says, walking over to his father.

Remi turns in surprise. "Sure," he says.

The fewer words, it turns out, the better. Hen's afraid to say anything much more to his father, afraid to slice what's left between them, the fragile tendon dangling from the severed hand of their affection. They've moved so slowly together over the years. They need so much time to recover from every gesture, every slight, every word. How will they ever get anywhere, with words so quickly misunderstood, feelings so easily hurt and time rushing by so fast? "What can I do?" he says.

"Give your brother a hand with those fence pieces, why don't you."

"Okay," Hen says. "Hey, it all looks great, Dad."

Remi looks up at him and nods. Hen sees the sorrow in his father's eyes as he glances over at Faye in the garden, still clinging to hope, as her clematis does to its pole. He feels the strangest mix of pity and love rush bitter through him. He'd give anything to see his father smile. He wants to be angry that his father can think only of himself at that moment, that he can't do anything to stop his mother from leaving. But what he does instead, is repeat himself. "Everything looks great," he says.

Buzz sits at the picnic table, yanking the nails out of the old fence boards. "So, congratulations, old man," he says to Hen. "You made it through the gates of high school hell."

"Just barely," Hen says.

"What's next?" Buzz says. "I haven't heard much college talk."

"U. Mass," Hen says. "Unless—"

Buzz shakes his head. "Man. Things sure have changed around here. In my day, you would've been rammed into some hole at Harvard by now. Grandpa Mercy's name still pulled some weight back then. You're a lucky S.O.B., you know that?"

"Why?" Hen says.

"The truth?" Buzz says.

Hen nods.

"I hated Harvard." Buzz yanks a nail from a board. "Every god-damned Ivy League crimson and white minute of it."

"Why?"

"I didn't belong there. I was a fish out of water, an imposter. Count your lucky stars, bro. This family hit the skids a long time ago and you were born just in time to be off the old rusty hook." Buzz tosses the board onto the pile.

"Might get drafted, never make it to college," Hen says. "Then I can really disgrace the family name."

"Right." Buzz raises his left hand. "Lucky me. Have to stay home and tend the family business with the old fake thumb."

"Do you mind?"

Buzz cups his hand. "What, the freaky appendage?"

"No," Hen says. "Minding the family store. You know, following in the old man's footsteps. Keeping the business going."

"Nah," Buzz says. "I actually like the work. Turns out I'm good at it. Who would have guessed it? That's irony for you. And this..." Buzz rubs his stubby thumb. "I'm used to it. It's part of me. Like the store."

"Dad's still on my back," Hen says. "About you and me running Potts Pro together. He won't let up."

"I'll take care of Dad." Buzz looks at him hard. "You've got plenty to worry about—college, the draft. You just take care of yourself, you hear?"

"You know about him and Mom, right?"

"Tory told me they're having a few problems." They look over at their mother in the garden, face smudged with dirt, her strong arms digging, tilling, working the earth.

"She doesn't love him anymore, Buzz. I don't know if she ever loved anyone."

"Only you, little brother," Buzz says, as another nail comes screech-ing free. "She only ever loved you."

In the olive house, as Chickie, Janie, and Seph prepare the lasagna for the party, Violet calls from the stationery store to check in.

"I know, Ma." Chickie hugs the phone to her cheek. "Pasta, cheese, sauce, pasta, cheese, sauce. Yes, I get it. Yes, I feel fine." She hangs up the phone, plunges her hand into a bowl of shredded cheese. "God, she'll always treat me like an idiot. It's such a drag, being the youngest. They don't really want you to grow up. They won't let you."

"Yeah, well, the oldest has to grow up too fast," Seph says. "We're the science experiments. I was a failure, so the bar was drastically lowered for you two. You can both thank me now."

"And woe the middle child." Janie scoops her finger through the bowl of ricotta cheese. "It gets ignored. Suffocated. Squished." Her palm comes down hard on the table. "Like a lowly, crawling bug."

"At least you guys had each other." Chickie flings handfuls of cheese over a layer of noodles. "I only had Hen."

"Whoa, baby, take it easy with that cheese," Seph says.

"Don't call me that," Chickie says.

Baby. The word's still everywhere, in the news, on the radio, on billboards, brazen on her sister's lips. Chickie's been counting obsessively, every time she hears it, sees it, reads it, keeping track in her brain. Thirty-six *babies* so far today. It's true. She'll always be the baby. She's flunking growing up. The list should add up, but it doesn't—done calculus, danced a ballet solo, ridden a motorcycle, gotten into college, had sex on a golf course, made a baby…unmade a baby. Shouldn't she feel like a woman by now? Chickie ladles puddles of tomato sauce on top of the cheese. Something's wrong. She's not growing right. She screwed up high school. It's a miracle Wellesley accepted her. She got word in the mail. They took the imposter, the Chickie who talked a good game, who aced the SATs, held her head high in the interview, kept her cool and didn't cave. She wore what Violet had laid out on the bed for her, the headband and the pantyhose, the ironed blouse. She played her cards right, came off confident, calm, opinionated, but not disrespectful. She'd been taught well. The admissions people nodded their heads approvingly. She knew it was working, that they were falling for it. One thing she'd learned from Violet was how to make a first good impression. But what work it was. And how exhausted she always felt afterward, wanting to climb under a blanket and sleep for a thousand years. Wellesley couldn't see that all it was getting was a screwed-up girl who couldn't get anything right, couldn't even say a decent goodbye to Elvis, a girl who's still trying to get back at her mother by making a mess of everything—the kitchen, her life, the lasagna. She keeps heaping on the cheese, tossing random noodles here and there, blobs of sauce. Cheese, cheese, pasta, sauce. Fucking pasta, sauce, cheese. *Whatever.*

"Just do it right, for Christ's sake, Chickie." Janie leans over to straighten the lasagna noodles in the pan. "It's for your party. At least try to make it look decent."

"What difference does it make what it looks like?" Chickie says. "It all ends up in your stomach anyway. It all ends up—"

"Okay, Chickie," Seph says quietly. "We get the point."

"So," Janie says. "You survived the Rule of Violet, Chick."

"You guys told me when I got my period, she'd lower the boom. But I think she actually lifted it."

"She was bound to run out of steam sooner or later," Janie says, shaking her head. "Man, she gave us such a hard time."

"She's different now," Chickie says.

"I hope you're right," Janie says, opening a giant box of tinfoil. "She's going to need all the tolerance she can muster."

"What do you mean?" Seph asks.

Janie pulls out a sheet of the shiny foil. "Can you two keep a secret?"

"Yes," Seph says, just as Chickie says, "No."

"Warren and I are engaged," Janie says.

"Oh, Janie, congratulations." Seph gives her sister a hug.

"Wow," Chickie says. "Way to get revenge."

"It's not about revenge," Janie says. "I just broke every rule in the old WASP book. I fell in love and I fell in love with a Black man to boot."

"What does it feel like?" Chickie asks.

"Fantastic, actually," Janie says. "It's a huge relief. I might be human after all."

Chickie hugs Janie too, then, impulsively, Seph. Seph pulls herself away and looks her up and down. "You're thin, kiddo. What's up? You're not pulling a Tory, are you?"

Chickie looks over at Janie. "Nah," she says. "My ulcer's been acting up, that's all."

"What are you talking about, your ulcer?"

"It's a joke," Chickie says. "But this burning…" She rubs her belly low.

"Still?" Janie says sharply.

"You're too young to have an ulcer." Seph looks over at Janie. "What do you mean *still*?"

"It must be angst," Chickie says.

"Angst? God, Chickie," Seph says. "Where do you come up with these words? Tell Violet, will you? See a doctor. Find out what's wrong."

"Nothing's wrong," Chickie says quietly.

"What did you mean, Janie, still?" Seph says. "Still what?"

"Let it go, Seph." Janie wraps tinfoil around her pan. "Let's just finish up the lasagna."

Chickie gives Janie a grateful look. Seph would've had plenty to say about the abortion—judgment, argument, counsel. She would've said out loud all the thoughts that are creeping in slow circles around Chickie's brain—the doubts and worries she doesn't dare let fly, the risks she took, the time she's wasted, the mess she's made of everything. She's still spotting, cramping, still feeling lousy. Maybe there's still part of a baby inside her, a part that will grow into a monster, a one-eyed mutant, no-limbed, brainless blob. The thick noodles slide slippery through her fingers. Chickie does it right this time. Pasta, cheese, sauce—pasta, cheese, sauce.

After six pans of lasagna are covered with tinfoil and packed away in the refrigerator, Tory swings by to pick up Seph. They walk to the Square to buy graduation presents for Chickie and Hen, gifts picked out already by Faye and Violet. Walking down Brattle Street, they pass Longfellow House and Design Research, then head into the heart of the Square.

"So, Victoria, how's the most beautiful of the Pottses doing?" Seph asks as they walk.

"Oh, just busy wasting away," Tory says. "Wasting my brain and my breath, generally making nothing of myself. And how is the prodigal Persephone?

"Oh, still building playdough castles, growing bean sprouts, writing unread masterpieces. Waiting to find out what I want to be when I grow up."

"What are you leaning toward?" Tory asks as they round the arc of Brattle Street to the kiosk.

"Narcissist, hedonist, guru." Seph laughs. "How 'bout you?" she says.

Tory lights up a filterless Kool and takes a drag. "Let's see. Masochist, character assassin, flounderer. Or I may just give it all up and become a nun."

"I've had that thought, too," Seph says.

They laugh and look at each other, trying to see what they've missed all these years, why they never saw it, how alike they were, how much they might have shared.

"No doubt about it," Tory says. "The Potts line is coming apart at

the seams. Janie with a Black man, the women bringing home the bacon, Hen going to a state school, or god forbid—"

"And that ain't all," Seph says.

"What do you mean?"

"Oh, nothing. Grandpa Mercy must be doing double somersaults in
his grave, that's all." Seph laughs. "Chickie told Ma she was thinking of
becoming a bag lady the other day and Violet got splotches on her skin.
'Course it could be all that extramarital sex."

"Persephone!" Tory feigns mock horror.

"She's only human, I suppose." Seph smiles wanly. "I try to keep
telling myself that."

"Hey, more power to her," Tory says. "At least she's seeing some
action. I don't think my mother's had any since the six-foot alien was
conceived."

"Your mom's a good egg, Tor. She's kind of a rarity these days."

"Everyone's a rarity these days," Tory says. "It's beginning to be such
a drag."

As they enter the smoke shop, the rich smells of tobacco envelop
them. Tory finds the marble chess set her mother picked out for Hen.
The man takes it from the glass case and sets it on the counter. Tory's
hand reaches out to lift a pawn, bone thin, translucent. She pulls it back,
curls it into a fist. "Could you wrap it, please?" she says. "Something in
a late sixties *Boston Globe*, maybe. It's a gift."

"Are you all right, Tor?" Seph asks. "Your hand was shaking."

"I'm fine," Tory says. "Just tired. Between things—men, mind-
sets. You know." She looks at Seph, fresh-faced, thinner than usual,
full-breasted like her mother, with Violet's deep green eyes. "You, on
the other hand, Persephone, look fantastic. What's going on?"

Seph grins.

"Sex," Tory says. "Oh my god, you're having sex. Great. Outrageous.
Orgasmic sex."

"Yeah, actually." Seph blushes. "I am."

"Who's the lucky guy?"

"It's not a guy, actually," Seph says.

"What? Oh my god, you're kidding." Tory laughs out loud. "Mercy,
mercy me."

Seph spins her finger around. "Another somersault in that grave."

"So tell me about good sex." Tory takes Seph's arm as they leave the
store. "Please. I crave details. It's been so long."

"Well, it's good," Seph says, still grinning. "Good sex is very, very good."

"Aye, aye, aye." Tory bites her lip and groans. "I can't even remember."

"You're not with anyone now, Tor?"

"I suppose he considers himself to be someone," Tory says half-heartedly. "But I've come to think of Phillip as sort of a subhuman species." She rubs her eyes. "Maybe I'm too tough on him. He's not such a bad guy. He tries too hard, but then again…" She sighs. "Maybe I don't try hard enough."

"God," Seph says. "The goddess crumbling? You're worrying me, Tory. I've never heard you talk this way before."

"I've never really felt this way before," Tory says, without inflection. "I wasn't exactly kidding, you know—about becoming a nun."

Cammie takes a long, even breath and turns her head on the pillow to look at the motel clock: 4:31 in the afternoon. And all is finally well. Almost. She slides out of the bed sideways, lands softly on her perfect size-five feet. Stretching her arms high, she catches a glimpse of herself in the mirror, admires her body's reflection. Not many people look this good in this green, god-awful motel light. But how could she not feel fantastic at this moment of victory? After almost two years. The armor finally cracked. The guy had stamina, you had to give him that. With willpower like that, along with her looks and her smarts, she could've ruled the world instead of conning two-bit gamblers and turning tricks at the racetrack. But, and you always had to keep this in mind—self-pity could suck you up like quicksand if you let it—this had been her choice. She was as smart as the next person. If she'd wanted to be a brain surgeon, she could've been a brain surgeon. It just wasn't the way things had turned out.

Cammie looks down at the guy stretched out on the bed. How many men she's gazed upon from this angle, from this remove. For the most part, they're a blur of smoke and stubble, a pile of rumpled flesh and cash. But this Remi Potts from across the river in Cambridge—he'd turned out to be a tougher, sweeter cookie than she knew. After that first day at the track, she'd pegged him as an easy target—a tortured, troubled guy—not so sure with women, not so sure of himself. Good with numbers; a feel for the track, the horses, the jockeys, or maybe, like he said, just hiding a damn good bookie out there. He came back that second Tuesday, nervous but willing. She anticipated the usual drill—work her wiles, bide her time, wait for the next payoff, take him to the motel, do her thing, and slip away. A few solid wins had come and gone, a few big losses, too, but he'd never caved. She'd almost felt sorry for him sometimes, but then she'd felt sorry for a lot of guys before she fleeced them, and for plenty who'd caught her and turned it right back on her—scalding water tossed on her arms once, a knife nearly piercing vital organs. Anyway, what does she care? All her vital organs are still intact. Her complexion's clearer, creamier, than any twenty-year-old's. She's still a pro; she's still got it. And her patience's finally been rewarded; this guy came through big time. Even though she had to cheat some. With the pills. With the stakes this high, she'd had no choice.

Cammie pulls a sheer silk stocking up over her rounded calf, admiring its line and form. This guy had really put her to the test, and of course a challenge was always more fun. You had to hand it to him. Not many men were strong enough to resist. She could tame the wildest, stubbornest of them—sticking them with her tranquilizer of love—she was famous for it—what she could do with her hands, her mouth, her body—it melted them, immobilized them, sapped them of all their strength and will and finally sent them off to dreamland. This was her two-fold power, the secret of her scam. She could make men sweat and writhe and beg; and then she could make them sleep. It was a matter of principle with her. Unless it was absolutely necessary, no pills were involved. She wasn't a criminal, just a damn good businesswoman.

Cammie pulls out her lipstick and gives her lips a quick smear. But this guy wouldn't crack. Two years. No sleep. No cash. No scam. She wonders why she stuck it out this long. Today she finally got her answer. They left the racetrack flying high. Twenty grand in cash. With this kind of money at stake, she'd had no choice but to slip him one in his victory drink at the bar. She looks down at Remi lying on his back, snoring gently. He's wearing a watch she's never seen. It was his brother's, he said, his twin brother's. They shared everything, he said. Full of surprises, this one. She never knew he had a twin. A polite guy, nervous, an insomniac probably, he'd be a real gentleman if only he wasn't so mad at the world, so scared. It figures he'd snore like this, just barely, discreet even in his sleep. Cammie feels a stab of pity, wonders what went wrong for him. Well educated. Well off. A handsome guy to boot. She never felt scared with him, even though it was true, if she were honest, she thrilled on the rough ones, the unknown, the danger. This guy was stuck somewhere in between the unknown and the danger. He'd only lost it that once, took a swipe at her after she came back from having the mumps. But he'd felt so bad about hitting her, he made it up to her a thousand times. Not with jewelry or dinner or anything like that, but with words. It was a different kind of offering and she'd enjoyed it. Words of apology, kindness…respect.

The comfort Cammie sometimes felt with Remi was a nice change, a relief. Sometimes she even let herself go and enjoyed the sex, the way he made her wipe her makeup off first, the clumsy pawing under the sheet, how he'd pour his heart out to her afterward, how much he loved his family, his plans to save them all, getting more excited as he spilled the details, the way his wife scrubbed the bottom of the pans but not the insides, the crooked part of her hair. It got him horny, his longing, his anguish; all of it got him hard. Whatever. It took all kinds. All ways. This guy never had any trouble getting it up. He was a man through and through. At least he had that going for him; not all guys his age could say that. If she'd let herself, she might actually have fallen for this one.

Keeping a careful eye on Remi, Cammie picks up his coat jacket and slides her hand into the lapel pocket. The wad of cash is tucked inside, as thick as the door to a cave full of thieves. She doesn't bother to count it. It's all there, she's sure, all but the thirty bucks or so he shelled out for drinks and the motel. Not a big spender, Remi—no flowers, no candy, no frills. He might be a cheapskate, a miser with the money, but damn if he didn't have a big, aching heart. Cammie's hand trembles as she pockets the cash. It's a miracle—someone up there has finally decided to look out for her—it's Remi's biggest win yet. Twenty grand. Two thousand down on another long shot. However he came to it, he sure knew how to pick them. He was delirious afterward, wanted to buy his wife a present on the way home—something big, something special. Asked her for ideas. Get her an ice maker, she advised. Everyone loved an ice maker. Poor guy. Wouldn't matter anyhow. It's clear to Cammie from all he's let slip, from all she's heard. It's too late. The wife's had it. She'll soon be long gone.

Looking one last time at Remi, Cammie feels a tug of something in her gut. It's not guilt. She's been around too long, more than paid her dues. But sometimes, when she's tired like this, a little off-kilter, her guard down, she thinks she might like to settle down. Maybe with one of them. Stay at home and cook some omelettes, hang the laundry up on a line. She'd like to reach out and touch this guy's face one more time, smooth his hair from his forehead, wake him up and shoot the breeze. But what would be the use? Such a good-looking guy. Such a sad guy. Wonder what the hell ever happened to him? As Cammie slips out the motel door, with her high heels in one hand and the wad of cash stashed warm against her breast, she almost wishes she could stick around to break his heart.

Nash blesses Faye for being so predictable, so true, for being exactly where he would have expected her to be at this certain hour on this night, sitting on her couch in the living room, reading a book, the rest of the family scattered to the winds. How reassuring it's been, the rippling mirage that's moved along with him all these years since that first day he saw her in the bookstore. And more than that, the true comfort and pleasure of her company since he got whacked on the head.

"Nash." Faye looks pleased to see him, puts down her book and picks up the deck of cards. "Back for revenge, eh? You're a glutton for punishment, I see." Nash smiles. Neither of them can admit how much they've enjoyed these scattered, random visits over the past months, the spirited games of Crazy Eights, each other's quiet, uncomplicated company.

"Not tonight, Faye. I'm a lost cause." He sits down next to her on the couch. "So, this is it," he says.

"What?"

"The end. With the kids." He lifts his hands. "It's all over."

"No, it isn't," she says. "It's just the beginning, Nash. For them. For us. We get another chance. To be something more again than just their parents."

"You're right." Nash feels his eyes well up. "I don't know why I feel so...helpless."

"What is it, Nash?" she says.

"Did I screw up, Faye?" he whispers. "When I found you in the bookstore? When I brought you home for Remi? Did I do the wrong thing?"

"No," she says. "You saved me, Nash. You and Remi both, the two of you. I've always wanted to thank you for that." He watches her lean toward him, feels her breath on his face. Just in the nick of time, he closes his eyes. She kisses him gently on the mouth. His arms come up around her and he kisses her back. Gently. Just so. Gently. Still not opening his eyes.

"I've been wanting to do that since 1943," she says, pulling away. "I'm sorry, Nash."

"I'm not," he says.

"I don't want to feel bad anymore," she says. "I don't want to feel guilty."

"I know."

"It won't happen again. I promise."

"You sure?" Eyes still closed, Nash smiles. Without confirmation from Faye's eyes, he can't gauge the flush in her cheek, the tone of her voice. He can't see the freckles on her nose or the creases at the edge of her eyes. He's unwilling to risk it, to break the moment with vision, a sensory snap. If he keeps his eyes closed, the kiss won't be real. It won't have happened; it will only have been felt. And he can keep it as visceral memory, the final sequel to the roller coaster ride. He feels Faye's body pull away, hears her walking toward the door. Leaning back on the couch, he feels his heart beating hard. He waits for a long time, until he's sure that when he opens his eyes, she'll be gone. If he can just hold out, eyes closed, safe in the arms of this old couch for long enough, the kiss will disappear, no cause for regret, or reflection, or guilt. Faye promised. It won't ever happen again. He can't even begin to hope. She is nothing if not a woman of her word. It's a long time before Nash realizes that he's sitting on Remi's couch, not his own, and that Faye has just walked out her own front door.

16

Graduation 1970 is a restless affair, postponed once already because of a bomb scare, plans still uncertain at the eleventh hour as a thunderstorm watch unfolds. Mrs. Lugbout presides in a peach-colored suit, an orchid pinned to her giant bosom, perfume wafting, jewelry jingling, curls newly tight and dyed. She's recently been appointed high school principal, taking Mr. Packer's place after he keeled over dead from a heart attack in the hallway the month before. A terrible tragedy, an unexpected twist of fate. Mrs. Lugbout holds down a rising smile, riffles through her papers, looks out over the front row of teachers. Miss Gladstone has a new suit, Mr. Harrington a new haircut. They sit together in the front row.

The sky is dark and restless, wind pulling up short in tight gusts, swirling leaves, bottle caps, and trash. The graduates file out from the gym, hanging on to their lifting hats, rising gowns, flapping ties. The SDS group huddles by the library with pamphlets and cups of coffee, still circling, chanting. Hundreds of fold-down chairs line the green, though it's finally lost all claim to the name, hardly a blade of grass left, bisected still by the cement path lined with broken benches, one of them the kissing bench where Hen kissed Cozmo's feet. A loudspeaker booms a screechy, incomprehensible welcome. The graduates gather by the stage. The Goodyear blimp circles slowly overhead. Families arrive in clusters. Some come in pastel ruffles, some in dark suits, some in cowboy boots and jeans. Some wear tie-dye, some velvet, some silk. Elvis Donahue's parents arrive in matching black leather pants and dark glasses. They've never set eyes on Chickie, nor she on them. Faye wears an Indian print cotton skirt and sandals, hair pulled back loosely with a batik kerchief. Remi wears a bow tie and sports coat, a nip of Jack Daniels tucked into his lapel pocket. Nash has on a new sweat suit from the store; he keeps reaching for pockets that don't exist. Violet comes straight from work in a pine-green pantsuit and matching pumps, a vermillion paisley scarf. Janie wears bold Marimekko, an elegant, afroed Warren by her side. Tory shows up in a miniskirt, lavender dress shirt, and man's tie, Buzz in a baseball cap and rumpled Prep Shop striped shirt, Lainey in Talbots green at his side. Hen wears black jeans, an Army-Navy T-shirt, and, true to his promise to Faye, he has washed and combed his hair. Underneath Chickie's white graduation gown, her leopard-skinned shirt and purple clogs glow. And Seph still hasn't arrived.

Vi looks out over Cambridge Street. "Where is she?" she says to Nash. "She's always late. She does it just to—"

"No, she doesn't." Nash's voice holds caveat, patience. "She'll get here when she gets here, Vi," he says.

Mrs. Lugbout adjusts her drooping corsage uneasily. This won't be like other graduation days, and not just because of the stormy skies. A ripple of apprehension zips up her spine and she cuts it off at the neck with a clenching of her jaw. She can't remember when things started to unravel the way they did. Only a few students come here anymore with gratitude and pride. Only a few care about upholding the seriousness, the sacredness of this day, keeping it a rose-pressed memory in their yearbooks. The winds have risen. The spirits of these children have long since flown from these fold-up chairs. The school, like the family, like the country, is going to rack and ruin. Mrs. Lugbout has ulcers now. And it's no wonder. Thirty-seven days of school canceled this year because of bomb threats, blizzards, racial tensions, political rallies. Door blown off the gym. Three former students dead in Vietnam; sixteen suspended for taking over the cafeteria in protest of the war. Nine students caught smoking pot in the bathrooms. Two girls with babies on the way. And just last week, a young biology teacher pushed brazenly down the stairs. This isn't a safe place anymore, no safer than the streets, no longer a hallowed place of learning, just a holding tank for children growing up too recklessly, too soon. This no longer feels like an institution of learning, and so, Mrs. Lugbout thinks, not without a stab of resentment, she can't truly or with any real triumph, as she's waited her whole life, feel the glory of being the high school principal.

Mrs. Lugbout stands to welcome the audience and introduce the mayor. The echoes of the mike squeak and bounce back against the crowd. The teachers shift in their front-row seats. They are all on trial this night. She looks at the graduates sitting in their chairs, so many of them slouched, defiant. There's that boy, Henry Potts, shot up now, gone to grunge and seed, and that strange cousin of his, dressed like a hippie, or a hussy, who can tell anymore? Accepted to Wellesley and doesn't even want to go. A perfect example of a waste of two promising young minds. The family sits in the sixth row. A motley crew. Who knows what really goes on in those old rambling houses off Brattle

Street? Maybe it's no wonder. The girl was so smart, and the boy used to be so utterly beautiful. Mrs. Lugbout remembers his smooth chest and swollen lip and shudders. Such a shame. All those brains and beauty starved. All that privilege wasted.

Still, Mrs. Lugbout holds her head high. She hasn't missed but two days of school in all of her nineteen years, one for jury duty and one for a secret she'll take to her grave. She graduated from this very school in 1932, went on to Boston College, worked her way up through the system. She's done her work here and she's done it well. She has a new dress, a clean carpet at home, an almost clear conscience, and in this day and age, that's close enough. She had her hair done today. The dye job isn't perfect—a little too blue—but then it always is. And they aren't all lost causes. There's Diane Downing, in the third row, beaming, a carnation pinned to her chest, a lovely girl, Radcliffe bound. And Donny Kemp, a brilliant science student and tri-letter athlete, off to Princeton in the fall. If they can only make it through the speeches, through the handing out of the diplomas. If only the rain holds and the SDS group stays in its corner. If no one misbehaves, if no one gets hurt, then the thunder can rumble and the band can play. They can fold up the chairs, lock the doors, move on to summer, to rest. The cycle, once again, will be complete. And perhaps by the fall—Mrs. Lugbout is never one to give up hope—the world will have started to tilt itself back to right, to the way it used to be.

The mayor promises a short speech and is held to it by the chanting and the boos. The valedictorian's hair hangs halfway to his knees and isn't clean. He speaks not of fond memories, but of ignorance and violence, not of looking forward into bright futures, but looking back into the darkness of tyranny and oppression. Not of counting our accomplishments, but counting our losses, our shames. The salutatorian is beautiful, angry, and Black. She wears an armband, raises her fist in a salute with a cry of "Black Power," bringing large patches of the audience to its feet with a dignified roar. Mrs. Lugbout starts to call the graduates' names. One by one they file across the stage to receive their diplomas. *Aaron, Roberta—Ablon, Curt—Ackerman, Aldous Reginald*," she calls out, as Monkey Man lopes toward her.

"Aldous Reginald?" Chickie says. "That's his real name?"

"Like Aldous Huxley," Hen says. "He asked for a hit of acid on his deathbed."

"*That's* the way to go," she says.

After getting his diploma, Monkey Man takes the microphone from Mrs. Lugbout and turns front to the audience. "Hey, listen up, everyone? I got something to say to my French teacher, Miss G., sitting right down there in the front row and I'm going to say it all in French, the way I know she'd want me to, so here goes…" He takes out a piece of paper from his pocket and clears his throat. "VOUS…ETES…UNE… BILLET…CHAUDE." Everyone looks over at Miss Gladstone, who's grinning from ear to ear. "And for those of you in the audience who don't speak French," Monkey Man adds, "that means, YOU ARE ONE HOT TICKET, MISS G.!" He hands the mike back to Mrs. Lugbout and jumps down off the stage, his graduation robe flapping open to reveal nothing underneath but a pair of shorts and untied army boots. Going up to Miss Gladstone, he pulls her up from her chair, wraps his arms around her and kisses her full and long on the mouth. The crowd starts clapping slowly and then goes wild. Monkey Man bends down to Mr. Harrington, who's sitting to Miss Gladstone's left. "Time's a wasting, Harrington," he says. "You better make your move soon." He flings off his cap and gown and throws them into the crowd. "You like my army boots, folks?" he yells. "They're my mother's. She let me wear them for the night."

"He just can't quit," Chickie says. "He'll never be able to quit."

"And we're only on the As," Hen says.

Mrs. Lugbout rolls through the alphabet. *Delvechio, Downing, Dorfman, Dyer.* Some don't rise; many aren't there. When a name goes unanswered, she simply moves on. A roll of caps goes off somewhere. Thunder rumbles in the distance. *Jackson, Jeune, Joffrey.* A policeman shifts his feet by the stage, looks up at the sky, then at his watch and back again to the sky. Mrs. Lugbout arrives at the Ps. *Pachelli, Pierce, Pinckney…Potts, Henry Dickinson. Potts, Minerva Warren.* A pocket of loud cheering erupts from the crowd. Violet raises her camera and snaps Chickie coming down off the stage, her white gown flowing open. *Click.* After the ceremony, Faye asks Hen to pose on the kissing bench, resisting the urge to wipe a smudge from his forehead. *Click.* "Now, both of you," she says. Chickie plops down beside Hen, puts two fingers up in a V behind his head, makes the vampire face. *Click.* "Be serious now. I want a *real* picture," Faye says. Just as her finger hits the button, Chickie leans over and kisses Hen on the cheek—*click*—the last shot on the roll of film Faye took to Nantucket that weekend in April, to take photos of the cottage and the beach to send to the real estate agent for the summer renters. They never got any pictures. The people took the place sight unseen. Funny, it's not like her, Faye thinks. She forgot to develop the film.

The party at Hemlock Street begins at dusk. Faye lights the Chinese lanterns. Nash sets up the old croquet set in the newly opened yard. Chickie and Hen play chess in the tree house and Remi tends bar, a chorus line of leggy bottles glinting on the makeshift table. Buzz balances the stereo speakers on the kitchen windowsill and puts on Taj Mahal, a generational compromise to start the evening off. The guests start to arrive, old friends of the family mostly, colleagues, neighbors, bridge and tennis partners. Jane introduces Warren around, getting ready to drop her bombshell. Tory flirts with a man who's suddenly appeared at her side, a stranger with thinning hair, a flat, puttied nose and beautiful shoes, replacing Melody, who has just as suddenly disappeared. Lainey passes around a tray of hors d'oeuvres. Buzz rolls a football in his hand, excited by the new expanse of the yard, looking for a player, a game. And Seph still hasn't arrived.

Up in the tree house, on the chessboard, Hen takes Chickie's queen.

"That's it. I'm doomed without her." She finds Nash's vodka bottle stashed in a hole in the tree, reaches for her pawn.

"Watch your bishop on king three, Chick," Hen says. "He's trying to tell you something and you're not listening."

"Well, then he's not enunciating clearly, is he?" She fixes herself a drink with a can of ginger ale. "You want one, Hen?" she says.

"No," he says. "Careful of my rook."

"Come on, celebrate, Hen. I see your sneaky old rook and I've got a plan. Just have one drink. It won't kill you."

"It'll just make a fool out of me." He gestures down to his father, who's rolling his hands the way he does when he's gearing up for the punch line of a bad joke. "That's all booze does. You sure you want to make that move?"

"No. J'adoube." Chickie yanks the bishop back to its square. "If I say j'adoube, I can take back my move, right?"

"Right," Hen says. "Is Elvis coming?"

"No, it's over," she says. "Kaput. Zappota. Fini."

"Did you ever tell him?"

"Yes, I told him."

"Good." Hen swoops up her bishop and attacks her king. "Checkmate, Chick," he says.

"Shit." Chickie takes a sip of her drink, examines the board. "Wasted, once again."

"They get wasted a lot at Wellesley?" Hen asks.

"Don't remind me," Chickie says. "I may have to kill myself first."

"I thought you wanted to go to Wellesley."

"No, Violet wanted me to go, and I guess I wanted to prove something to her. But now the joke's on me. I got in."

"Won't be so bad."

"Ha," Chickie says. "A bunch of snotty little rich girls, just like me, only snottier, and richer. I shouldn't have moved my knight there, right?" Chickie groans. "I'll drown at Wellesley, with all that blonditude and snot. Oh, now I see what you were saying about the rook. I could've moved my pawn there." She replays the moves on the board. "They don't even have a dance department. What was I thinking? I should've applied to Bennington. That's what I wanted to do, but she said it wasn't a real college and part of me believed it. I should have moved here, right? I should've...should've. Shit. I *hate* that word." She takes another sip of her drink. "Part of me still believes my mother knows what's best for me." She knocks over her king in defeat. "How screwed up is that?"

"Good game, Chick." Hen lies down on his back on the tree house floor.

"Liar." Chickie sweeps her hair off the nape of her neck, clips it up in a barrette. "Let's hit the road, Hen. Let's just split."

"What. You mean run away from home? That's a little first grade, Chick, don't you think?"

"It wouldn't be such a big deal." Chickie downs the last of her drink. "We're both eighteen. Grown up, supposedly." She looks down into the yard, as the party starts to simmer. "And this doesn't feel like much of a home anymore."

Violet wears red and eats lasagna, more than she should. She flirts with Les Parker, but only out of habit, not for the kill. She straightens out her skirt, straightens out her brain. She and Nash will go on a diet tomorrow. She looks over at him. From a distance, he's still a good-looking man. If he lost five pounds, maybe eight... She sees the possibilities now, with the yard opened wide. Maybe Nash and Remi could put up a tennis backboard; she'll cut down on her hours at the club. Her serve's gone to pot, since... Ah, what the hell. A Japanese garden in the far corner, a goldfish pond. Her mind wanders. A swarthy landscaper with a broad back. No. She can't risk the landscaper. She'll have to leave the arrangements to Nash. She pulls her dress away from her sticky skin. Three thoughts converge suddenly in her head: It's hotter out than she realized. Les Parker's in much better shape than Nash. And Seph still hasn't arrived.

Nash is the only one to see Tory leave midway through the party, slipping down the flagstone path on the arm of the stranger into the night. Adrian. No one but Tory ever knew his name. At the airport she kisses him goodbye. He feels his bussed cheek as he watches her head for the departure gate, bewildered not for the first time that day. She'd called early that morning out of the blue, asked him to this family gig. He'd dressed carefully, brought some extra cash, remembering the one night they'd spent together a few years back, the feel of that glorious hair and silky skin, her throaty, jabbing whispers, the strange, dark places she'd taken him. But she barely spoke to him all night at the party, pulled this airport stunt at the last minute, wouldn't even say where she was going, just asked to be chauffeured. Like a fool, he'd half hoped she would ask him to go with her at the last minute, hand him a plane ticket and fly off with him into the sunset. Beware the power of beautiful women, he thinks, wiping the lipstick off his cheek. Tory blows him a kiss as she disappears through the airline gate. All eyes turn to see who'll catch it. People still stare at her, though soon there won't be much left to see. He felt her bones when he embraced her, felt a chill. He shivers, suddenly relieved to have her gone. This, the stranger thinks, might be the most beautiful girl in the world, but also the most unlucky, the most dangerous. He feels for his untouched wad of cash in his pocket, glances down at his shoes, and heads for the escalator down.

But Tory, sitting in the window seat of Row 22 on Flight #1985 to New York, feels more rational, more at peace than she ever has before, knowing that maybe for the first time in her life, she's acknowledging her true feelings. Acting on them. Maybe there *is* something to this touchy-feely stuff, she thinks, as she opens her carry-on bag. It's there, her masterpiece. She made it behind closed doors back on Hemlock Street while everyone else was running around getting ready for the party. A diorama. They used to make them at the Shady Lane School— dinosaurs, volcanoes, the frozen tundra. Her father rewarded every grade of A with a five-dollar bill and that was a lot of money in those days. She'd always kept a stash. Tory wasn't much of an artist, but she'd enjoyed making the diorama that morning and remembers each step with satisfaction. First, she cut down one side of a shoebox, then drew a black and white chessboard on the remaining three sides with a magic marker. She labeled the diorama "The Marriage of John" in fancy, curli-cued letters. She took three chess pieces from an old set of Hen's, found a rusted saw in the carriage house, borrowed some glue and labels from her mother's study. She glued the pieces in place with labels at their feet: John, the White King, standing in the middle; The Nameless Bride at his side, a white queen gauged and disfigured with a knife. Off to the side lay the black queen, decapitated, her crowned head glued tilted on the board beside her, a red trail of blood streaming from her neck. Labeled, in her very best handwriting—Queen Victoria with Dripping Head.

Tory drinks a nip bottle of coffee brandy on the plane and eats a saltine to settle her stomach. She takes a cab from the airport to John's brownstone in midtown and leaves the package with the doorman, be-fore walking the thirty-six blocks north to her own apartment on the Upper West Side. She knows the dangers of walking the city alone at night, without an escort or at least a can of mace. She knows she left the party without a word, not saying goodbye to her parents or her brothers or to anyone at all. Her parents will call her headstrong, impossible. Adrian will call her selfish, maybe even cruel. And John will call her sick and twisted, suffering from some fancy condition in one of his psychi-atry textbooks—narcissistic personality disorder or some such thing. He'll see her gift as spite and not surrender, revenge and not regret. He won't understand that it's just her warped way of saying goodbye, that she really did feel something. That it's all right. She's always been mis-understood, mistrusted. It's easier just to leave it that way. She's always been able to call the shots, control the distance, pick and choose. And she likes it that way. All the boys. All the men. They'd all come running again if she so much as lifted her little finger.

It's just too hard being with you, Tor, John said when they broke up. *I don't think I could ever end up with someone who's so afraid of herself, so unwilling to be in touch with her feelings.* She'd joked, put her hand to his crotch, asked him if she was getting in touch with any feelings now. He'd pushed her hand away, almost in disgust. She remembers now and cringes. She has feelings all right, and since that moment John left her, they've spiked her fairly raw. She'll let him know exactly how that last fling of his arm, that last glance of pity and disdain, made her feel. The diorama will be congratulations, gift, proof, confession, punishment enough.

Tory feels the coarse damp heat of the summer evening as she walks through the New York streets. The sweat pools in her collarbone and drips down the hollow of her back. She kicks one sandal off onto the sidewalk, the other into the gutter. She loosens the tie and tosses it onto the pavement. Her linen jacket lands on the hood of a silver car. She sees a man on the street corner, another hailing a cab, one fiddling with the lock on a brownstone door, two cops sitting in a cruiser up the street. Slowly, she starts to unbutton her shirt. For the moment, all the men are occupied; they pay no attention. For a moment, she's invisible. She understands. It takes a lot to raise an eyebrow in Manhattan on a full-blown summer night; this island's seen it all. At the corner of Broadway and Sixty-Second, she slides off her shirt and throws it back over her head. By the time she hits Sixty-Third Street, the cop in the driver's seat has turned over the ignition in the cruiser. Tory feels herself shrinking with each piece of clothing shed, each block passed. She pulls down one strap of her bra, then another. It's puzzling. The men still haven't raised their heads—the guy selling pretzels on Sixty-Sixth, the bum on the grate on Sixty-Eighth, the businessman waiting for a bus on Seventy-Third. They all seem to be in another world. She unclasps her bra, lets it fall. The police siren sounds behind her, but she doesn't hear it. She's finally spotted the one she wants, the one who'll keep her from shrinking too far—a man playing the sax on Seventy-Fourth Street—"Strange Fruit." How perfect. She laughs. Victoria Abbott Potts. The strangest fruit of all. She unzips her skirt just as the cop car pulls up behind her. The sax player doesn't see her yet. She understands. His music's taken him far away, and, as visions go, she's still so small. But soon she'll grow up out of this heat, the sudden desire she has for this beautiful man and his music, grow back into her life-sized, willful self. The two cops come up from behind and take her by the elbows. Tory turns around, barefoot and naked from the waist up. "You'll have to come with us, miss," one of them says. Tory nods. She understands. They want her to go with them, want her to take them to a warm, dark place and make them feel good. She can do that. "Sure," she says, touching the cop's arm. "No need to put the handcuffs on, Sergeant. Really. I promise. I'll cooperate. I'm all yours." The other policeman puts his jacket around her shoulders. She pulls the zippered edges close, thanks him for his kindness. By then a crowd is all around. Tory sees them all—every boy she's ever cast a spell on, ever loved—all gathered here to send her off, to wherever it is that she and the sax player will go when he's finished his song, wherever it is these guys are taking her. The cop bends her head so she won't bump it getting into the cruiser. Taking one last look out at the crowd before the tinted window closes, Tory waves.

By midnight, back on Hemlock Street, the guests have thinned. The storm's passed out to sea, but another one follows on its tail. From up in the tree house, Nash watches Remi weave a drunken path through the yard in his old corduroy coat and bow tie, still playing the host: a word here, another drink, an avuncular slap on the back. Nash waits for his brother to pass by under the oak tree.

"Hey, Rem," he says. "Up here."

Remi looks up. "Nash? That you?"

"Come on up, big brother. Survey the old estate with me."

"I don't think I can manage that damn ladder," Remi says, looking up. "My back's out again. Tell you what. Put in an elevator and I'll stop by for a drink sometime."

"You're not an old man yet, Remi. Climb the goddamned ladder."

Remi climbs slowly, grimacing, poking his head up into the tree house, hoists himself up with a groan and sits down beside his brother. "So, you finally made your goddamned tree house."

"Hen helped," Nash says. "He's good with his hands. I never knew that."

"He's a good kid," Remi says.

"He's a good man," Nash says.

Remi nods. "Nice view from up here." He dangles his legs over the side. "If you lean this way, you can see right down Laura Chapin's dress."

"Dirty old man," Nash says. "Remember the first time, Remi, that girl in the Dodge. What was her name?"

"Marcia Lacey," Remi says. "Silver belt. Pink sweater. One hell of a nerve."

"She took pity on us." Nash beats his fists on his chest. "Made men out of both of us in ten minutes flat. She must've set a record."

Remi laughs, a short, hard laugh. "You got anything to drink up here?"

Nash lifts the empty vodka bottle. "Looks like the kids found my stash."

"Where are the kids?" Remi asks.

"Long gone," Nash says.

"Tweedledum and Tweedledee," Remi says. "Remember when the old man used to call us that?"

Nash shakes his head. "You remember all that stuff, Rem. I lost it a long time ago. And the concussion didn't help. Or maybe I've just let it all go."

"I could stand to lose some of it," Remi says, rubbing his forehead.

"I'm going to miss having the kids around."

"They're not going far. You wait and see. Ten years from now they'll still be hanging around with their dirty laundry, looking for a hot meal. Kids these days don't really grow up. Have you noticed, Nash? They don't worry about the future. But surprise, the future's here, isn't it? It's all so goddamned different. We grew up so fast. We had to."

"Did Hen talk to you, Rem?"

"About what?"

"The draft."

"Sure. We've talked about it. He's my son, isn't he? Of course we talked about it. Goddamned right."

"He doesn't want to go."

"'Course he doesn't. He's a healthy, normal kid. That shrink even said so. He's scared, that's all. Who wouldn't be?"

Nash nods, slowly. "I think Hen's got a real conviction about this, Rem. He really doesn't want to support this war."

"He may have to. Listen, Nash—"

"I know." Nash raises his hands. "He's not even my kid and—"

"Don't put words in my mouth."

"They're my words," Nash says. "Hen's your son and I can't possibly know how you feel. But I do know that this war is one colossal horror show. Rem, it's got to stop."

"But here's my question." Remi's voice starts to slur. "How the hell... can you know, Nash, how this war will measure up? Until all the rest of the wars have been fought? Until the very end?"

"This war's rotten to the core," Nash says. "Those kids are over there with bombs and napalm, stoned and bewildered, taking random orders to kill. And now the cops are killing protesters over here. This war's tearing both countries apart. I could never, in good conscience, send anyone over there. Let alone someone I care about as much as—"

"I wouldn't be sending him, for Christ's sake, Nash. There's a draft on. Uncle Sam calls, you come running, you do your duty."

"Duty, Rem?" Nash says.

"Listen," Remi says. "All of my kids have been snailing around their whole lives. I just keep waiting for them to *do* something. Buzz is finally pulling himself together. And I just want Hen to take responsibility for something for once in his life."

"I think he has," Nash says. "Give him some credit, Rem."

Remi runs his fingers along the creases in his forehead. "Why the hell do you think I'm such a terrible father?"

"Neither one of us has been so great."

"Faye's leaving me, Nash. Did you know that?"

Nash's head snaps left. Remi feels a dark thrill to have blurted it out like that, to shock his brother so. Maybe now that he's said the words out loud, they can't hurt him anymore. The mantle of his pain can now rest safely in the palm of Nash's hand.

"What do you mean she's leaving you?" With the memory of Faye's lips on his, Nash feels a rush of fear.

"Any minute now, she's about to vanish. I'm just waiting for it to happen." Remi waves his finger back and forth: *tick, tock, tick, tock.*

"What are you talking about?" Nash says.

"Apparently...Faye's had enough. Enough of me." Remi lifts his shoulders in a drunken shrug. "Little bit, you know. Little bit of old Remi goes a long, long way."

"Oh, it's a joke. You're drunk. Down. You two had a fight."

"I'm drunk all right," Remi says. "But it's no joke, Nash."

"It's always a possibility. Marriage is tough, Rem. We're all hanging on by a thread."

"Ours broke," Remi says bluntly.

Nash's eyes scan the yard. "Look, there's Faye." He points. "Over by the bar. Talking to Bill Randall. She looks fine. She looks great, as a matter of fact."

"Doesn't she?" Remi says. "Doesn't she look *fantastic*?" His wobbly voice stops up short. "She's here now, you see. For the kids. For Hen. But it's not really her. And afterward, she'll be gone. She's going to fly away..." Remi points to a tree branch. "Just like that bird over there. Flap her wings and fly away."

"You're serious."

"I have never...ever...been anything but serious," Remi says. "And if you don't know that about me by now, little brother—"

"How did this happen?"

"Jesus, Nash." Remi's hair's gone nearly white. "Don't you get it? You're not responsible. It wasn't your marriage, even though you arranged the whole goddamned thing. Even though you watched over it like a hawk. It was mine, Nash. It was my fucking marriage. And it just, plain…" His hand falls at the wrist. "Broke," he says.

Nash stares at his brother and tries to conjure up the face of Remi as a young man, as a boy. But he sees nothing but his own shadow, feels his own heartbeat, his own breath. Suddenly he can't remember anything he and Remi have ever really done together. He remembers the feel of Violet's sure hands on his back, the clutch of Chickie's baby arms around his neck, the sound of Seph's voice as she read out loud from one of her tragic, rambling stories, Janie's hoarse voice telling knock-knock jokes, over and over again. He runs two fingers along his forearm to find the old scar, to unearth the memory. Remi bears a similar scar, on the same arm. This, Nash remembers.

They were boys, eleven or twelve, wrestling in the garage. In those days after their father died, they played hard, played rough. During an argument, Nash pushed Remi into a storm window leaning up against the garage wall. The glass shattered and a jagged edge tore deep into Remi's arm.

"I'm sorry," Nash said, as the blood started spewing from Remi's arm. "I didn't mean to push you so hard, Rem. I didn't see the window. I'm sorry."

"Get away from me," Remi yelled. "Don't touch me. I'm bleeding. You did this. And I'm probably going to die."

As their mother came running from the house, Nash took out his red pocketknife—the one Remi was so jealous of—turned away, and carefully cut his own arm, the same cut as Remi's, in the same place, at the same angle. His mother looked over as she led Remi away, just as he finished cleaning the blade of the knife on his pants, and flung him a look of horror. He held his arm up tight against his chest, turned his eyes away. He didn't want anything from his mother, any scolding, any sympathy. He only wanted her to make Remi stop crying, make his cut stop bleeding.

In the dim light of the tree house, Nash can just make out the scar on Remi's arm. It's not as neat as his; Remi's cut was deeper, more ragged. They got stitched up together at the Mount Auburn Hospital, side by side on a metal table, and when it was over they got ice cream cones at Brigham's and stayed home from school the next day, read comic books, and relived all the blood and gore. Remi was happy by then, forgiving, the martyred, wounded hero.

"I'm really sorry, Rem." Nash kept apologizing for days. "I didn't see that window behind you. I swear. You were really brave. Your cut was tons worse than mine." Remi played tough then, said it hadn't hurt much, that it was no big deal. He never even asked about Nash's cut, how he'd gotten it, how they both ended up getting stitched up together that day. As with so many other experiences in their lives, it just seemed natural that they'd shared it.

Up in the tree house with his brother, Nash waits to see if there's more to come. He's been expecting it, the slow leaking of Remi's conscience, bits and pieces of the bleeding truth. He runs his finger over his scar and looks over at Remi, who's doing something like crying now, though the liquor's dried him out completely. "Son of a bitch," Remi says. "Son of a goddamned bitch."

"More like sons of a bastard," Nash says. "We got half a lousy draw, Rem. That's just the way the cookie crumbled." He puts his hand on Remi's back, trying to feel his brother's pain as he always has before, to find a way out for him, a solution, a salve. He tries to feel the sorrows of a man whose pride's been battered, whose son's life may be in peril, whose wife is deserting him. But he can't feel anything but a chilling calm, a desperate desire to hold on to all he's got. Nash watches his brother's head rise up from his chest, his hand wipe his eyes dry. And he feels nothing but relief, a profound, selfish joy. The two of them are floating down a fast-moving river and he's caught on to the fallen trunk of a tree. He can't let go. He can't swim after Remi, can't try to save him, because if he does, he'll drown. It's as simple as that. That clear. Maybe, Nash thinks, as Remi's body slowly stills beside him, this is what it feels like to be a single child.

Near one o'clock, the clouds finally break, and a warm rain hits the earth in big, splattering drops. The last straggling guests run for their cars. The Chinese lanterns riffle and bleed. Rain pelts the pizza boxes and the paper tablecloths, staining everything pink and green. And as the yard empties of humans, the birds return in squawking circles.

In the upstairs bathroom of the olive house, Violet peels off her wet clothes. She hears the door opening before she sees it. Nash is there, inside, before she can cover her naked self.

"I eat too much," she says, reaching for a towel.

"I don't care how much you eat." Nash wipes his wet hair from his brow.

"Lord, what *do* you care about?" Violet says, wrapping the towel around her body.

Nash takes one finger of her hand and kisses it. "I care about this little piggy, the one that went to market…" He raises the next. "And this one I'm even more fond of, the one that stayed home…"

"Nash, please."

"I like the way you look." Nash drops her hand. "I always have. Ever since the first day I saw you in the Quad. It was snowing. You were wearing a white hat and those ugly green stretch pants. Your thighs were incredible."

"Dirty old man." Violet tucks in the towel to the side of her left breast. "How do you remember such things?"

Nash lets go of her hand. "Those thighs were not to be ignored," he says.

Violet smiles. She feels so strange, like she used to as a girl, when her brothers were tall hairy beasts, watching her dress at the stove on a winter morning, watching her inch by inch, moment by moment, growing slowly into a woman. Nash's hand comes toward her again, rotates her arm, runs a finger up the winding path of a blue vein. Violet watches it climb.

"Are you all right, Nash?"

"I'm fine."

"Something's different. Strange. You're…" She puts her hand up to his forehead, as if to feel for fever. "Oh my god, you're sober."

"If you quit having affairs," he says. "I'll quit drinking."

"No fair. You're a better quitter than I am."

"Maybe." Nash raises mock doe eyes. "But I bet you never loved any of those guys like I love my whiskey."

"Guys. You say it like you don't begrudge them a thing, like they were your best buddies."

"Were they?" Nash asks, letting her arm fall.

"No," Violet says quietly. "Never."

"Good," he says. "So what should I begrudge them? They're wherever they are. And we…" He kisses her on the mouth. "Are here."

Vi pulls the slipping towel up over her chest. "God. I want that. What you have."

"What?"

"That distance. That ability to detach, to rise up over the chaos."

Nash shakes his head. "We're human. Flawed. Why beat ourselves up about it?"

"It's kind of difficult to feel desirable here," Violet says.

"Don't try to feel desirable, Vi." Nash untucks the towel, lets it fall. "Just try to feel good."

Vi wraps her arms around her naked body. "I didn't touch him, Nash, I swear."

"Who didn't you touch?"

"The ball boy. Andrew. Not even once. I swear."

"I believe you," Nash says, taking her into his arms.

Making love in the bathtub is something Vi always imagined she'd do furtively, with a lover. She never would have pictured herself and Nash rolling up against the faucet, knocking the shampoos off the edge, rubbing oil all over each other as the water streamed over them. She smooths his face as she sits astride him, her stomach in folds, one for each child she's borne, her breasts hanging full and low. Working her way backwards, she bends her head and takes his cock into her mouth, seeing the same look of surprise he wore when they used to do this in the back seat of a car before they were married. When he's hard, she lifts her hips, positions herself on him, eases herself down. Nash arches his back and groans. Dirty sex, her mother would have called this, dirty under the glow of the neon light, in a strange place, dirty unless your husband asked you for it. Dirtier, if the woman was on top, if she made the first move. Filthy, if she made noise. A slut if she enjoyed it, if she cried out, if she came. Nash pushes up hard into her, again and again. Bullshit. Violet tosses back her head, feels the heat and shiver rise. Even then she hadn't bought it. Her poor mother never had a chance. Violet wasn't thinking about love when she married Nash. The shudders overtake her as she comes. But, thank god—she takes a long, deep breath—he was.

Outside, in the backyard, Remi and Faye are left face to face in the tapering rain, each holding a garbage bag.

"We can clean up the rest tomorrow," Faye says, squashing a stack of dirty paper plates into her bag.

"Right," Remi says. "You coming in?"

"You go on ahead," Faye says. "I'll be in in a bit."

"It's raining, Faye. You're getting soaked."

She doesn't answer, doesn't turn.

Remi runs his hand through his hair. "I'm glad I know," he says. "I would've felt like such an idiot if I didn't."

"Know what?"

"That you're going to walk out of here. That you're not coming back."

Faye twists her garbage bag closed at the neck.

"When were you going to tell me?" Remi asks.

"Soon." She gestures with one hand. "When all of this was over."

"It'll never be over," he says. "That's the thing, Faye. It just keeps on going and going—"

"I was going to tell you soon."

"Well, you don't have to," he says unsteadily. "Because you see…I already know."

"I'm sorry," Faye says. "I'm—"

"I know. I told you. I know. I knew. You don't need to…nothing." Remi starts to walk unsteadily back to the house. "It's over. I know it. Over and done with. A dead horse and all." He turns back to her. "You see, Faye, the thing is…" he says. "I already knew."

Faye stands alone in the empty, ravaged yard. She hears the sound of her own breathing, shallow and ragged. The racoons begin their scavenging. The oak tree's lower branches sway. The sky closes up and holds the rain back in again, letting loose only an occasional thick, warm drop.

After escaping the party, Hen wanders the Square. He passes Adams House, an old Harvard dorm at the corner of Bow and Arrow, and remembers the pool. A bunch of them had snuck in after graduation rehearsal the week before. Someone knew of an unlocked entrance, an old lock easily jimmied with a kitchen knife kept hidden on the ledge above the door. Chickie had led the pack. The pool room was sunlit, stained-glassed, intricate tile mosaics lining the floor. You half expected to see nightingales and butterflies swooping down from the rafters. Kicking off her clogs and skirt, she dove in gracefully and swam the length of the pool underwater, hair streaming behind her, silver earrings flashing in the angled slabs of light that flooded through the windows. The others tore off their clothes and jumped in too, whooping and hollering. Chickie hopped up onto the other side of the pool. The security guard caught them then, appearing at the door with a feeble, stuttering

"Hey!" Laughing, dripping, stoned, half-naked, they all fled into the sunlight of Bow Street, pulling on their clothes and shoes as they ran, as the guard sputtered after them, too many, too fast to catch, the echoes of their laughter trailing away. Hen felt ashamed, not so much of what they'd done—it wasn't such a terrible crime—but of who he was, who he was turning out to be, as he looked back at the guard's helpless face, the uniform, the hunch of his frail back, the weak cry and hopeless chase. They weren't screwing Harvard by sneaking into the pool; they were only screwing the old man.

Now, after midnight, with most students gone home already for the summer, the dorm is quiet. The EXIT sign glows red above his head. Hen runs his fingers along the ledge of the door and eases off the knife. Jiggling the lock, he slips inside the dark and steamy pool room. Two columns of underwater light slice the still water. The silence is absolute. He remembers the children in the *Twilight Zone* who dove down into the backyard pool to escape their bickering parents and never came back up. He takes off his T-shirt and jeans and slides into the water. His nipples go tight, not with cold, but with memory, the guard's lost eyes, Melody's breasts, Chickie's wet body, his mother eating a corn chip. Pushing himself off the edge, he tries to make it underwater down the length of the pool. Three fourths of the way, he comes up gasping for air. Catching his breath, he turns over and floats on his back, looks up into the dome of the tiled ceiling, into the silence in his own head, the sudden emptiness of his brain, that clear feeling he used to be able to summon at will when he was younger.

As Hen floats on his back in the pool, his mind wanders. He thinks of the party back home, all the parties, all the alcohol poured and drunk on Hemlock Street over the years, enough to fill ten swimming pools this size. He's suddenly grabbed by a fear of his own smallness, the family circus in the backyard, the clown faces, the exaggerated senses of self-importance, as if they were the only ones ever to have eaten home-made lasagna, thrown a party, graduated from high school. Almost four billion people on the planet. How few ever collided. The faces of his small world dance through his brain. Lugbout. Paul Dunphy. Monkey Man. Arthur at Hazen's grill. Buzz. Tory. Chickie. Dropped by fate's hand onto the same, bite-sized slice of the earth, they cluster together on its shouldered, cheesy edge. The other three billion and odd plus are total strangers, no more than exotic, floating ideas. Whether this is comforting or terrifying, Hen can't tell. Every one of these people has helped to shape his fate: Melody; Plato the poet; the man at the drugstore in New York; John, the chess master in the Square; Cozmo at the kissing bench; whoever's about to draw his number in the draft lottery. They've etched the lines of his fate, put him into context, perspective. They make his story true. Had he hung suspended in space forever, alone, as he wanted to when he was a kid, he would never have been real. Chickie was right. All you really could believe in was people, and gravity *was* cool. It's still true, he could never shoot anyone, he's sure of it. But mostly, goddamn it if he just doesn't want to die.

Back in his room, Hen finds a message from Chickie at his window. Unclipping it from the pulley, he reads, *Leaving tomorrow. Early. Nantucket. I'll leave the back door open. Come with me.* Hen looks out at her window, at the rising light on the horizon, and feels the sudden urge to disappear through the crack of the still, gray dawn.

Wait for me, he writes back. The note sails across on the pulley, a white flag in the dark, to Chickie's rattling window. *I'm coming with you, Chickie. Wait for me.*

17

Chickie and Hen hitch to Woods Hole and catch a late-morning ferry to Nantucket. The season's not in full swing yet, and the boat's nearly empty—a few stragglers, a family of noisy boys, the odd pair of lovers draped over a lifeboat, a big shaggy dog. The seagulls swoop and hover, squawking dismally, begging in an uninterested crowd. No cameras today, no sandwich crusts, no treats, no *oohs*, no *aahs*. A couple sits hunched in the wind, smoking cigarettes, reading identical copies of *The Magus*. With a long blast of its horn, the ferry backs slowly away from the dock. The storm that never fully broke the night before still brews. A lone white sail is etched against the water. The rig of a scalloping boat moored in the harbor bobs in the ferry's wake. Rounding the bend, the boat's motor revs and the hull shudders. As the ferry picks up steam, the wake gushes hard.

Out on the bow, Chickie remembers riding this boat for all these years, the metal railing level first with her chin, then her chest, and now her stomach, so many summers, coming tight and pale, leaving loose and golden—so many rides. "What'd you write in your note?" she says to Hen.

"Said I needed to get away for a while." He flicks a leaf from the bottom of his boot over the side. "What'd you say in yours?"

"I told them I was with you. That college might have to wait." Chickie lights up a butt. "Doesn't really matter what you say."

"You sure the renters aren't there yet?"

"Not until the July Fourth weekend," Chickie says.

"Damn." Hen thrusts his hands into his jean pockets. "I forgot the keys."

"It's not locked." Chickie twists her hair up into a knot on the top of her head. "The cottage is never locked," she says.

"I hope there's firewood," he says. "I don't know if that window ever got fixed. Something weird happened the weekend my parents were there. I hope we'll be warm enough. We better stop and get some food."

"Will you stop worrying?" Chickie says. "We're supposed to be celebrating, remember? Hey, let's not stay in the cottage tonight. Let's get a room in that motel up on the north shore, The Blue Moon. We can get out the bikes and ride down. I hear they have vibrating beds."

"I don't want to spend my money on some sleazy motel," Hen says.

"It's off-season. So we blow twenty bucks. Come on, it'll be an adventure."

Hen throws back his head and groans. Another one of Chickie's crazy ideas he can't say no to, even after all these years.

The woman at the check-in desk at the Blue Moon gets chatty after they've handed over the money for the room.

"Potts?" She peers over her glasses to read their names in the register. "Any relation to those twins who come out here every summer?"

"They're our fathers," Chickie says. "We're first cousins."

"Someone was up that way in March," the woman says. "Fixing up the cottage. Left a broken window. Mitt Carver went to board it up. Don't know what happened. Whoever it was left fast, but no sign of any trouble. Found a watch out on the deck. I think Mitt Carver still has that watch." She looks the two of them over. "I always wondered. You do with twins, don't you. Are they identical?"

"Pretty much," Chickie says.

"Hmph." The woman's voice hardens as she gives them the twice-over. "Your parents know you're here?"

In Room 6, the walls are cardboard thin. Murmurs float through from Room 4, a room in which Violet lay the summer before with an island bike courier, a would-be sculptor who licked fudge sauce from her navel. There are cheesy lighthouse paintings on the walls, brown wall-to-wall carpeting, a metal box with a money slot at the side of the bed, bottles of oils and lotions, an AM radio.

"Hey, check this out," Chickie calls from the bathroom. "Some weird toilet without a seat."

"No Bible here." Hen opens the drawer of the nightstand. "Just..." He picks up a heavy book. "Oh, man. Can you believe this? *The Ecstasy of Sex*."

"Ooh la la. Let me see." Chickie comes over and takes the book. "Man, what a find. Wanna go out and pick up a few friends, Hen, have an orgy? We've got the manual, right here."

"Aren't you forgetting something?"

"What?"

"You can't have sex yet, Chickie."

"Says who?"

"The pamphlet. From the clinic."

"God, did you memorize that thing?"

Chickie slips a quarter into the slot next to the bed. With a clunk, it starts to shake and quiver. "Come on!" she shrieks. "Get on! It's a gas!" She jumps up and down on the vibrating bed, her head barely clearing the ceiling. "Relax, Henry," she says. "We're here to have fun, remember?"

Hen's palms are sweating. "How can I relax?" he says. "It smells like a bus station in here." The couple next door starts to argue.

I told you. I don't want to.

You never want to. You fucking never want to.

Fuck you.

"Another happy couple heard from." Chickie makes a microphone with her fist. "Live from America's Sleazy Hotel Number 3,456!" She jumps off the bed, rummages in her bag and pulls out her bikini. "I'm going down to the beach for a swim," she says. "You coming?"

"I didn't bring a bathing suit," Hen says.

"You didn't bring a bathing suit to Nantucket?"

"I forgot it. Jesus, I'm here, aren't I?"

"Come on, Hen. Let's walk down to the cliffs then, go to the cave. Get fried clams. Go skinny-dipping when it gets dark."

"I'll stay here," Hen says.

"Fine." Chickie starts to pull off her shirt. "I'm getting into that ocean."

"Chick-ie." Hen groans.

"What?" She whirls around, her arm halfway out of a twisted sleeve, back and belly bared.

"Change in the bathroom, will you?"

"Sor-ry, Mr. Modesto."

Chickie comes out of the bathroom in her bikini, hair bouncing down over her shoulders and pale back.

"Be careful," Hen says as she heads for the door. "Those waves are big."

"I like them big." Chickie bounds out the door onto the beach, her towel flying behind her, sand flying up at the heels. At the water's edge, she hesitates for a minute, then plunges in. Hen fiddles with his chess set at the open door, keeping his eyes on Chickie as she jumps up with the swell of each wave, then dives back down into the next, smoothing back her hair each time she resurfaces, her legs poking up like a wishbone in a handstand, riding the curls of the waves, running back up onto the sand, two cartwheels to the door, shivering, stomach and legs covered with goosebumps, the color of filleted salmon.

Hen waits at the door with another towel. "You're crazy, you know that," he says. "When it comes to water, you're out of your mind."

"It feels great," Chickie says, breathless. "I like being out of mind. God, if I could just live in the water forever. I *must've* been a fish in another life."

"There's a bunch of guys who jump into the Boston Harbor every New Year's Day." Hen rubs Chickie's back with the towel, trying to warm her. "The L Street Brownies. You should go down and join the crowd."

"Violet always wanted me to be a Brownie." Chickie heads for the bathroom, untying the top of her suit, still shivering. "Man, I feel it now," she calls out. The bikini top lands a stringy heap on the floor. "I'm freezing. You want to go buy some soda for the vodka in the vending machine, Hen? There's one down the hall."

Hen stops in his tracks. "What vodka?"

"My dad's." Chickie pokes her head out of the bathroom door. "I took a bottle from the liquor cabinet. He won't miss it."

"You don't need vodka, Chick," Hen says.

"Of course I don't need it. I want it," she says.

After a hot shower, Chickie sits on the bed in her T-shirt and underwear, her hair up in a towel like a sheikh, sipping vodka and ginger ale from a plastic cup. Hen turns on the TV.

"You going to wear those boots all night?" she asks.

Hen shrugs. "Till I have a reason to take them off."

"It's almost summer." Chickie pulls the towel off her head, leans over the bed, and whips her hair back and forth. "Think they're shitting bricks yet back home?" she says.

"Probably." Hen starts to unlace his boots.

"Might miss the old Fourth of July picnic this year."

"Wouldn't be the end of my world," Hen says.

"Are you mad at me, Hen?" Chickie takes a sip of her drink.

"For what?" He looks up.

"For anything. Anything that's ever happened."

"No," he says. "I'm not mad at you, Chickie."

"I didn't make you come."

"Of course you didn't."

"So." Chickie runs her fingers through her wet, tangled hair. "Why *did* you come?"

"To get away, that's all."

Chickie takes a bite of a peanut butter cracker. "Why didn't you like Elvis?" she says.

"I didn't *not* like him, Chickie. I could have cared less about the guy. I just didn't get it, you and him together. It didn't make any sense."

"You thought he was stupid, didn't you?"

"You said it, not me."

"People used to think that about you, too, you know. They'd pat you on the head like a puppy and talk to you as if you were some kind of moron. Because you didn't talk for so long, because of the way you looked. Like a little angel. Without a brain under all those curls. Elvis wears black leather and smokes too much dope, so people think he's a thug. But he's not, really."

"So what did *you* like about him?" Hen says.

Chickie stretches out long on the bed, points her toes. "I guess in the beginning, I liked him because he liked me," she says. "And the Norton didn't hurt…" She lifts up her legs, then lets them flop down again. Her wet hair drips down onto her T-shirt. Hen turns his head away. He remembers when they used to sleep in a pup tent together out on the beach at the cottage. They'd press up together to keep warm. She used to smell like cinnamon candy and salt and smoke from the driftwood fires they'd made on the beach. Tonight she looks almost like a kid again, the old Chickie, untouched, untangled. She used to be all his, and he used to be enough for her. Now she's empty, restless. She's running away—from Elvis, from the abortion, from her mother, from Wellesley. She asked him to come, she needed company, courage, but they won't be together for long. Hen's leg jerks with a jolt of premonition. Chickie's about to go somewhere far away. He can tell. She's thinking about it right now—how she might get there, who she might meet along the way. Her eyes flicker; her breasts rise and fall with each breath. She sings along to the radio, Marvin Gaye. Hen rubs his eyes—*what the hell is going on?* Chickie, too, is like oobleck, softened now by the ocean and the hot shower and the booze. But if he tries to corral her, grasp her too tightly, pummel her with too many questions and words, she'll harden and turn away.

A rush of loneliness and desire surges up in Hen's belly and scares him half to death. They're alone. Chickie's getting drunk. He can tell by the way she's starting to sway, starting to melt, starting to sing. She gets up to dance in front of the full-length mirror, crooning into her fist, still in her T-shirt and underwear, her belly flat and brown. God. He can't turn his eyes away. She used to take care of him. It's true. And all he ever wanted to do was to take care of her in return, smooth the crinkled lines of worry from her face, slow the flood of chatter, yank the drink glass from her hand. He gets up from the edge of the bed, paces and sucks on motel ice cubes from the fake leather ice bucket. Chickie reaches for the sex book and starts to read out loud, just as the couple next door starts going at it.

"Wow, great timing." Chickie puts her ear up to the wall. "Now we can do some research." She leafs through the pages of the book. "Says here you got your moaners—that would be Violet—and your heavy breathers—my dad, probably, and then there's the silent, suffering types—your mom, perhaps?"

"Don't, Chickie."

"Sorry." She takes a sip of her drink. "And then you got your grunters. That would be these two." She gestures with her cup toward the wall. "Right here behind door number four."

"I wish they'd quit it." Hen's teeth crack an ice cube. "I wish you'd quit reading that book." He watches Chickie's shirt ride up as she sits back down on the bed, her legs folded up underneath her in a pretzeled bend, underwear hugging the crease of her thigh.

"Interesting sex facts." Chickie rests the book on her crossed legs. "Thirty-five percent of couples engage in post-coital conversation, forty percent enjoy a post-coital cigarette. Fifty percent of women douche... ah, that's what that thing in the bathroom is, the old crotch washer..."

Hen grits his teeth. "Why the hell did we come here?" he says.

"I thought it would be fun. I forgot what a drag you can be sometimes."

He rakes his hand through his hair. "You can't keep doing this to me, Chickie," he says.

"Doing what? You *are* mad at me. Why don't you just admit it?"

"You can't keep dragging me to places like this, talking to me that way. You can't keep making me feel—"

"Feel what?" Chickie sits up straight, flushed, indignant. "You're always blaming me for what you're feeling. Jesus, Hen. Why can't you just admit you're actually feeling something all by yourself, just because you are. Damn, did you know a woman can have up to six orgasms in one hour?" She flips through the pages of the sex book, suddenly caught up short. "Oh my god, look at this picture. That's not physically possible, is it?" She turns the book upside down for him to see. "You're a guy. *Is* it?"

Hen shuts his eyes on the drawing, bites his tongue as he crunches hard on another ice cube. He feels his father's rage burning inside of him. He knows it's his father's because he no longer sees the book just as a book, but as a weapon. For an instant, he imagines slamming it down on Chickie's head to make her be quiet, to make her stop drinking, to be still.

"I mean if it's hard, how can it bend like that, and if it's soft—"

"Chickie!" His hoarse voice grazes the loaded air. "Stop reading that goddamned book!"

"The clitoral orgasm is far more common—" She reads on, oblivious. "However, the *vaginal* orgasm—"

"Chickie!" Hen's hand reaches out before he can stop it, grabs the book by its spine and flings it to the floor. He takes her by both arms and shakes her. "Stop it!" he says.

"Hey!" Chickie's drunk; puzzled eyes rake over him, her body folded inward. "What the hell is your problem?"

Hen feels his breath come fast, closes and opens his eyes. Closes. Opens. The room spins; he's sick to his stomach. He lets go of Chickie, lifts his arms. "I gotta get out of here," he says.

"Why?" Chickie gets up off the bed.

"I almost hurt you." He spreads out his trembling hands. "I came this close—"

"No." She takes his hands. "You didn't hurt me, Hen. The book got wrecked. That's all. It's no big deal. It's cool. I was teasing you. I pushed you too hard. You blew a fuse. Maybe I am a little wasted. I'm sorry. Hey, don't freak out, Hen. Please don't freak out on me."

He looks up at the ceiling, tugs at his hair, breathing fast. "I almost hit you, Chickie." He slams his fist down on the bureau top. "I'm *fucked.* Just like he is. I'm just like him." His own voice comes to him, what he told his father when they were playing pool. *I'm a pacifist. Violence is never the answer.* "I'm such a hypocrite. Such a jerk. I could've really hurt you, Chickie."

"Stop saying that." She strokes his arm. "You didn't hurt me. The book got wrecked. I'm fine."

"I almost whacked you, Chickie." Hen picks up the vodka bottle. "And if you weren't drunk out of your skull, you'd know it."

"I'm not drunk out of my skull."

"You can't drink half a bottle of booze and not be drunk." His voice breaks. "It's a fact, Chickie. Deal with it."

Chickie lifts a hand to his face and strokes his cheek. He pulls her hand away. "What's wrong?" she says. "Oh my god, Hen. What's happening? Why are you so upset?"

"Why am I so upset?" Hen fights the tears that pulse hot in the corners of his eyes, a slow tremor overtaking his whole body as the answer surges through him. "Because I love you, Chickie. I fucking love you. That's why."

Her arms wrap around him. "I love you too," she says.

"No." He closes his eyes. "Not like that. I mean I love you the wrong way."

"What wrong way?" They both look down at the sex book on the floor, open to a drawing of a man pushing himself into a woman from behind. Chickie kneels down and closes it.

"I said it," Hen says in a flat, dazed voice.

"You didn't mean it." Chickie is suddenly softened, suddenly sobered. "There is no wrong way, Hen."

"Yes, there is." Hen takes her hand at the wrist, presses her palm to his burning cheek, closes his eyes. "There could be."

"You're just feeling weird because we're here in this creepy place." Chickie's voice is soothing, far away. She strokes the back of his neck, his face, his hair. "Because of the book, and the vibrating bed. And the grunters. Because we left home. Graduation. The party. The draft lottery. It *is* weird here. Let's go back to the cottage. Light a fire. Drink cocoa. Play cards like we used to."

Hen keeps his eyes closed. "Let's get married, Chick," he says.

"What?" She laughs, sputters, pulls her hand away.

"Cousins do." He won't open his eyes until he's done. "We're eighteen. Nobody could stop us."

"Our kids would be all screwed up, Hen. You're crazy."

"You said you didn't want any kids."

"I didn't mean *ever*. I do want kids someday. I love kids."

"So why'd you do it, Chickie? How could you walk through that door?"

"I told you. I wasn't ready to be a mother."

"So how the hell did it happen?"

"Why does everyone keep asking me that same stupid question?" Chickie sits down on the edge of the bed. "I must've forgotten to take the pill two nights in a row, maybe three. I can't remember. It's no fair. The girl has to remember…I'm no good at remembering stuff like that."

"Stuff like what? Not making a baby?"

"You didn't deal with it either, with Miss Mondo Tits there. It's not what I was thinking about when—"

"When what?"

"Nothing, all right? I'm tired of thinking. When you're fucking, you can escape everything. That's what I like about sex. It makes me feel so…empty."

"Empty?" Hen says. "You felt empty? God, I felt like I was about to explode."

Chickie sits back down on the bed. "What were you thinking about when you were doing it with Chesty Morgan, then. Come on. Tell me, Hen."

"No."

"Come on. I want to know. All the gory details."

"I was thinking about hockey and the war, and my mother and father. I was even thinking about you. That's how screwed up I am, Chick. You want to know just how screwed up I am? The whole time…" He tries to keep his voice steady. "The whole time I was driving to New York, waiting for you at the clinic, all that time, waiting for you to come back through that door, I was wishing it was mine. I was jealous, Chickie. I wanted it to be a baby, and I wanted it to be mine."

"Oh, Hen." She touches his back from behind. For one moment, she even thinks, why not marry him. She'd always be loved, always be safe. Her eyes catch sight of the red marks his hands left on her arm. Always.

"Lie down with me," she says, stretching out on the bed on her side. "Come on, I'm tired. It's getting dark."

Hen lies down next to her, puts one arm around her from behind, smells the ocean and the baby oil and the vodka and the shampoo.

"It wasn't a baby yet," she whispers.

"I know," he says into her hair. "I'm sorry, Chickie. I know."

"I couldn't have taken care of it," she says. "It wouldn't have been fair. I didn't love Elvis. It was an accident, a mistake."

"I know," he says, putting his hand on her belly. "It's over with. It's done, Chick. Shh. You're fine. It's okay. It's all over now."

"So why do I feel so bad?" she says.

"I made you feel that way." Hen tightens his hold. "I'm an idiot. I couldn't let it go. It just made me crazy. I'm sorry. I couldn't keep my mouth shut. I couldn't keep my hands—"

"I didn't even cry, Hen. Why didn't I even cry?"

"You're not a crier," he says. "You never were."

"But it was my baby," she whispers. "It was—"

"No." Hen puts a finger to her lips. "It wasn't a baby yet. Remember?"

Hen buries his face in Chickie's hair, remembering how she used to hold out the tips for him to smell when she tried out a new shampoo, commanding him to rate it from one to ten, one being garbage and ten being a rose. He feels the hard ridge of her back as she moves to fit the curve of his body. He feels her butt moor in his crotch. He feels her fingers making tracks on his arm. He feels his belly seize, his whole body go hard.

"I love you, too, Hen," Chickie murmurs. "You're the only one. You know that. And when they pick the draft numbers—"

"Shhh." He sweeps her hair away from her neck.

"I'm not going to let you go."

"Okay." Hen presses his lips to the nape of her neck, wills every part of himself to be still. He repositions his hand carefully on Chickie's stomach, feels it rise and fall. With each new breath comes a wave of thought. Ideas roam free; actions have consequences. As long as his brain keeps cool, keeps his hands in check. As long as Chickie stays still, doesn't shift her weight. It'll be all right. *J'adoube.* He'll keep saying it. Over and over again. Nothing bad will happen. He can take it all back. *J'adoube.* They can ride their bikes back to the cottage tomorrow and then go back home.

But Chickie *does* move, does turn slowly to face him, and he has no control over that. She *does* lift the bottom of his shirt and she *does* speak. "Take it off," she says, going into the Noxzema lady's voice. "Remember that day, Hen, at the kissing bench, with Cozmo? Take it *all* off."

"I do," Hen says. And what can he do but obey, quickly slinging off his shirt, then coming back down close to Chickie on the bed. She brings her hands up to his chest. "You're so smooth," she says. "You've always been so smooth."

"Chick."

"I just want to feel you." She runs her hand across his belly. "I've always just wanted to feel you this way."

"God." Hen feels the heat well up inside him, the impossible, raging desire. His belly seizes as he lifts his head. His lips come forward, touch hers, tentatively. A question. She responds, with a slip of a tongue inside his mouth. He's on top of her now, he's kissing her, his hand slides down her belly low.

"No," Chickie says suddenly, stopping his hand.

"Why not?" Hen says. "I meant it, Chick. I love you. I'll always love you. I'll do whatever you want, be whoever you want me to be."

"Why would you ever do that?" She strokes his back, his shoulders.

"I don't know," Hen says. "I don't care anymore."

"Yes, you do," Chickie says. "You do care. You will."

"Chickie." Hen buries his head in her neck. "Please, Chickie, listen to me!"

"No, Hen," Chickie says. "It would ruin it. You know it would."

"Ruin what?" Hen feels his heart start to crack as she murmurs and turns away. *Ruin what? Ruin what? Ruin what?*

"Everything," Chickie says.

'Round about the time Chickie plunges into the ocean in Nantucket, Violet and Faye cross paths in Harvard Square. A mime mimes. A church clock chimes. A singer wails raspy, wan Dylan, *de rigeur* for street musicians these days. Violet's slowly making her way home. She grabbed a bite at work and stayed late to go over the books, afraid, excited to face Nash after the night before in the bathroom, not sure who she'll find in the armchair—the drunk, slumped and snoring, the one who's watched her come and go for so many years, or the other man—the sober one who pinned her to the bathtub floor, the one with clear eyes waiting for better, for more. Violet doesn't know anymore what to expect of the man who made her come three times in as many hours and who, at breakfast when she said, "I may be late tonight," answered, "I'll wait up for you."

Faye comes to the Square from the opposite direction. She's been walking since she closed Clay City at five o'clock, not hungry or tired, not ready yet on this first night alone to go back to her new apartment. She hadn't planned on leaving Hemlock Street so soon, but by forcing the truth from her the night before, Remi had given her the break she needed, the final unwitting shove. No time like the present. It's always been one of her favorite expressions, the last aphorism she may ever choose to live by. For now, finally, the present has arrived. She got up early, before anyone else was awake, left a letter for Hen on the kitchen counter, and mailed two others, one to Buzz in Allston, one to Tory in New York, trying to explain. The words felt selfish, hard. Inadequate. But true. She won't give in to the old feelings. Doubt. Guilt. Remorse. Sentiments of the weak—of women, it's often said.

"Faye!" Violet calls out as they nearly collide. "I barely got a chance to talk to you at the party. How do you think it went?"

"I think the kids had a good time. And that's what counts. You must be so proud of Chickie, Vi, Wellesley and all."

"She got her act together in the end. No one was more surprised than I was. 'Course we always knew she had potential. The SAT scores must have done it. Certainly not her GPA. What are Hen's plans?"

"Little up in the air right now." Faye smiles wanly. "U. Mass will have him. Meanwhile, the draft lottery… Let's keep our fingers crossed."

"Hen always seems to land on his feet."

"He does, doesn't he?" Faye says.

"Are you all right, Faye? You look so pale."

"I'm fine," Faye says. "But you should know, Vi. I've left Remi."

"What?" Violet gasps.

"Today, actually." Faye's voice steadies. "I left Hemlock Street today. I'm moving out."

A thrill clutches at the top of Violet's spine. "Oh my god," she says. "What happened?"

Faye throws up her hands. "There's just nothing left," she says.

"Oh, Faye. I never dreamed. You live so close to someone all those years. It can happen to anybody, can't it? Believe me, Nash and I are hanging by a thread."

"At least you two always knew how to have fun," Faye says.

"It's true." Vi smiles. "Come on. Let's go somewhere and have coffee, Faye. Or better yet, a stiff drink. I'm in no rush. I told Nash I might be late."

Faye puts her hand on Vi's arm. "Another time," she says.

"Right." Violet feels the loss hard, not so much of a friend, but a long-time ally.

"I wanted to thank you, Vi," Faye says.

"Whatever for?"

"I always felt better, knowing you were there. Next door. Leading the charge. Doing your own thing, as the kids say. It kept me going sometimes."

"Oh, come on, Faye. I'm just a—"

"Don't be so hard on yourself, Vi."

"All right," Vi says quietly. "I won't if you won't." She looks quizzically over at Faye. "By the way," she says. "I like what you've done with your hair."

Vi stands alone after Faye walks away. She feels suddenly unmoored, as if all the truths she's recently uncovered have just revealed more of their crusted layers in a cruel, repeating dream. How naive, how smug she's been, to think that with her grand confession, she's made everything right? Faye's left Remi. So where does that leave her? Seph never showed up for the party, never even called. What does it mean? Should she be worried? Is Seph trying to punish her? Is it all her fault? Has she done enough to try and make things better between them? Has she done enough for anyone, for herself? Can she really be faithful to Nash, be true? Does she even want to? She can't go home yet. The reunion with Nash will have to wait. She walks the arc of Brattle, past Woolworths and Potts Pro, closed up tight, up to Nini's Corner. At the courtyard she sits down and watches a lone Hari Krishna dance. Where's the rest of his group? she wonders. Why is he dancing all alone? How did he get here from there, from a little boy with crooked teeth and a comic book collection to this pigtailed, robed effete? She tries to see past the robe, past the gaping, chanting mouth, the risen eyes. She watches his legs under his robe, muscled and graceful. The hands playing the tambourine are beautiful and strong. Seph's hands did things that way, too, carefully, with authority—playing the piano, arranging her books on her shelf, playing a game of cards. The Hari Krishna suddenly breaks concentration, looks over at her and smiles. Violet feels a hopeless sense of loss, a sudden surge of power. Making eye contact with the Hare Krishna, she slowly nods her head. He comes over to her, lays his hand on her arm. "Let me take you to our temple," he says. "You will find what you are looking for there."

Remi dips into the Blarney Stone, breathless. The bar hasn't changed much over the course of thirty years, only gotten more so. It used to be casual, hip. Now it's almost seedy—the wooden booths sticky, the glasses dull and scratched like train windows, the smoke thicker, the bartenders younger and younger. He and Nash used to come here back in the fifties, and yet, wasn't he just here playing pool, that night when

Hen confronted him about hitting Faye? *If you ever...* Man, he'd never seen that kind of fire in the kid's eyes before. You had to admire him for it.

"Evening, sir." The kid behind the bar's not much older than Hen. He knows Remi as a regular, a guy who comes into the bar two, three times a week, after the dinner hour, and stays until closing time, drinking himself blotto. To the young bartender, Remi has the air of a lost and lonely man. This guy doesn't come here for the music or the company or a pickup, or even the small talk. He doesn't play the jukebox or read the paper or even look at women. He just comes here because he has nowhere else to go. The bartender might not be surprised to know that the man who sits hunched on the bar stool hour after hour has a quick temper, a pain in his gut, a great and stubborn love for his wife, secrets grown so big they may kill him.

Remi settles on a bar stool and waits for his breath to settle. He's just seen Faye and Violet talking on the street corner near Potts Pro. He saw how Violet's face jolted when Faye told her. He felt embarrassed that she'd heard the news that way in an open square with pigeons pecking at her feet, furious that Nash hadn't had the decency to tell her privately. Had he no respect for his feelings? Or had Nash simply not believed him when he said Faye was leaving, refused to accept that the marriage he'd forged had failed? And Remi was angry, too, that Faye felt so free with her news that she'd drop it like peanut shells on the pavement. She wore jeans and an embroidered Mexican blouse. And some terrible new short haircut, like a mangy dog's. After Faye and Violet parted ways, Remi ducked around the corner of Palmer Street, hugged up against the wall of an alleyway behind the Coop. He needed alcohol. He needed the dark. For the first time in as long as he could remember, he had a longing for his mother.

Sitting at the bar, after the whiskey warms him, Remi fills with the rage of his humiliation and shame, to have been abandoned once again—deserted, betrayed, emasculated by all the people who were supposed to have loved him and made him strong, but who only left him broken—his father, the girl in the Dodge—all of a sudden, he can't even remember her name—his brother, his children, his poor, dead mother...and now, finally, his wife. He's so stunned, so shaken, he's almost forgotten the even bigger problem of the day, can barely summon his terrible secret to the forefront of his brain, the fact that he gambled against the deed to Potts Pro, gambled and *won*, by god, and then was fleeced by a scheming, two-bit whore. A bigger fool even than he ever imagined. Twenty grand gone in the literal blink of an eye. Stolen by a woman he'd made love to every Tuesday since the fall, except for those three when she had the mumps, a woman he'd almost come to care about—to trust.

"Usual, sir?" the bartender asks.

"No, actually," Remi says. "Give me a vodka and soda, with a slice of lemon. It's what my mother used to drink."

"Change of pace, eh?" the bartender asks.

"That's right, change of pace." Remi squeezes the lemon into his drink. How on earth could any of this have happened? He's lost everything. He can't understand. He truly can't. He only hit Faye that once. In all those years. And he's tried a thousand times to say how sorry he was about that day on the beach, even though he's still and truly mystified by her outrage—she'd come on to him, hadn't she, done a striptease on the sand? All he'd wanted to do was make love to her, make love to his wife. When had that become a crime? Still, he'd promised to talk things out, seek professional help if she wanted him to, maybe that shrink Hen had talked to. He seemed a good sort. Remi even promised, in a moment of desperation, that he'd never touch her again. If only she wouldn't leave him. But maybe he never said that last part out loud. Maybe he'd never told her how much she meant to him, how much he loved her. How completely. How unconditionally. Maybe he never said anything at all.

Too many times he's invented his own disasters, been the messenger of his own impending doom. His emotions terrify him—too unpredictable, too fickle, too strong. What else, really, could he have said to stop Faye from leaving? In the end, all he'd wanted her to know was that he'd gladly give her anything, anything. Except... The only thing he couldn't bear for her to have—and why was that such a threat for him?—was her freedom. That's what a shrink would try getting at, his desperate need to control. What the hell was he so afraid of? God, if he only knew. This must be his final punishment for not being a good enough son, father, husband—for not being a good enough man.

Remi looks down through his drink glass to the other side of his life. He sees the parts of himself and Faye that their children have taken with them—Tory's polished beauty, Buzz's fierce loyalty, Hen's moral outrage and fragile heart. The kids will have to watch out. They could all get their hearts busted; the apples never fall far from the tree. And then Remi sees the losses and the shames: Buzz never whole, never fully confident without that thumb; Tory with no humility and maybe even a death wish; and Hen, who just can't seem to tackle anything head on. Now he's run off with Chickie. Stupid, scared kid. *Had to get away for a while,* the note said. Get away where? Doesn't Hen know there's no escape? Not to Nantucket or into a chess game or Canada or outer space? Doesn't Hen get it yet, that there's nowhere to hide?

Remi woke up alone this morning. No signs of Faye's ever having slept. The kitchen was unusually clean. He found a note from Faye to Hen on the counter, and Hen's note to them both out on the hallway table. She must have missed it on her way out. All day Remi's kept the secret. He didn't call Faye at Clay City to tell her. Silence. It's the last ace up his sleeve and he's going to hold on to it. Later, when he gets home, he'll call her and give her the news. She left her new phone number printed neatly on a sheet of paper in the kitchen—Faye at Apartment 423-1987. Capital A. The scarlet letter of her emancipation. Soon she'll have gone to sleep in her new bed. Knowing Faye, it's too soon yet for a lover. He'll tell her calmly about Hen, how he's taken off with Chickie. She'll ask him when he found the note. He'll tell the truth, how he kept the news to himself, how he needed time to think, how they need to talk. He'll explain a little about the gambling, the money, his plans to get it back, or no, maybe not everything just yet. She'll be worried, frantic, about Hen. He imagines the loaded silence on the phone after he tells her the kids are gone, and before she finally speaks. Remi orders a whiskey and takes a cleansing swig. At first Faye will blame him, berate him, maybe even cry. He'll imagine how beautiful she is in her fright on the other end of the line, even with that terrible haircut.

"What do you want me to do, Faye?" he'll ask her.

"Let's go find him, Remi," she'll finally say. "Let's go find our beautiful boy."

Near closing time, the bartender shuts off the neon sign and hangs the pool cues up on the rack.

"That time already?" Remi says.

"One o'clock, sir, Mr…."

"Potts," Remi says, holding out his hand. "Remington Atwater Potts. Nice to meet you."

"Well, it's actually goodbye, Mr. Potts, sir." The bartender shakes Remi's hand. "I may not be seeing you again for a while."

"Why's that?" Remi's voice slurs. "Or, should I say, why's that…not?"

"I enlisted," the bartender says. "I'm going home to spend some time with my family before I head out."

"Home," Remi says flatly. "Where's home, son?"

"Buffalo."

"Buffalo," Remi says thickly. "Your parents…in Buffalo…must be very proud."

"I guess so, sir."

"I've got a son," Remi begins. "I've got two sons, in fact. And one of them, the one who might be of any use here, to old Uncle Sam, well, I'm told he's decided not to go. I'm told"—Remi waves a drunken hand—"that he's a pacifist, that he can't support this war."

The bartender laughs uneasily, wipes the bar with a wet rag. "Who's telling you all this stuff, Mr. Potts?"

"My brother. My identical twin brother. Apparently, he knows my son better than I do. Apparently, my son trusts my brother more than he does his own father. Apparently—"

The bartender tips the stools. "I've really got to close up now, sir," he says.

Remi stands up, puts on his coat. He looks at this clean-cut kid on his way to war via Buffalo, a throwback to another era, sober, industrious, polite.

"What's your name?" he asks.

"Chris."

"Tell me something, Chris. What do you think of a guy like my son, a guy who's thinking of skipping out?"

"Oh, I wouldn't—"

"No, please," Remi says. "No right or wrong answer. No judgments. Nothing. Just a question. Man to man. A simple question."

"Well, the way I see it, sir," Chris says. "Maybe this war wasn't such a good idea in the first place. But we're in deep now and we've got to finish the job. We're the strongest nation in the world."

"We certainly are."

"It's our responsibility to take charge." Remi hears the voice of his grandfather, his own voice speaking to Hen, the echoes of a slowly disappearing logic. "We've gotta hang in there, sir. It's our duty."

"And what exactly is our duty, Chris?"

He doesn't hesitate. "To serve our country, sir. In whatever way we can."

"I'm with you there," Remi says, as Chris reaches for the broom. His head swirls. "But the thing is, see, Chris, I've been thinking, see... we're *killing* 'em. Tons of them. Thousands and *thousands.* And they're killing us right back. And *we're* killing us and *they're* killing each other and...you got to wonder sometimes..." In an explosive, drunken flash, Remi sees what a waste it would be to lose a boy like this, or Hen, or any human life for something as cloudy and blind as patriotic fervor or national pride run amok. And when the flash is gone, Chris is left, assured, articulate, all limbs intact—a boy any father would be proud of. "Where the hell's it ever going to end?"

"I don't know, sir, but I'm going to go ahead and do my part."

"Good man." Remi shoves a fifty into the bartender's hand. "Here," he says. "Take this, Chris."

"No, sir, please. I can't."

"Take it, please. Humor an old man. An old patriot. Do something fun in Buffalo, Chris. Before you head out. Live it up. Have a ball. Life's short." He lifts his hands in a helpless gesture. "You kids don't believe it, but it is."

"Well, thanks, Mr. Potts," Chris says, pocketing the bill. "Thank you very much, sir. I'll be sure to put it to good use."

"You just take care, Chris," Remi says, buttoning up his coat. "You take care of yourself, you hear?"

At the door of the plum house, Remi fumbles with his key in the lock and stumbles over the threshold into the dark.

"Hen?" he calls out. "Faye? Buzz? Tory?" What strange names they have, these people he's lived with all these years. His sons. His daughter. His wife. *Ex*-wife. *Ex, ex, ex.* He picks up a glass from the drink caddy, winds up and smashes it hard against the living room wall, reassured by the certainty of cause and effect—the expected crash and shattering of glass. There's no one home, no sign of human life at all. Remi picks up a piece of glass from the floor and draws it lightly across the jagged scar on his arm. Where is everyone? And what was his plan? Who was he going to call when he got home? What disaster has befallen them? Has time run out? Is he the last man left in the world? Drunk beyond memory, hurt beyond reason, he forgets that Hen's run off, that Faye's left him, that Cammie stole his money, that Buzz and Tory are long gone. "Faye!" he calls out again. "Faye! Tory! Hen! Hello? Where the hell is everyone? Is anybody home?" *Home. Home. HOME?* There's no answer, nothing but the hum of the refrigerator, the ticking of the clock, the whirring of a ceiling fan, the crunch of glass underfoot. Remi pushes through the swinging door into the kitchen, opens the screen door, and looks out into the backyard, the party tables still standing, a few streamers hanging limp, the tree house in shadow, Faye's old kiln. He starts over to his brother's house.

"Nash!" he calls out. "You over there? You home? Nobody the hell else is. Everyone…flew…the goddamned coop!" He stumbles across the yard and starts to bang on Nash's back door. "Nash, you in there? Nash? Goddamn it. Open up. It's me, Remi! Let me in!" He pushes through the unlocked door into his brother's empty kitchen. "Shh," he says to the dishwater-gray cat. "Shh, you. It's only me." Nash will be back. He's probably just out for a walk. He'll wait for him, drink a glass of water, sober up a bit. When Nash gets home, they'll talk—about the kids, the store, the houses, the future. He'll come clean about the gambling, Cammie, the deed to the store, though why does he have this feeling Nash already knows it all? And then they can start all over again—walk to the store like they used to do, get back in shape, maybe even get a dog. Remi smiles as his plans take shape. Nash will be angry for a while, about Faye, the breakup. He—Nash—will blame himself before he's able to forgive him—Remi. That's always the pattern; he'll have to give Nash time. But Nash can't hold a grudge for long. Soon they'll be back to normal, going to baseball games, working side by side at the store, drinking gin and tonics and playing bridge. Slowly Buzz will take over—who knows anymore what Hen's future holds—and slowly he and Nash will ease out of the business. Retire together. Nash has already begun. That knock on the head really changed him. He's so laid back these days, so…peaceful. Remi could use some of that, this goddamned *peace* everyone keeps talking about. Maybe the two of them will take up golf. Nash will find him some cheerful women, pick-you-up types who'll suggest hobbies and sew suede patches on the elbows of his old sweaters, drag him to the symphony, insist on routine sex. It's what he's always needed, someone to make him over, push and pull him, keep him in some kind of line. Someone more like Violet. Come to think of it, maybe he won't even need another woman. Violet's perfectly capable of taking care of both of them, except for the sex, and maybe he's just too old, too exhausted for sex anymore. She'll fuss over him, scold him, do his laundry, make his coffee, his lists. She's always been itching to organize him, to manage him. He wouldn't have wanted such a wife, but maybe they'd have stood a better chance. He'd wanted Faye. Pretty, quiet Faye. Faye never once tried to mend or prep or change him. Maybe if only she had. Maybe Nash will help him win her back. He's always had a way with her, a special bond. What the hell. Remi bends down to open his brother's liquor cabinet. All he knows is, all he ever wanted was Faye.

Remi climbs up the back stairs with a glass of whiskey and goes into his brother's bedroom, a room he's never more than glanced into all these years. He sees Nash's clothes strewn on the bed, Violet's makeup on the dressing table, Nash's change and wallet on the bureau. He picks up an old photograph of the four of them at a Harvard football game before the kids were born, a key ring, a book of matches, a clip-on tie. These belongings of his brother's are so familiar to him; in a way, they might as well be his. He opens Nash's bureau drawers and rummages: cufflinks, ChapStick, suspenders, the red pocketknife, lists, matches, handkerchiefs, pills. He picks up the knife, opens it, and runs his finger over its blunted blade. He smells his brother's shirts, his ties, his sweaters. He fills his arms, flops down on the bed. There's no telling how long he lies there, his face buried in the heap of Nash's belongings. There's no telling how drunk Remi is, how he's supposed to feel, what his next move should be. There's no way of knowing if, in swallowing the last sip of that last glass of whiskey, Remi has finally had his fill. There's no telling how or when or why he finally rouses himself from his brother's unmade bed, creeps back down the stairs wearing Nash's Red Sox cap, and slips out the back door, stumbling…all the way home.

18

Nash reads Chickie's note over again in the armchair. He's alone in the olive house. It's the dead of night. He dozed off for a while. Vi never returned his call at work and still hasn't come home. He promised he'd wait up. The clock strikes two. The kitchen faucet's dripping. A familiar hum starts up in his ears, a hum he's sometimes attributed to the refrigerator, and other times simply to the chaos in his brain. It's always been so crowded in this house, so gloriously noisy. For so many years, a person could find no peace here. Arguments, commotion, spats, giggling, Slapjack, Seph and Janie bickering, Chickie on a tear, the hypnotic murmur of the baseball crowd on TV, the revving of Elvis's motorcycle, Hen slamming the screen door, the Pratts and Pendletons for bridge, Remi coming in to borrow the WD-40. Now Nash can hear the venetian blinds lapping against the windowpane, a faint dog's bark from afar. Now an argument would look elsewhere for a venue, a card shark elsewhere for a game. Where the hell can Violet be at this hour?

The note, folded in four, has been captive in Nash's pocket all day. He smooths it out carefully on his leg.

"M & D—Gone off for a while. College may have to wait. Wellesley's all wrong for me. I need some time to think. Don't worry. I'm with Hen."

It took Nash a while to decipher the *M* and *D*. Mom and Dad. He runs his fingers over the letter. It almost breaks his heart to be the *D*. Chickie's handwriting has never improved, not since her second-grade teacher called it chicken scrawl and sent her home with a stack of blue-lined notebooks to practice—*the quick brown fox jumps over the lazy dog* a thousand times. And Chickie, furious and grumbling, insisting that no self-respecting fox would ever jump over some stupid, lazy dog. Nash isn't comfortable with secrets, and maybe that's why he feels so uneasy. He should have told Violet right away. Maybe that was wrong. But he'd felt instantly possessive of the scribbled note he found on the kitchen table this morning, of the knowledge—Chickie and Hen run off—as if it were somehow owed to him. He couldn't resist the temptation, for once, to be the first one to know something important in his family—to react, to take charge. This may be the first and last chance Nash ever has to hold a family secret hostage.

Remi's news about Faye's leaving shook him badly. But he can't worry now about his brother's broken marriage. He doesn't want to miss his second chance with Vi. Last night notwithstanding, they're not done talking, negotiating. She rejects forgiveness, sees it as passive condoning and resignation. But what else does he have to give? She persists with this strange idea that marriage is some kind of contest of character, that he's trying to outdo her in tolerance, fidelity, wisdom. A good Protestant, long used to running the treadmill of guilt, Violet still claims she wants to be punished. And yet she's adamant that she's committed no crime. And he agrees. So why the push for atonement? Penance can't crawl forward on its knees without being summoned by blame. These old family values are so hardwired, so tough to cut through. He'll do what he can, what has to be done. He'll improvise; he'll act. He'll say, how could you, you shouldn't have, how can we, we must. Vi wants him to be a man. He'll rant and wring his hands so that she'll know how much she's loved, how far that love goes in forgiveness. And maybe the feelings Vi speaks of will catch up with him someday. But for now, if Vi wants jealousy, he'll give her passion. If she wants anger, he'll give her heat, if she truly wants change, well, then, he'll give her his undivided attention.

Nash shifts in the chair. It's a relief, in a sober moment, to discover selfishness tugging at him, guilt gnawing at the edge of his bones. The truth is, he's not really thinking about Remi, or the kids, or even Vi; he's thinking about himself. He's always wondered where it was hidden, the selfish side that's tortured Remi, driven him for so long, for better, more for worse. Nash knows why he doesn't want to tell Vi about Chickie just yet. Because once he tells her, last night will be no more than a dream. She won't want to make love with him that way again. She'll be scared, paranoid, frantic; she'll feel ashamed. They'll have to go out and find Chickie. Vi will bring danger to the forefront—their baby girl in danger—the pervert in the alleyway, the thief on the street, the madman on the train. And somehow their wanton sex of the night before will be at fault. They'll have to blame and punish themselves. Be responsible. Sober. *Guilty.*

Nash can't bear to miss the second part of this second chance with Vi. He can't wait to have her that way again—steamy, shy—him sober and hard under the glare of the bathroom light. For the second night in a row he hasn't touched a drop of booze. Probably the first time since he was sixteen. He's drunk on something else—anticipation, uncertainty, those cold tiles on the bathroom floor. His selfish side jitterbugs, jives. He stares at the whiskey bottle, at Chickie's note. *Don't worry,* it says. He obeys the note's command. Maybe he *is* hopelessly naive, as Violet always claims, but deep down inside, he senses that Chickie *is* okay. No serious runaway leaves a note, and besides, she's with Hen. Whatever risks each might take on their own, neither would ever put the other in harm's way. In this way they've always taken care of themselves. Tonight Chickie's still just a headstrong kid run off with her favorite cousin. Tomorrow, she'll be a missing child.

Sitting there in the armchair, as the minutes tick by, the fears begin to take hold, that Vi's left him too, that Chickie's in danger, that in the end he'll be punished for his weaknesses and failures, for keeping this last secret, the secret of Chickie and Hen. What is it about him, this place, that sends all the women away? First Seph, then Janie, then Vi, or who knows which of them really left first, now Chickie. All of them, running in and out of the darkness, in search of someone, something. Don't they understand that here they are home, that without them this house is nothing but an empty, echoing shell? Nash gets up and paces. It's not a friendly universe after all. Chickie's been restless, unhappy. She's smoked dope, made love. Had an abortion. He can read behind her bravado, her cool. He's seen a similar lost and restless look in Remi's eyes. He's never intervened between Violet and the girls, always considered the mother-daughter bond sacred. As their father, he's always thought he had nothing to offer them. But that's just a cop-out. He hasn't wanted to feel Chickie's pain, or her confusion, all these years. He's been a coward. He bought into that myth about daughters needing their mothers more than their fathers. No wonder women haven't made it to the outfield yet. The mothers need to get out there and learn how to play baseball and the fathers need to stay home and listen to their children, dare to feel before they speak.

As Nash's older daughters—Seph and Janie—rise from a distant place in his mind, guilt and regret overwhelm him. He laments their losses, their frustrations, their cynicism. He's never been much good to them. He let them go without a second thought. Janie—solid and stubborn, the middle child. A chip on her shoulder, but strong enough to have held out for a life chosen by, worked for, herself. And Warren was a good man. They'd be equal to the tough tasks of a challenging marriage, both practical and tough as nails. And Seph, such a sweet and gentle child, turned inward, turned away, turned hard. So much expected of her so soon. He understands how Seph's gifts overpowered her, threatened her, how all she ever wanted was her own identity, not one Violet had laid out for her like a fancy outfit on the bed. She will forever agonize, waffle, brood, but lives well as poet, activist, androgyne, Jamaica Plain saint. She'll end up with a houseful of cats, maybe, a clear conscience, hopefully a good lover, a good friend, and in the end, with wisdom to spare. She'll be as happy as she feels she has a right to be, which in the end may be a far sight more than the rest of them. And his brother. Nash thinks of Remi as his brother now, and not his twin. His older brother by almost three minutes. He can no longer be responsible for Remi, no longer be half a spirit, half a conscience, half a mind. At nearly fifty, being the other half of Remi is something Nash can no longer do.

Nash looks out into the yard. On any other night, spooked by the echoes in his brain, he would have sought comfort and company in a bottle. He would have mixed himself a drink, brought a bag of pretzels out into the living room and settled back into his armchair to let his thoughts run hazy and free. He's always needed booze to think about the hard things, to dull their edges—his children, Vi, the war. He needed whiskey to feel anger, outrage, sex, joy, and then more and more of it not to feel any of them too much. He thinks of getting up to pour himself a drink, but his mind refuses to put the idea into motion, won't raise his body up to take him to the liquor cabinet in the kitchen. He sits a dead and sober weight in his chair and takes on the feelings, the noises, the contradictions, the accusations, the pleas—one by one as they assail him—fending off each one with the shield of his sober clarity. His arms won't lift him. His mind floats.

"So what about the drinking?" Vi asked the night before, after they'd risen from the bathtub and fallen, wrinkled and tired, into the unmade bed.

"I'll cut down," he'd said. "It's high time I did."

"You can't be half an alcoholic." She ran her finger across his chest. "Any more than I can be half a nympho." She wasn't accusing, not pointing that finger, but still, the words pressed in hard, reminding them both of their other failed marriages—his with booze, hers with strange men, turning slowly sour, bringing less pleasure and more obeisance, never satisfied, the way Vi felt with the men, she tried to explain, gulping more and faster, losing the taste, the warmth, the tingle of the hand on the inside of the thigh, sinking to the bottom, the feel of the liquid on the throat, running down into the belly, spilling out, coating, chilling muscle and bone. After a time, feeling nothing anymore.

Nash folds up Chickie's letter. He closes his eyes and dozes off again, feeling the presence of someone nearby, the waltzing spirits of all those who've come and gone through the house over the years. He hears honking, banging, laughing, footsteps, sirens, whistles, booms—the echoing chatter of his life, his armchair dreams. The noises are garbled, distorted. His worst fears are met in an armchair dream. He's the one, the crowning fool that pushes the red button on the Oval Office desk and sends the missiles blasting. The troops flood out into the night—by land, by sea, by air. A fierce battle ensues. A violent storm finally diverts the bombs into the Bermuda Triangle. When it's over, the fallen men rise up into the sky. From their bodies fly off the helmets, belts and jockstraps, medals, guns and knives, pipes and baseball caps, watches and wallets, all of their bourbon and spare change. The flotsam and jetsam of men spin in space as their bodies fall back down through the clouds into a frostbitten sea, naked and shorn in their army crewcuts. The women wait in rowboats, the women who've always been bare, essential, unarmed, impervious to the cold, strong in the forearm and spirit, the caretakers, the warriors, the defenders. The women lift the men into the lifeboats and row them to a warm lagoon where they bathe and tend them—weak and twisted, waterlogged, wretched. And when the men have healed and rested and are strong again, the clouds shift to reveal a clear blue sky and the men take back their children and lift them high in their arms. And it's the girl children who hold their heads the highest, whose backs are the straightest and strongest, whose voices ring truest, most clear; it's the women that look forward, without hesitation or fear. In his armchair, Nash stirs at the sound of the screen door closing, footsteps on the stairs. "Vi?" he whispers, sleepily. "Chickie? Janie? Seph?" No answer. Nash thanks a god he's never spoken with before for giving him daughters. To be a man with daughters, sober and clear, was to be a lucky man. In the end, with his family wandering the night, Nash gives up on peace and settles, in the grip of his weary armchair, for possibility. As he drifts off again, in the corner of one eye, the next dream begins with the rising of a tiny flame.

Hen takes the subway stairs two at a time and comes up into the quiet morning Square. He's on his way home after a crazy trip to Nantucket with Chickie. They left the motel in the middle of the night, rode their bikes back to the cottage, and slept a few hours until daybreak before they split. He left her on the road, hitchhiking, walked down to the ferry dock, and took the first bus back to Boston from Woods Hole. And here he is. Today's the day. The guy at Nini's Corner takes a *Globe* out from under the brick. Hen hands him a quarter. He sits down at an outdoor table in the courtyard with a cup of coffee. Scratching his itchy face, he could swear he feels the bristling of a first real beard. He opens the paper and turns to page three—the full page listing of draft lottery numbers, printed top to bottom. He finds his birthday, October 26th, and runs his finger along the white space until it hits up hard against the print. His eyes register the number—three digits—move away, slide back again to verify. Double O…Shit. Top ten. He takes another look to be sure, swallows hard, and tosses the paper down on the table, lottery numbers belly down. SEVEN. *Seven, seven, Double O SEVEN.* Goddamn. His draft number's come up, low and dangerous—and it's not just any number, it's James fucking Bond's. He runs his hand through his hair, breathless, and tries to remember who he was before this moment, what was on his mind. Home. That had been his plan. To break the news about the draft, good or bad, visit his mother at Clay City, see what his father was up to, check in with Nash, go home. But now what was the rush? No one was waiting for him anymore. He left a note. He's eighteen, 007. A man of mystery, power, adventure. An international playboy and spy. *Ha!* His whole life's been busted apart. Chickie's on the road. Melody's history. His parents are breaking up. And now he could be on his way to Vietnam. So what's another hour? Or two or six or seven?

A few tables down, the chess master sets up his board. Hen heads over. For now, his time's still his own. A game of chess will calm him, steady his course, ready him for his next move.

"Hey, man." The chess master gestures for him to take a seat. "How you doing?"

"Not so good," Hen says. "I just drew number seven in the draft lottery."

"Bummer. Uncle Sam doesn't mess around these days, does he? What are you going to do?"

"Don't know yet." Hen sets up his pieces. "Canada. CO. I haven't wrapped my brain around it yet. Have to come up with a plan."

"I'm pushing thirty," the chess master says. "They got no use for an old dog like me."

"Just dumb luck, I guess," Hen says with a shrug. "We're born when we're born is all."

"Luck's part of it," the chess master says. "The rest is kismet, man, just plain old fucking fate."

Hen brings out his first pawn. The pieces are wooden, unfamiliar; the squares wiggle and squirm before his eyes. He blunders on move five, loses a quick game. "Sorry," he says, holding out a crumpled dollar bill. "I guess I'm worthless on the board today."

"Hey, keep it, man," the chess master says, pushing the money away. "No way I could sleep tonight, knowing I took cash from Double O Seven when he was down."

As Hen walks away from the courtyard, a man in a business suit and tie slides into his vacated seat and picks up the newspaper Hen left behind, open to the draft lottery page. His eyes glide over the sea of numbers, which don't seem to interest or concern him. He leafs through the pages that follow—murder, corruption, disaster—eyes landing finally on a small item in the lower left-hand corner of page eight.

MAN TRIES TO RESCUE TWIN BROTHER IN LATE NIGHT BLAZE

Firefighters rushed to the scene of a three-alarm blaze on Hemlock Street early this morning where identical twin brothers were found unconscious on the ground floor. One of the twins was resuscitated at the scene and the other was rushed to the Mount Auburn Hospital where he was pronounced dead at 2:11. A neighbor reported smelling smoke shortly after 1:30 a.m. By the time she went to investigate, the house was engulfed in flames. The twins lived next door to each other. It is not clear in whose house the fire started, or whether one twin tried to come to the rescue of the other. At press time, the surviving twin was being treated for smoke inhalation and second-degree burns and was under heavy sedation. There were apparently no other inhabitants home at the time of the blaze. The names of the victims are being withheld pending notification of the family. A small red pocketknife was found in the pocket of the deceased.

"Wow," the man says, whistling low.

"Wow what?" asks a woman at the next table over.

"Big fire last night down by the river," the man says. "Drove by on my way to work. Saw the rubble. Whole place burned to the ground. Identical twins in the house. And only one of them made it. That has to be tough on the survivor. They say twins have that ESP thing, you know? If one of them gets hurt, the other feels the pain, even if they're miles apart. Wonder how that works when one of them dies."

"How terrible," the woman says, spreading jelly on her bagel. "That it could all end that way. It's just so sad."

Hen cuts over to the river and walks the path along the shore. Under a mackerel sky, the heat's quickly rising; it's going to be another scorcher. He passes the walking bridge, where he and Chickie used to hunt turtles, where he used to come biking with his father and a reddish dog he can barely remember. As he walks, his head starts to clear. The shock's worn off a bit. It always does after the first gut-wrenching punch. Lucky seven. Couldn't be much worse. But what a strange relief to have this day come, his number finally drawn. He hasn't turned into a pumpkin or a chicken or a dead man yet. He's still standing whole and strong. He can step in and take charge of his life, make a decision, shape his own fate. *Do* something, by god. He thinks of Chickie taking off down the road that morning in Nantucket, kissing him goodbye. "See you back at the ranch, Henry," she said. "I need a few more days of freedom. Maybe a few more weeks. Who knows? I'll call you. Don't take any wooden nickels."

"They've been telling us that our whole lives," he said. "What the hell does it even mean?" Chickie shrugged and stuck her thumb out. A car stopped right away. He watched her run to catch the ride, the strings of her bikini top streaming out of her backpack—a skittish, barefoot bird—and watched her fly away.

Hen starts to whistle as he walks, not a real song, just a tune that arranges itself in disparate notes on the curl of his tongue. Whistling. He can actually hear himself whistling. Be a man, Remi has told him so often. And so he is. Plato the poet approaches from the opposite direction on the river path. Déjà vu. They seem to move in the same vicious circles. Hen stops him. "Hey, are you named after the philosopher?" he says.

Plato laughs and shakes his head. "No way, it's just a nickname," he says. "My brother Jerome gave it to me. I used to eat the stuff at school."

"Dig it, man," Hen says. "That stuff was *good*." He gives Plato the peace sign, and steady on his course, starts to make his way upriver—home.

Chickie looks over at the boy in the driver's seat, a crooked front tooth and uncombed hair, a strong, lanky build and striped shirt—a handsome guy who doesn't care what he looks like, Hen-like—a guy after her own heart. "Hey, thanks for picking me up," she says.

"No problem," the boy says. "Where you headed?"

"Anywhere," she says. "I've got no plans. I'm Minerva, by the way."

"Floyd," he says. "I've got a joint. We could smoke it and go bowling or something."

"Bowling?" Chickie snorts. "That's all you got for me, Floyd? Bowling?"

"Hey, it's an island," he says with a shrug. "There's not much else to do. Five more miles, we drive off into the drink."

"Cool." Chickie pulls her legs up under her in the lotus position, looks out at the ocean as they drive. She feels the waves covering her toes, her knees, her waist, taking her under, taking her in. Looking over at Floyd, she tracks the stripes on his shirt, the ripple of his arm muscle, the sleepy, willing look in his eyes.

"What?" he says, shifting his hands on the steering wheel, suddenly self-conscious. "What are you looking at me like that for?"

Chickie smiles. "Just wondering, Floyd," she says, "how far you can swim."

ACKNOWLEDGMENTS

Thanks to Elizabeth Graver, Pagan Kennedy, Lauren Slater, Audrey Schulman, Scott Campbell and Ed Hardy for their work on the earliest drafts of the novel. Thanks, also, to Lane Zachary, Irene Skolnick and Richard Parks for their championing of the book during the long journey from pen to page. I'm grateful to Jaynie Royal and all the remarkable women at Regal House Publishing for taking a chance on this book. I couldn't have asked for a better editor than Pam Van Dyk, who lent her fine and discerning eye to the novel. Credit for all things chess-related goes to Al. Lastly, my thanks always to Sofia, Anna, Natasha, Ian and Isla… the lights of my life.